D0607303

THE
BLOOD
OF
INNOCENTS

Center Point
Large Print

Also by Sean Lynch and available from Center Point Large Print:

Death Rattle
Cottonmouth

This Large Print Book carries the Seal of Approval of N.A.V.H.

THE BLOOD OF INNOCENTS

THE GUNS OF SAMUEL PRITCHARD

SEAN LYNCH

CENTER POINT LARGE PRINT
THORNDIKE, MAINE

This Center Point Large Print edition
is published in the year 2021 by arrangement with
Kensington Publishing Corp.

The text of this Large Print edition is unabridged.
In other aspects, this book may vary
from the original edition.
Printed in the United States of America
on permanent paper.
Set in 16-point Times New Roman type.

ISBN: 978-1-63808-084-8

The Library of Congress has cataloged this record
under Library of Congress Control Number: 2021940860

*This book is dedicated to
Marc Cameron and Gary Goldstein,
two hombres who know their way
around a good western story.*

CHAPTER ONE

East of Lawrence, Kansas. August, 1874

"They're not more'n a couple of miles ahead of us," Pritchard said, as he stood. He'd dismounted his big chestnut-colored Morgan, Rusty, and knelt to more closely examine the horse droppings left by a trio of riders he and his deputy had been tracking for the past two days.

"Will we overtake them before they get to Lawrence?" Strobl asked, in his Austrian accent.

"Likely," Pritchard replied. "We've still got a few hours of daylight left. I'd surely prefer to brace 'em afield. If we have to take 'em in town, it could get a mite messy."

Strobl nodded his assent. Both men had seen far too much innocent blood spilled during their lifetimes. As a result, each fervently wished to avoid gunplay near non-combatants whenever possible.

Atherton, Missouri, town marshal Samuel Pritchard, who was also the sheriff of Jackson County, and Deputy Marshal Florian Strobl were tracking three saddle tramps who'd passed through earlier that week.

Atherton was a booming lumber-town, bustling

7

Missouri River port, busy stopover on the Chicago, Burlington and Quincy rail line between Kansas City and St. Louis, and certainly not unfamiliar with horseback transients. But the three trail-dust-covered men who rode in were evidently unaware the town of Atherton was marshaled by Samuel Pritchard—formerly known as Smokin' Joe Atherton. Had they known, it's unlikely they'd have chosen Atherton as the place to do what they'd done.

Assuming the alias "Joe Atherton" as a teenager after he survived being headshot and buried prematurely in a shallow grave, Pritchard fled his hometown, went on to fight for the Confederacy as a horseback guerilla, served ten years as a Texas Ranger, and earned a reputation as the most lethal gunfighter on the frontier. The fact that Pritchard also stood six-and-a-half feet tall, was heavily muscled from a youth spent hauling lumber at his father's mill, and sported an ominous bullet-hole scar on his forehead over his right eye, did little to diminish his fearsome reputation.

When he finally returned home to Atherton last autumn, three years shy of his thirtieth birthday, Pritchard resumed his true name. He also avenged his murdered parents, and along with his childhood friend Ditch Clemson, wiped out the ruthless gang of murderers and thieves who'd ruled Atherton like Pharaohs since before the war.

8

In the months following the Battle of Atherton, as it became locally known, Pritchard had also been forced to stave off an onslaught of bounty-killers in a brazen attempt to wrest control of his family's considerable assets from his younger sister, Idelle, the town's acting-mayor. This became known as the Second Battle of Atherton.

The spring of 1874 had been a particularly bloody time for the citizens of Atherton. Like most towns straddling the one-time border between North and South, its citizens were still suffering from the lingering after-effects of the Civil War almost ten years later.

As a lawman, Pritchard fought hard to bring a measure of peace to war-weary Atherton, and his determined efforts were finally beginning to bear welcome fruit. In the short time since he'd resigned his post as a Texas Ranger and pinned on a town marshal's star, Atherton had become a relatively safe place. Despite the First and Second Battles of Atherton, thanks to his fists, guns, and even-handed skill at enforcing the law, it was once more safe to walk the streets.

His loyal friend Ditch, in addition to marrying his sister, had been elected to replace her as mayor. Ditch's shrewd business acumen, acquired as a successful Texas cattleman in the years following the war, greatly contributed to the community's prosperity.

Fighting alongside Pritchard to bring peace

and justice to Atherton was Florian Strobl, a European duelist who'd originally arrived among the flock of gunmen who'd come to collect a bounty on his head before the Second Battle of Atherton. A disgraced Austrian Count exiled to America, Strobl had switched loyalties after Pritchard spared his life. He subsequently joined the marshal as his deputy, and in that role set out with his boss after a trio of kidnappers and murderers two days previously.

Three strangers rode into Atherton, an otherwise unnoteworthy occurrence, and settled in at the Sidewinder, a restaurant and saloon operated by a local clan of Romanichals. After dining on steak and consuming two bottles of whiskey, the newcomers, claiming to be cowhands hailing from the Oklahoma Territory but whose hands suspiciously lacked the callouses of working men, took particular notice of the buxom, teenaged, waitress serving them dinner.

When one of the drunken men, none of whom were less than thirty years old, grabbed the fifteen-year-old girl, clamped a filthy hand over her mouth to suppress her screams, and proceeded to drag her out into the alley behind the Sidewinder, his two companions kept the other patrons at bay with drawn pistols. They also helped themselves to another bottle of whiskey as they followed their companion and his struggling captive out through the back door. Needless to say, no effort was made by the men to pay for their meals and drink.

The saloonkeeper, Manfri Pannell, and one of his adult sons, Vano, came running from the kitchen. They stormed into the alley just as the cowboy who'd first grabbed the girl stripped her of her dress, tearing the garment entirely from her body.

Manfri and Vano, both sturdy, muscular men, ran to the girl's aid. The other two cowboys, despite their drunkenness, sensed the duo advancing behind them. Both gunmen spun and fired.

Manfri was struck in the shoulder. A .44 slug spun him around and sent him tumbling to the ground. His son Vano was struck squarely in the belly by a bullet fired from the other cowboy's .45. Like his father, he collapsed.

"You idjits," the first cowboy scolded. "Them shots'll bring the law down on us fer sure."

"What was we supposed to do?" one of the other two cowboys retorted. "Let them two yokels whomp us?"

"We'd best git," the third cowboy said, holstering his gun. "I'll go around front and fetch our horses."

"What about her?" the second cowboy asked, pointing to the terrified, gagged, and naked teenager, still trapped in his companion's thick arms.

"We'll take her along with us," he said with a leer.

Pritchard had been out in the county serving an arrest warrant on a livestock thief when the incident occurred. When he rode back into town after dark, with his passive prisoner in tow, he was greeted at the jail by a crowd of townspeople bearing grim news.

One of Pritchard's only two full-time deputy marshals, Toby "Tater" Jessup, reported what transpired. Tater, a kind-hearted, middle-aged, former liveryman, tearfully relayed what Doctor Mauldin had reported to him; that Manfri Pannell would recover, but his son Vano had succumbed to his belly-wound shortly after being shot.

Manfri Pannell and his entire immigrant, Romanichal, clan, had been personally shepherded into Atherton by Pritchard himself. He considered Manfri and his family more than friends.

The girl, named Vadoma, was one of Manfri's nieces. She was last seen, nude and sobbing, on the back of one of the horses as the trio of intoxicated cowboys rode hell-bent-for-leather out of town. All three riders fired their pistols indiscriminately at shop windows, lampposts, and anything else they believed would dissuade pursuers as they galloped out.

Pritchard wasted no time. He turned over his prisoner to Tater to be locked up, retrieved his

12

Winchester from the jail, loaded his saddlebags with provisions, grain, ammunition, and an extra canteen, and re-mounted. Deputy Strobl, who had been awaiting Pritchard's return, and Mayor Ditch Clemson, a veteran of the late war who'd grown up with Pritchard and fought alongside him too many times to remember, and who'd been deputized on more than one occasion, joined him.

The portly Tater halted Pritchard, Strobl, and Ditch with a raised hand before they departed. He extended three sets of manacles to the mounted marshal.

"Ain't you forgettin' these, Marshal?" Tater asked. "They're for your prisoners."

"Won't have need for 'em," Pritchard told his deputy.

The three lawmen rode wordlessly out of Atherton, heading west. None were strangers to hunting armed men.

Chapter Two

The cowboys had several hours' start on Pritchard, Ditch, and Strobl, but left an easy-enough trail to follow, even at night. Pritchard and Ditch had grown up in the woods along the Missouri River, and knew every inch of ground for twenty miles in all directions. Five miles west of Atherton they found the girl.

Vadoma lay on a patch of grass near a creek, quietly crying, which was how they located her in the darkness. She was still naked, and covered in bruises and welts. After her three captors took turns violating her, they stole her shoes to slow her return to town.

The oldest of Vadoma's assailants, the leader of the trio and the one who'd initially grabbed her at her uncle's inn, had drawn his revolver, cocked the hammer, and placed the barrel against her head.

"You're gonna deliver a message to the posse which'll be a-comin' after us," he said.

Vadoma nodded, her eyes tightly shut.

"You're gonna tell whoever is a-comin' after us to stop comin'," the leader said, as his partners fastened their britches. "You're gonna remind that posse that we didn't kill you, even though we could've. You're also gonna let 'em know if they don't heed this warning, we'll be waitin' up the trail for 'em. If'n they find us, we'll plant 'em all. Can you remember to tell 'em that?"

"I'll relay your message," the girl said in her British accent. Her Romanichal Tribe heralded from England, and had emigrated to America less than two years before. "But it will make no difference. The marshal will disregard your warning. He will hunt you down. He will shoot all of you like the dogs you are or hang you from the nearest tree."

"We ain't afraid of no tinhorn marshal from no backwater, Missouri town," one of the other cowboys scoffed. "Nor of any posse of shopkeepers and stable boys."

"The marshal was once a Texas Ranger," she said. "He's known far and wide as a killer of men."

"She's lyin'," the third cowboy said to his companions. "Tryin' to put a spook into us 'cause we done had our way with her."

"What's this marshal's name?" the leader asked.

"His name is Samuel Pritchard," Vadoma answered. She opened her eyes and looked up at the man holding a gun to her head.

"Never heard of him."

"He used to go by another name," she said. "Perhaps you have heard of that one?"

"What name would that be?"

"Joe Atherton."

"Joe Atherton?" the youngest cowboy said. "You're tellin' me Smokin' Joe Atherton is the marshal of that hogslop of a town back there?"

Vadoma nodded. "It is said he took the name of his hometown during the war."

"Now I know she's lyin'," the other cowboy said. "Ain't no way a famous pistoleer like Smokin' Joe is the sheriff of no backwoods river town."

"What's this marshal look like?" the leader asked.

"Tall as a barn, and as wide in the shoulders," Vadoma answered. "He's young. He's not even thirty years old. He has white-blond hair, blue eyes, and a bullet scar on his forehead."

"Is that so?" The youngest cowboy laughed. "Tall as a barn-hah! A bullet hole in his noggin! Sounds like she's describin' the booger man. Does he sport horns and fangs, too?"

"Shut up," the leader snapped. He prodded Vadoma with the barrel of his revolver. "You ain't fibbin'? You tellin' us the truth?"

"You already beat me, defiled me, and are going to shoot me," the girl said defiantly. "What do I gain by lying?"

The gun was removed from her head. "Get mounted," the leader said to the other two cowboys, as he lowered the hammer.

"Maybe we'd best finish her?" one of the other

16

cowboys said. He drew his own revolver. "It ain't savvy to leave the bitch above ground. She knows our faces."

"Put that lead pusher away," the leader barked. "Nobody's givin' her a pill."

"What're you afraid of?" the cowboy said. "You don't actually believe her made-up fairy tale, do you?"

"I saw Smokin' Joe gun a man in the Oklahoma Territory," the leader said, "a few years after the war. He was with a company of Texas Rangers. He wasn't much more than a kid then. A giant of a kid. But she's described him, dead-on, all right."

"She's probably heard campfire stories," the second cowboy argued. "She's only repeatin' what others have told her about his appearance."

"Maybe not," the leader said. "I heard tell a while ago Smokin' Joe had given up the Rangers and was sheriffin' somewhere's up north under a different name." He holstered his revolver. "Get mounted, like I told you."

All three cowboys climbed aboard their horses. This time their leader pointed his finger, and not his gun, at Vadoma.

"You remember what I told you to tell that posse," he admonished her. "Smokin' Joe or not, anyone who comes after us is gonna wish they didn't."

"I'll tell them," the naked, abused, girl said. "Have fun looking over your shoulder."

17

Ditch wrapped the exhausted Vadoma in his coat and gently put her up on his horse. It was agreed since he was married, and his wife, Pritchard's sister Idelle, was due to give birth in a few months, he should be the one to escort her back to Atherton.

"Soon as I drop her off in town with Doc Mauldin and her folks," Ditch said, "I'll turn around and catch up to you and Florian."

"Don't bother," Pritchard said. "You'll be needed in Atherton. With me and Strobl gone for who knows how long, it'll be just you and Tater to look after the town. What if some other hard cases ride in? You're a solid gun hand, and we both know the only thing Tater's ever wrestled with is indigestion."

"But Samuel," Ditch protested, "there's three of 'em, and—"

"No 'buts,' " Pritchard cut him off. "I've faced worse odds a hundred times over, and you know it. As much as I welcome your company, you belong back in Atherton lookin' after your pregnant wife and our town. You're not just a part-time deputy, Ditch, you're the mayor, remember? Now get goin'."

Pritchard's logic was irrefutable. Ditch nodded to Strobl and his friend and began leading his horse, with Vadoma astride, back toward town.

"I told those three animals you'd be coming

after them, Marshal," Vadoma suddenly spoke up. "I told them it was Joe Atherton on their trail. I said you would find them and shoot them like dogs or string them up. I hope you aren't angry with me for saying such a thing?"

"Of course not," Pritchard soothed. "Marshal Pritchard, or Smokin' Joe, it don't matter a whit. Those boys'll get what's comin' to them for what they done to you and your family. You have my word on the matter."

"My word, as well," Strobl said.

"You just get on back to your folks and get to healin'," Pritchard said.

"Thank you, Marshal."

Pritchard tipped his hat to Vadoma and climbed into the saddle. Strobl took the cue and followed suit.

"Let's ride," he said to his deputy.

CHAPTER THREE

Just as Pritchard suspected, the fugitive cowboys skipped over Kansas City. He figured they'd guess a posse would presume they'd head straight for the nearest big town to blend in and hide out. Instead, the cowboys stayed well north of Kansas City as they headed west, toward Lawrence. The sign they left indicated they were pushing hard, trying to put as much distance between themselves and anyone trailing them.

It was late afternoon, on a blazing hot Kansas prairie a few miles east of Lawrence, when Pritchard and Strobl spotted them. Three riders, a thousand yards ahead in the haze and dust.

Pritchard withdrew his .44-40 from the saddle scabbard and levered the action. Strobl withdrew his Henry .44 and likewise chambered a round. Pritchard had bequeathed the Henry to his deputy after acquiring the 1873 Winchester.

In addition to his rifle, Pritchard was armed with a brace of .45 Colt Single-Action Army revolvers, both sporting custom, five-and-one-half-inch barrels. Pritchard had no way of knowing that the Colt factory wouldn't offer such guns, which would eventually become known as the Artillery Model, as regular production items for another year. He'd won his pair of custom-barreled Colt pistols in a shooting contest in Abilene, Kansas, at the end of a cattle drive, before returning home to Atherton the previous summer.

Pritchard always carried at least two pistols, a habit developed as a horseback guerilla during the war. Since being bound, forced onto his knees, and shot in the head, he swore an oath that never again would a gun be aimed at him without the ability to shoot back. Consequently, after being dug up, rescued, and nursed back to health by Ditch, he devoted himself to the study of the one-handed gun with religious zeal.

Since his "resurrection," as Ditch mockingly called it, at seventeen years old, Pritchard dedicated a portion of each day to drawing, aiming, and dry-firing his pistols. Just as some men shaved, bathed, or prayed as part of their daily constitutional, Pritchard dutifully practiced each day with his revolvers.

As a youth, Pritchard had already demonstrated extraordinary skill as a rifle marksman. He'd also been the county fair's bare-knuckle wrestling champion every year since age thirteen as a result of his great size and strength. His extremely large hands, uncommonly powerful physique, and natural athletic ability, in concert with his ability as a sharpshooter, aided him significantly in his endeavors to become a competent pistoleer.

Before long he was uncannily gifted, with either hand, in the use of his revolvers.

His skill with weapons was soon tested in the crucible of combat during the war and further honed by his years as a Texas Ranger. By the time he was twenty-seven, more than a decade after he'd been "executed," Pritchard, under the alias Joe Atherton, was widely acknowledged as one of the most skilled, and deadly, pistol fighters in all of the Americas.

Before he'd acquired the Colt .45s, Pritchard's preferred weapons were a pair of 1863 Remingtons converted to accept metallic .44 cartridges by a Dallas gunsmith. The guns had been a gift from Ditch. He'd used those guns, along with the Henry rifle now in Florian Strobl's capable hands, to avenge the murder of his beloved fiancée, Caroline.

Deputy Florian Strobl was also armed with two revolvers. His guns, nickel-plated Chamelot-Delvigne revolvers, made up for their anemic, eleven-millimeter, cartridge by being double-action in design. Strobl carried the weapons in dual shoulder-holsters under his tailored riding jacket, unlike Pritchard, who slung his guns across his narrow hips in a set of traditional, hand-tooled, holsters suspended from a pair of cartridge-laden belts.

"How do you want to play this hand?" Strobl asked.

"Only one way to play it," Pritchard said. "Straight at 'em. If they haven't spotted us yet, they soon will. This Kansas ground is flat as a nickel, and there ain't been a tree nor brush for miles. If we can see 'em, they can see us. Likely the only reason they haven't eyeballed us yet, I'm guessin', is they're hung over and exhausted."

"Won't they make a run for it when they see us?"

"They will," Pritchard conceded, "but it won't make any difference. Our horses have been eatin' grain, not grass. We'll catch up to 'em easy enough."

Pritchard's horse, Rusty, was twelve years old, stood eighteen hands tall, and had been his faithful companion through countless battles, raids, and frontier skirmishes since the day he fled Atherton as a youth. The highly intelligent animal had a nose for action, and its ears were perked up now, anticipating the imminent fight.

Strobl's mount, a deep-black, medium-sized, quarter he'd named Schatz, was spirited and reliable, as well. The elegant Strobl stood six-feet tall, but had a slender build, and could easily count on Schatz to run down most other horses. Particularly those horses that had been ridden hard by fugitive longriders with little rest for the past two days and fed nothing but bone-dry prairie grass while on the move.

"They lit out of Atherton before they provisioned up," Pritchard added. "I heard they ate a good meal at the Sidewinder, but that was two days ago. Those three fools are likely just as hungry and tuckered out as their horses. You ready, Deputy?"

"But of course," Strobl said nonchalantly.

"Let's go get them sons-of-bitches," Pritchard said, spurring Rusty to a trot. Deputy Strobl, astride Schatz, followed closely on his heels.

CHAPTER FOUR

Pritchard and Strobl got within two-hundred yards before the three cowboys, slumped in their saddles, finally heard the sound of approaching hoofbeats and looked back. When they spotted the twin riders fast approaching, they immediately spurred their horses to a full gallop.

The lawmen had been steadily advancing on them with their own horses at a measured trot. As soon as the three fugitives took off, Pritchard and Strobl spurred Rusty and Schatz to a full gallop, as well. The lawmen's eager horses instinctively raced to catch their fleeing counterparts. In no time, the distance between pursuer and pursued began to shrink.

Both Pritchard and Strobl knew that accurate gunfire, even with a rifle or carbine, was nearly impossible from atop a galloping horse at much beyond point-blank range. Nonetheless, when Pritchard and Strobl narrowed the gap to less than one-hundred yards, the marshal took aim and fired several rounds from his Winchester.

Strobl understood what Pritchard was doing. Though unlikely to hit any of the fleeing riders ahead, the shots would rattle them and prompt the fugitives to spur their nearly-spent horses to even greater effort, quickening their impending collapse.

Sure enough, after a little more than a mile of all five mounts charging at full gallop, Pritchard and Strobl watched as one of the cowboy's horses crumpled forward to the ground. Its rider was tossed over the saddle and went sprawling on his face in the dry, Kansas, dust.

By then, Rusty and Schatz had closed the space between the lawmen and fugitives to less than one-hundred feet.

The downed cowboy's two companions, less out of loyalty to their stranded comrade and more from the inescapable realization that their own foaming horses were only steps from similar catastrophic failure, suddenly brought their mounts to an abrupt halt.

"What are they doing?" Strobl asked, as he and Pritchard reined their horses back to a trot. Less than fifty feet now separated the lawmen from the downed horse and rider, and another twenty-five from his two partners. The pair of cowboys hastily dismounted.

"Their horses are played out," Pritchard said, as he and Strobl slowed theirs to a walk, "and they know it. They're either gonna surrender or make a fight of it."

The thrown cowboy, minus his hat, struggled shakily to his feet. He held one shoulder and appeared to be in pain.

"I'm Marshal Pritchard," Pritchard called out, as he halted Rusty, "of Atherton, Missouri." Strobl pulled Schatz alongside him. "This here's my deputy." Both lawmen held their rifles at port arms. The hammers were back, and their fingers near the triggers.

"You're all wanted men," Pritchard continued. "Throw down your irons and throw up your hands."

None of the three cowboys made an effort to comply.

"You rode all the way from Missouri," the leader called out, "to arrest us for pirootin' with a knee-high saloon trollop?"

"She weren't no painted cat," Pritchard said, "and you know it. She was an innocent young kid slinging hash at her family's tavern."

"You said you were a Missouri lawman, didn't ya?" the cowboy next to the leader said, changing the subject. "This here is Kansas. You ain't got no legal authority here."

"Same authority you have to kidnap, rape, and murder in Missouri."

"Who'd we murder?" the leader asked.

"Barman at the Sidewinder," Pritchard said. "Shot dead in the alley tryin' to rescue his young cousin. He was a friend of mine."

"Didn't know he expired," the leader said. "It wasn't our intention to plug no barkeep. It was his own fault, though. If'n he didn't want his

27

lamp blowed out, he should've minded his own business. Ain't no law against havin' a few drinks and cavortin' with a townie skirt. Weren't no cause for a ruckus."

"A fifteen-year-old girl disagrees. So do I."

"We didn't hurt her," the leader said. "Not much, leastways. We didn't do nothin' to her wasn't gonna be done sooner or later."

"I reckon she views what you did to her a mite differently."

"We could've plugged her," the other cowboy insisted, "but we didn't. She's still above the snakes, Marshal. Don't that count for somethin'?"

"I didn't ride all the way to Kansas to listen to your bobbery," Pritchard said. "Lose them barkin' irons."

"You're Smokin' Joe, ain't ya?" the leader spoke up. "The famous Texas Ranger and man-killer. I watched you bed a feller down in Oklahoma a while back." He spat in the dirt at his feet. "Looks like that little Missouri strumpet was tellin' us the truth." He grinned at his two partners. "Whaddaya know, boys? We're bein' arrested by a gen-u-wine hero of the Confederacy."

"Who I was," Pritchard said, "don't matter a whit. What matters is that I'm done jawin' with killers of unarmed men and molesters of women. Put up your hands and be taken prisoner peaceable, or make your play. This is your last warnin'."

"What if we do give ourselves up?" the leader asked. "You gonna march us all the way back to Missouri to stand trial before a judge and jury?"

"Nope," Pritchard said. "I'm a-gonna hang you. Today."

All three cowboys started laughing. "Hell, Marshal," the leader said between guffaws. "What're you gonna hang us from? This here's Kansas. We ain't seen a tree in miles." More laughter followed.

"Why don't you let me worry about where I hold my lynchin' bee?" Pritchard said.

"I don't believe I'm gonna allow you to stretch my neck," the leader said.

"I'm in agreeance," the cowboy standing next to him said.

"You can go to hell, Smokin' Joe," the wobbly, hatless, cowboy said. He clumsily drew his revolver and raised it at Pritchard.

Quick as a flash, Pritchard shouldered his Winchester and shot him through the neck. The cowboy fell back to the Kansas dirt which he'd risen out of only a moment before. He lay on his back, gurgling, as his death rattle trickled out with his blood and his life.

The other two cowboys drew as one. Strobl's Henry boomed first, since Pritchard was busy cycling the lever on his rifle. The trio's leader was instantly felled by a shot to his chest.

The last cowboy standing dropped his gun

and raised his arms before Pritchard could fire. "Don't shoot," he begged. He was the youngest of the three. "I ditched my thumbbuster. I ain't armed no more."

Pritchard and Strobl dismounted. Both men lowered the hammers on their rifles and returned them to the saddle scabbards. The surviving cowboy stood rigid with an expression of fear on his face. His hands were extended above his head.

The hatless, throat-shot, cowboy expired in less than a minute. The leader, shot through the lungs with one of Strobl's .44 rimfires, was gasping for breath, but still alive and conscious. Pritchard kicked his revolver out-of-reach and stood over him.

"I'm gone goslin', Marshal," he said, spitting blood. "You done cashed me in. You got any whiskey in your saddle to ease my journey?"

"I've got whiskey," Pritchard admitted. "But I ain't bestowin' any of it on the likes of you. I'm right partial who I drink with. Besides, you'll be eventuated momentarily. It'd be a waste of good spirits to pour 'em down your worthless gullet."

"Indeed, it would," Strobl agreed.

"B-bastards," the dying cowboy sputtered, spewing more blood. "Missouri t-trash, the b-both of you."

"Actually," Strobl said cheerfully in his Austrian accent, "I hail from considerably farther east."

Pritchard removed the saddle from Rusty. Strobl did likewise with Schatz. Then they busied themselves collecting the cowboys' three discarded pistols, unloading them, and depositing the weapons into their saddlebags.

The surviving cowboy stood in the stifling heat with his hands above his head, afraid to move. "What're you gonna do with me?" he finally asked, his voice trembling.

"Where was that last tree we passed?" Pritchard asked Strobl, ignoring the cowboy's question.

"The last tree we passed was about two miles back," Strobl answered. "It was a very small tree, though. Entirely unacceptable, I suspect. I saw one which would be suitable for our purposes approximately five miles ago."

"I remember it," Pritchard said. He turned to the cowboy. "Round up your horses. We'll water 'em, grain 'em, rest 'em a spell, get a bite to eat, load up your friends' carcasses, and be on our way in the mornin'."

"Where're we goin'?" the cowboy asked, knowing the answer but hoping he was wrong. "Into Lawrence?"

"Nope," Pritchard answered matter-of-factly. "Goin' to find that big tree we passed a few miles back. Can't have a necktie social without a proper tree, can we?"

"You're gonna string me?"

"That's what I said," Pritchard answered.

31

"But I done surrendered?"

"That was your choice," Pritchard said. "You could have gone out game."

"Don't I even get a trial?" the cowboy pleaded.

"You surely do," Pritchard answered. "You get the same trial you gave Manfri Pannell, his son Vano, and his young niece, Vadoma."

"You can't," the cowboy sobbed. He sagged to his knees and clasped his hands together as if in prayer. "You can't just string me up like a common horse thief. It ain't right. You're lawmen, ain't ya? Lawmen ain't supposed to throw necktie parties. Don't you fellers gotta follow the law?"

"Of course, we've got to obey the law," Pritchard said evenly, "in Missouri." A hard grin spread across his thin face. "Like you said a minute ago, this here's Kansas."

CHAPTER FIVE

A sizable crowd of townsfolk gathered at the train depot, on the outskirts of Atherton, to greet Marshal Pritchard and Deputy Strobl when they disembarked. Pritchard wired Ditch from the telegraph office in Lawrence to notify him of their impending arrival.

After resting overnight on the prairie east of Lawrence and enjoying a supper of pemmican and whiskey, of which their prisoner got none, Pritchard and Strobl rose at dawn. Pritchard took the first watch, and he and his deputy alternated shifts during the night guarding their forlorn prisoner.

They lashed the carcasses of the two dead cowboys onto their own refreshed horses, put their morose captive, who said his name was Chuck, onto his horse, mounted up, and headed west to find a hanging tree. As it turned out, they never got the chance to use one.

Chuck, who began crying softly soon after their departure, quickly descended into wailing hysterics. He lamented his two friends, whom he faulted for his fate, cursed Pritchard and Strobl for their unforgiving cruelty, and reserved his foulest insults for the "gypsy whore" he evidently believed lured him and his now-deceased companions to their doom. Even though his hands were bound in front with a rawhide strip, Pritchard made the blubbering cowboy ride slightly ahead to keep an eye on him. Deputy Strobl and the two corpse-laden horses brought up the rear.

"It would appear Chuck blames everyone but himself for his predicament," Strobl remarked, as the distraught cowboy continued his tear-filled, obscenity-laced, tirade.

"If he's lookin' for sympathy," Pritchard said, "he'd best look elsewhere."

Less than a mile after beginning their journey, the hysterical cowboy glanced over his shoulder with panic in his eyes. He suddenly spurred his horse and took off. As he fled at full gallop, he continued to simultaneously wail and swear.

Pritchard halted Rusty. Strobl brought Schatz and the packhorses up alongside.

"We were never going to reach that tree, were we?" Strobl asked, pointing his chin at the back of the cowboy riding furiously away. "You expected him to run, didn't you?"

"Had a notion," Pritchard admitted, as he withdrew his Winchester from its scabbard. He thumbed the hammer back, since the weapon already had a cartridge chambered from the previous day's action. He shouldered it, and placed the front sight in the center of the fleeing prisoner's back.

"Auf wiedersehen, Chuck," Strobl said, as Pritchard squinted, exhaled, and squeezed the trigger.

Fifteen minutes later, after they'd rounded up Chuck's horse and roped his remains over the saddle, the lawmen re-mounted, turned around, and headed west into Lawrence, less than ten miles away.

The caravan drew solemn stares as they rode into town. Two lawmen pulling a train of three cadaver-loaded animals wasn't a particularly common sight. Pritchard checked in with the town marshal, a salty old veteran named Art Rankin, whom he knew well. Then he bought two passages on the next eastbound train and fired off a telegram to Ditch advising his friend that he and Strobl would be arriving in Atherton later that night.

Marshal Rankin offered to dispose of the bodies, but Pritchard declined. He paid the ticket clerk extra to have the three horses and their burdens loaded onto the livestock car. The Lawrence marshal didn't need an explanation why.

Both marshals, one young and one old, were each experienced enough to recognize the value in returning bad men, whether dead or alive, back to the town they'd violated. It's the reason hangings were conducted in public. Often it wasn't feasible to return captured fugitives or their remains back to the places they'd committed their crimes, due to practicalities of time and distance in running them to ground.

But Pritchard and Marshal Rankin believed that providing surviving victims, such as Manfri Pannell and Vadoma, and the loved ones of dead victims, like Vano Pannell's wife and children, a measure of satisfaction in seeing justice served merited the additional effort.

Just as important, Pritchard, like all frontier lawmen worth their flint, knew returning the macabre trophies back to Atherton, and burying them under markers identifying them as the murderers they were, sent a potent warning. Their gravestones would serve as talismans, and portend of the fate awaiting those contemplating lawbreaking in Jackson County.

"Welcome home, Samuel," Ditch said. As mayor, he'd positioned himself at the front of the crowd and was the first to greet the marshal and deputy as they stepped off the train.

"Howdy, Ditch," Pritchard answered. The men shook hands. Ditch shook Deputy Strobl's, as well. Manfri Pannell stepped forward. He was surrounded by his wife and most of the members of his Romanichal clan. Vadoma stood beside him. One of her eyes was black, but she appeared in good health and a far cry from the naked, beaten, and brutalized young woman they'd found on the trail. Manfri's eyes were hollow with grief, and his left arm was suspended across his chest in a sling.

"I'm deeply sorry for the loss of your son, Vano," Pritchard said, removing his hat. The bullet scar on his forehead showed ominously in the depot's lamplight. Manfri gave Pritchard's shoulder a squeeze with his good arm, and smiled as well as a man who'd recently lost a son could.

All eyes looked past Pritchard toward the livestock car, where the freight handlers slid open the door and began off-loading animals. First Schatz, and then Rusty, were led down the ramp, followed by the horses belonging to the three cowboys. All were turned over to liverymen and escorted to the town's stable.

Pritchard motioned to Simon Tilley and his son Seth. Atherton's two undertakers were seated in their wagon, parked at the edge of the crowd. They maneuvered it around to the livestock car's open door. Old Simon remained in the seat while Seth dismounted to help the freight handlers load three tarpaulin-wrapped corpses into the back of the wagon.

"Is that them?" Manfri asked. "The men who murdered my son?"

"I believe so," Pritchard said. "But in truth, Manfri, that's for you and Vadoma to say. At least one of you has to identify the bodies, to make it legal." He looked at Vadoma. "But only if'n you're up to it?"

"You don't have to," Manfri's wife, Sabina, said to her niece. "Manfri can look upon them and speak for you both."

"It's all right," Vadoma said. "I want to look at their faces. I want to remember them for always as they are now. Dead and rotting. Not as they were . . . when they . . . while they were . . ."

Manfri put his good arm around Vadoma's shoulders. "We will look at them together," he said.

Pritchard gave a nod to Strobl, who politely removed his hat, extended his elbow, and escorted Vadoma, followed by Manfri, over to the wagon. One by one, Seth Tilley peeled back the tarpaulins to reveal the slack faces of three dead men. Vadoma spoke first.

"It is them," she said. "May their souls burn in hell."

"Those are indeed the men who shot me and my son," Manfri confirmed.

Pritchard nodded again and Seth re-covered the bodies. Sabina led Vadoma, who had begun to cry, gently away.

"How did they die?" Manfri asked.

"Like the cowards they were," Pritchard said. "Know if I could've brought 'em back to swing in the town square for all to see, I would've. They chose to go out game, leaving Deputy Strobl and myself no choice but to bed 'em down."

Judge Eugene Pearson, in his formal suit and

38

standing with Ditch at the head of the crowd, stepped forward. Pearson had served honorably on the side of the Union during the war, possessed a "no-nonsense" demeanor, had a reputation for being a fair magistrate, and was respected by all in Atherton.

"Is that how these three men came to their ends?" he asked Deputy Strobl.

"On my oath, Your Honor," Strobl answered. "Marshal Pritchard was forced to shoot one of them down as he was being fired upon, and I another for the same reason. The third surrendered, but then later tried to flee on horseback, forcing us to shoot him to prevent his escape."

"Knowing the character of Marshal Pritchard," Judge Pearson announced, "and of his deputy, I hereby declare these killings lawful and justice served. If anyone has evidence or testimony to the contrary, speak now, or forever hold your peace."

No one spoke. "Very well," the judge declared. "Case closed."

"Thank you," Manfri Pannell said to Judge Pearson, "for bringing justice to my family."

"It wasn't done only for you," Judge Pearson said. "It was done for all our families in Atherton."

Manfri gathered his clan. Once he and his relatives departed, old Simon Tilley, a senior member of the town council and also respected by all in Atherton, stood up in the wagon.

"You've done a man's work, Marshal Pritchard, ridin' those filthy bastards to justice. I'm sure I'm not alone in sayin' my only regret is they didn't get to swing from a noose in the town square. But what's done is done, and now it's my turn to go to work. I presume you want these men sunk in Sin Hill and not the Churchyard?"

"Damn straight," Pritchard said. "Cheapest eternity boxes you've got. Plant 'em close to the road, where their markers can be read by passers-by. County will pay for their plantin', just like always."

Atherton's main cemetery, a tree-filled glade commonly referred to as the Churchyard by the locals, sat on the high side of town overlooking the river valley. During the war, it had expanded greatly, with sections divided by familial affiliation, religious connotation, and by allegiance to either North or South.

Situated slightly below the Churchyard, close to Atherton's main road and separated from the larger cemetery by a wrought-iron fence, was Sin Hill. This resting place was reserved for those deemed unfit to lay in repose among decent folk. Sin Hill contained the final remains of former Mayor Burnell Shipley, Sheriff Horace Foster, Marshal Elton Stacy, deputy and gunslinger Eli Gaines, and more than two-dozen other men of

40

bad character and violence put down by Pritchard or his deputies since his fateful return home.

"And their grave markers?" Tilley went on. "Wood or stone?"

"Stone," Pritchard said. "Lasts longer. Mark 'em as the murderers they were. And there'll be no doo-dads to adorn their holes." Flowers or other graveside decorations were not permitted in Sin Hill.

"It'll be done as you say, Marshal."

The crowd dissipated. Ditch offered Pritchard an envelope.

"Telegram came in for you yesterday," he said. "It's from Jefferson City."

"What's this about?" Pritchard asked, accepting the envelope and opening it.

"It's a summons," Ditch said. "Governor Woodson wants to speak with you."

CHAPTER SIX

"Mr. Quincy will see you now," the receptionist said to the tall, lean man waiting in the lobby. She was young and very attractive.

"Thank you," the man replied. He stood, extinguished his cheroot in an ashtray on the receptionist's desk, picked up his black, wide-brimmed, Boss-of-the-Plains Stetson, and strode through the big mahogany door into the office.

The Quincy Detective Agency was head-quartered in a stately brick building situated on St. Louis's waterfront. The owner's office was a large wood-paneled room with a magnificent view of the Mississippi.

Dominic Cottonmouth Quincy rose from behind his imposing desk to greet his guest. He was a medium-sized man in his fifties with graying hair going white at the temples. His eyes were slightly red and watering, and his nose had obviously been badly broken in the recent past and improperly set. He was wearing an expensive suit and highly polished shoes. He shook the newcomer's right hand with his left, since his own right arm was missing below the elbow.

"Thank you for coming, Mr. Bonner," Quincy said in his Irish brogue.

"A personal invitation from the illustrious Dominic Quincy is difficult to decline," Bonner said. "Especially when that invitation includes stage fare from the Oklahoma Territory, a train ticket from Kansas City to St. Louis, and one-hundred dollars, just to meet with you. Not many men where I come from would pass on such an invite."

Quincy motioned to one of the high-backed leather chairs facing his desk. "May I offer you a drink?"

"Whiskey, if you've got it."

"Scotch?"

"Even better."

"Do you know why I summoned you?" Quincy asked, as he filled two glasses from a crystal decanter.

"I can guess," Bonner said, adjusting his brace of 1872 Open-Top Colts and taking a seat. One of his guns was worn on his right side, the other cross-draw. He tossed his hat on Quincy's desk. "May I smoke?"

"By all means," Quincy said, handing a glass to Bonner. He took his own glass and returned to his chair behind the desk. Both men lit cigars, Bonner a dirty-brown cheroot retrieved from an inside pocket and Quincy a thick cigar taken from an ornately engraved box on his desk.

"Captain Laird Bonner," Quincy said, once he'd clipped the end of his cigar and got it fired up. "A successful Indiana farmer before the war. Educated, too, I'm told, at the University of Pennsylvania. Served with distinction as a member of Colonel Minty's 7th Pennsylvania Cavalry—the Saber Brigade. If I'm not mistaken, you led the charge at Reed's Bridge during the Battle of Chickamauga?"

"I was there," Bonner said, lighting his smoke, "during that bloody September. Can't say I served with distinction. I was still breathing after the fight, whereas a lot of better men weren't. That's all the distinction I remember."

"Your humility is admirable," Quincy said. "My sources inform me your skill on the battlefield is matched only by your ruthlessness."

"Sources?"

"You forget, Mr. Bonner, I run a nationally renowned detective agency."

"What else do your sources tell you?" Bonner asked.

Before answering, Quincy produced a handkerchief and wiped a trickle of snot that had secreted from his nostrils and dribbled over his mustache. "It is my understanding that when you returned home to Indiana after the war," he went on, "you found your daughter had died of typhoid fever and your wife had run off with a newspaperman from Fort Wayne."

Bonner squinted at Quincy through the smoke from his cheroot, but otherwise his expression didn't change.

44

"It is my further understanding," Quincy continued, tucking the handkerchief away, "that you hunted the lovebirds down. You caught up to them in a rooming house in Cincinnati. Both, not coincidentally, ended up being shot dead. According to newspaper accounts of the incident, your wife's paramour was shot deliberately and your wife died accidentally."

"He pulled on me first," Bonner said, without inflection.

"And your former wife?"

"She got in the way. Believe it or not, the bullet which ended her was fired from her boyfriend at me. It was her bad luck to have taken up with a lousy shot."

"Indeed," Quincy said. "In any case, you were cleared of all charges in the matter."

"Do you have a problem with the way I handled my personal affairs?" Bonner said.

"Not in the slightest," Quincy said. "In fact, I consider it a mark in your favor."

"A mark in my favor?"

"Absolutely," Quincy said. "Just as I consider your chosen profession since the war a mark in your favor, as well. By some accounts, Mr. Bonner, you are the best professional bounty hunter in the Americas. By all accounts, you are the most lethal. It is said that very few of the bounties you collect are paid on live prisoners."

"I find dead men easier to corral," Bonner said.

"Indeed," Quincy repeated.

"You were about to tell me why you wanted to speak with me," Bonner said.

"A moment ago, you told me you could guess," Quincy said. "Indulge me."

"You want to hire me to hunt down and kill Smokin' Joe Atherton," Bonner said.

"Your guess is correct," Quincy said. "Although he no longer wears that name. Atherton's now a Missouri lawman, who goes by his true name, Samuel Pritchard."

"I recall hearing a rumor to that effect," Bonner said.

"What do you know about him?"

"Never met him, personally," Bonner began. "I only know what I've heard. They say he's young, under thirty, six-and-a-half feet tall, has blue eyes, is built like a brick outhouse, and has a gunshot scar on his forehead over his right eye. Not exactly an easy fellow to lose in a crowd."

"You describe his appearance perfectly," Quincy said. "What have you heard about his history, character, and temperament?"

"As far as his history goes, I've heard he fought for the Confederacy as a horseback guerilla and spent his years after the war notching his guns for the Texas Rangers. He's reputed to have planted more men than pneumonia. I've also heard, from those who would know, that his skill with all manner of firearms, particularly pistols, is unmatched. They say the only thing which outstrips the speed and accuracy of his revolvers is his willingness to use them."

"His character?"

"They say he's an honest man," Bonner said. "I've heard no rumblings of a weakness towards drink, gambling, or women."

"And his temperament?"

"Folks say he doesn't court trouble, but when it comes courting him he's unafraid to meet it. The notches on his guns also speak to that."

"You're well-informed," Quincy said. "Why do you think I want Atherton—er Pritchard—dead?"

"I don't care. Whatever the reason, it's yours."

"Not the least bit curious?"

"Didn't say that," Bonner said. "Just saying a man's entitled to his reasons. If he wants to keep them private, that's his business."

"Again," Quincy said, "I ask you to indulge me?"

"You bought the ticket," Bonner conceded, "so I'll answer. I recall hearing a rumor about your detective agency placing a bounty of ten-thousand dollars on Pritchard's head. I happen to know you're facing criminal charges for attempting to orchestrate his demise, for which you're currently out on bail, awaiting trial, so there must be at least some truth to it. There was also, I believe, mention of a woman's involvement."

"A woman was involved," Quincy confirmed.

"Whatever the motivation to end Pritchard, yours or hers," Bonner said, "in my profession ten-grand gets attention. But since I haven't heard anything about Pritchard's death, and I'm here in your office, I can only assume the effort didn't bear fruit."

"Once again, Mr. Bonner," Quincy said, exhaling smoke, "your assumptions are largely, but not entirely, correct. For the record, the woman involved meant a great deal to me. And I did put up ten-thousand dollars on Pritchard's head, but the money wasn't mine; it was hers."

"An unusual arrangement," Bonner said.

"Not really. Pritchard killed this woman's husband in the New Mexico Territory while he was riding with the Texas Rangers as Smokin' Joe Atherton. She employed me and my agency as an intermediary in her quest for justice."

"You mean vengeance, don't you?"

"A distinction without a difference," Quincy said dismissively.

"Not necessarily," Bonner countered. "If Atherton—I mean Pritchard—killed her husband while he was a Texas Ranger, he likely did it lawfully and for good reason."

"She was inclined to disagree."

"Now I know the reason for you posting the bounty on Pritchard," Bonner said. "Where is this woman now?"

"She is dead. Killed, like her husband, at the hands of Samuel Pritchard."

"And your reason for wanting Pritchard dead? Retribution for the woman's death?"

"Partly. Three months ago, Pritchard came into this very office, broke my nose, and shot off my right arm." He lifted the stub for emphasis. "As you can imagine, I take such affronts personally."

"Understandable," Bonner said. "Just as one can understand why Pritchard might take it personally that you put up ten-grand, even if acting on behalf of a client, to have him killed."

"You sympathize with him?"

"I didn't say that. I only said I understand why a man would harbor hostility towards someone paying to have him put down. What I don't understand, Mr. Quincy, is why you're still alive? From what I gather about Pritchard, or Smokin' Joe Atherton, whichever name he uses, most people who cross him aren't usually so lucky."

"Perhaps I'm not so easy to kill?" Quincy said.

"Perhaps," Bonner said, "perhaps not. No offense, Mr. Quincy, but if Pritchard was close enough to rid you of your gun arm and rap you one in the beezer, he certainly could have finished you off. I suspect you are above ground only because he chose not to end your life."

Quincy's face reddened, and his nose began to leak again. Once more the handkerchief came out.

"Will you take the job?" he finally said, after wiping his nose.

"Twenty-thousand dollars," Bonner said.

"That's outrageous," Quincy said. "Out of the question. Three months ago, I put up ten-thousand dollars—"

"You paid ten-thousand dollars," Bonner interrupted, "of someone else's money for a job that didn't get done. All your client got for her cash was to have it confiscated by the government, a platoon of bounty hunters and private detectives got put to rest, and Smokin' Joe Atherton carved a few more notches on his guns, one of which was hers. Not exactly a profitable return on your client's investment, or a sterling advertisement for your agency's services, I'd say."

"I'm not sure I like your tone," Quincy said.

"I'm not trying to insult you," Bonner said. "I'm simply speaking plain truth. If I'm hearing you correctly, you want me to go, alone, after a fellow you spent ten-grand to send an army of bounty-killers and detectives after?"

"Ten-thousand dollars is a fortune," Quincy said. "Twenty is a king's ransom. All I'm asking you to do is to kill one man. I know, for a fact, you've killed men for a fraction of that amount."

"I have," Bonner admitted. "But every man I ended was a wanted criminal with a reward bounty posted on his head. I never broke the law. You're asking me to commit a crime by killing a lawman who may have wronged you, but committed no crime himself. A man that ten-thousand-dollars' worth of hired guns couldn't put down."

"What makes you think I'd pay twenty-thousand-dollars to you when I can hire a dozen others who would do the job for half?"

"Because you're desperate, Mister Quincy. You're running out of time and can't afford the publicity."

"Not many men speak to me so disrespectfully," Quincy said, his eyes narrowing.

"It's not my intention to be disrespectful," Bonner said. "The fact is, you can't put out an open bounty on Pritchard because you're out on bail awaiting trial for previously paying to have him killed."

"If Pritchard is dead, there will be no one to testify against me at trial," Quincy said.

"True," Bonner agreed, "but if word got out that you're attempting to have him silenced again, your bail would be revoked, you'd be arrested, locked up, and this time held without bail, despite your money and political connections. That's why you can't afford to solicit more than one bounty-killer for this job. You can't risk loose talk."

"You're a bold man, Mister Bonner," Quincy said. "I'll give you that."

"I'm also a practical man, Mister Quincy. So

are you. Twenty-thousand is my price. Half up front, and half on delivery of proof of Pritchard's demise. Take it or leave it."

Quincy stared for a long minute across his desk at the man opposite him.

"You know I have no choice," Quincy finally said, "but to take it. Do we have a contract?"

"We do," Bonner said.

"Shall I draw up papers?"

"If it isn't cash, paper is meaningless."

"Then I'll arrange for a down payment of ten-thousand-dollars cash in the morning," Quincy said.

"That is satisfactory."

"Do you know why they call me Cottonmouth?" Quincy asked.

"No," Bonner said. "But I can guess."

"Everybody thinks it's because I strike like a serpent," Quincy said. "In truth, I was given the name when I commanded a fleet of riverboats under General Blair, during Sherman's siege of the Yazoo Valley. Cottonmouth Quincy they called me. The River Snake."

"I remember hearing about atrocities committed during that campaign," Bonner said. "Sherman ordered his men to destroy every grist mill, silo, and grain barn, and tear down every building they could find for wood to fuel their boats. I also heard he ordered wholesale attacks on unarmed civilians."

"I did all that, and more," Quincy said. "Which

52

means I shouldn't have to warn of what would happen should you elect to abscond with my money and not complete the task for which you're being employed."

"I need no such warning," Bonner said. "Just as I would be remiss in failing to disclose the fate awaiting you should you fail to fulfill your end of the bargain once the job is done."

Dominic Cottonmouth Quincy stood and raised his glass. Laird Bonner followed suit.

"To Samuel Pritchard's head," Quincy said, "on a silver platter."

"To twenty-thousand dollars," Bonner countered. Both men drank.

CHAPTER SEVEN

"It's good to see you again, Samuel," Governor Woodson said, as he shook Pritchard's massive hand. "Lord, but you're a strapping brute." He stepped back to appraise him. "Still tall as a tree and fit as a fiddle, I see. Isn't Marshal Pritchard fit as a fiddle, Henry?"

Governor Woodson addressed this remark to Missouri Attorney General Henry Ewing. Both men greeted Pritchard as he entered the governor's office.

"He's as fine a specimen of manhood as the Great State of Missouri ever produced," Ewing agreed, shaking Pritchard's hand.

Pritchard arrived by rail in Jefferson City the night before, lodged at a local hotel, and was up, shaved, breakfasted, and in the governor's mansion by nine o'clock. He was attired in his least-worn button-front shirt, his best pair of dungarees, his neckerchief with the fewest holes in it, and had shined up his boots, cartridge belts, holsters, and Jackson County Sheriff engraved star. His well-worn, wide-brimmed, Stetson rested in his massive left fist. This manner of dress left him, despite his unique size, largely indistinguishable from many other cattlemen, lawmen, or cowboys inhabiting the region. This was by choice.

Pritchard was by no means a pauper, having in excess of ten-thousand dollars in his Wells Fargo Bank account. He'd refused any of the inherited wealth he recovered from the Burnell Shipley faction after they murdered his father and plundered his family's lucrative lumber business, leaving his sister Idelle to manage the Pritchard's financial interests.

Some of Pritchard's savings were accrued from wages he'd earned during his years as a Texas Ranger, but most of the funds were accumulated by the various rewards and bounties he'd collected on the countless outlaws he'd corralled or buried during his stint with the hard-riding Texas Rangers.

Pritchard chose his Spartan life deliberately, having lived out of a saddle since fleeing Atherton at seventeen to enlist in the Army of the Confederacy. His time as a Ranger after the war did little to abate those simple habits. His sole attempt to purchase property and settle down as a respectable landowner and family man ended with the murder of his beloved fiancée, Caroline, and soured him on the prospect of further attempts to put down roots. Other than Rusty, his saddle, guns, and a few clothes, he owned nothing that couldn't be lashed to a single horse.

"I got your telegram, Governor Woodson,"

Pritchard said. "I apologize for my delay in arriving. When your wire came, I was afield on a pressing criminal matter."

"So I've been informed," Woodson said. "Three craven cowards murdered an unarmed man in cold blood, and then kidnapped and attacked a young girl. Nasty business. It is, however, my understanding you recovered the young lady, alive, and dispatched the three outlaws with your usual trademark efficiency. Judge Pearson wired me the details."

"I'd have brought 'em in for trial if I could've," Pritchard explained. "Weren't my call."

"I'm sure you would have," Woodson said, reaching up to pat Pritchard's shoulder, "but Eugene noted in his telegram that justice was more than properly served by their deaths. I have no reason to doubt his, or your, judgement in the matter."

"What can I do for you?" Pritchard asked, as Woodson gestured for all three men to take seats.

"Right to it," Ewing said. "I like a young man with purpose."

"There is a grave problem vexing the State of Missouri," Woodson began. "A mystery whose origin is causing great consternation among not only the good citizens of this state, but the denizens of the states of Iowa, Nebraska, Illinois, and many other eastern territories. I suspect the true nature of this enigmatic trouble might be something that you, Samuel, may be uniquely suited to resolve."

Pritchard walked into Perkins's Diner, ducking his head to get through the doorway as he entered. A trio of patrons looked up from their breakfasts and waved as he came in.

Ditch Clemson, Judge Eugene Pearson, and his sister Idelle, Ditch's wife, were already dining. Idelle was petite, beautiful, five years younger than Pritchard, and shared her older brother's white-blond hair and blue eyes. She was also five months along in her pregnancy and noticeably showing.

Pritchard shook Ditch's and the judge's hands, gave his sister a hug, and joined them at their table.

"Didn't expect you back in Atherton so soon," Ditch said.

"Got in on the midnight special," Pritchard said. Dady Perkins, the diner's owner, approached without being summoned and poured him a cup of coffee. "Slept in the jail."

"I don't know why you don't take a room in the hotel." Idelle said. "We own it, remember? It would surely be much nicer accommodations than that rank old jail."

"The jail ain't old," Pritchard corrected. "Hell, it's barely broken in."

Atherton had constructed a new jail within the

past year, and Pritchard kept a small room with a cot in back.

"Maybe so," Idelle said, "but it's still no place for a respectable man to call home."

"What'll you have, Marshal?" Dady asked.

"Whatever you recommend," Pritchard smiled at her. "Extra-sized portions."

"The steak and eggs are especially good today," she said, "and the biscuits are as sweet and flaky as they come. At least that's what Tater Jessup tells me."

"If anyone would know," Pritchard said, "it's Tater."

Deputy Toby Jessup, affectionately dubbed Tater by his fellow Athertonians due to his physique and affinity for spuds, was usually the first customer in line when Dady opened her door for business each morning at five o'clock.

"What did the governor summon you for?" Ditch asked around a mouthful of hash browns. "Must have been something pretty important."

"Why don't you ask Judge Pearson?" Pritchard said. "He evidently knew why I was summoned by Governor Woodson before I left for Jefferson City."

"I had an inkling," Pearson admitted, "but wasn't certain. In any event, Silas—I mean Governor Woodson—wanted to speak with you in person on the matter. I thought it best to allow him to explain the situation himself."

"I ain't complainin'." Pritchard grinned. "Was nice to get out of town for a day or two."

"So what did the governor want?" Idelle demanded. "I'm fit to burst with curiosity."

Pritchard took a slow sip of coffee to goad his sister before answering. "Seems like there's been a passel of homesteaders lately who've set off for California on the Oregon Trail from the trailhead here in Missouri who ain't never been heard from again. Lots of concerned relatives are powerful worried about the fate of their loved ones and the loss of their families' fortunes. These folks have been writin' to their congressmen. The governor's bein' nudged to act."

"What's the big mystery?" Ditch asked. "Not everyone who sets out by wagon from Independence makes it all the way to California. You should know that, as a former Texas Ranger, as well as anyone. The Oregon's a hardship-riddled trail, filled with all manner of woe. Brigands, hostile Indians, biblical weather, tainted water, and disease, to name only a few. Of those hardy souls who set out upon it, who's to know for certain how many actually reach their destination?"

"True enough," Pritchard admitted. "But the governor seems to believe, based on what he's hearing from his constituents, that an 'especially inordinate,' as he called it, number of pilgrims have disappeared along the Oregon Trail."

Pritchard, like everyone else in Atherton, knew what Ditch was referring to. The Oregon Trail, starting in Independence, Missouri, only ten miles south of Atherton, was the jumping-off point for homesteaders, pioneers, prospectors, and fortune-hunters seeking a better life in either California, or farther north in the state of Oregon. The trail meandered west from Missouri, through the States of Kansas and Nebraska, and into the Territories of Wyoming and Idaho where it eventually split west of Fort Hall either north to the Oregon Territory, or southward to California.

Since the war, the railroads had made significant progress in advancing the great American migration westward, and the journey west by rail could be made in under one-hundred hours. But at over eighty dollars per ticket, and at a time when the average yearly wage in the United States was less than two-hundred dollars, the trip to California by train was out-of-reach for most working families. In addition, many people heading out west to start their lives anew weren't traveling with only a suitcase. Most were packing all their worldly possessions, including livestock, furniture, and valuables, which required a wagon and team to pull it. Thus began the advent of the great, post-war, wagon-train migration westward on the Oregon Trail.

"The bulk of folks who meet their end traversing the Oregon are probably done in by disease, or the Sioux, Cherokee, or Cheyenne, to name only a few of the hostile tribes roaming the Oregon," Ditch said. "The Indian Nations have been riled up something fierce ever since the railroads began laying down tracks all over their lands."

"That's what the governor thought, at first," Pritchard said. "But reports from the army don't indicate any more than the usual number of raids, skirmishes, and attacks. And the fact that none of these pilgrim families seem to get word back to their relatives, once they get west of Cheyenne, is troubling."

"What do you mean?" Idelle asked.

"It's common for those traveling on the Oregon to send a wire or letter back to their eastern relatives once they reach Cheyenne. Sometimes it's to ask for money, or just to let their families know they're all right. Since many of the missing folks did just that, we know whatever befell them occurred after reaching Cheyenne."

"Now that you mention it," Idelle said, "there're a couple of families from right here in Atherton who've had relatives go missing on the Oregon in the past couple of years. The McIntoshs and the Fennermans both come to mind. Bob and Shirlene McIntosh set out last summer with their four kids and a herd of stock. The Fennermans had three of their own kids, a couple of cousins, and both sets of parents in three wagons, along with that prize bull Jim Fennerman was always bragging about. None of them have been heard from since."

"According to the governor," Pritchard said, "it's the same story all over Nebraska, Iowa, and Illinois. Folks set out west on the Oregon Trail and not long after clearing Cheyenne they vanish without a trace. He provided me a list of the names of the known missing."

Pritchard withdrew a piece of paper from his pocket and handed it to Judge Pearson. The paper was covered on both sides, top-to-bottom, with family names. Each name was listed alphabetically.

Judge Pearson whistled and handed the paper back to Pritchard. "That's a lot of missing people. Are you going to do it?"

"Do what?" Idelle asked, a puzzled expression on her face.

In answer, Pritchard withdrew a Deputy U.S. Marshal's badge from his pocket and set it on the table.

"I reckon so," Pritchard said.

CHAPTER EIGHT

"What's gotten into you?" Idelle said, as she walked with her brother, Ditch, and Judge Pearson across the street from the diner to the jail. "You only came back home last year! Why do you want to leave again? Good Lord, Samuel," she scolded, "we just put this town back together! Atherton is finally becoming prosperous and peaceful, and you want to run off and abandon it?"

"Who said I was leavin' Atherton permanent?" Pritchard protested. "I'll only be gone a few weeks. I've been appointed Deputy U.S. Marshal by the governor and tasked with an important mission. Atherton can surely do without the likes of me for a spell. You just said so yourself, Idelle; this town's prosperous and peaceful again. Deputy Strobl, Tater, and Ditch are as capable a trio of hombres as you'll find anywhere in the territory, and there are plenty of other good men in Atherton who'll take up arms if called. The fort will stand while I'm gone, little sister. Ain't like I'm indispensable."

"The Pannell family might say different," Ditch said.

"What befell them was tragic, but not

commonplace," Pritchard said. "It's the kind of thing that could befall anyone in any frontier town, whether the marshal's there or not."

"I'd still rather have you here," Idelle said. "Most in town would agree with me."

"I won't be gone much more than a month," Pritchard insisted, "two at the most. I'll be back before the first snow. Governor Woodson has asked for my help, and—"

Idelle cut him off. "You could have said no. You could have suggested he find someone else."

"The governor felt I was the best man for the job," Pritchard said. "Who am I to dispute the wisdom of the chief executive officer of the State of Missouri?"

"Just because trouble comes courting," Idelle said, "doesn't mean you have to offer it a seat in the parlor."

"Idelle—"

"Give it up, Samuel," Ditch said. "There are two theories about arguin' with a woman. Neither of 'em works. Both apply double to your sister." Pritchard laughed, and Idelle punched Ditch in the arm.

"Got no choice," Pritchard said. "I already gave the governor my word."

That ended the debate, and Idelle, Ditch, and Judge Pearson all knew it.

Pritchard opened the jail's door, and the quartet entered. Florian Strobl was seated at the desk across from Tater. Both held cards in their fists. A pile of matches, standing in for poker chips, lay stacked between them.

There were only two prisoners in the jail; a local drunk sleeping off a bender, and the livestock thief Pritchard and Strobl had rounded up a few days previously.

Upon Idelle's entry Strobl instinctively stood, extinguished his cigarette, and bowed slightly. Tater looked up at him irritably.

"What's all the formal hoo-haw for?" Tater grunted. "It's only Idelle; ain't like the Queen of Sheba waltzed in. I'm on a roll, Florian. Sit yerself back down and play yer hand."

"Forgive my fellow deputy, Mrs. Clemson," Strobl said in his Austrian accent. "One might presume Deputy Jessup was raised by wolves, except that wolf packs typically exhibit better manners. Not to mention hygiene."

"Hi-what?" Tater demanded. "There he goes, usin' that fancy Eu-rope-ean mumbo-jumbo on me again." He turned to Ditch. "What did he just say?"

"He said you could use a bath." Ditch chuckled.

"What for?" Tater said. "I already done took a bath a Saturday ago."

"Actually," Strobl corrected, "I believe it was two Saturdays ago. At least."

"Whose countin'?" Tater grumbled.

"Gonna be leavin' you boys for a while,"

Pritchard announced, as he removed his sheriff's badge and replaced it with the U.S. Marshal's star. "Got a job to do. Leavin' on the noon train to Cheyenne. Ain't exactly sure when I'll be back. Likely no more than a few weeks. You two will be in charge of protectin' the town while I'm gone."

"U.S. Marshal." Tater whistled. "What's this all about?"

"Gonna be headin' out west, on the Oregon Trail, as a favor to the governor." He nodded to Judge Pearson, who explained the particulars of the mission to Deputies Strobl and Jessup while Pritchard went into his room and began to pack. It didn't take long.

The judge was just finishing his explanation when Pritchard emerged a couple of minutes later. His bulging saddlebags, bedroll, and canteens were slung over one shoulder.

"If what the judge says is true about all kinda folks goin' missin' on the Oregon Trail," Tater said, "shouldn't one of us go along with you? What if it is warring redskins or a pack of highwaymen? You can't take 'em on all by your lonesome?"

"My orders aren't to start a war, Tater," Pritchard said. "The governor tasked me with finding out what's befallen some westward pilgrims who're overdue, that's all. I'm on a fact-finding mission; nothin' more. Ain't expectin' any bloodshed."

"Horse feathers," Tater said. "If that was true, why is the governor sending you, and not some regular U.S. Marshal out of Jefferson City? You're savvy enough to know it ain't what you expect to find that'll kill you; it's what you actually find that'll plant your bones. Or worse, what ends up findin' you."

"My pungent co-worker is not wrong," Strobl said. "Perhaps one of us should accompany you?"

"Not necessary," Pritchard said. "Besides, after what happened to the Pannells, I don't want to leave Atherton down any more deputies. I'll be all right."

"As you wish," Strobl said.

"Deputy Strobl will be Acting Sheriff in charge of peacekeeping in my absence," Pritchard announced, "which makes you, Deputy Jessup, Atherton's Chief Deputy."

Tater stood and puffed out his chest, which still left it lagging well behind his considerable belly.

"If'n trouble arises in town which requires extra manpower," Pritchard said, "Deputy Strobl is hereby authorized, with the approval of both Mayor Clemson and Judge Pearson, to deputize and arm as many men as are needed to quell it. Any extra costs will be paid for by the State of Missouri, by order of the governor."

Pritchard retrieved his Winchester from the gun rack and tucked several boxes of .44-40 cartridges for his rifle, and .45 Colt for his revolvers, into his saddlebags. Then he set the weapon and his bags by the door, opened his desk, and removed a bottle of whiskey and five glasses.

He poured five shots, while Idelle wrinkled her nose, and distributed them among the men. Even before the pregnancy, Idelle rarely drank, and only wine when she did.

"Until our trails cross again," Pritchard toasted, raising his glass.

"Here's to safe travels," Judge Pearson said.

"Here's to keeping your scalp," Ditch said.

"Zum Wohl," Strobl said.

"Don't squat with your spurs on," Tater said last, as the men downed their shots.

CHAPTER NINE

"Can I help you, mister?" Tater asked.

A tall, lean, man wearing a long coat, a wide-brimmed Boss of the Plains, and sporting two holstered revolvers entered the jail. When he opened his coat to extract a cheroot from an inside pocket, he revealed a U.S. Marshal's star pinned to his vest.

"Name's Marshal Will Johnson," the man said, as he lit his smoke, "out of Illinois. I'm looking for either the Jackson County sheriff or the Atherton town marshal."

"They're one and the same man," Tater said. "His name is Samuel Pritchard. But you're a mite late, Marshal. He left town more'n a week ago, on official business out west."

"When do you expect him to return?"

"Don't rightly know," Tater said. "Could be a few weeks, could be longer. Is there something I can do for you?"

"I'm hunting a wanted man," the marshal said, "I have reason to believe Marshal Pritchard might be quite familiar with him. I was hoping to enlist his help, or at least ask him a few questions about the fellow."

"Looks like you're out of luck, Marshal."

"Maybe not," the man said. "As it turns out, the fugitive I'm hunting is likely heading west also. You wouldn't happen to know exactly where in that direction Marshal Pritchard was destined, would you?"

"I know he took the train to Cheyenne," Tater said, rubbing his whiskers, "and from there he'll be ridin' the Oregon Trail to Fort Hall. Where Marshal Pritchard is bound after that is between him and the governor."

"The governor?"

"That's right," Tater said loftily. He tucked his thumbs under his suspenders and stuck out his chest. "Marshal Pritchard's on some kinda special mission, on di-rect orders from Governor Woodson hisself."

"You don't say?" the man said.

"On my mama's grave," Tater swore. "Governor Woodson thinks mighty highly of Marshal Pritchard, that's a fact."

"Evidently so," the man said. "Say, Deputy—"

"Chief Deputy," Tater corrected him, puffing out his chest further.

"Chief Deputy," the man continued, "if you don't mind me asking, what's the nature of this special mission Marshal Pritchard's on for the governor?"

"Well," Tater said, "normally I'd be keepin' such matters under my hat, but with you bein' a U.S. Marshal and all I guess it wouldn't hurt none to tell you. Marshal Pritchard's lookin' into the disappearance of some homesteaders who've gone missing on the Oregon Trail west of Cheyenne. Quite a few pilgrims have vanished, I understand. Lot of folks are worried about their loved ones."

"I've never met Marshal Pritchard myself," the man said, "but from what I've heard tell of him the governor couldn't find a better lawman for the job."

"You can say that again," Tater agreed.

"Thank you for your time, Chief Deputy," the man said. He tossed his cheroot in the spittoon, turned, and opened the door.

"Oh, Marshal," Tater called after him. "What's the name of that fella you're a-huntin'? If you'd like, I can keep an eye out for him in case he comes passin' through Atherton?"

"Don't bother yourself," the man said. "The fellow I'm after is already well west of here." He touched the brim of his hat and departed the jail.

Deputy Strobl passed the man as he entered the jail.

"Who was that?" Strobl asked.

"U.S. Marshal named Johnson," Tater said, "out of Illinois." He got up from behind the desk to pour them both coffee.

"What business did he have in Atherton?"

"Wanted to speak with Marshal Pritchard about a fugitive he's a-trackin'. I told him Samuel was

71

on business out west. He seemed like a real nice feller."

"Unfortunately for him," Strobl said, accepting a cup from Tater. "Marshal Pritchard is gone."

"His bad luck, I reckon," Tater said.

CHAPTER TEN

"What's the holdup?" Pritchard asked, dismounting Rusty.

"That's exactly what it is," the wagon master answered. He was a weathered-looking man of more than middle age with craggy features, long mustaches and a beard, and the rough hands of a laborer. He was cradling a single-barreled shotgun across his chest, and one side of his jaw was distended with tobacco. "A gosh-darned holdup. Who're you?"

"Name's Pritchard," he said. "Came ridin' up the trail and found you folks dead-stopped. Mite early in the day to be haltin' your wagons, ain't it?"

"Take it up with these fellers," the wagon master said, pointing his chin at the riders blocking the trail.

Pritchard had set out alone on the Oregon Trail from Cheyenne after arriving in the Wyoming Territory by train. While in town he stocked up on provisions, and spoke with a local blacksmith who informed him that a forty-wagon caravan of Hoosier Quakers had departed from Cheyenne three days prior.

Five days later, Pritchard caught up with them.

A line of covered wagons, followed by a herd of over three-hundred cattle, oxen, and horses, was stopped on the trail a day's ride east of Fort Laramie. It was mid-day, and the wagon train shouldn't have stopped before sundown.

Pritchard was challenged by a horseman as he approached. He showed his badge, introduced himself, and was escorted forward to the front of the halted column.

As Pritchard and his escort galloped the length of the stopped wagon train he noted the occupants of the wagons. They were certainly the Quakers from Indiana he'd been told of in Cheyenne. He saw plenty of women, children, and more than a few elderly folks. By their dress and mannerisms, he recognized them as members of the Religious Society of Friends. Almost all the men appeared to be herders or farmers, and none were armed. All gawked at the giant lawman as he and his big red Morgan rode past.

At the front of the column, they found the man with the shotgun Pritchard took for the wagon master. He was arguing with a group of five men sitting astride horses and blocking the trail. Four of the mounted men had their rifles out of their scabbards, but weren't pointing them at anyone. The fifth horseman, obviously the group's leader, rested a Smith & Wesson Russian Model loosely across his pommel.

"This fella came ridin' up on us," Pritchard's

74

escort reported to the wagon master. "Says he's a Missouri lawman."

The wagon master appraised Pritchard as he dismounted, and answered his query by telling him why their wagon train had stopped.

"Me and the wagon boss here are conductin' a little business," the leader of the group of five riders said to Pritchard. "Ain't nuthin' for no Missouri lawman to concern hisself over."

"Don't mind me," Pritchard said, smiling and resting his thumbs in the front of his cartridge belts. "I don't plan on interferin' with your business."

"That's a right healthy perspective," the honcho rider chuckled. "Especially when you're outnumbered." He turned his attention back to the wagon master.

"If'n you and your wagons want to pass," the leader said, "you gotta pay the toll."

"What toll?" the wagon master said. "This here's open range. There ain't no toll."

"You're wrong," the leader said. He was a hard-faced man who was missing one of his upper front teeth. "It's five dollars per wagon, a dollar a person, and two-bits for each head of livestock. I'm in a good mood today, so I won't charge you for dogs or goats."

"That ain't no lawful toll," the wagon master said, spitting tobacco juice. "Hell, there ain't even a bridge nor gate to pass through."

75

"Nonetheless," the leader said, "you've gotta pay."

"We ain't got that kind of money," the wagon master said. "These here are poor Quaker farmers and workin' folks. All they've got in the world is the few knickknacks they're totin' in them wagons."

"We'll just have to work out a trade, won't we?" the leader said. "You got livestock, don't you? We'd be happy to take your herd in payment."

"You got women, don't ya?" one of the other riders called out from behind the leader. "I know you do, 'cause I can smell 'em." The other riders broke out in filthy laughter.

"I'll tell you what I'll do," the leader grinned. "Because I'm a generous man, I'll make you a special deal. You voluntarily give us half your herd, and let me and my boys pick out five of your prettiest womenfolk to piroot with, and I'll consider your toll paid in full. You and your wagon train full of religious sodbusters can be on your merry way."

"Those ain't respectable terms," the wagon master said, "and you know it. What you're offerin' is pure thievery, and worse."

"The alternative," said the leader, "to not payin' our toll, is we'll shoot your spud-diggin' carcass, along with anybody else who tries to stand against us, burn your wagons, take the whole herd, have our way with your womenfolk anyways, and leave those we don't plug to starve out here on the prairie. Do you fancy those terms any better, mister wagon master?"

The wagon master looked to Pritchard.

"Don't look to Missouri law," the leader said. "This here's the Wyoming Territory."

The wagon master gripped his shotgun tighter.

"That one-pop scattergun ain't gonna do you any more good than that lonesome, yeller, lawman," the leader taunted.

"Ain't you gonna do nothin'?" the desperate wagon master asked Pritchard. Pritchard smiled innocently back at him.

"What do you say, Missouri lawman?" the leader challenged. He cocked his revolver, though kept it across his lap. "You're one of the biggest fellers I've ever seen, and I see you're wearin' pistols. Are you a hero? You gonna take a hand in this?"

"It ain't my decision to make," Pritchard said.

"That's a right sound position for a lone lawman so far from home," the leader said. "This ain't none of your business. No use catchin' a bullet on someone else's account, is there? Let these wagon-bound folks decide their own fate, I says."

"It ain't their decision, either," Pritchard said.

"Huh?" the leader said. "What are you talkin' about?"

"I've gotta consult the marshal," Pritchard said.

77

"I'm only the deputy marshal. The marshal's the one who's gotta decide."

"What marshal?" the leader asked. "I don't see no other marshal."

"Marshal Rusty," Pritchard said.

Pritchard walked over to his horse. "Marshal Rusty," he began, speaking into Rusty's ear. "There's five highwaymen who are a-tryin' to shake money out of these here travelers. They're demanding half their herd, and a turn with some of their women, or else they'll shoot men down, despoil womenfolk, and burn wagons, leavin' oldsters, women, and children afoot to perish on the prairie."

The four riders behind the leader burst out laughing. "He's talkin' to his horse," one of them cackled.

"The lawman's takin' orders from a four-legged critter," another hooted. The leader shook his head and laughed, too.

"What do you want me to do?" Pritchard asked Rusty. He put his ear next to his horse's mouth.

All five horsemen were belly-laughing uncontrollably now. The wagon master looked quizzically at Pritchard; a peace officer seemingly taking direction from a horse.

Pritchard nodded, patted Rusty's neck, and turned back to face the five horsemen.

"Marshal Rusty's made his decision," Pritchard said.

"What did the 'marshal' tell you to do?" the leader of the five horsemen asked, wiping tears from his eyes with the back of his gun-hand. His companions were still laughing hysterically.

"He told me to kill all you sons-of-bitches," Pritchard said, drawing both revolvers simultaneously so fast they seemed to materialize in his hands.

Before the leader of the five horsemen could react, Pritchard shot him in the center of the face. And before the dead man hit the ground from atop his horse, the two nearest riders were also struck by the lightning-fast, and deadly accurate fire from Pritchard's Colts. One took a bullet in the forehead, and the other through his right eye.

The fourth fired a hasty shot at Pritchard with his Henry carbine, but he'd already ducked behind the leader's spooked, riderless, horse and the shot went wide. As the gunman was levering the action of his weapon for another shot, Pritchard popped up over the saddle and put two .45s into his chest. He tumbled to the ground like his three companions before him.

The fifth rider had enough. He dropped his rifle, reined his horse around, and spurred it to full gallop away from the wagon train. Pritchard leisurely holstered his revolvers, strode casually over to Rusty, and retrieved his Winchester from the scabbard. He levered the action, shouldered the gun, took aim, let out a breath, and placed his finger on the trigger.

"You can't just shoot him in the back," the wagon master protested.

"Watch me," Pritchard said, as he squeezed the trigger.

CHAPTER ELEVEN

"You just shot that feller in the back," the wagon master remarked, as Pritchard returned his Winchester to Rusty's saddle-scabbard.

"Yep," Pritchard said, "I most surely did." He began extracting the empty cases from his left-hand revolver and reloading it.

"Not very sportin' of you," the wagon master said.

"True," Pritchard said. "But last I checked, neither is rape, murder, rustlin', and thievery."

"What kind of lawman are you?"

"One that plans to stay above ground," Pritchard answered. "Do you know this country?"

"Nope. This is my first-time takin' a wagon train west of Cheyenne, and my last time herdin' Quakers, that's for sure."

"I ain't familiar with this country either," Pritchard said. "But you can be sure that bandit I just shot is."

People slowly emerged from the wagons. They began to assemble around Pritchard and the wagon master. Most stared in awe at the tall Missourian. Pritchard smiled pleasantly at them. Parents covered their small children's eyes to prevent them from viewing the bodies of the four highwaymen lying on the ground. Several young women and girls smiled back at him.

"What, exactly, are you a-gettin' at?" the wagon master said.

"That fleein' bandit eyeballed your forty wagons and fat herd," Pritchard explained, loud enough for all to hear. "If'n I let him go, how long do you think it would take for him to round up another batch of banditos and set up a proper ambush somewheres ahead on the trail? And you can bet your front teeth he'd learn from what happened today. After watchin' four of his compadres shot to pieces, likely as not he and his new gang wouldn't ride out in the open to make their demands again. They'd pick a spot where they could ambush you with rifles from hidin'. They'd stampede your herd, pick off your menfolk, and then abuse the womenfolk and children at their leisure. By the time they finished, and rode off with your stock and valuables, there'd be nothin' left of your pilgrimage but smokin' wagons and the carcasses of your family, friends, and neighbors a-rottin' on the prairie. You ain't in Indiana no more."

"How can you know for certain that's what he'd do?" a pretty young woman about thirty asked.

"I can't," Pritchard admitted, "and neither can any of you. Do you want to bet your lives on the intentions of a highwayman?"

"Once you put it that way," she said, "I reckon not."

"You've got farmers in your company, don't you?" Pritchard asked, looking at the assembled men. He holstered his left-hand gun and turned his attention to his right-hand Colt.

"We do," the wagon master said. "Most of 'em, in fact."

"Then you'll know how to dig. Get a crew of men to start diggin' a big hole. Ain't no time nor need for individual graves. Round up the dead men's horses, recover their saddles, guns, ammunition, and anything else which might be of use, dump their worthless remains in the hole, cover 'em up, and we'll be on our merry way. Shouldn't take more'n an hour or two."

"You want us to put these men to rest without a proper Christian burial?" a matronly woman in a bonnet said.

"Those boys look like proper Christians to you?" Pritchard asked.

"They do not."

"Not to me, neither," Pritchard said. "What they looked like, and might well be, was the scoutin' element of a larger force of bandits. Even if they weren't, do any of you want to stick around here awhile and take that chance?"

"I reckon not," the wagon master said. "For a Missouri lawman," he said, "you sure seem to know a lot about Wyoming bandits."

"Spent my time after the war rangerin' in Texas," Pritchard said. "Dealt with my share of bandits. Way I see it, bandits is bandits, whether they're from Texas or Wyoming."

"By your appearance," a heavy-shouldered man in a straw hat said, "and by the way you handled them pistols you're a-packin', I'd say you've dealt with a mite more than your share."

"There're those who'd be inclined agree with you," Pritchard said. "Some of 'em are even above ground." He re-holstered his second re-loaded revolver.

"It'll be done as you say," the wagon master said. He barked orders, and men scrambled to comply.

"My name's Ned Konig," he said, lowering his shotgun and extending his hand to Pritchard. "I'm bein' paid to lead these Quaker folks from their church in Bloomington, Indiana, to California. I reckon we all owe you a debt. Without your savvy, and guns, we'd be in a world of trouble about now. Is there anything we can do to repay you?"

Pritchard shook Ned's hand and introduced himself properly. "I'm travelin' to California myself, on official government business," he explained. "If'n you don't mind the company, I'd like to ride along with you. I heard some mention of hostile Indians plaguing the Oregon Trail awhile back in Cheyenne, but in truth, I suspect the greater threat is highwaymen of the sort who just braced your wagon train. In either case, there's safety in numbers, as they say."

"We'd be right honored to have you accompany us."

"Now hold on, Ned," a small, stern-faced, man in spectacles spoke up. "You ain't authorized to invite this feller along with us. We've only got his word for who he is, and what his intentions are. We'll have to convene a meetin' of the church council and consult Reverend Farley, before we invite a stranger into our company."

"The hell we do," Ned said, spitting tobacco juice at the man's feet. "You may be a church deacon back in Bloomington, Mister Wilson, but I'm the boss of this here wagon train. We ain't got time for no church social. If it wasn't for Marshal Pritchard's arrival, we'd all likely be feedin' the crows."

"What's so special about him?" Deacon Wilson scoffed, staring hotly at Ned but gesturing at Pritchard with his thumb. "Far as I'm concerned, he's nothing but a vicious gun killer no different from those poor souls he just shot down. And he's from Missouri, for heaven's sakes. He probably fought on the side of the Confederacy."

"Ain't no 'probably' about it," Pritchard said.

"War's over," Ned said. "And if you can't tell the difference between this man standin' before you and them brigands that just tried to stick us up, you're even stupider than you look."

"I doubt he's even Christian," Wilson argued. "And on top of that, he was talkin' to his horse.

Not only is that a sign of an addled mind, it's the devil's work. It's downright blasphemous!"

"Maybe so," Ned said, "but when those boys rode up on us with their guns skinned, and blocked our way, Marshal Pritchard was standin' next to me a-facin' 'em. I seem to recollect you, and the rest of that church council you hold in such high regard, includin' that overfed Reverend Farley, a-hidin' out in the wagons with the womenfolk and chilluns."

Wilson's face flushed behind his glasses.

"The Reverend and I are both God-fearing Quakers," Deacon Wilson declared, "and conscientious objectors to the use of violence against our fellow man. We are not gunfighters or killers."

"You ain't much use, either," Ned said.

"Perhaps in your eyes," Deacon Wilson retorted. "But in the eyes of God—"

"God ain't in charge of this here wagon train," Ned cut him off. "I am. The marshal rides along with us. Them's my orders, and they're final. Go tell that to the reverend and the rest of your church council, if you like. If'n they'll come out from behind their women's petticoats, that is. And while you're at it, tell 'em to grab shovels and get to diggin'. They might as well do something useful; they damn sure didn't fill their hands with guns when trouble came a-courtin'."

"I'm reporting your behavior to Reverend

Farley and the elders," Wilson said, and stormed off.

"You do that," Ned said to his back.

"An addled mind?" Pritchard grinned, once Wilson was gone.

"Don't worry none about him," Ned said, wiping tobacco spittle on his sleeve. "Deacon Wilson is just like the rest of those fools he calls the church elders; all fire and brimstone when givin' a Sunday sermon, but plumb useless as teats on a boar for anything else."

"Evidently he found my conversin' with a horse a sinful undertaking."

"Of course, he would," Ned grinned back. "He's too dimwitted to know that your horse wasn't really talkin' to you, and you was just usin' conversation with the animal to distract those bandits to get the jump on 'em. A nice trick, if'n I say so myself."

"Don't say it too loud," Pritchard said. "My horse is a mite sensitive. He might overhear you and take offense."

CHAPTER TWELVE

"I recall him," the tall blacksmith said. "Feller that big ain't hard to remember. A regular giant. A full head taller than me, and I ain't exactly short. What'd you say his name was, Marshal Johnson?"

"Pritchard," Johnson said. "Marshal Samuel Pritchard."

"That's him all right," the blacksmith said. "Real nice feller. Sittin' atop as stout a Morgan as I've ever seen. Fine lookin' animal."

"What did he want?" Johnson said.

"Nothin' but information," the blacksmith said. "Inquired about a wagon train that pulled out of town a few days before he arrived. Batch of Hoosiers, headin' to California. I did some work for 'em, fixin' up a couple of their Conestogas."

"And Marshal Pritchard went after them?"

"Can't rightly say where he went after he left my shop," the blacksmith said. "He just thanked me and rode off."

"How long ago was this?"

"Not more'n a week, at most."

"I thank you, as well," Johnson said. He mounted his horse.

"Say," the blacksmith said, "if'n you don't

mind me askin', why is one marshal a-trackin' another all the way from Missouri to Cheyenne?"

"I've got some bad news to deliver," Johnson said, as he rode off.

"Would you care for some dinner, Marshal?" a young, feminine, voice asked. "It's fresh and hot."

Pritchard paused from brushing down Rusty to find a very pretty blond girl about eighteen years of age standing behind him with a heaping plate of beef stew in her hands.

"Thank you kindly," Pritchard said, "but I haven't earned a meal that hearty today. Best serve all the others before offerin' up any victuals to me."

"Ma said you'd say something like that," the girl said. Pritchard noticed a group of four or five girls of similar age watching the interaction from what they thought was a position of concealment behind a nearby wagon.

"Ma also said a man your size needs to eat. She told me I wasn't to take 'no' for an answer."

"What's your name?" Pritchard asked.

"Becky," the girl said. "Becky Matheson."

"I'm Samuel Pritchard," he said, introducing himself.

"I know," the girl said. "You're the Missouri marshal everyone's talking about. I watched you shoot down those outlaws the other day."

"I'm sorry you had to see that."

"I'm not," Becky said. "Ma says she's glad somebody had the sand to do it. I am, too."

"You tell your ma I'm grateful for her generosity," Pritchard said. "But that chow should be placed at your father's table."

"My pa's dead," Becky said, looking down. "He got gunned down in our hardware store last winter by men just like the ones you shot. It's why we packed up with Grandpa and are heading out west to California to start anew."

"I'm right sorry for your loss," Pritchard said, accepting the plate.

"They never caught them," Beck said. "The men who shot Pa, I mean. They got away. That's why I didn't mind seeing you shoot down those highway robbers. I'd like to think one of them was the man who shot Pa."

"Where shall I return the plate when I'm finished?" he asked.

"We're three campfires from the lead wagon," Becky said. She ran to meet up with the other girls behind the wagon. All looked over their shoulders at him, giggled, and scurried off.

Pritchard tilted his hat back, sat down, and began to eat. The stew was delicious. He was, in fact, hungry as hell.

Three days had passed since he'd first encountered the wagon train on the Oregon Trail and joined the travelers. Since then he'd been helping wagon master Ned Konig move the caravan along as best he could. He and Rusty scouted the trail ahead, and convinced Ned to double the number of men riding herd and guard for safety, but since most of the men wouldn't carry guns the extra guard was of little value.

Ned explained to Pritchard that the Hoosiers he was hired to escort to California were Quakers and sworn pacifists. They believed it was a sin to raise a hand against their fellow man, even in self-defense. He further explained that since almost all were farmers most owned firearms, but of the single-shot, hunting, variety, such as shotguns and small-bore rifles used only to pot game. None of the men were veterans of the war, as conscientious objectors objected to all war on religious grounds. Few, if any, had ever fired a military rifle or handgun, believing such implements to be the tools of the devil.

Pritchard had known Amish folk in Missouri, so he was familiar with the pacifistic theology. Now he understood why Ned stood alone to face the five highwaymen, and with only a single-shot scattergun for armament. Ned himself claimed to be agnostic, and laughingly told Pritchard the color of pacifist money was the same as anybody else's and just as easy to spend.

When Pritchard asked Ned how he felt, traveling with over one-hundred pacifists across hostile country, the old wagon master shrugged.

91

"I take it with a grain of salt," he said. "Most of them Indiana Bible-thumpers I'm a-haulin' to California claim to be teetotalers, too, but that's a claim could be challenged. One of the barrels in the back of those church wagons is filled with rye whiskey. For medicinal purposes only, they tell me. Hah!"

Pritchard could sense relief in some that he was accompanying the wagon train and resentment and hostility in others. The resentful ones were mostly a group of stiff-necked, older, men he presumed were the church elders. Ned, for his part, was a competent and affable leader, and more than once expressed his gratitude that Pritchard, and his guns, were in their company.

The wagon train made steady progress, but little better than ten miles a day. Ned complained to Pritchard about the pace.

"It's more'n five-hundred miles from Cheyenne to Fort Hall," Ned explained to Pritchard as they rode point together earlier that day. "It's September. At this pace, it might be November before we get to the fort, especially with us stoppin' every Sunday for Sabbath. Like I already told you, I ain't never been this far west. I hear tell mountain winters come early, are fierce as hell, and can swallow up a wagon train like a hog gobbles a corn nubbin. Last thing I want is to be stranded in an Idaho Territory blizzard."

Pritchard finished the stew, washed it down

with water from his canteen, and cleaned the plate as best he could. "I'll be back in a while," he told Rusty, as he righted his hat and headed into the main encampment.

It was twilight, and Pritchard felt more than saw the many eyes on him as he walked past the wagons and their occupants settling in for the night. He recognized Becky Matheson, seated with her friends at a campfire near a large wagon. She waved as he approached.

"Evening, Marshal Pritchard," Becky said.

"Brought your plate back," he said. "And I told you, my name is Samuel."

A woman suddenly emerged from within the wagon. She stepped gracefully down and faced Pritchard, blowing an errant lock of blond hair out of her face as she descended.

"I'm Jolie Matheson," she said. "I see you've already met my daughter Rebecca."

"I'm Samuel Pritchard," he said. "I have you to thank for the delicious meal."

"Figured after all you've done for us, you could use something more to eat than whatever's in your saddlebags." She smiled, showing even, white, teeth.

Jolie Matheson was tall at five-foot-seven, and a strikingly handsome woman. She was broad-shouldered, narrow-waisted, long-legged, large-busted, though lean in figure, and clearly descended from Nordic stock not dissimilar from

Pritchard's own lineage. Her hair was blond, like her daughter's, and both shared large, expressive, brown eyes. If Pritchard had to guess, based on Rebecca's age, she had to be at least thirty-eight, which put her more than ten years his senior. But no man he knew, regardless of age, would have declined to give Jolie Matheson a second look.

Rebecca took the plate from Pritchard. "May I offer you a cup of coffee, Marshal?" Jolie said.

"Thank you," Pritchard said. "But only if you'll call me Samuel. The only people who call me 'Marshal Pritchard' are the folks I lock up. Hell, even my deputies call me by my first name."

"Have a seat," Jolie said, as she poured the coffee.

Pritchard nodded, removed his hat, and sat on one of several chairs set up around the campfire. Once his Stetson came off, the gunshot scar on his forehead over his right eye became clearly visible in the dancing firelight. Rebecca and her friends gasped. One of them, a pigtailed brunette a bit younger than Rebecca, pointed at his head and declared, "Lookit! He's been shot in the melon!"

"Girls!" Jolie scolded. "Your manners! Apologize to Samuel, this minute!"

"No apology necessary," Pritchard waved her off. "I take no offense. I'm used to it."

"How can you get shot in the head," another of Rebecca's friends couldn't help blurting, "and still be alive?"

"Easy." Pritchard grinned at her. "There ain't no vital organs in my noggin. Bullet passed through my skull like it was goin' through an empty closet."

The girls' eyes widened and their jaws dropped.

"That's enough," Jolie said, suppressing her grin and clapping her hands together. "Rebecca, run along and get yourself washed up for bed. The rest of you gals get on back to your folks."

"Goodnight, Samuel," Rebecca said, as she ran off with her friends.

"You'll have to forgive my daughter," Jolie said, as she sat across from him with her own cup of coffee. "She wasn't raised to forget her manners."

"She's a fine young lady," Pritchard said, "and no forgiveness is warranted. She's a credit to your parenting."

Both sipped coffee. "Tell me, Samuel," Jolie began, "if you don't mind me asking, how'd you happen along on the Oregon Trail heading west? Rumor has it you hail from Missouri."

"Line of duty," Pritchard said. "I'm on an errand for the governor."

"How's your family feel about you being so far from home?"

"Only family I've got is a sister, and she's married to my best friend. He takes plenty good care of her."

"No wife or children of your own?"

95

"No, ma'am," Pritchard said. "I haven't exactly lived a life which favors puttin' down roots."

"What's goin' on out here, Jolie?" a man's voice demanded. Pritchard looked up to see a tall, bearded man about sixty years of age enter the camp carrying an axe and a bundle of firewood. He was accompanied by the diminutive Deacon Wilson. Pritchard set down his coffee cup and stood to greet them.

"I was just getting acquainted with Samuel," Jolie answered. "Samuel, this is my father-in-law, Jebediah Matheson."

Pritchard extended his hand. Instead of taking it, the older man glared at Pritchard, abruptly dropped his load of firewood and the axe, and made an elaborate gesture of withdrawing his pipe and tobacco pouch from inside his coat pocket.

"I know who you are," he said, looking at his pipe. "You're that young Missouri lawman who shoots men down without blinking. Not to mention without arrest, nor trial, nor remorse."

"Pa!" Jolie exclaimed.

"It's true," he said around his pipe, "ain't it?" Jebediah's eyes were bloodshot and watery, and Pritchard could smell the heavy odor of whiskey emanating from his breath.

"It certainly is," Deacon Wilson chimed in. "Saw it myself with my own two eyes." He too, Pritchard noted, exhibited signs of having

96

partaken, though he didn't appear as intoxicated as Jebediah Matheson.

"Surprised you saw anything at all," Jolie muttered, "cowering in your wagon."

"It's the Lord's place to judge matters of life and death, boy," Jebediah said, pointing his pipe at Pritchard like a gun. "It is for the Lord alone to take life. Not you, nor any mortal man. Says so right in the Good Book."

"Weren't judgin' anyone," Pritchard said pleasantly. "Was only tryin' to stay above the snakes."

"Jesus would see it differently."

"I can't speak for Jesus," Pritchard said, "but I don't recollect seein' him on the trail that day, facin' those gunmen."

Jebediah smirked. "You know what the Good Book says about killin', don't you?"

"Last I checked," Pritchard said, "bible verses don't stop bullets."

"There he goes with his blasphemy again," Wilson said, clicking his teeth. "The man's a murderous, Southern heathen. You ought to be ashamed of yourself, Jolie," he admonished her. "What would your husband say, if he could see you consorting with a gun killer?"

"He wouldn't say anything," Jolie replied hotly. "He's dead."

"My son was a peaceful, God-fearing, Quaker," Jebediah said. "I won't stand for his name or memory to be sullied. Not by you, daughter-in-law, nor any two-gun Confederate ruffian."

"Nobody's sullying Robert's name," Jolie insisted. "You're right, Pa. My husband was a peaceful, God-fearing Quaker. He didn't know how to make a fist nor fire a gun. Do you know what he got for his peace-loving, God-fearing Quaker, ways? Gutshot by a saddle tramp behind the register of his hardware store for a handful of coins, that's what he got. And when he died, after three days of screaming agony, he left his wife and daughter nothing. We had to sell everything we had, including the cottage and store, just to buy the wagon and team to take us to California. So don't you lecture me, Pa, about besmirching the name of your son and my dead husband. I loved him as much as you. But speaking truth isn't sullying."

"If you were my wife," Jebediah said, glaring at his daughter-in-law, "I'd give you the back of my hand. A woman's duty is to stay quiet and obey her menfolk."

Jolie scoffed. "I've no such duty," she said. "Especially when the men are as narrow of mind and limp of spine as you. And I'm not your wife, God rest her long-suffering soul. If you ever try to lay a hand on me, you'll—"

"Ungodly insolence," Deacon Wilson cut her off, shaking his head. "Very unbecoming of a Quaker woman. What a terrible example to set for her young daughter."

"I'll thank you to mind your tongue about Rebecca," Jolie said.

"As a church deacon, I have a duty to look out for the welfare of my flock."

"My daughter and I aren't yours to tend," Jolie said. "My participation in your congregation ended with my husband. We're only traveling with your church as a way to get to California."

"That's exactly her problem, Jeb," Wilson said. "Jolie has strayed from the path. She is too long without a man. Without a firm masculine hand to keep her in her place, a woman can become too spirited. She's the proof."

"You're only saying that, Deacon, because I've rejected your advances," Jolie said. Wilson's face turned bright red. "You'd fancy nothing more than to be the man to put me in my place, wouldn't you?"

"As you can plainly see," he said, ignoring her question, "disgraceful behaviors, like the rebelliousness she's displaying this very minute, are the inevitable result of a woman left to her own devices without a God-fearing man's steady rule."

"Amen," Jebediah said.

Others seated around nearby campfires began approaching to witness the escalating argument.

"Your refusal to consider Deacon Wilson's generous offer of courtship isn't Christian," Jebediah noted. "Especially with him bein' one of the most eligible bachelors in the church. And his bein' kind enough to show interest in you, despite your bein' widowed, to boot."

"I don't want his kindness," she said, looking at the deacon with disdain, "nor attentions, nor any other part of him."

"Do you hear the boldness in her tone?" Deacon Wilson said. "Shameful, I tell you."

"Shameful, indeed," Jebediah said. "Why, any other self-respecting Quaker widow would jump at the attentions of a fine man like Deacon Wilson. Why you won't is a source of concern to me and the other elders."

"I don't need to explain myself to you," Jolie said, "or anyone else."

"A single woman, especially one with a child, is an affront in the eyes of God," Deacon Wilson said. "You need a man."

"Let me know when you find one," Jolie said, "and maybe I'll consider his offer."

Wilson's lip curled into a sneer. "You see what I mean?" he said. "The woman has no respect for her betters, and speaks like no Quaker woman should. Satan's hooks are digging in."

"There's wisdom in your words, Deacon," Jebediah said. "Go fetch me a hickory switch. The devil is going to be expunged from this woman, this very minute, as you said, before her shameless wickedness infects my only granddaughter."

"Won't need to get a switch," Wilson said. "I

have a quirt right here with me." He handed his short riding whip to the older man.

"I am thirty-eight years old," Jolie said, "and have a right to speak my mind as much as any man. And I'll not be whipped by anyone, man, woman, or beast. Certainly not by the likes of you two drunken, sanctimonious fools."

"You are all witness," Deacon Wilson exclaimed, elevating his voice for the onlookers to hear, "to the infectious poison of Satan's own sin within this woman. It is every righteous Christian's duty to see such wickedness purged before it spreads."

Jebediah smacked the whip against his thigh. "Stand and take your due, woman," he commanded. "As a church elder, I order you—"

"I will not," Jolie interrupted him. She stepped back, squared her shoulders, stuck out her chin, and put her hands on her hips.

"Mama!" Rebecca called out, pushing her way through the crowd. She wore a worried expression on her face. "What's going on?"

"Stay back, Granddaughter," Jebediah ordered her. "This is no place for a child." Rebecca ignored her grandfather's order and ran to her mother, embracing her.

The crowd of spectators had grown larger, as more of the wagon train's members noticed the commotion. Soon most of the people in camp were surrounding the Matheson campfire.

"Remove that child from her mother's arms," Jebediah commanded, as he again cracked the whip. "God's work must be done."

"No!" protested a tearful Rebecca, clinging even tighter to her mother. Deacon Wilson stepped forward and reached for Rebecca's arm. "Come, child," he said. "This is for your mother's own good."

"That's enough," Pritchard said. He moved between the deacon and the two women.

"Stay out of this, interloper," Jebediah said. "This is God's business."

"I will not," Pritchard said, echoing Jolie's words. "Don't know much about God's business, but I reckon a pair of drunken bullies whippin' a defenseless woman is something he'd have no part of."

"Step aside!" Jebediah boomed.

"Not a-gonna," Pritchard said. "First man who lays a hand on this woman, or any other, is gonna be eatin' his mornin' grits without teeth."

"You foul infidel," Deacon Wilson said. His body was trembling with rage, and the liquor he'd consumed had overtaken his judgment. He swung clumsily at Pritchard, who caught the fist in one of his large hands.

As Wilson shrieked in pain, Pritchard easily twisted the tiny deacon's wrist until the screaming man was bent nearly backward. Pritchard then grabbed him by his belt, hefted him off the ground, and hurled him bodily through the air. The church official thudded to rest in a tangle of arms and legs fifteen feet from where he'd originally thrown his ill-advised punch at Pritchard's head.

Jebediah roared and lunged, raising the quirt above his head. Pritchard blocked the blow with his left forearm, receiving a torn shirt-sleeve and a shallow gash for his effort, but prevented the dual rawhide ends of the short whip from striking his face.

When the infuriated Jebediah recoiled the quirt to launch another lash, Pritchard snatched it from his grasp. He tossed the quirt aside, spun Jebediah around, planted the heel of his boot squarely in the seat of the church elder's pants, and pushed. The old man fell on his face amidst the load of wood he'd earlier dropped.

The crowd gasped and murmured. Deacon Wilson slowly stood up, rubbing his bruised wrist. His hat was missing, his glasses were hanging from one ear, and he was covered in dust.

Jebediah Matheson pushed himself up and turned to face Pritchard. His face was a mask of fury as he realized his previously discarded axe lay at his feet. He snatched it, raised the implement up, and charged at Pritchard, a guttural snarl emitting from behind his bared teeth. He was only a couple of yards from Pritchard when a single gunshot rang out.

Pritchard drew his right-hand Colt and fired, the .45 caliber slug striking the haft of the axe. The steel head flew off, and the impact of the bullet as it shattered the descending axe-handle sent Jebediah stumbling harmlessly past the tall marshal, to end up on his belly in the Wyoming dust once more.

No one in the crowd said anything as the gunshot's echo faded into the night. Jebediah looked up blankly at Pritchard. His anger had transformed into stunned disbelief.

"What was that you were telling me," Pritchard said, as he extracted the empty cartridge case from his revolver and reloaded, "about it bein' only the Lord's place to take a life?"

CHAPTER THIRTEEN

The following days were somewhat awkward for Pritchard in the wake of the incident at the Matheson camp, as the wagon train continued its journey west on the Oregon Trail.

Pritchard continued to act as Wagon master Ned Konig's second-in-command, to the chagrin of many of the menfolk. Most of the women, however, seemed more than willing to forgive him whatever transgressions he'd committed in preventing the corporal punishment of Jolie Matheson at the hands of her former father-in-law.

Pritchard continued scouting, riding herd, and guarding the train as the caravan steadily plodded westward. Many of the men cast disparaging glares as he and Rusty rode back and forth along the train, but many more of the women, particularly the younger ones, cast him sidelong glances of a different nature.

Other than an afternoon squall, and a particularly challenging creek that burned a full day getting the wagons and herd safely across, the weather held, and the trail was solid. It wasn't until more than a week after the incident at the Matheson camp that Pritchard again found himself in trouble.

It began one morning, as the train passed a shallow gulch. There, along the trail, they found a small band of Indians encamped. Pritchard and Ned halted the train, and both men rode forward to investigate. Pritchard kept his Winchester across his lap, and Ned, who'd traded his single-shot scattergun for one of the Henry rifles recovered from the highwaymen they'd encountered, rode alongside him.

As they neared, Pritchard recognized the Indians as Cheyenne. It was a party of only about twenty or thirty, almost exclusively women and young children. The absence of braves was overt.

All looked weak and malnourished. There were several ragged tepees, and a fire burning in the center of a pit with what looked like a prairie dog roasting on a spit. An ancient, stooped, brave, the only adult male in the party, stood to greet the horsemen.

The old man said in excellent English, "I am Avanaco."

"I am Samuel," Pritchard said, returning his rifle to the scabbard. "This here is Ned." Avanaco nodded.

"Where are all your menfolk?" Pritchard asked.

"The Dog Men are gone," Avanaco said. "Making war with the Crow and the White-Faced Devils. They have not returned for two moons now. We have little to eat, since there is no one to hunt. I am too old to fight and hunt, so I remain to care for the squaws and little ones." He lowered his weathered face. "In truth, it is the squaws and little ones who care for me."

"Why do your warriors fight the white people?" Ned asked.

"The White Devils are killing the herds," Avanaco answered, as if everybody already knew the answer, "to kill the Cheyenne."

"Huh?" Ned asked Pritchard. "What's he talkin' about?"

"The U.S. Army," Pritchard explained, "under orders from the president, in addition to outright killin' and lodge burnin', has hired an army of buffalo hunters. They aim to wipe out the herds, starve out the Sioux and Cheyenne, and drive 'em from their lands."

"God almighty," Ned said. "I used to hunt buffalo. I find that plumb shameful."

"It's workin' pretty well, too," Pritchard said. "While the braves are out fightin' to keep their homes and hunting grounds, their women, old folks, and young'uns are left defenseless on the prairie. Those who don't succumb to starvation or disease, are captured and relocated to a reservation by the army."

"What if they don't want to go?" Ned asked.

"They're usually shot dead on the spot," Pritchard said. "Sometimes whole villages at a time."

"Jesus, Mary, and Joseph," Ned said. "They're

just gunned down without mercy? Women and kids?"

"They say President Grant lost his stomach for mercy after Captain Jack cut General Canby's throat out in California," Pritchard said. "Mercy's in pretty short supply on both sides of this war."

"I didn't realize there was a war," Ned said.

"There ain't," Pritchard said, "in Indiana. Evidently nobody told 'em here in Wyoming."

CHAPTER FOURTEEN

"What in Hades is going on here?" Reverend Farley demanded. "Why are we stopped?"

"Ned Konig and Marshal Pritchard halted the wagons," Deacon Wilson answered, "to frolic with heathens!"

"We did not," Ned retorted, "you slow-witted ninny."

Ned had ridden back to the wagons and signaled for them to come forward. Once the wagons reached the small Cheyenne camp, he halted them again. Pritchard rode to the rear of the train, where the herd was loitering, and roped a cow. He ordered a herder to rope another, and to follow him to the front of the train.

"What do you intend to do with those cows?" Farley asked Pritchard, once he'd stormed to the front.

Reverend Winston Farley, as head of the church, was the official leader of the group of Indiana Quakers. He was tall, obese, and affected a sanctimonious posture at all times. He ruled with an iron fist, and no decision was made without his say-so. It was Farley who'd hired Ned Konig, a decision he'd come to regret.

"I'm fixin' to give these two cows to the Cheyenne," Pritchard said, matter-of-factly.

"You are not," Farley said. "These cows belong to the church. They are not for you to do with as you please, and certainly not to be given away as tokens to ungodly savages we encounter along the trail."

Once more, all the occupants of the wagons disembarked to witness Pritchard engage in a conflict with a church elder, this time, their leader.

"They're human beings, not savages," Pritchard said. "Women and children, and they're starving."

"They are not God's children. They are godless heathen. Their plight is no concern of ours."

"Rather a narrow interpretation of your Good Book, wouldn't you say, Reverend?"

"Return those two animals to the herd," Farley ordered.

Pritchard reached into his pocket and withdrew a gold coin. "Those two cows wouldn't get you twenty dollars apiece in Wichita," he said. He flipped the coin at Reverend Farley, who caught it. "That's a fifty-dollar gold piece. I just bought 'em, and I'm givin' 'em to the Cheyenne."

"They're not for sale. Not at any price."

"For heaven's sakes, Reverend," a woman called out. "Those poor Indians look like skin and bones. It's only a couple of steer. They're hungry. We have plenty more cattle."

110

"It's the Christian thing to do," another woman said. Other females in the company murmured their assent.

"Silence!" Reverend Farley bellowed. "I decide what conduct is Christian in this flock and what is not. I need no advice from upstart women who don't know enough to mind their tongues, and whose men evidently can't keep a firm enough hand in their own homes."

Farley pointed his finger accusingly at Pritchard. "Deacon Wilson was right," he said. "Your presence has infected our womenfolk. Because of you, they feel compelled to speak freely, without obtaining their husband's consent, as if their voices carried the same weight as men. This appalling display of wickedness shall not stand."

"I'm only tryin' to lend a hand to those in need," Pritchard said.

"You may hide your godless ways in a cloak of kindness, Marshal," Farley said, "but I see through your wolf's clothing. You're deliberately sowing discontent among my flock, especially the women, and nudging them towards temptation and farther from God."

"If'n you say so." Pritchard shrugged. "You're the expert on God, not me. And here I thought I was only givin' a little beef to some starvin' folks out on the prairie."

Five men emerged from the crowd and stood

111

behind Reverend Farley. All were middle-aged, hard-faced, and carrying guns. Not their usual, small-caliber hunting rifles, but the big-bore revolvers and carbines confiscated from the road agents Pritchard shot.

Farley tossed Pritchard's coin back to him, which he caught with his left hand.

"As you can see, Marshal," Reverend Farley gloated, "we've been planning for this moment since the night you interfered in the Matheson family's affairs."

"You didn't plan well enough," Pritchard said, his easy smile vanishing. Behind him, Ned slowly eased his Henry rifle from his saddle. Avanaco moved to stand next to Pritchard.

"You will drop your guns, Samuel Pritchard," Farley commanded. "Then you will mount your horse, ride your sinful soul away, and never return."

"If'n I don't?"

"Then you will die," Farley said.

"This ain't gonna go the way you planned, Reverend."

"Put those guns down," Jolie said, stepping forward. "What's gotten into you men?"

"Silence, woman," Farley shouted at her. "You are the very Judas goat who led us to this place, where men must take up arms to defend their women from your rebellious wickedness."

"You're a fool," Jolie said. She pointed at the armed men. "You're all fools."

Pritchard looked, one-by-one, at each of the farmers holding a gun. Some had rifles, others revolvers. None were pointing them at him. Jebediah Matheson had eyes burning with anger and hatred, a couple looked confused, but the rest had darting, nervous eyes, belying their fear.

"Have any of you ever killed a man before?" he asked the group. No one answered.

"I can't rightly recall the exact number of men I've killed," Pritchard said.

"This does not surprise me," Farley said.

"It ain't like pottin' game," Pritchard said, "shootin' a man."

"You may as well enlighten us," Reverend Farley said. "Seeing as how you'll be on your way, or dead, in a moment's time."

"It's a messy business, I can tell you that," Pritchard said. "And just 'cause a feller gets shot, don't mean he's out of the fight. Hell, I've been shot more'n a few times, myself." The uneasy expressions on the armed men became more pronounced. "You'd all best know, I take gettin' shot at, or shot, right personal. Every single man who ever shot at me is under the snakes. That's a stone fact."

"We are not afraid," Reverend Farley said, inflating his chest. "We have God on our side."

"That's good," Pritchard said, " 'cause the first one of you who so much as twitches is gonna meet him directly."

"Bold talk," Reverend Farley said. "As you can see, we are many. You, Marshal, are but one."

"Two," Ned Konig said, leveling his rifle and stepping beside Pritchard, opposite Avanaco.

"I'm disappointed in you, Ned," the reverend said, shaking his head.

"My pappy once told me the same thing," Ned said. "I got over it."

"You're outgunned, Marshal," Farley said. "Ride away."

"It ain't how many guns you have," Pritchard said. "It's what you can do with the ones you've got."

Pritchard suddenly tossed the gold coin into the air above their heads. Faster than the eye could track, he drew his right-hand Colt and fired. Before the coin landed in the dust at Reverend Farley's feet, he'd re-cocked his revolver and drew his left-hand gun. Both were leveled with the hammers back.

The unexpected shot startled one of the farmers holding a rifle so badly he dropped it.

"Which of you boys wants to make a widow of your wife?" Pritchard asked. "I ain't a-wastin' another bullet. Next shot I fire hits meat."

Reverend Farley slowly bent down and retrieved the coin. An approximately .45 caliber hole was drilled through its center.

"By the way, Reverend," Pritchard said. "Before

114

I shoot any of your boys, you'll catch the first bullet. That's a Texas promise."

Large beads of sweat had begun to form on Reverend Farley's florid face. He rolled the coin between his thick fingers.

"This is folly," he finally said, holding the coin aloft for all to see. "Behold the supernatural nature of his wicked eye, and Lucifer's power in his sinner's hand. Surely this man is one of the Devil's own disciples. Lower your guns, men. Go back to your wagons."

The relieved farmers did as they were told. Pritchard holstered his left-hand gun and reloaded his right. Farley approached him.

"Satan is strong within you, Marshal," he said, examining the coin, "but the power of God is strong within me. This is not over between us."

"Let's hope for your sake, Reverend," Pritchard said, "it is."

"Give these savages the beef," Farley ordered, "and let's be on our way."

"That was my intention all along," Pritchard said innocently. "To ease the suffering of my fellow man. Kinda surprised, as a so-called Christian, you don't understand that."

Ned lowered his rifle and turned over the two cows to Avanaco.

"Tell me something, Marshal?" Farley asked. "If not accursed by Satan, why were you so willing to die, just now, merely to feed a handful of hungry savages?"

"The why don't matter," Pritchard replied. "Question is, Reverend, if you ain't accursed by Satan, why were you so willing to die to starve them?"

CHAPTER FIFTEEN

"That was a mite too close to gunplay for my tastes," Ned remarked, as the wagon train and herd again got moving. Pritchard continued to receive hostile glares from some of the men as they drove their wagons past.

"For my tastes, too," Pritchard admitted.

"Would you have really shot 'em?" Ned asked. "And the reverend too, despite him bein' unarmed?"

Pritchard removed his hat and wiped his brow. The sun was high and hot. "Weren't my call. The day after I got this here pistol-ball mark," he said, pointing to the scar on his forehead, "I swore any man who raised a gun against me would die before, if not alongside, me. If the good reverend had been successful in incitin' one of his followers to make a move, I'd have honored my oath. I'd have gunned whoever pulled on me, sure as hell. Then I'd have shot Reverend Farley along with him, on general principle."

"You're certainly a man of your word," Ned said, spitting tobacco juice. "Ain't nobody can say otherwise. I reckon the reverend and his boys knew it, too, which is why they turned tail."

"By the way," Pritchard said, "thanks for throwin' in. You didn't have to take a hand."

"What was I supposed to do?" Ned grinned. "Let 'em start up a shootin' gallery on you without invitin' me? I've kinda grown accustomed to your company. Would hate to see you run off or shot full of holes."

Pritchard gave the older man a slap on the shoulder and replaced his hat. "Me, too," he said. The last of the herd moved past, leaving a billowing cloud of dust to envelope the Cheyenne encampment.

Ned wiped dust and tobacco spittle from his mustaches and beard on a sleeve stained brown from many a previous wiping. "Gotta admit," he said, "now that we're alone and can speak freely, I'm startin' to get a mite nervous. Can I have a private word with you?"

"What's on your mind?"

"Plenty," Ned began. "Weather's a-changin', I don't know this country, this train's movin' too slow for my likin', we've got too few guns, and even fewer men with the grit to use 'em. We've already been visited by one gang of bandits, Avanaco tells us the Cheyenne and Crow are a-fightin' each other in the vicinity, not to mention on the warpath against us 'White-Faced Devils,' and to top it all off, half the men in camp want to see you run off or dead." He spit again. "You may not know it, but these are the sort of

118

troubles that keep a wagon master up at night."

"They're righteous concerns," Pritchard agreed.

"But what's really got me vexed," Ned said, "is why you haven't ridden off and left us?"

"Why ever would I do that?" Pritchard said.

"Don't try to buffalo an old buffalo hunter," Ned said. "You don't need this grief and we both know it. You can surely take care of yourself, as you've demonstrated well enough. Ridin' alone, you could make better'n thirty-or-forty miles-a-day. You could be in Fort Hall in a week. You could ride on, and leave me and this bunch of Indiana Bible-thumpers in your dust."

"Why don't you quit askin' me to dance," Pritchard said, "and kiss me? What's really on your mind, Ned?"

"All right," Ned said, "I will. You told me you were headin' out west on official business, and I heard you tell Jolie Matheson you were on a mission for the governor of Missouri."

"So I did," Pritchard said. "I'm still a-listenin'."

"Your mission wouldn't be investigatin' the disappearance of wagon trains travelin' on the Oregon Trail, would it?"

"What makes you ask?"

"Rumors I've heard," Ned said. "Before I left Bloomington, I heard folks talkin' of their loved ones gone missin' on the Oregon Trail. Lots of rumors, Samuel. More than the usual numbers of travelers lost to Indians, and bandits, and cholera,

119

and other hazards, they say. Word is, the wagon trains just vanish. It's why I got paid so well for this trip. These Quakers couldn't find any other wagon masters willin' to take on the job."

"So why'd you take on the job?"

"Money was too good. Also, I got no kin. Figured I might as well head out west, find a place where it don't snow, and make a new start for myself someplace warm all year-round."

"Fair enough," Pritchard said. "What do you make of the rumors?"

"Don't rightly know what to think," Ned said. "Usually, when a wagon train sets out west on the Oregon and tragedy befalls it, some word eventually gets back. Survivors, or an army patrol, or trappers, or hunters, discover some inkling of their fate. Signs of a massacre or bones and such. But according to what folks are a-sayin', lately wagon trains on the Oregon Trail are just droppin' off the edge of the world, never to be seen again."

"There's truth to those rumors," Pritchard said. "Wagon trains on the Oregon heading west have indeed been disappearin'. I've been dispatched by Governor Woodson to ferret out why."

"I suspected as much," Ned said, slapping his thigh. "That would surely explain why you're a-taggin' along with the likes of us. Not that I ain't glad to have you."

"Now you know."

"I thank you for your honesty," Ned said.

"I'd appreciate it," Pritchard said, "if you kept my business under your hat. It wouldn't do anyone in our company any good to have 'em know there's even a spark of truth in rumors about vanishing wagon trains."

"Of course not," Ned said. "You can count on me."

"I already know that."

"We'd best mount up," Ned said, "and get ourselves caught up to the wagon train before it vanishes on us." Pritchard and Ned climbed into their saddles.

Avanaco, who was holding the guide ropes for the two cows, had been standing close enough to overhear their conversation.

"Hahoo, Samuel of the White-Faces," Avanaco said. He waved with one hand and held up the guide ropes with the other. "Your gift will not be forgotten."

"It was my honor to make your acquaintance, Avanaco of the Cheyenne," Pritchard said. He tipped his hat, and he and Ned spurred their horses.

"Beware the falling whiskey," Avanaco called after them.

"Been told that before," Ned chuckled over his shoulder. "More'n once. So long!"

"Nė-sta-évà-hóse-vóomàtse," Avanaco said, to himself, as Pritchard and Ned rode off. "We will meet again."

CHAPTER SIXTEEN

"Where do you think you're going?" Deacon Wilson demanded, as Jolie and Rebecca Matheson, along with a number of other women and girls, walked away from the parked wagons toward the creek. He was dressed in his good black suit, carrying a Bible, and leading most of the wagon train's other members in the opposite direction, toward where Reverend Farley had set up his pulpit. "The prayer meeting is the other way, in the clearing, up yonder."

"I know where the meeting is," Jolie said. "And where I'm going is none of your business."

"Mind your disrespectful tone," Wilson admonished, cognizant of the audience of churchgoers with him, "when speaking to a church deacon."

"When you mind your own damned business," Jolie said, "I'll be happy to."

"Your day of reckoning is coming, Jolie Matheson. Sooner than you know."

"Brave talk," she retorted, "coming from a man who threatens women but hides under their skirts in a wagon when danger beckons."

The red-faced deacon stormed off.

It was Sunday. Instead of breaking camp at

dawn, packing up, and moving the wagons and livestock west, Ned Konig was compelled to keep the caravan and herd where they'd camped the night previously while the entire day was consumed with religious observation.

Pritchard and Ned were lounging at the rear of the wagons, near the herd. They typically camped and slept there each night when not on watch, underneath the trail wagon, away from others. Both men had already breakfasted. Ned was seated on the ground, sewing up a hole in one of his socks. Several other ragged socks waited their turn at his elbow. Pritchard was conducting his daily pistol practice.

Since age seventeen, as close to each day that he could, Pritchard spent at least ten minutes, and sometimes as much as half-an-hour, drawing, aiming, and dry-firing his pistols. He worked each hand methodically, aiming at a coin he'd place at ten paces. Back in Atherton he practiced dry-firing inside the jail, and once-a-week rode Rusty out-of-town to practice with live ammunition. There he also practiced distance-shooting with his Winchester. Florian and Tater had grown accustomed to his unique daily ritual, as Ditch had before them.

"It's plumb foolhardiness," Ned complained, spitting tobacco juice as he spoke, "if'n you ask me. Here we are, a-wastin' perfectly good daylight sittin' like frogs on a lily pad with hawks overhead, smack-dab in the middle of unfamiliar, hostile territory. This nonsense happens every Sunday. We oughta be a-movin'."

"Folks are entitled to their religious observations," Pritchard said. "At least we're near water this particular idle Sunday. We can go fishin' this afternoon while the reverend preaches."

Ned had chosen their campsite well the previous day. The wagon train was stopped along a creek, surrounded by a strip of woods, at the edge of a large glade. Pritchard had shot a pair of turkeys there the night before.

"I don't mind their damned prayer meetings," Ned grumbled. "I just don't understand why in hell they can't conduct 'em around the campfire once we've stopped for the night?"

"Reverend Farley says Sunday is the Sabbath," Pritchard said. "Claims it's supposed to be for restin' and praisin' God. Me, I was raised not to waste anything, least of all the hours in a day."

"To hell with what Reverend Farley says," Ned shot back. "That blowhard claims the Good Book says whatever he wants it to say. If'n he's hungry, he claims the Good Book says to eat. If he's thirsty, he claims the Good Book says to drink. He claims the book commands all the women in his flock to do whatever their menfolk say, and that all of 'em, men, women, and children, have to do whatever he says."

"I reckon the reverend interprets the Good

124

Book," Pritchard said, "to say whatever tickles his fancy at the time."

Ned finished a stitch and bit off the end of a thread. "I seem to remember Reverend Farley a-claimin' the Good Book authorized him puttin' an end to you?" He picked up another hole-filled sock.

"Don't know much about the Good Book, myself," Pritchard admitted. "But if folks are foolish enough to take a man like Winston Farley's word for what the Bible says, and not cipher it out for themselves, shame on them."

"That's a sermon I'd like to hear preached to Reverend Farley's flock." Ned laughed.

"Why aren't you attending the ceremony?" Pritchard asked.

"Two reasons," Ned said. "The first is, me and God have an understanding. If'n he don't stick his nose into my feedbag, I won't nuzzle my snout into his."

"And the second reason?"

"Reverend Farley's screechin' voice. Hearin' that man speak is liable to cause me to upchuck my biscuits and gravy."

Pritchard laughed as he wiped his revolvers down with an oiled rag and reloaded them. "I think I'll mosey on down to the creek, he said. "Get in a shave and wash up." He collected a bar of soap, his razor, and a towel from his saddlebags.

Ned winked at him. "Your sudden need for cleanliness wouldn't have nothin' to do with Jolie Matheson bein' down at the creek, would it?"

"Enjoy your needlepoint, Ma'am," Pritchard said, as he walked off to the sound of Ned's laughter behind him.

"Don't cut yourself, Marshal," Jolie said.

Pritchard looked up from where he was squatting at the edge of the creek. He was stripped to the waist, and had shaving soap over half his haw. His hat, gun belts, and button-front shirt were draped over a nearby tree branch.

"I'll try not to slice my own throat," Pritchard replied, standing to greet her.

Jolie had her hair down, and her blouse unbuttoned enough to reveal the tops of her bosom. She'd obviously just finished her own washing ritual.

She approached and looked up at the extremely tall lawman. She couldn't help but notice the multiple gunshot scars across his broad, muscular chest and taut abdomen. Her gaze stopped when she saw the scabbed gash on his left forearm, where her former father-in-law had struck him with the quirt.

"This needs to be cleaned," she said, taking his arm and examining the raw-looking wound.

"It's all right," Pritchard said. "It looks nasty, but it's shallow. It'll clear up in no time at all. I'm a right quick healer."

126

She ran a hand over his chest, feeling the scars. "Apparently so," she said.

"Where're all the other womenfolk?" Pritchard asked, though he'd already scouted the creek and knew the answer.

"Rebecca, and some of the other women who've also had a bellyful of the reverend and his flock of dullard sheep, are upstream doing some washing. Thought I'd take a walk."

"I'm glad you did."

"I never actually thanked you for what you did for me," Jolie said, pointing to his forearm.

"Nothin' to thank me for," Pritchard said. "I don't abide the abuse of womenfolk."

Without asking permission, Jolie took the razor from Pritchard's hand. "Sit down," she commanded. "You're too tall for me to reach."

Pritchard did as she asked. She faced him and began to finish the job of shaving he'd only partially completed. Pritchard tried not to stare at her breasts, which were only inches from his nose, but failed miserably. Jolie caught him, and suppressed a smile.

"There," Jolie said, as she finished. "Smooth as a baby's bottom." She wiped his face with the towel over his shoulder and stepped back, allowing him to stand. "I didn't even draw blood."

"Maybe not," Pritchard said, "but you sure got my blood up."

"So do something about it," Jolie said.

Pritchard took the razor from her, tossed it aside with his towel, and pulled her to him. An instant later his mouth was on hers. She responded in kind.

He put one hand on the small of her back, and with the other grabbed a fistful of her hair. She dug her nails into his back, and met his kiss with the fire of her own.

"I warned you, heathen," Reverend Farley's contempt-filled voice said. "It ain't over between us."

CHAPTER SEVENTEEN

Pritchard found himself surrounded by a half-dozen men. This time, they were pointing their guns directly at him. The group had obviously crept up while he and Jolie were distracted in the throes of their kiss.

"What in the hell do you think you're doing?" Jolie demanded. "Have you men gone insane?"

"Funny you should mention hell," Reverend Farley said. "For that is exactly where harlots such as the likes of you, Jolie Matheson, are doomed to go."

"You can go to hell yourself, you fat hypocrite," she hissed. "And all you men who call yourselves God-fearing Christians can go right along with him."

"Helluva prayer meeting, Reverend," Pritchard said.

"We weren't meeting," Farley said, "we were planning. Remember when you told me I didn't plan our last encounter well enough?" He withdrew the fifty-dollar gold piece Pritchard had shot and held it up to his eye, like a monocle. "I took your advice, Marshal Pritchard."

Jolie was pulled from Pritchard's grasp. No one

leered at her harder, or hungrier, than Deacon Wilson.

"What would your wives say?" Jolie asked them.

"After we finish dealing with you," Farley said, "they'll say nothing. They'll let their men speak for them again, as before. Our women will return to the proper Quaker ways they held to before the arrival of your paramour, the heathen gun-killer from Missouri."

"Who's holding the guns now?" Pritchard asked.

"What do you intend to do with us?" Jolie demanded, standing up.

"You'll know soon enough," the reverend said. "Bring them."

Pritchard's revolvers, boots, hat, and shirt were collected, and he was prodded barefoot and shirtless from the wooded creek toward the wagons by several men with guns. Jolie was escorted by a pair of burly farmers who held her tightly at each elbow. Reverend Farley led the parade.

When they got back to the wagons, Pritchard saw Ned was also being held at gunpoint. The entire wagon party was assembled in a semi-circle around him. All of the Indiana pilgrims were clad in their Sunday best. A trickle of blood ran down the tough old wagon master's face.

"Looks like they bushwhacked you, too, Ned," Pritchard called out.

"They caught me unawares," Ned replied. "Sorry, Samuel."

"Nothin' to apologize for," Pritchard said. "Leastways you got to put up a fight. I got caught with my pants down."

"Looks like we underestimated them Quaker's penchant for violence," Ned remarked.

"Honest mistake," Pritchard said. "These boys didn't show this much grit when faced with armed bandits bent on theft, rape, and murder."

"Silence!" Reverend Farley commanded, halting the column at a large oak tree near the front of the wagons. Pritchard looked up to find a rope, ending in a noose, slung over a stout branch.

"What in God's name are you planning to do?" Jolie gasped.

"Only what must be done," Reverend Farley said.

"Mama!" Rebecca cried. She tried to run to her mother but was restrained.

"Leave my daughter be!" Jolie shouted. She struggled vainly to break free of the thick arms that held her.

"Samuel Pritchard," the reverend began, in his most officious voice, "you have been found guilty by a vote of the council of church elders of the sins of blasphemy, inciting wickedness, and the ruination and despoiling of Christian womenfolk. How do you plead?"

131

"What does it matter?" Pritchard shrugged his massive shoulders. "Them things I'm accused of ain't crimes, and you know it. They're made-up by you and your loco tribe of religious zealots, none of whom got the sense to realize you're even more loco than they are."

"Speak your vile blasphemy while you can, Marshal," Farley said. "Your days of doing Satan's work are coming to an end."

"I understand my fate's sealed," Pritchard said, pointing to the rope with his chin, "but what do you intend to do with Jolie?"

"That depends on her," Farley answered. "If she acknowledges her sin, prostrates herself in shame, begs forgiveness, and marries Deacon Wilson, she may, in time, after an appropriate period of shunning, be allowed back into the flock."

"If you think I'm going to prostrate myself before you," Jolie said, "and wed that little rodent of a deacon, you've got another thing coming."

A ripple of snickers wafted through the assembly as Deacon Wilson's face flushed with embarrassment.

"Then you will hang alongside the marshal," Farley said.

"You'd hang an innocent woman?" Ned asked.

"I would purge my flock of Satan's influence," Farley corrected him. "It is my Christian duty."

"Why you fat, gutless, yellow son-of-a-bitch,"

Ned spat. "If'n I wasn't hogtied I'd whomp you so hard your mama would show bruises."

One of the farmers holding a rifle behind Ned slammed the stock into his kidney. Ned grunted in agony and fell to his knees. Pritchard responded by instantly lunging forward and kicking the rifleman squarely in the groin. He moved so fast, no one had a chance to stop him.

Pritchard's kick was so powerful it lifted the man, who weighed over two-hundred pounds, several inches off the ground. He lost the rifle, clasped both hands to his crotch, and collapsed in a whimpering heap. Five men rushed to pin the bound Pritchard against a wagon, and they were barely able to accomplish the task.

"The sooner we get the Lord's work completed," Reverend Farley announced, "the safer we'll be." He turned to Jolie. "What's it going to be, woman? Repentance or the rope?"

In answer, Jolie Matheson spit in Reverend Farley's face.

"Put up another rope," Farley said, a smile slowly breaking across his features, "and bring another horse."

Men complied with the reverend's command. Two horses were led to the tree, and another noose was tossed over the branch. Jolie's hands were tied behind her back, and she and Pritchard were hefted onto horseback by many rough hands. The nooses were placed around their

133

necks by a pair of horsemen who stood by with quirts holding tight to the horses' reins, awaiting a signal from the leader of their church to whip the mounts out from under them.

"Mama!" Rebecca sobbed hysterically. "No! Mama!"

"Take the girl away," Farley ordered. The hysterical Rebecca was picked up by a pair of burly men and hauled off.

Deacon Wilson rushed forward to Jolie, his face twisted in anguish. "You don't have to do this," he beseeched. "Repent your sins, Jolie. Join me in matrimony and return to God's grace."

"I haven't sinned," Jolie said. "And if it's a choice between a rope and your greasy affections, I'll take the hemp necktie."

"Your sin is pride," Wilson said. "Do you wish to die for it?"

"And your sin, Deacon, is the same as my husband's was; being too weak and stupid to know that Reverend Farley is using all of you to advance his own, sick, lust for power."

Deacon Wilson lowered his head in defeat and stepped back.

Many of the faces in the crowd looked uneasy. Most of the women were ashen-faced, and more than a few of the men appeared nervous, as well. Yet none dared speak up; not with Reverend Farley's eyes ablaze in righteous anger and his most loyal followers standing behind him bearing guns.

"I condemn this pair of unabashed sinners to the smoldering fires of hell," he said, "and their cursed souls to eternal damnation for the sins of—"

"Oh, shut up," Pritchard interrupted, "and get on with it. I am truly sick of hearin' your mouth, Reverend Farley. Ned was right; your voice gives a feller cause to upchuck."

Jolie turned to Pritchard, seated astride the horse next to her. "Aren't you scared?" she asked. Her voice was calm, but tears ran down her face.

"Naw," Pritchard said. "Been killed before. Buried and dug up, too. Besides"—he smiled at her—"a man could do worse than spend his last day in your arms."

Despite herself, Jolie smiled back at him.

"Do you have any last words?" Reverend Farley asked Jolie.

"Take care of my Rebecca," Jolie said. "I'll be waiting in hell to greet those who stood witness to my murder, yet call me a sinner."

"And you, Marshal? Any final words?"

"Kiss my Missouri ass," Pritchard said.

"Then to hell you both shall go," the reverend said. He nodded at the men attending the horses beneath Pritchard and Jolie, and raised his right hand above his head. The horsemen lifted their quirts, awaiting the drop of Reverend Farley's arm.

Reverend Farley's right hand suddenly exploded into fragments of meat and bone. An instant later, a booming gunshot was heard echoing across the glade.

CHAPTER EIGHTEEN

A 550 grain, .50-90 cartridge, fired from a Sharps rifle at a distance of less than fifty yards, struck Reverend Farley's upraised hand at a velocity of just under fifteen-hundred-feet-per-second. The stunned reverend slowly lowered his hand and discovered it essentially missing below the wrist. Blood spurted in a geyser over his Sunday frock coat.

"I'm sorry to break up your lynching party," a man's voice called from out-of-sight in the woods bordering the creek, "but stringing up a lawman and a defenseless woman during Sunday morning services isn't exactly Christian behavior."

One of the farmers wielding a Henry rifle began wildly firing in the general direction of the voice. He got three shots off before his head exploded in a cloud of red mist and he dropped lifelessly to the ground.

Still staring at his missing right hand in shocked disbelief, Reverend Farley slowly sat down. No one else moved.

"Put down your guns," the voice ordered from the woodline, "all of you. Do it, or I'll keep on shooting."

The armed parishioners looked to their reverend for guidance. They found him sitting cross-legged in the dirt, mumbling Bible verses to himself, and staring numbly at the bloody stump that was once his right hand.

"How many of 'em do you think are out there?" a farmer holding a shotgun asked.

"How many of 'em do you need?" another farmer, carrying a revolver, answered. They both set their guns on the ground. All the other men bearing arms quickly followed suit.

With Farley useless, the men looked vainly to Deacon Wilson. He was busy vomiting on a nearby wagon wheel.

"Take those ropes off their necks," the voice continued. "Get them down from those horses, and cut them loose."

The two horsemen removed the nooses from Pritchard and Jolie, and cut the bonds from their hands. Ned, too, was released. Pritchard dismounted and gently lifted Jolie to the ground. Rebecca ran to her, and he turned the dazed woman over to her daughter's care. Both Rebecca and Jolie began crying in each other's arms.

Ned recovered Pritchard's Colt revolvers and handed them over. Then he found his Henry rifle, and approached the burly farmer who'd butt-stroked him in the gut. The wagon master wordlessly slammed the stock of his rifle in the man's face, shattering his nose and sending him sprawling.

"You finished?" Pritchard asked him.

"Hell," Ned said, staring hotly at the rest of the formerly armed Quaker men, "I'm just gettin' started."

"Save it for later," Pritchard said. "You in the woods," he shouted toward the woodline, "with the rifle and the sharp eye? My name is U.S. Marshal Samuel Pritchard. It's safe to show yourself and come on out."

"I know who you are," the voice said.

"I'd surely like to meet you face-to-face," Pritchard hollered, "and thank you for savin' my life."

"I believe I'll stay here in the weeds and remain anonymous for the time being," the voice said. "Don't worry, Marshal. We'll meet again."

"Fair enough," Pritchard said. "I look forward to making your acquaintance, and thank you kindly for your marksmanship."

"You're welcome," the voice said. "I'll be on my way now, Marshal. If anyone in your company attempts to track me, I'll be forced to demonstrate my marksmanship again."

"Don't worry none," Pritchard said. "We won't be moving until tomorrow. You're free to go on your way unmolested. You have my word."

"So long, Marshal Pritchard," the voice said.

Pritchard turned his attention back to the wagon train and surveyed the scene before him.

The wife of the farmer who'd been headshot

by the mysterious marksman in the woods lay sobbing over his body. Three burly farmers were attempting to hold a thrashing and howling Reverend Farley still, while a woman bound his wrist with a tourniquet. Jolie and Rebecca Matheson concluded their tears of relief and wiped their eyes, still clinging to each other. Everyone else stood dumbstruck and silent.

"Ned," Pritchard said, loud enough for all to hear, "I want you to collect every firearm in this camp. Every last gun. I want 'em unloaded and locked up in the lead wagon. From here on out, if I catch a man with a gun I'll shoot him dead on the spot."

"You heard the marshal," Ned barked. "Fetch your irons. Shotguns, squirrel rifles, pea shooters, it don't matter. I want every lead pusher in this wagon train on the ground at my feet. Move!" The men began to head off to their wagons to comply.

"Disregard that order," Deacon Wilson suddenly spoke up. He walked up to Pritchard, holding his glasses and hat in one hand and wiping his mouth with a handkerchief with the other. He had vomit spittle on his shoes. At the sound of his voice, all the men halted.

"You've no authority here, Marshal," Deacon Wilson said. "With Reverend Farley incapacitated, I am in charge of this flock. I will give the orders from now on."

"Here's my authority," Pritchard said. He launched a haymaker into the diminutive deacon's jaw. The force of the blow, which Pritchard kept at about quarter-steam due to the deacon's small stature, still sent Wilson flying backward through the air. He landed flat on his back, a dozen feet away, out cold before he hit the ground.

"Get movin'!" Ned yelled. "If'n every gun in this camp ain't at my feet in five minutes, I'm a-gonna shoot me a pilgrim." Once more the men scrambled to comply.

Pritchard slipped into his boots, belted on his cartridge belts and holsters, and put on his hat. Shirtless, he checked his guns, ensuring they were still loaded, then holstered them.

He spotted a group of men standing idle, watching the reverend as he moaned and thrashed.

"Why aren't you fellers fetchin' your guns?" he asked.

"Don't own no firearms," one of them replied.

"Then quit gawkin' and make yourselves useful," Pritchard said. "Get a fire goin'. We'll need to cauterize the reverend's arm, lest he bleeds out. Do you have any whiskey?"

"We're Quakers, Marshal," a woman said indignantly. "We don't condone the drinking of demon spirits."

"That ain't what I asked," Pritchard said.

"There's a barrel of whiskey in the reverend's

wagon," Ned told him. "All the menfolk know it."

"Get a canteen and fill it," Pritchard ordered one of the men. "Bring it back here as soon as you can." The man went off.

Ned stood with his rifle at port arms, and Pritchard with his hands resting on the butts of his twin-holstered Colts, as the Quaker men returned and lay their weapons on the ground before them. All were careful not to point their guns in Pritchard's or Ned's direction.

"That was a pretty timely shot," Ned whispered to Pritchard, as the men lined up and turned in their weapons, "if'n I say so myself. Dead accurate, too. Took the Reverend Winston Farley's booger-hook clean off'n his arm."

"I reckon if that mysterious sharpshooter wanted to," Pritchard said, "that buffalo gun of his would've taken the reverend's head clean off'n his shoulders."

"You ain't got a guardian angel, do you, Samuel?"

"If'n I do," Pritchard said, "I don't know who he is."

CHAPTER NINETEEN

"Care for some coffee, Samuel?"

"I care more for your company." Pritchard smiled, standing as Jolie entered his and Ned's makeshift camp. She was carrying a tin coffeepot and looked stunning as the firelight danced on her long, blond hair. She filled his cup.

"Would you like some coffee, Ned?" Jolie asked.

"No thank you, Ma'am," Ned said, rising to his feet. "I believe I'll check in with the guard. "Ever since we saw them redskins yesterday, I've been a-lookin' over my shoulder." He bit off another chaw of tobacco from the plug in his pocket. "I ain't afraid to admit it," he continued around his distended jaw, "but I sure will be glad when we finally get to Fort Hall." He put on his hat and coat, picked up his Henry rifle, and trudged off into the darkness. He was already wearing a pistol.

In the ten days that had passed since he'd been taken prisoner, and Pritchard and Jolie had nearly been lynched, Ned had been wearing a sidearm, something he hadn't done before.

Once all the guns in camp were collected and safely tucked away in the lead wagon, and the Quaker who'd been headshot was buried, Pritchard issued Ned one of the confiscated revolvers taken off the dead highwaymen. He selected one in good condition, field-stripped, cleaned, and loaded it, and ordered Ned to wear the weapon at all times in a belt holster stuffed with cartridges. Ned didn't object.

Pritchard also cleaned and loaded one of the other revolvers, a Smith & Wesson Russian .44, and discretely gave it to Jolie. He told her to keep it hidden and with her always. She didn't object, either.

Pritchard issued a rifle to each of the Indiana Quakers riding herd, and one to the watchmen he posted on guard every night in camp at the start of his shift. These men, specially selected by Ned, were not among Reverend Farley's most ardent loyalists. Ned hadn't forgotten the faces of the men who'd tried to string Pritchard and Jolie up.

It had been a busy and eventful ten days. As Pritchard had promised the anonymous marksman, the wagon train spent the remainder of that Sunday where they were. Reverend Farley spent that night in his wagon, whimpering in fevered agony in the wake of having his wrist cauterized. Ironically, it was Jolie who had the most medical experience in the group. It was her healing skills that quenched the reverend's bleeding and saved his life.

Even with a canteen of whiskey in him the reverend hollered like a stuck pig, as Ned described it, when they put his arm into the campfire coals. He was still moaning the following morning, at dawn, when the wagon train moved out. Deacon Wilson, sporting a broken nose and two black eyes, steered Reverend Farley's wagon, minus the whiskey barrel, while the reverend himself convalesced in back.

With Pritchard and Ned in charge, the wagon train and herd began moving each morning at dawn, and didn't stop until the sun was almost below the horizon. He allowed a one-hour pause on the following Sunday, for a simple prayer service, and then moved the train and herd out again.

Reverend Farley, who hadn't spoken to Pritchard since the previous Sunday, said nothing in protest. But when Deacon Wilson approached Pritchard to complain that Sunday was the Sabbath, and under God's law should be set aside for a day of rest, Pritchard merely told him he could stay and pray if he wanted to, but the wagon train was moving on.

Pritchard also insisted the wagons assemble in a circle each night, another departure from previous routine, ostensibly for protection from the wind. In reality, the formation was to aid in staving off raiders, whether bandits or Indians, should any be encountered.

These changes Pritchard implemented were appreciated by Ned, but initially by very few others. The new schedule meant folks had to arise much earlier, which was vastly different from their previous lackadaisical routine under Reverend Farley's command, and retire much later.

When some of the Quakers complained, Ned reminded them it was already well into September and unless they wanted to winter on the frozen prairie, the wagon train needed to pick up its pace.

And pick up the pace it did. Under Pritchard and Ned's leadership, and constant prompting, the wagon train advanced over one-hundred-and-sixty miles in less than ten days. On the ninth day after the near-lynching Ned announced at dinner, after consulting his compass and map, that the wagon train had crossed into Idaho Territory.

This was of little consolation to the weary travelers. What wagon master Ned Konig didn't have to announce was what everyone already knew; that it was at least another hundred miles to Fort Hall. One hundred more miles of hardship and danger or worse.

The nights were getting colder, the terrain rougher, and the supplies thinner. If these things weren't enough incentive to motivate the wagon train to push forward as hard as possible, Indians had been spotted shadowing them, filling the Hoosier wagoneers with fear and dread.

Two days earlier, while scouting ahead of the train, Pritchard spotted three horseback Indians off in the distance observing the caravan from a ridge overlooking the trail. He notified Ned and rode to the rear of the column where the livestock was being herded along by several of the Quaker men. Sure enough, also off in the distance, Pritchard noticed two more Indian riders trailing them from behind.

Both groups of riders were too far away for him to be sure, but Pritchard thought they were Crow by their long beaded hair. He knew the Crow to be generally friendly toward whites, though mortal enemies of the Sioux and Cheyenne, who were at war with the White-Faces.

The Indians, if indeed Crow, continued to shadow the wagon train, off-and-on, all the next day. When they went unseen, it prompted hope among the pilgrims that they had departed.

Pritchard and Ned, however, were not reassured. They knew, even when out-of-sight, the Indians were still with them. Sure enough, the native riders would inevitably be spotted again, both ahead and behind the column, and the travelers' hopes would once more give way to anxiety and fear.

There were other things Pritchard noticed as he scouted ahead of the wagon train during the past ten days; horse droppings, for one. They were from a single horse, and always at least a day old.

He also found the occasional stub of a burned-out cheroot. He surmised his guardian angel was also heading west on the Oregon Trail, ahead of the wagon train.

Ned had no sooner departed the camp, after Jolie's arrival with the coffee, when Pritchard tossed his cup aside, swept her into his arms, and hoisted her into the nearest unoccupied wagon. He happened to know this particular cart's owner was standing a watch with the herd, which was why he'd chosen to make his campfire near it.

Every night before bed, Pritchard and Jolie briefly reenacted what was interrupted by Reverend Farley's lynching party two Sundays past. The giant Missouri lawman and the buxom Indiana pilgrim kissed each other with a fevered passion, whenever and wherever they could conceal themselves from the judgmental eyes of their fellow wagoneers.

"Hello, Samuel," Ned called out, long before he re-entered the camp. Ned was no fool, and a good sport. By unspoken agreement he always announced his return to camp to give the big lawman and and Jolie time to collect themselves after a romantic embrace.

By the time Ned arrived with a party of men following behind him, Pritchard was leaning nonchalantly against the side of the wagon, leaving Jolie to return to her daughter.

"The reverend and some of the church elders

would like a word with you," Ned said, as he walked into the radius of the campfire's illumination. Behind him were the Reverend Winston Farley, Deacon Wilson, Jebediah Matheson, and several of the churchmen Pritchard knew to be loyal to them. One of the men, like Deacon Wilson, had a broken nose and racoon eyes from where Ned had clouted him with his Henry rifle.

"What can I do for you, Reverend?" Pritchard said. It was the first time he'd spoken to Farley in ten days, since the florid preacher had lost his hand.

"I want to speak to you about the guns," Reverend Farley began.

"Ain't nothin' to discuss," Pritchard said. "They're locked in a box, I've got the key, and that's where they'll stay."

"You've got guns," Farley protested.

"You're damn right," Pritchard said. "And when I said I'd plug the first one of you Bible-thumpin' Quaker outlaws I catch puttin' his hand to one, I meant it."

"That's hardly fair, Samuel."

"The name's Marshal Pritchard to you, Reverend. You'll want to remember that when we get to Fort Hall."

"What happens in Fort Hall?"

"That's when I arrest you on charges of attempting to murder a U.S. Marshal."

Reverend Farley's eyes widened. "Charges?"

"You didn't think I was gonna give you a pass on tryin' to stretch my neck?" Pritchard said. "Even if they don't hang you for tryin' to end me, I guarantee you'll get the rope for attemptin' to lynch the innocent, widowed mother of a teenaged girl."

"I don't subject myself to the laws of man," he said. "I follow God's law."

"Good luck offerin' that defense before a territorial judge," Pritchard said.

I thought," Farley said, holding up his stump of a hand, "because of what happened to me, we were now even."

"Not a chance," Pritchard said. "Besides, I wasn't the one who took your hand." Farley suddenly looked like he was going to throw up.

"We need those guns," Deacon Wilson insisted.

"I thought you conscientious objectors didn't approve of guns, even in self-defense," Pritchard said. "Oh, my mistake, evidently you do believe in guns when you're using them to commit a lynching." He chuckled.

"Killing a savage heathen isn't the same as killing a human being," the deacon pronounced haughtily. "An Indian has no Christian soul."

"I ain't sure they'd want one," Ned said, after spitting tobacco juice, "if'n it's anything like yours."

"There are savages about," Wilson pleaded.

150

"We've all seen them following us. You've seen them, too. They could strike at any moment."

"I've seen a few Indians," Pritchard admitted. "So far, I ain't felt threatened. Can't say the same for you and your flock, Deacon. Sorry, but the guns stay locked up."

"Without those guns," the church elder with the broken nose spoke up, "we don't stand a chance if the savages attack. You're signing our death warrant."

"Then you know how I felt sittin' astride a horse with a noose around my neck. Now get out of here, all of you, and get to bed. We move out, as usual, at dawn. And you'd all best remember what I told you; I get an inkling one of you is creepin' up on me with a knife, or a shovel, or an axe, like your good Christian friend Jebediah, I'll shoot that feller dead and anyone in the vicinity along with him. You have my oath on it."

All but Ned turned and left. Once they'd gone, Pritchard helped Jolie out of the wagon. Her hair was mussed, her face flushed, and her clothing disheveled, but she was nonetheless just as stunning as when she'd arrived in their makeshift camp.

"Care for a drink?" Ned asked. He tilted back his hat, rested his Henry rifle against the wagon, and sat down near the fire, which was beginning to fade. Pritchard threw on another log as Ned unlimbered his canteen.

151

"Don't mind if I do," Pritchard said, accepting the canteen from Ned. He took a swig of whiskey and offered it to Jolie, who declined with a wave of her hand. She sat down beside them.

"I hate to admit it," Ned said, after taking a slug of whiskey himself, "but them Quakers might be right. With Indians sniffin' about, maybe we should distribute the guns?"

"Wouldn't make no difference," Pritchard said, shaking his head. "Other than our guns, this company's only got a few decent weapons and but a handful of cartridges for each. Those Indians have been watchin' us for the better part of two days. If'n they're gonna attack a train as big as this one, you can bet they'll do it in force. A few extra guns won't make much difference. Not to mention, we don't know if any of these conscientious objectors can even shoot."

"I'll wager the good Reverend Winston Farley can shoot well enough," Ned said, "even with his left hand, to put a pistol-ball into you while you're a-sleepin.'"

"I wouldn't take that bet," Pritchard agreed.

"I can shoot," Jolie said. "My father taught me when I was a little girl, before he passed."

"Here's hopin' you won't have to," Ned said, taking another gulp of whiskey.

"I'll drink to that," Pritchard said, accepting the canteen.

CHAPTER TWENTY

Other than a torrential rainstorm, and a brief stop to replace a broken wheel on one of the wagons, the next three days were largely uneventful. The days were less warm, the nights growing increasingly colder, and the wagon train made good progress. The Quakers put another fifty miles behind them. On the fourth day, however, after not seeing their Indian shadows for over twenty-four hours, things changed dramatically.

At mid-morning, under a cloudless sky, Ned, who was riding point, noticed a rider approaching on the trail ahead. He waved to Pritchard, who rode to the front of the column to join him.

"Rider a-comin'," Ned said, pointing to a speck on the horizon with a large dust cloud behind it.

Pritchard extracted a telescope from his saddlebag, extended it, and put the device to his eye. It had been a gift from his former commander in the Texas Rangers, Captain Tom Franchard.

"Single horseman," he said, squinting through the lens. "Comin' in at full gallop."

"What's that big cloud of dust behind him?" Ned asked.

"Indians," Pritchard said, his voice flat and

hard. He collapsed the telescope. "A helluva lot of 'em. Get the wagons in a circle, Ned. Do it quick. They ain't but a couple miles out; they'll be upon us in no time. Also, I reckon I stand corrected; you'd best distribute those guns. I trust you know who to give 'em out to."

"What about the herd?"

"We'll have to leave it where it is," Pritchard said. "No time to corral 'em. We can round 'em up later, if'n there're any of us left to do it."

Ned rode back toward the train at a gallop, hollering orders.

Fifteen frantic minutes later the wagons were arranged in a wide circle, and their teams unhitched. Ned unlocked the crate containing the guns, and handed them out to those he felt were the most skilled with firearms.

Pritchard ordered the terrified women and children to lie under their wagons, and to open their water barrels and ready buckets to quell fire. He then strategically placed those few men with guns to form a defensive perimeter.

Of the one-hundred-and-twenty-seven pilgrims in the wagon train, just under forty were men of fighting age. The remainder were women, children, and males too young, old, or infirm to fight.

Jolie ran to Pritchard, fear on her face. "You can see them clearly now," she gasped. "There's hundreds of them. What's going to happen to us?"

"Don't know, for sure," he said. He leaned in close and kept his voice low. "Do you still have your pistol?" She nodded.

"Keep it handy, and don't waste bullets shootin' at Indians," he told her. "I've done my share of Indian fightin'. Maybe we'll fend 'em off, maybe we won't. If'n we don't, and they overrun us, it'll mean I'm dead and gone. Hear my words, Jolie; neither you, nor Rebecca, nor any of the other womenfolk will want to be taken. The death you'll endure, after what they do to you first, you can't imagine. You'll have to end your daughter, and then yourself. I'm sorry, but that's just the way it is."

"I know," she said. She kissed him and ran off to find Rebecca.

Of the forty, able-bodied, adult males, fewer than twenty were armed with guns. And the vast majority of those were fielding small-bore hunting rifles suitable for small game, such as rabbits and squirrels, and game-bird shotguns useless at more than twenty yards. Some of the other twenty men wielded axes, shovels, or other makeshift weapons. At least ten of the men stood apart with Reverend Farley and Deacon Wilson, refusing to take up arms of any kind and fight in keeping with their religious holdings.

Pritchard was busy stuffing his pockets with cartridges from his saddlebags when Ned rode up and dismounted.

"We're as ready as we can be," he said, ejecting a glob of tobacco juice, "to receive a coupla' hundred screamin' redskin visitors, which ain't very ready. You can see 'em plain, now. They're Crow, all right, and painted up for war. There's a passel of 'em, that's for sure."

"What about that single rider?"

"He looks to be a white man, just ahead of 'em, ridin' for dear life. He'll be here any second."

"Tell the boys on the perimeter not to shoot him and to let him in when he arrives," Pritchard said. "If he's who I think he is, he's handy with a gun and brought one with him." Ned jogged off to relay Pritchard's orders.

The sound of thundering hoofbeats from hundreds of horses approaching at full gallop reverberated across the prairie. Other than the soft crying of children and some sobbing women, no one spoke. The terror within the circled wagons was palpable.

Reverend Farley and Deacon Wilson approached Pritchard. Farley looked scared. Wilson looked terrified. "A word, Marshal, if you please?" Farley said.

"Make it quick, Reverend," Pritchard said, adding a sixth cartridge to each of his revolvers and topping off his Winchester. "I'm powerful busy this mornin'."

"I was thinking," the reverend began, "that a peaceful resolution might be reached? Perhaps a delegate could go out to meet with the savages and come to some kind of mutual accord?"

"Help yourself, Reverend," Pritchard said. "Can't guarantee you'll reach an accord with the Crow, but I can guarantee you'll be among the first to have your hair lifted."

"I wasn't suggesting I be the one to conduct the parlay," the reverend said. "I have no experience in Indian matters."

"Who then exactly were you proposin' to nominate?" Pritchard smiled.

"I was thinking," Farley continued, "that with your wide-ranging experience as a law officer and Texas Ranger, you might consider such a course of action yourself?"

"You conscientious objectors bewilder me," Pritchard said. He had to speak louder to be heard over the noise of the approaching Crow horses. "You won't take up arms against bandits, but you'll take up arms against a lawman and a defenseless woman? You won't take up arms against hostile Indians, nor parlay with them, but you'll happily nominate another to go out and parlay with 'em on your behalf while you cower behind those who will take up arms?"

"The way you make it sound," Reverend Farley said indignantly, "I'm practically a coward."

"Ain't no practically about it, Reverend," Pritchard said.

One of the two wagons facing the trail was

pushed aside by several men, and the solo rider burst in. The horseman was a tall, lean, man in his mid-thirties, wearing a black duster and black Boss of the Plains. His horse, a black Quarter, was foaming. Pritchard and Ned met him as he dismounted.

"Welcome, not-so-stranger," Pritchard said.

"I don't mean to be rude, Mister," Ned said, "but I surely wish you hadn't brought all them redskins with you. Especially since you were kind enough to rile 'em up before arrivin'."

"I'm Will Johnson," the man said. He shook dust off his coat, exposing a pair of Open Top Colts at his belt and a U.S. Marshal's badge on his chest. He opened his canteen and took a long pull.

"We can get acquainted later," Pritchard said, "if we're still alive. How many braves are there?"

"Over two hundred, is my guess," Johnson said. "Encountered them about an hour ago, heading due east on the Oregon Trail, making straight for your wagon train."

"Over two hundred braves?" Ned whistled. "The army officer in Cheyenne said there weren't no war parties that big out here."

"Maybe back in Cheyenne," Johnson said, "there aren't. Here in the Idaho Territory, I'd say that army officer misspoke."

Pritchard pulled the Shiloh-Sharps rifle out of Johnson's saddle scabbard and examined it. His and Johnson's eyes met.

"I won't ask if you're any good with this rifle," Pritchard said, "because I already know you are. How're you fixed for ammunition?"

"I've got about one-hundred rounds."

"You'll be needin' every one of 'em," Pritchard said. He handed the rifle to Johnson. "Pick your spot. I trust you'll know when to begin shootin'."

"You can count on me."

"Here they come," Ned said, over the sudden sound of Crow war-cries.

CHAPTER TWENTY-ONE

The first of the Crow warriors to reach the encircled wagons came in a straight line, directly at them. Pritchard, Johnson, and Ned each scored direct hits with their first rifle shots, and three Crow braves tumbled from their horses. The remainder of the Quaker men all fired reflexively, blasting out an aimless volley. No other Indians fell.

"Hold your fire!" Pritchard yelled at them. "Save your ammunition for when they breach the wagons and get inside the perimeter!"

"Get inside the perimeter?" Reverend Farley exclaimed, his voice cracking in terror. "They'll get inside?"

"Why are you worried, Reverend?" Pritchard said, as he squeezed another shot and was rewarded by another brave falling dead from his horse. "Ain't you got God on your side? Why don't you preach a sermon at them Indians? That ought to stop 'em cold."

"It'll sure enough give 'em a headache, leastways," Ned said between shots.

A stream of bullets, mostly fired from Henry rifles and Spencer carbines, along with a hail of arrows, rained into the wagon train fortress. Two of the Hoosier men fell; one by gunshot, one by arrow.

Pritchard, Johnson, and Ned continued to aim and fire. Each of their rifles, Pritchard's .44-40 Winchester, Johnson's .50-90 Sharps, and Ned's .44 Henry, all made distinctly different reports. Yet in the cacophony of pounding hoofbeats, voluminous gunfire, ear-splitting war-cries, and wailing, terrified women and children, the variances went unnoticed.

What Pritchard did notice, however, was that significantly less than half of the mounted Crow were armed with rifles. The remainder were armed with bow and spear.

"Concentrate your fire on the braves with firearms!" Pritchard shouted to Johnson and Ned. Both men signaled they understood.

Though accurate rifle fire from horseback was difficult, it was still more accurate than bow and arrow, and consequently the greater threat. All three men knew that once the Crow were afoot, the rifles in their hands would become infinitely more deadly. Soon brave after brave bearing a rifle was lying dead on the Idaho prairie.

The Crow quickly figured out a direct frontal assault was not going to work as long as the three sharpshooters behind the wagons continued their deadly accurate shooting. As expected, they then adjusted their tactics and began riding around the wagon train in a wide circle, searching for a crack in the defenses.

Assisting Pritchard, Johnson, and Ned in their efforts was the fact that the Crow, like almost all mounted plains Indians, rode their horses bareback. The Crow were excellent horsemen, but without stirrups or reins, stopping, starting, and turning were more difficult, and thus slightly slower. At the moment when a brave was conducting one of these maneuvers, they made superb targets, which the three riflemen exploited to good effect.

"Right fair shootin'," Pritchard said to Ned, as the wagon master felled another mounted brave.

"Spent my youth huntin' buffalo on the plains of Nebraska," Ned answered, explaining his marksmanship. "Had to learn to shoot. Ball and powder cost money."

All three reloaded continually, and as rapidly as they could. Pritchard and Ned would fire a few, then reload a few, with the goal of not allowing their weapons to run dry. Johnson's weapon was a single-shot breech-loader, but his nimble fingers and skill helped him maintain a volume of fire not significantly slower than the repeaters.

"Look yonder," Pritchard shouted to Johnson, "about a half-mile out. Just south of the trail. Do you see him?" Pritchard pointed to a rider wearing a war bonnet, holding a long, feathered, lance, and sitting astride a painted horse.

"I see him," Johnson said. He dropped from the kneeling-supported position he'd been shooting from and lay prone. "It isn't going to be easy," he said, "aiming through all this dust."

"Generally speakin'," Ned said, spitting tobacco and firing again, "nothin' about this day strikes me as particularly easy."

Johnson spent a moment adjusting the rear sight, then shouldered the weapon.

"Can you really hit that feller all the way out there?" Ned asked.

"We'll find out," Johnson said, as he fired. More than a full second later, the bonneted Crow fell from his horse. Johnson immediately resumed his kneeling position. It was easier to rapidly reload than from the prone position, and his targets were now much closer.

"Right fair shootin'," Ned said to Johnson, repeating Pritchard's compliment. "Though I must admit, I enjoyed your shot on the reverend's mitten just as much."

A faint smile cracked Johnson's face.

A man screamed behind them, and Pritchard turned to see several Crow warriors inside the perimeter on foot. One had buried his tomahawk into the skull of an unarmed Quaker. More warriors were entering from all sides.

"They're gettin' in!" Ned called out.

"All right, boys," Pritchard commanded the armed Hoosier men. "Time to join the festivities.

Don't shoot until you've got a redskin dead in your sights, and be ready with your knife or pike afterwards."

General combat erupted all around them. Pritchard continued to steadily shoot Crow horsemen off their mounts, outside the wagons, but his rate-of-fire diminished significantly due to the need for him to occasionally turn around and shoot a brave advancing on him inside the perimeter. He looked to Ned and Johnson, and discovered they were in the same quandary. They would shoot outward at the Crow horsemen, and before they could reload and fire again, had to come about and engage a brave behind them within the perimeter with their pistols. The inescapable fact, plain to Pritchard, Johnson, and Ned, was that the wagon train was being overrun.

The Indiana wagoneers fired their collection of paltry weapons and braves collapsed. The fighting then became hand-to-hand, as none of the armed Quakers had a chance to reload. Many of them fell, but most not before sinking an axe, or hoe, or shovel into one of their killers.

Pritchard watched Johnson butt-stroke an Indian about to stab him, and saw Ned gutshoot another with his revolver, his Henry rifle lying at his feet.

Pritchard's rifle clicked empty, but before he could reach into his pocket for another cartridge a yowling brave leaped at him, his war-club raised over his head with both hands. He ducked, and the club swung harmlessly past. Pritchard side-stepped, drew, and shot the club's owner in the temple with his Colt.

It was pandemonium inside the perimeter. Crow warriors and Indiana Quakers fought furiously with one-another, locked in mortal combat. Some of the braves were attempting to drag women, old men, or children out from under the wagons.

Pritchard thought of Jolie and Rebecca and drew his second revolver. He fired systematically with both guns, as he navigated the field of battle, felling braves right and left. He spotted Jolie, through the haze of gunsmoke and dust, being dragged by the hair out from under a wagon. Her daughter Rebecca held on to her legs, engaged in a desperate game of tug-of-war with a Crow brave determined to scalp her mother. Jolie was trying to draw the Smith & Wesson revolver Pritchard had given her, but it was snagged in her dress.

Pritchard aimed and fired, but his right-hand Colt clicked on an empty cartridge case. He fired his left-hand gun and achieved the same result. Holstering his guns, he drew his Bowie knife and charged.

Just as the Crow brave's blade was about to descend upon Jolie's forehead, Pritchard thrust his razor-sharp Bowie in an uppercut that buried the knife, hilt-deep, under the Indian's chin.

"Get back under the wagon!" Pritchard commanded, as Jolie retreated. He withdrew his bloody knife from the dead brave's neck and pivoted to face two more advancing braves, one armed with a spear, the other with a tomahawk.

The tomahawk-wielding brave struck first, slashing at Pritchard's head. He dodged the swipe, losing his hat in the process, and inserted his knife into the man's belly. As the other brave jabbed with his spear, Pritchard spun the gut-sliced Crow warrior in front of him, and the already mortally wounded Indian absorbed the strike from his fellow tribesman's spear.

Unfortunately, Pritchard wasn't able to pull his knife out before the now-unarmed Crow warrior, who wasn't as tall as Pritchard but outweighed him, tackled him. Both men tumbled to the ground, face-to-face, with Pritchard on the bottom.

Powerful hands clamped around Pritchard's neck, squeezing, choking, and trying to strangle the life from him. But Pritchard's powerful hands encircled his adversary's neck, too. The two men, one white, one red, then engaged in a lethal contest; a test to determine which of them was physically stronger and could withstand more abuse. The prize each man sought was his own life.

For almost a full minute the duo dueled. Pritchard, who as a youth had been the annual Jackson County Fair's wrestling champion until he was forced to run off and join in the war, eventually gained the upper hand. But instead of slowly twisting the life out of his opponent, he chose instead to snap his neck.

A nearly exhausted Pritchard had just rolled the lifeless body of the huge brave off himself, when he looked up to find the Reverend Winston Farley standing over him. He held a Colt revolver, with the hammer back, in his only hand. It was aimed at Pritchard from a distance of only a few feet.

"They'll be no charges levied against me at Fort Hall," he smirked, his eyes already gleaming with triumph.

"I gather you're no longer a conscientious objector?" Pritchard said, catching his breath.

"Not today, Marshal Pritchard. Good-bye."

A pistol shot rang out, but no bullet entered Pritchard. Instead, a hole appeared in Reverend Farley's forehead. It was created when the .44 rimfire bullet fired by Jolie Matheson's Smith & Wesson revolver into the back of his skull exited out the front.

Pritchard rolled out of the way as Farley's body fell forward and came to rest where he'd been lying an instant before.

"I thought I told you to get back under that wagon," Pritchard said, as he stood.

"I think it's only fair to warn you," she said, staring down at the reverend's corpse, "I don't always do what I'm told."

CHAPTER TWENTY-TWO

"Any minute now," Ned said, pointing at the Crow horsemen milling in the distance. They appeared to be rallying for another assault on the wagon train.

Pritchard, Johnson, and Ned stood back-to-back, in the center of the interior of the circled wagons, reloading their revolvers. All three were drenched in sweat and spattered in blood, though none of the blood was their own. Surrounding them lay over thirty dead Crow braves, as well as seventeen dead Quaker men, among them Jebediah Matheson, four dead women, and two dead children. Outside the perimeter were the bodies of over seventy more Crow warriors, one of them a chieftain who'd been shot with a Shiloh-Sharps rifle from a distance of more than a thousand yards.

After their initial onslaught was repelled, and all the warriors who'd breached the interior perimeter were killed, the Crow pulled back. The survivors within the circled wagon train hoped they'd had enough, and the Indians would ride away, but it was clear to Pritchard, Johnson, and Ned they were only re-grouping for another attack.

After reloading their revolvers, the trio

recovered their rifles and began to reload them.

"I ain't got many cartridges left," Ned said.

"Me either," Johnson said.

"I'm runnin' a little short myself," Pritchard said.

"How many of 'em you reckon we killed?" Ned asked.

"A little over half," Johnson said.

"Not nearly enough," Pritchard said.

Women and children sobbed all around them, and the few men who were wounded but not killed cried out in agony. Some had been partially scalped.

Jolie approached with her daughter. They were holding hands.

"Are they gone?" she asked.

"No," Pritchard said, "They're only gettin' set for another go at us."

"Can we hold them off?"

The expressions on Pritchard's, Johnson's, and Ned's faces was all the answer she needed.

"Get yourselves back under the wagon," Pritchard said softly. "Be ready with your pistol. You know what to do." She nodded, brushed Rebecca's hair from where her daughter's tears had plastered it against her face, and departed.

Deacon Wilson, covered in dust, minus his glasses, and wearing panic on his face, stumbled over. "They're still out there!" he cried. "Over a hundred of them!"

"Our eyes work just fine," Ned said.

"There's too many of them!" he blubbered, stating the obvious. "We don't stand a chance!"

"Why don't you say it a little louder?" Pritchard said. "There might be a child under a wagon somewheres who ain't fully terrified yet."

"We have to surrender!" the hysterical deacon said. "It's our only chance!"

"That's no chance at all," Pritchard said. "The Crow don't take prisoners, you fool, they take scalps. Unless you're a squaw, that is, and frankly, in your case, I'm beginning to have my doubts."

Ned laughed out loud.

"This is all your fault, Ned!" Deacon Wilson wailed. "You led us into this trap!"

"There's only one Oregon Trail," Ned chuckled. "Where else was I gonna lead you? Your mistake, Deacon, was thinkin' a passel of peace-lovin' Indiana Quakers armed with little more than prayers could safely travel it. My mistake, was takin' the money to guide you. Looks like we were both addle-headed, don't it?"

"A curse on your soul, Ned Konig," Wilson sobbed. "And on yours, as well, Marshal."

"I feel slighted," Johnson said.

"Get out of my sight, Deacon," Pritchard said. "I'll not spend my last moments listenin' to your prattlin' gab. Another word, and I'll put a bullet to you myself."

"Use your knife," Johnson said. "Save the bullet for the Crow."

"Amen," Ned said, spitting tobacco juice.

Deacon Wilson started to retort, then thought better of it.

"Evidently he ain't as stupid as he looks," Ned said, as the deacon scampered off.

"He couldn't be," Pritchard remarked.

"Here they come," Ned said. "Good a day to die as any, I reckon, and better than most." He stuck out his hand to Pritchard. "Likely won't get a chance to say 'good-bye' later. So long, Samuel. It's been an honor knowin' you. Just met you, Marshal Johnson, but the same goes for you, too."

"We ain't dealt out yet, Ned." Pritchard grinned, ignoring the wagon master's outstretched hand. "We've still got a few chips on the table, and some cards to play. Save the good-byes for when we're busted."

The blood-curdling sound of more than a hundred war cries erupted once more, as the mounted Crow warriors again charged the wagon train. Pritchard, Johnson, and Ned all knelt and began firing.

Crow braves at the head of the pack plummeted from their horses, one after another, as bullet-after-bullet fired from Pritchard's, Johnson's, and Ned's rifles found their mark. When they fell, their bodies were instantly trampled by the wave of horsemen following behind them.

"Yee-haw!" Ned cackled, as he felled another Crow brave and watched him churned up beneath the hooves of his fellow warrior's horses. "That'll slow 'em down some!"

The trio of riflemen continued their deadly fusillade. Before the main body of Crow horsemen reached the wagons, nearly two-dozen more dead Indians lay among their lifeless brethren.

"That's it for me," Johnson announced, opening the breech of his Sharps. "I'm down to my pistols."

"Me, too," Ned said, tossing his Henry aside and drawing his revolver. "I'm plumb out of rifle fodder."

Pritchard felled another Crow, and then another, before his Winchester clicked empty. He set it aside, and drew both Colts.

"Okay boys," Pritchard said, "now it gets personal." He looked back and saw Jolie, huddled under a wagon. With one hand she covered Rebecca's eyes. In the other, she held her Smith & Wesson Russian .44.

When the Crow horsemen got to within ten yards of the circled wagons, they leapt off their horses and rushed on foot. The dust cloud created by the sudden halt of over seventy-five animals swept over the wagon train, creating cover for their advance. They'd obviously learned from the folly of their original attack in which they rode in too close to the circled wagons, presenting excellent targets, and suffered extensive casualties as a result.

As the first Crow braves reached the makeshift barricade of the wagons, Pritchard, Johnson, and Ned fired their revolvers point-blank. More braves fell.

An arrow struck Johnson in the thigh, and he fell to one knee. Ned shot the bowman in the face with his revolver's last shot. Pritchard dropped an Indian-per-shot with his Colts, watching them topple dead at his feet, but he was soon holding empty pistols.

Pritchard dropped his guns, drew his Bowie, and began to slash and stab. Ned swung an axe, rending flesh, and Johnson, still on one knee, thrust and struck with a Crow lance he'd pried from the limp hands of a dead warrior. Dozens of enraged Crow closed in around them.

Pritchard risked another quick look over his shoulder at Jolie, and found several warriors slowly surrounding her. She'd placed the barrel of her pistol against Rebecca's head, and was thumbing back the weapon's hammer.

Suddenly the sound of a bugle, blasting loud and clear, reverberated across the battlefield. The Crow braves instantly ceased their attack.

A bewildered Pritchard, Johnson, and Ned watched, each panting from exertion, as the Indians silently backed away from them.

In the vacuum left by the absence of war cries, and the sounds of battle, the bugle's music rang out.

"That's mighty strange," Johnson remarked, as the Crow warriors clambered back over the wagons and departed out-of-view.

"What is?" Pritchard said.

"That bugle," Johnson said. "It's playing 'retreat,' not 'charge.' "

"I ain't complainin'," Ned said, spitting tobacco juice between pants. "Long as them redskins go away, I don't care if that horn is playin' 'Camptown Races.' "

Pritchard recovered his revolvers and immediately began to reload. Ned and Johnson followed his lead.

Jolie and Rebecca ran to Pritchard, crying tears of joy and relief. He took both in his arms. "What happened?" Jolie asked him. "I almost had to—"

Pritchard silenced her. "You didn't. That's all that matters."

Ned busied himself pulling the arrow out of Johnson's thigh. Fortunately it hadn't sunk in too deep and missed the bone. He cleansed the wound with whiskey from his canteen, bandaged it, and took a long pull before handing it over to Johnson.

"What's going on?" someone asked, as the stunned Quaker women, children, and surviving men emerged from under the wagons and began to assemble.

"Don't rightly know," Ned told them.

Pritchard detached himself from Jolie and her daughter and walked to the edge of the circled wagons. What met his gaze when he looked out into the prairie was a most inexplicable sight.

A troop of more than one-hundred mounted U.S. cavalry soldiers were stopped in a column before them. The Crow warriors were standing docilely beside the horse soldiers, as if part of their unit. At the head of the column was a goateed captain carrying a saber. Alongside him rode a corporal holding a bugle.

"You boys ever see anything like this before?" Pritchard asked Johnson and Ned, who'd joined him. "It almost looks like—"

"—the Crow who attacked us are under the army's command," Johnson finished Pritchard's sentence for him.

"Hell and tarnation," Ned spat.

CHAPTER TWENTY-THREE

The Crow braves pushed two of the wagons apart and the cavalry captain entered the wagon train's inner perimeter on horseback. The rest of the cavalrymen dismounted, and fanned out with their Trapdoor Springfield rifles across their chests at the ready. The Crow warriors followed behind them.

"I am Captain Mason," the captain announced, "assigned to Fort Hall." He sheathed his saber. "This wagon train, and all those within it, are hereby impounded."

"Impounded?" Ned asked. "What does that mean, 'impounded'?"

"It means," Pritchard said, "we're his prisoners."

"You will surrender your arms," the captain declared, "and accompany us voluntarily, or be disarmed and rounded up by force."

As Mason said this, all his men shouldered their rifles and took aim at Pritchard, Johnson, Ned, and the rest of the Quaker survivors.

"What should we do?" Ned asked.

"Not much we can do" —Pritchard shrugged, unbuckling his gun belts—"with a hundred guns a-pointin' at us." Johnson and Ned did likewise.

"Sergeant," the captain called to one of his men, "you know the drill. Have a detail search the wagons and confiscate all firearms. Have another detail collect the livestock, and hook teams up to the wagons in preparation to move out. Police up all the bodies, and load them into the wagons. We'll depart as soon as these tasks are completed."

"What's goin on?" a confused Ned asked Pritchard and Johnson, as U.S. cavalrymen and Crow braves lowered their weapons and scrambled to comply with the captain's orders.

"Looks to me," Johnson said, "like this army captain is going to take us away whether we want to go or not."

"And erase any sign we were ever here," Pritchard observed. "Certainly any sign a battle was fought."

The captain rode up to Pritchard, Johnson, and Ned, and dismounted. "Who was in charge here?" he demanded.

"I'm Ned Konig, the wagon master," Ned said, barely containing his rage. "Why in the hell did you let them Crow attack us, Captain? They're with you, ain't they? We've got innocent folks— women and children—dead because of your folly!"

"How many people are in your party?" the captain inquired, ignoring Ned's questions. Ned looked fit to burst.

"We had one-hundred-and-twenty-six pilgrims alive and well this mornin'," Ned said through gritted teeth, "before your Crow pony soldiers came a-visitin'. I reckon we've got considerably less now."

"Corporal," Mason called out.

"Sir," the corporal reported.

"Get me a complete head count," he ordered. "And let me know how many are wounded."

"Right away." The corporal saluted.

"You folks put up quite a fight," the captain remarked, surveying the scene. "You took out half of my Crow war party."

"If'n there'd been a few more of us," Ned retorted hotly, "and a few more guns, we'd have wiped 'em all out."

"Doubtful," the captain said. "There're plenty more Crow braves where they came from." Ned glared at the captain and spat tobacco juice at his feet.

"Easy, Ned," Pritchard said to the infuriated wagon master. "Don't give 'em a reason."

"But Samuel," Ned argued, "that captain plumb just admitted them Crow were under his command! Why, it's the same as if his soldiers attacked us!"

"This ain't the time," Pritchard placated the fuming wagon master. "There'll be another."

"Best listen to your large friend's advice," Captain Mason said to Ned. "I'd hate to see you get shot today, especially after surviving the Crow's assault."

"Why you, yellow-bellied—"

"Back 'er down," Pritchard stepped in and cut the enraged wagon master off. "I ain't any less off my oats than you are about how things played out," he whispered to Ned, "but catchin' a bullet doesn't do anybody any good. Keep your head. Folks are countin' on you."

Ned's shoulders slumped. He nodded, and stayed silent.

"I may not show it, Cap'n," Pritchard said, "but I'm just as hornet-mad as the wagon master. Why did you sic those Crow on us, anyways?"

"You surely are a big one, aren't you?" Captain Mason said. "And what a unique scar you have on your forehead. Is that from a gunshot?"

"I cut myself shavin'."

"I'll bet. What's your name?"

"Name's Samuel Pritchard, from Missouri."

"You fought for the Confederacy, I presume, during the War of Rebellion?"

"I did."

"And you?" Captain Mason asked Johnson.

"Name's Will Johnson, if it's any of your business. I fought for the Union. I'd also like to know why the army's permitting hostile Indians a free hand to attack a civilian wagon train."

The captain smiled under his mustaches. "You'll have the answers to your questions soon enough, gentlemen," he said. "Sergeant," he again called out, "what's the count?"

"Eighty-nine total survivors, Captain," the sergeant reported. "Sixty-three females, half of them just girls. Of the remaining twenty-six males, six are badly wounded, and half of them are only boys."

"The guns?"

"Odd, Sir. We've found only about twenty-five guns, and no ammunition to speak of. Most of the firearms we collected were squirrel shooters and bird shotguns. We did find a whole crate of Bibles, though."

The captain smiled. "A religious party? Let me guess. Conscientious objectors on religious grounds?"

"Quakers," Ned affirmed, "all from the same church in Bloomington. They don't believe in harmin' their fellow man. Which makes massacring them a right cowardly act."

"I take it you three men," Mason went on, ignoring Ned's jibe, "are not Quakers, nor conscientious objectors?"

"Not by a country mile," Pritchard said.

Mason put his hands on his hips and appraised Pritchard, Johnson, and Ned. "That would mean you three did the lion's share of the fighting, if not all of it?"

Neither Pritchard, Johnson, nor Ned answered him. The captain shook his head in disbelief.

"Three guns killed well over a-hundred Crow warriors," he said. "If I didn't see the bodies myself, I'd hardly believe it."

"That was only one mornin's labor," Ned couldn't contain himself from blurting. "Just think how many of you murderin' bastards we'd have killed with a full day at our disposal."

"Put these three in chains," Captain Mason ordered. "They appear to be the only men in this wagon train capable of putting up a fight."

CHAPTER TWENTY-FOUR

Pritchard, Johnson, and Ned were each manacled at the wrist. They stood and watched, under guard, as the wagon train prepared to move out.

All of the dead bodies, both Crow and Quaker, were piled into the wagons. This left no room for living passengers, who were lined up, also under guard, behind the wagons, which had been re-hitched to teams of horses. The livestock had been collected and was being shepherded by a combination of Crow horsemen and U.S. cavalrymen.

A group of Crow, under supervision of the corporal, spread out and walked the entire battlefield, collecting arrows, spears, debris, cartridge casings, and any other remnant of the Indian attack.

"They're cleanin' up," Pritchard noted.

"Removing any trace of the attack," Johnson said. "After the first snow, probably not more than a month from now, there'll be no sign of the battle at all."

"It would seem to anyone investigatin' our fate," Pritchard said, "that this particular wagon train was just swallowed up and vanished."

"Never seen anything like it," Ned commented. "Indians, working along with the army."

"I have," Johnson said. "During the war. More than a few tribes were allied with Union forces, the Crow in particular. Those bonds only got stronger after the war, when the army began fighting the Sioux and Cheyenne, who are the sworn enemy of the Crow Nation."

"You seem to know a lot about such affairs," Ned said. "What did you do in the army?"

"Survived," Johnson said.

Once all the wagons were loaded and readied, the herd was gathered and all the prisoners were lined up in a column of twos, Captain Mason strode over to where six badly-wounded Quaker men were laid out on the ground. All had been shot at least once by either bullet or arrow, and two of them had been partially scalped. Three were unconscious, one mumbled prayers, and the other two moaned deliriously in pain. Their anguished wives and children were separated from them by a line of cavalrymen with rifles, and begged for their loved ones to receive medical attention.

Captain Mason gestured to the sergeant. He and six cavalrymen approached. The sergeant pointed to the wounded men on the ground, lined the troops up, gave a terse order, and all six wounded men were executed by a single volley from six Trapdoor Springfield rifles at point-blank range.

The Crow whooped and shrieked in glee. Some of the remaining prisoners wailed and cried out in horror at the execution.

Captain Mason drew his revolver, pointed it skyward, and fired. "Silence!" he commanded.

"I am sorry you had to witness that spectacle," he began in a loud voice, once the Crow and prisoners had quieted. "But I want you to remember it well. Those men were dying and could not be saved. They were of no use to us and had become a burden. Now you all know what happens if you become burdensome."

He holstered his revolver and continued. "We'll be moving out momentarily. You must keep up with the wagons and stay ahead of the herd behind you. Do not falter. We will not stop until nightfall, and will start again at dawn. Anyone who fails to keep up will suffer the same fate as these men."

Captain Mason nodded to the sergeant. His men began to load the six fresh corpses into the already weighed-down wagons.

"Ready Sir!" the sergeant reported.

"Move out!" Captain Mason said, mounting his horse.

A pair of cavalrymen rode ahead to scout the way, followed by Captain Mason and a squad of his troopers. The wagons, each driven by a cavalryman, went first, then the prisoners, and next the horses and cattle followed. A line of mounted soldiers bordered each side of the caravan, and the Crow contingent rode behind the herd. Pritchard, Johnson, and Ned walked at the rear of the column of prisoners, between the wagons and the herd.

"How far do you suppose it is to Fort Hall?" Ned asked.

"Maybe thirty miles," Pritchard said. "Except it don't matter how far away Fort Hall is."

"Why not?"

"Because we ain't goin' to Fort Hall," Pritchard said. "Fort Hall is due west. If you ain't noticed, we're heading north."

"So we are," Ned said. "I wonder why? Ain't nothin' north of the Oregon Trail but uncharted territory."

"As far as we know," Johnson said. "There must be something that direction we don't know about, or they wouldn't be taking us there. At least water."

"You three," a cavalryman barked from his horse above them, "button them lips, or I'll button 'em for you."

The caravan plodded onward throughout the afternoon. Other than the braying of livestock, and the quiet sobbing of the marching prisoners, the only sound was the creak of wagons under strain and the steady pounding of hoofbeats. Pritchard noted Jolie and Rebecca, in the middle of the pack of prisoners ahead, trudging along in silence. He also noted how many of the cavalrymen found an excuse to ride past them, leering at the pretty mother and daughter, and the other attractive women prisoners within the column.

Johnson was obviously in some pain, due to his wounded thigh, and walked with a noticeable limp. But he kept pace with Pritchard and Ned, and never complained once.

"What're we gonna do?" Ned discretely asked Pritchard and Johnson, when the cavalrymen weren't paying attention.

"Not much we can do," Pritchard said quietly. "We're outnumbered, unarmed, and chained up. We've got to bide our time and wait for a chance to deal ourselves a hand."

"What if that card ain't in the deck?"

"Then we'll cheat," Johnson said. "Pritchard's right. We've got to lay low right now. Wait for the opportunity to act."

By dusk, several of the smaller children were near exhaustion. Pritchard carried a pair of toddlers, and Ned and Johnson a child each. The older prisoners staggered along as the caravan progressed, and even the younger, stronger ones, like Jolie and Rebecca, were beginning to falter.

Just as the sun began to drop below the horizon, Captain Mason halted the train. He ordered the wagons circled and posted sentries. Male prisoners, including Pritchard, Johnson, and Ned, were ordered to collect wood for a fire.

The women were ordered to prepare food. Once the fire was going, and the meal was readied, Captain Mason and his men lined up to eat, followed by the Crow braves. By the time the last brave had gone through the line, there was very little food left.

"There isn't enough for all of us," one of the women complained. "The children are hungry."

"You'll take what you get," the sergeant told her, "and be grateful you're gettin' anything to eat at all."

The captive Quakers divided the paltry leftovers among themselves and began to pray.

"Lookit that," one of the cavalrymen chided. "Them Bible-thumpers are givin' thanks to the Lord for their daily bread." His fellow troopers laughed.

"You can bet they won't be thankin' the Lord Almighty," another cavalryman said, "when they get to where they're goin'. They'll be prayin' for salvation." More raucous laughter ensued.

Pritchard, Johnson, and Ned, who'd forgone their meals to allow more for the women and children to eat, sat apart from the main group of prisoners under a double guard. They were silently sipping water from tin cups when Captain Mason, his sergeant, a corporal, and a pair of troopers approached.

"You," Mason pointed to Pritchard. "On your feet."

Pritchard slowly rose to his full height, which was at least a head taller than Mason and his men.

"That's him all right," one of the troopers said. "I'd swear to it."

"No doubt about it, Sir," the other trooper added. "I thought it was him when I first saw him earlier today. Now I'm sure of it. I watched him shoot a feller who pulled on him down in Nacogdoches about five years back. Drilled him twice before that feller could even clear leather. That's Smokin' Joe Atherton, no doubt about it."

"You lied to me," Captain Mason said. "You said your name was Samuel Pritchard."

"That's because my name is Samuel Pritchard," he said.

"You're still lying," Mason said. "My men tell me you're a Texas Ranger and gunfighter named Joe Atherton."

"I started using that name during the war, and for almost ten years thereafter," Pritchard said, "to protect my family. Returned to my true name when I left the Rangers."

"Sounds like a dishonorable act, to me," Mason said. "Abandoning your family's name, and hiding like a coward behind an alias."

"I reckon it's not as honorable as promptin' a bunch of murderin' redskins to attack a wagon train full of innocent Quakers, and starvin' a bunch of women and children," Pritchard said, "but then again, I ain't an officer and gentleman in the U.S. Army, neither."

"Mind your tongue," the sergeant, whose name was Greenwald, said.

"Or what?" Pritchard said. "You'll chain me up and starve me?"

"I'll whip you like the rebel dog you are," Sergeant Greenwald interjected.

"Bold talk," Pritchard grunted, "for an armed man runnin' his mouth at a chained, unarmed, prisoner."

"At ease, Sergeant," Captain Mason said with an ominous smile. "There's no need to correct Mister Atherton's attitude now."

"The name's Pritchard," he said.

"Whatever your name is," the captain said, "your attitude will no doubt change once we arrive in Whiskey Falls."

CHAPTER TWENTY-FIVE

At dawn, the wagon train once again moved out. After a cold night spent sleeping on the hard ground, the troopers and Crow breakfasted on cold jerky. The shivering prisoners dined on cold water.

The Idaho sky was overcast and threatened rain that never came, as the caravan continued north. The going was slower, since there was no dedicated trail, and by noon the train and herd was at the foot of a steep grade. The next several grueling hours were spent slogging the wagons and herd uphill. By late afternoon the troopers, wagons, prisoners, herd, and Crow braves crested the summit and beheld the valley below. From the top of the ridge, they had a bird's-eye view.

"Hell and tarnation," Ned exclaimed, looking down into the valley. "There's a town down there!"

"Sure ain't on any map I've ever seen," Pritchard said.

"I doubt it's on any map at all," Johnson remarked.

A mile beneath them, split through its center by a wide stream beneath a flowing waterfall, was indeed a town. Most of the buildings looked shabbily erected, as evidenced by their canvas roofs, and appeared to have been in place for no more than a season or two.

The streets were dirt roads, with tents and smaller encampments surrounding the larger central buildings, giving the community the appearance of a large mining camp, stockyard town, or trading post.

On the near side, closest to the waterfall, was what looked like the opening of a mine. Dozens of shirtless men could be seen laboring in the vicinity. On the far side of the town was a giant corral, housing what appeared to be many hundreds, if not over a thousand, head of cattle and horses. Beyond the corral was a large field containing dozens of covered wagons, stages, freight wagons, and buckboards. A narrow trail, just wide enough for a single wagon, switchbacked its way down into the town.

Captain Mason ordered his bugler to blow three short blasts on his horn. Three faint bell rings could be heard in response from the town below. The captain signaled for the wagon train and herd to begin moving down the precipitous trail.

It took the remainder of the daylight for the caravan of troopers, wagons, prisoners, livestock, and Indians to descend the rugged path to the flatlands and reach the dirt road leading into the town. When they arrived, they were greeted at the outskirts by a pair of men with rifles. They

191

nodded to Captain Mason and waived the caravan past.

Over the sentries was a large wooden sign that read, WHISKEY FALLS. Beneath it, someone had scrawled in the phrase, "ABANDON ALL HOPE, YE WHO ENTER HERE."

"Dante's *Divine Comedy*," Johnson commented, as he passed the sign.

"Dante's what?" a confused Ned said. "I sure don't see anything sacred or humorous."

Captain Mason led his caravan down the center of the main road. In the middle of town was a large, open space with a raised, wooden stage. Behind the stage, looming over it, was a gallows.

Mason halted his column in the town square. "Sergeant Greenwald, have the Crow move the herd to the stockyards." The sergeant barked orders, and the herd was shepherded past the stopped wagons.

A man came out of the largest building, flanked by two other men, and mounted the steps to the stage. He was tall, over six-feet, but outweighed Pritchard's two-hundred and thirty-pounds by at least another thirty. He looked to be approximately fifty-years-old, sported a full, red beard, and red shoulder-length hair to match. He wore knee-high boots, a pair of belt pistols in cross-draw holsters, and a wide-brimmed hat with a feather in the band.

The men with him were just as unique. The

man on his right dwarfed him. He looked to be a couple of inches taller than even Pritchard, and weighed at least three-hundred-and-fifty pounds. He had a shaved head, handlebar mustaches, and wore an enormous buffalo coat that only enhanced his enormity. In one gargantuan fist he carried a large mallet.

The other man was shorter than average, with a thin, wiry, frame, a pencil-thin mustache, and small, furtive, rodent-like eyes. He wore a suit and vest, a bowler, and a pair of ivory-handled Colt revolvers; one strong-side, and the other cross-draw, like Johnson. Both of the men, the giant and the runt, stood a deferential two paces behind the burly, red-haired man in the wide hat.

"I know him," Johnson whispered, pointing to the red-haired man. "That's Lieutenant Henry Marleaux."

"Who?" Ned whispered back.

Before Johnson could answer, Captain Mason dismounted and strode to the edge of the stage. He saluted the red-haired man standing above him, who acknowledged the cavalry officer with a wave of his hand.

"Why is a captain saluting a lieutenant?" Pritchard asked.

"Fair question," Johnson said.

"You've brought in a somewhat smaller load this trip, Captain Mason," the man said, surveying the caravan assembled before him.

"Winter's coming on soon," the captain said. "Traffic on the Oregon Trail is beginning to peter out. Still, I brought over forty wagons, more than a-hundred horses, and three-hundred head of beef."

"Nicely done," the man said. "How many workers?"

"Just over eighty, but most are female. Only about twenty or twenty-five males, but half of them are adults."

"We'll find a use for them," the man said. "Gold? Money? Guns? Liquor?"

"No gold, very little cash money, few guns, and almost no liquor," Captain Mason said. "We did find a case of Bibles, though. Evidently this wagon train is comprised of Quakers hailing from Indiana."

"Crossing the Oregon without guns, gold, money, or liquor," the man said, shaking his head. "They must be Quakers, for that kind of stupidity is indeed a true act of faith. Do your men know what to do, Captain?"

"Same as always," Captain Mason said. "At first light we'll dump all the bodies in the old mine shaft, park the wagons, corral the herd, deposit all the firearms in the armory, and put all the other goods and sundries into the storehouse."

"Very good, Captain. I expect you'll join me at the saloon for a drink later tonight?"

"I'll be there."

The red-bearded man put his hands on his hips and addressed the exhausted, anxious, prisoners. "My name is Henry Marleaux," he announced in a booming voice. "Welcome to Whiskey Falls."

"I own this town," Marleaux went on. "I'm sure many of you have questions. Don't fret. The answers you seek will come to you soon enough. All you need to know, for now, is that I own you, too. All of you. If you work, and do whatever else me or my men tell you to do, every minute of every day, you will remain alive. If you don't, you will suffer and die. It's that simple."

Marleaux snapped his fingers, and two men emerged from a building dragging a third. The man being dragged was in his fifties, thin, shirtless, and filthy. He struggled feebly, but had no strength to resist. He was escorted roughly to the gallows, pulled up the stairs, and placed beneath the noose. One of the men bound his hands, and the other put a noose over his head.

The newcomers huddled together, appalled at what they were witnessing.

"Once-a-week," Marleaux continued, "I select the laziest son-of-a-bitch in Whiskey Falls and throw him a necktie party. This man was assigned to work in the mine. He didn't carry his share of the load, but he ate his share of the food. Tonight, for his sloth, he'll dangle at the end of a rope."

Without turning to look behind him, Marleaux again snapped his fingers. The lever was pulled and the man fell through the trapdoor, twitching and jerking until he twitched and jerked no more.

The new prisoners gasped, shuddered, and held each other. Some began to weep.

"There's one more thing you'd best know," Marleaux said. "There is no escaping Whiskey Falls. Even if you evade my men and the soldiers, and get out of town, you are surrounded by steep terrain on all sides. The Crow, loyal to Captain Mason and his troopers, are camped in the hills all around us. They have standing orders to kill anyone leaving this valley without my permission. I'm sure you're all well aware by now of the Crow's ability to kill. Incidentally, for every scalp they collect, they'll earn a bottle of rye whiskey."

"Right hospitable place, this Whiskey Falls," Ned said under his breath.

"Line up the newcomers, Captain," Marleaux said. "Let's see what we've got."

Sergeant Greenwald ordered his men to form the new prisoners into a line. Marleaux and his two contrasting assistants, with Captain Mason on their heels, walked slowly past each one, appraising Whiskey Falls' newest residents.

Children clung to their mothers, and the few surviving men to their wives, as Marleaux made his examination. He paid particular attention to the women, noting their ages, general condition, and comeliness. He stopped at Jolie, who held Rebecca and glared defiantly at him.

"Where's your man?" Marleaux asked.

"Long dead."

"Don't worry," Marleaux said, a wicked grin lighting his face, "we'll find you a new one every night, won't we boys?"

"More than one," Captain Mason said. The sentries and soldiers within earshot issued hoots, catcalls, and whistles.

"Put the men to work in the mine, the small boys at the stable, and for now, the women and girls in the mess hall," Marleaux said. "I'll select women for the comfort house tomorrow. Be sure and check them for hidden valuables they might have concealed on their person before bedding them down. I don't want any hoarders."

Marleaux stopped at the end of the line when he reached Pritchard, Johnson, and Ned.

"Why are these three in chains?" he asked.

"These three men staved off my Crow assault all by themselves," Captain Mason answered. "Killed over a hundred warriors. They'd probably be killing braves still, if they hadn't run out of ammunition."

"One hundred braves?" Marleaux said, rubbing his whiskers. "I take it these men aren't Quakers and object to killing, like the rest?"

"No, Sir," Mason said. "These three are definitely not the 'turn the other cheek' type. The older one is the wagon master, and claims to hail from Indiana. The very large one claims to be a

Missourian named Pritchard, but we sussed him out as a former rebel and Texas Ranger named Joe Atherton."

"Smokin' Joe Atherton?" Marleaux said, lifting his eyebrows. "The legendary mankiller?"

"That's what my men tell me," Mason said. "Never met him before, myself, but I've heard of him. He certainly put down enough Crow braves to earn the credential."

"I've heard tell tales of Smokin' Joe," Marleaux said. "Oleg," he addressed the huge, bald, man, "this man Atherton is reputed to be one of the toughest bare-knuckle fighters on the frontier. They say he killed a man once with a single blow."

"Not impressed," Oleg harrumphed in a thick, Slavic, accent.

"What do you think, McKinnon?"

"Just 'cause he's a big Texican, don't mean he's to be feared," the smaller man in the bowler said in a Scottish accent. He drew his right-hand Colt, twirled it on the trigger-guard, and re-holstered. "A bullet will end his days, just like anybody else."

"Careful," Marleaux said. "He's also supposed to be the deadliest pistoleer still above ground. It's said his guns have ended more men than the typhus."

"Maybe we'll have to find out for ourselves just how deadly he is?" McKinnon said.

"Maybe," Marleaux said. He pointed at Johnson. "What about him?"

"This one claims to hail from Illinois," Captain Mason said. "Says his name's Will Johnson. Also claims to have fought for the Union."

"He fought for the Union, all right," McKinnon interjected, "but he doesn't hail from Illinois. And he damned sure isn't named Johnson."

"You know him?" Marleaux asked.

"Hello, Daniel," Johnson said, before McKinnon could answer. "Been a long time."

"Indeed it has, Laird," McKinnon said. "Looks like you've got yourself into a bit of a pickle."

"So it would seem."

"Who is he?" Marleaux demanded.

"His name is Captain Laird Bonner," McKinnon explained. "He fought for the Union. He's from Indiana, not Illinois."

Pritchard and Ned exchanged quizzical glances.

"How do you know him?" Marleaux said.

"By professional association," McKinnon said, a smile starting across his face. "He's a bounty-killer, just like me."

CHAPTER TWENTY-SIX

Pritchard, Ned, and Laird Bonner, formerly known as Will Johnson, were escorted under guard to one of several large tents used to house prisoners. The manacles were removed from their wrists and replaced with leg irons, which allowed them to walk only in short steps and made running impossible.

The evening meal had already been served so they were given a bowl of cold corn gruel and a cup of water, and told to bed down on the plank floor wherever they could find space. They were further advised they could exit the tent to use the latrine, but only if they announced themselves first. If caught outside their tent without permission after the hours of darkness they would be shot on sight.

The trio found a spot in one corner and sat down. "Bon appetite," Bonner said, as they consumed their gruel.

"I don't know about you fellers," Ned said, "but I'm a-startin to get the feeling Whiskey Falls isn't a particularly pleasant place."

"Could be worse," Pritchard said, taking a sip of water. "We could've had our hair lifted back on the Oregon Trail, courtesy of the Crow."

"True enough," Ned agreed.

Pritchard nudged a fellow prisoner dozing beside him. "We're new here," he said. "I'd surely appreciate learnin' what can you tell me about Whiskey Falls?"

"Ask somebody else," the prisoner grumbled. "I'm trying to sleep. You'll find out a lot more than you want to know about Whiskey Falls soon enough."

Pritchard grabbed the man's hair and yanked him up to a sitting position. "I'm askin' you, friend," he said, "and I'm askin' now. Don't make me ask again."

"Okay, okay," the prisoner protested, not realizing Pritchard's size until fully awake. "What do you want to know?"

"Tell me about the place," Pritchard said, releasing his grip on the prisoner's hair.

"Ain't much to tell," he grumbled. "You just entered the ass-end of hell."

"Go on," Pritchard said. "How come nobody outside this valley knows about Whiskey Falls?"

"It weren't here until a couple of years ago," the prisoner said. "A party of prospectors struck a vein of silver hereabouts. They were headed into Fort Hall with their first payload when they got waylaid by Henry Marleaux and his gang."

"We met him," Pritchard said. "Who is he?"

"I can answer that," Bonner said.

"Why should I believe you," Pritchard challenged, "given you lied to me about your name and occupation?"

"That's an odd question," Bonner said, "coming from a man who used an alias for ten years."

"Okay, Mister Bonner," Pritchard said. "We'll talk about your name later. We've got more pressing concerns right now. What do you know about this Marleaux feller?"

"Lieutenant Red Henry Marleaux was second-in-command at the prisoner-of-war camp at Fort Sumter, in Andersonville."

"He helped run that God-forsaken hellhole?" Ned said. "What went on there was a sin against God and Man. Atrocities abounded. But it would certainly explain how the a son-of-a-bitch knows how to run a prison camp."

"After they hung his commanding officer, Captain Wirz, for war crimes," Bonner continued, "Marleaux fled and disappeared. He hasn't been heard from in years and was presumed dead. In fact, there's still a ten-thousand-dollar bounty on his head."

"I suppose you would know," Pritchard said, "since you're a bounty-killer."

"I can explain why I lied to you," Bonner said.

"I can guess," Pritchard said, turning back to the prisoner. "What more can you tell me about Henry Marleaux?"

"Marleaux runs a gang of thirty-or-so renegade ex-soldiers from both sides of the war," the prisoner went on. "They jumped the claim, killed all the prospectors, and took over the silver mine."

"That still doesn't explain the appearance of a town out in the middle of nowhere," Pritchard said.

"Marleaux needed workers to run the mine after he took it," the prisoner said. "So he worked out a deal with the troops at Fort Hall, which ain't but twenty miles away. He's a clever bastard, that Henry Marleaux, you've got to give him that."

"What sort of deal did he make with the army?"

"The troops at Fort Hall are supposed to be fightin' the Cheyenne and Sioux with the help of the Crow. But when they aren't fighting the Cheyenne and Sioux, Captain Mason has his troops and their Crow lackeys raid wagon and freight trains traveling the Oregon Trail."

"How's that connect Mason to Marleaux?"

"Marleaux pays Mason, in silver, and the Crow in liquor and trinkets. Captain Mason's cavalry constantly patrols the Oregon Trail, looking for wagon trains and freight caravans. When his troops find one, he sends in the Crow to attack it. Once they conquer it, he takes it, and diverts it north to Whiskey Falls, which is well off the Oregon Trail and hidden within this valley."

"That's exactly what happened to us!" Ned exclaimed.

"You're right," Pritchard said to the prisoner, but more to himself. "This Marleaux feller is a clever bastard. As criminal enterprises go, he's put together one helluva smart operation."

"You don't know the half of it," the prisoner said. "The captured trains provide Marleaux with a steady supply of materials and livestock to support his kingdom, but most importantly, it gives him fresh workers for his mine. That's where all the able-bodied men, like me and you, end up. Most of the women and kids he puts to work in the stables and the kitchens. The prettiest gals he puts into his 'comfort house,' as he calls it. It's nothing but a saloon, bordello, and gaming hall. Marleaux even has a roulette wheel in there. You'd be surprised what he gets off freight trains heading west, especially the amount of liquor he confiscates. They say it's why he named the place Whiskey Falls. The barrels of whiskey keep falling into his lap."

"He sounds like Blackbeard the Pirate," Ned said. "But instead of raiding ships on the high seas, he raids wagon trains on the Idaho prairie."

"All I know," the prisoner said, "is Henry Marleaux is an evil cur who thinks nothing of murdering and enslaving men, women, and children, and that nobody who ever comes to Whiskey Falls as his prisoner leaves alive."

"I presume," Pritchard said, "Marleaux also relieves the troopers of the silver he's paid them in his saloon, gambling hall, and whorehouse when they come back into town?"

"You'd be right," the prisoner said. "Marleaux takes back the very silver he pays out to have his booty brought to his doorstep in whiskey, cards, and women."

"A right enterprising feller, this Marleaux," Ned said.

"Henry Marleaux created Whiskey Falls, and he's making money hand-over-fist here," the prisoner conceded. "And he protects it. He'll crush anything, or anyone, who gets in his way, with plenty of suffering along the journey."

"What can we expect tomorrow?" Ned asked the prisoner.

"You three will be sent into the mine, like me," the prisoner answered. "You'll move dirt and rock from dawn till dusk. If you had wives or daughters in your wagon train, they'll be assigned to the kitchen or whored out. Your possessions, and maybe even yourselves or your relatives and children, will eventually be sold to the highest bidder during the next auction."

"What auction?" Pritchard asked.

"Once a month, Marleaux opens up Whiskey Falls to a collection of gangs, slavers, corrupt ranchers and farmers, outlaw trappers and traders, Indians, soldiers, and just about anyone else looking to buy human flesh or stolen goods. He holds an auction on that big stage in the town square, and sells all the booty, animals, and slaves he's collected since the previous month to the highest bidder. He trades in everything—wagons, livestock, guns, and even people. Pretty women, as you can imagine, go for a premium."

"It sounds like the Roman market of olden times," Bonner observed, "held outside the Colosseum before the gladiatorial bouts."

"When's the next auction?" Pritchard said.

"Any day now. You saw how full the wagon lot and the stockyards were when you came in? It's been several weeks since the last auction day, and Marleaux's inventory of stolen booty is building up. Also, the snows are coming and he knows it. Soon the Oregon Trail is going to dry up, and that includes buyers heading into Whiskey Falls. He'll want to make as much money as he can before he has to close up shop for the winter."

"How long have you been here?" Pritchard asked.

"Five months. I was hauling barrels of bourbon to California from Kentucky in a fifty-wagon freight train when we got jumped by the Crow. More than half of the men in my party were killed outright. The bulk of the barrels are still in his warehouse. Marleaux sells most of the whiskey, but keeps some of it to stock his saloon and pay off the Crow."

"I don't suppose you've tried to escape?"

"Good luck," the prisoner scoffed. "Every once in a while, someone gets desperate and makes a run for it. If the sentries don't shoot you on the way out of town, the Crow, or Captain Mason's cavalry, will. And that's not taking into account the terrain, weather, or the Sioux or Cheyenne war parties you'd have to contend with once outside this valley. Besides, where are you going to escape to? The nearest place is Fort Hall, which puts you right back in Captain Mason's lap."

"Marleaux has it worked out perfectly," Pritchard said. "He's the emperor of his own private empire right here in the Idaho Territory."

"And we're his slaves," Ned said, shaking his head.

"Everyone who's tried to flee," the prisoner said, "has ended up back in Whiskey Falls with their head on a pike in the town square for everybody to see, minus the scalp. As you probably noticed with the hanging earlier, Marleaux favors public discipline."

"It keeps the prisoners in line," Ned said.

"He learned his lessons from Andersonville well," Bonner said.

"Thank you," Pritchard said. "I apologize for disturbing your slumber." The prisoner turned back to sleep.

"What're we gonna do?" Ned asked Pritchard and Bonner.

"Whatever it takes," Pritchard said. "Get some sleep, boys. I've got a feelin' we'll be a-needin' it tomorrow."

CHAPTER TWENTY-SEVEN

Pritchard had been awakened at dawn, along with Ned, Bonner, and more than fifty other male prisoners in his tent, by a pair of Henry Marleaux's armed gang. They lined up the chained men and led them outside to a mess line where they were fed beef-laced corn meal and fresh water.

After breakfast they were marched in a shuffling gait, due to their leg irons, to the mine's entrance less than one-hundred yards away. They relieved the prisoners who'd been working the twelve-hour night shift, taking their picks and shovels from them, and entered the mine.

The prisoners ending their shift were filthy, exhausted, and ranged in age from fifteen to the mid-sixties. All shared one thing in common, a look of utter despair.

Once in the mine, they followed a line of candles to stations deep within the various tributaries where they were ordered to dig. Other prisoners hauled out what they chipped away in wooden carts for filtering in the slew at the creek outside the mine.

Talking was supposedly not allowed, but men were able to conduct hushed conversations when the armed guards were distracted or in another part of the shaft. Pritchard, Ned, and Bonner remained together, laboring away in the semi-darkness.

"This is great fun," Bonner said sarcastically, a couple of hours into their shift. Their guard had moved down the line to converse with another.

"Did some gold mining once," Ned said, "in Colorado. Weren't no more fun than this."

"How'd you make out?" Pritchard asked, as he chipped away with his pick.

"I just told you I only did it once." Ned chuckled. "That oughta tell you how well I made out. For what it's worth, there ain't no more silver in this here dirt than there was gold in my claim in Colorado."

"What do you mean?" Pritchard said.

Ned bent and scooped up a handful of dirt. "Might have been some silver here once, but this mine is played out. It was probably only a small silver deposit, and the prospectors who found it must have thought it led to a deeper vein. Don't see any sign they found one." He lowered his voice even more. "We ain't diggin' for silver, fellers. Were just movin' dirt."

"I wonder if Henry Marleaux knows his mine has dried up?" Bonner said.

"You earn your silver in a different way, don't you?" Pritchard said.

"You've pocketed money collecting bounties," Bonner retorted, "so I'm told."

"I've collected reward money as a Texas

Ranger, sure enough," Pritchard admitted. "But I've never hunted a feller solely for the money, and I never killed a man unless I had to."

"Splitting hairs, aren't you?" Bonner said. "Whether you're wearing a badge, and the blessing of the governor, or out to line your pockets on your own, hunting wanted men is hunting wanted men, wouldn't you say?"

"I'm not a wanted man," Pritchard said. "And you ain't gettin' paid to bring me to justice at the nearest hoosegow. You're bein' paid to deliver my head."

"What makes you think I'm hunting you?" Bonner asked.

"I'm also not a fool," Pritchard said, putting down his pick and turning to face Bonner. "Bird-doggin' our wagon train? Posin' as a lawman under an assumed name? That was all part of your plan to get me to Fort Hall, or some other town farther along the Oregon Trail, where you could kill me under witness to verify the bounty."

"If that's true," Bonner said, "why did I save your life?"

"You took that fancy rifle shot at Reverend Farley's hand to keep me from bein' lynched. You couldn't very well collect a bounty on my head if somebody else did me in."

"Fair enough," Bonner said. "I told you last night I'd explain, and I will."

"I'm listenin'."

"I was hired to bring in your head, just as you say," Bonner admitted. "That's the honest truth."

"That's a foul thing you're admittin' to," Ned said in disgust. "And here I was, takin' a likin' to you. Plannin' to murder a feller like Samuel, you oughta be ashamed of yourself. But runnin' into that Crow war party threw a horseshoe into your works, didn't it?"

"It did indeed," Bonner said. "I barely got back to your wagon train with my scalp."

"And wouldn't have it on your head now," Ned pointed out, "without me and Samuel."

"I'm aware of that," Bonner said solemnly. "And I'm grateful."

"How much?" Pritchard said. "What's the price on my head?"

"Twenty-thousand dollars," Bonner said. "Ten up front, and ten on delivery of proof of your demise at my hand."

"Hell and tarnation!" Ned couldn't contain his voice. "Twenty-thousand dollars!"

"Keep quiet down there!" a guard's voice called out. "Less jabberin' and more workin', unless one of you boys wants to dangle from Red Henry's gallows."

"Sorry," Ned whispered, once the guard had moved on. "I got a little excited. Twenty-thousand dollars is a helluva lot of money." He winked at Pritchard. "I might be tempted to end you myself for that amount of coin."

211

"Who put up the money?" Pritchard said.

"That's supposed to be confidential," Bonner said. "I'm not to disclose such information, ever." He looked directly at Pritchard. "But I figure since you saved my life, you're entitled to know. The bounty was put up by a one-armed man who owns a detective agency in St. Louis. His name is—"

"Cottonmouth Quincy," Pritchard finished the sentence. "I should've known. He hired men to have me done in before, but did it with somebody else's money. I'm the feller who clipped his arm and bent his beak."

"That's what he told me," Bonner said. "I suppose I don't have to tell you that Mr. Quincy dislikes you intensely."

"I'll say," Ned whistled. "Twenty grand buys a lot of grudge."

"So what's your plan?" Pritchard said. "Are you still going to do me in?"

"As you can see," Bonner said, holding up his shovel, "I'm presently not in a position to advance my financial interests at the expense of your health. When my situation improves, who knows?"

"Who knows?" Pritchard repeated.

The men worked in silence another hour before the trio of guards came for Pritchard.

"You," the man with the rifle addressed Pritchard, "with the bullet hole in your noggin'?

Smokin' Joe, or whatever the hell your name is? Henry wants a word with you. C'mon."

Pritchard looked at Ned and Bonner, put down his pickaxe, and followed the rifleman, who was accompanied by two other armed men, out of the mine.

He was escorted across town, squinting in the sunlight until his eyes adjusted from the darkness of the mine to the largest building in town.

The main part of the building contained a great hall with a bar, plenty of tables, chairs, the roulette wheel he'd been told of, and other furniture of a mixed variety that had been absconded from various wagon trains. Ten or fifteen soldiers were lounging about, along with a similar number of armed men in civilian clothing Pritchard assumed were members of Marleaux's gang.

There were also a number of women, some quite attractive, clad in fancy dresses and shoes. Pritchard could only assume the clothes, along with the women wearing them, were stolen from wagon trains, as well.

Seated at a large table in the center of the room was Henry Marleaux. His hat was off, his feet were up on the table, and his jumbo-sized frame was leaning back in his chair. A bottle of whiskey and a half-full glass were set out before him. Behind him, at a separate table, sat Oleg and McKinnon, who was still wearing his bowler and smoking a cigarette.

213

Pritchard was led before Marleaux. "Good morning, Marshal Pritchard." He smiled. "How are you enjoying your stay in Whiskey Falls?"

"The goose-feather mattress I slept on last night was a bit lumpy," Pritchard said, "and my mornin' coffee was a mite cold. Otherwise, Whiskey Falls is a right hospitable place."

"A sense of humor." Marleaux laughed. "I like that."

"It's all he's got left," McKinnon said from behind Marleaux. "Look at him." He spat. "He's nothing but a tiger without claws. And a dusty one, at that. Famous mankiller, indeed. Scratchin' in the mine like a gopher, that's what your famous mankiller is doing now."

"I don't think Mr. McKinnon likes you very much," Marleaux said.

"I'm heartsick at the very thought," Pritchard said. "Pint-sized weasels with loose mouths always give me the painted shivers."

Marleaux laughed again. McKinnon's face reddened. He got up from his seat and approached Pritchard, who stood more than a foot taller.

"You might want to show a little respect," he said. He drew his right-hand revolver, spun it on the trigger-guard, and finished the flourish by pointing the gun up at Pritchard's face.

Faster than the eye could track, Pritchard simultaneously snatched the revolver with his left hand and slapped McKinnon across the face with

214

his right. The blow sent the Scotsman's cigarette from his mouth, and his bowler from his head, but left him standing dazed and bloodied where he stood. He also found the barrel of his own ivory-handled revolver, now with the hammer cocked, pressed against his forehead.

A dozen guns were suddenly drawn and pointed at Pritchard. Marleaux's hand reflexively grabbed the butt of one of his own belted pistols.

"And you might want to be careful where you aim your popgun, little feller," Pritchard said to McKinnon. "It's impolite to point a pistol at your betters." He lowered the revolver's hammer and set it gently on the table in front of Marleaux.

A furious McKinnon drew his other pistol, cocked it, and once again aimed it at Pritchard's face. Pritchard stared evenly down at the enraged gunman.

"That'll be quite enough, Daniel," Marleaux said.

"I don't take that from any man," McKinnon hissed.

"Evidently Marshal Pritchard doesn't, either."

"Either pull that trigger," Pritchard said, "or put that lead-pusher away. If'n you don't, my next move won't be to slap you silly. It'll be to end you."

"Put your pistol away, Daniel," Marleaux ordered. "Now."

McKinnon reluctantly holstered his gun.

Marleaux nodded to the others in the saloon and everyone else holstered their weapons, as well.

McKinnon picked up his other gun from the table, and his hat from the floor, and returned to his seat. He wiped his bloody mouth on his sleeve and glared at Pritchard while he poured himself another drink.

"You certainly take chances, Marshal," Marleaux said.

"What's the worst that could happen?" Pritchard shrugged. "If your pet pistoleer shot me, at least I wouldn't have to return to diggin' in that infernal mine."

"I gather you don't like working in my silver mine?"

"Would you?"

"No," Marleaux said, "as a matter of fact, I would not. Have a seat, Marshal."

Pritchard sat.

"May I offer you a drink?"

"Don't mind if I do," Pritchard said. Marleaux gestured to a hostess, who scurried over with another glass, refreshed Marleaux's drink, and poured one for Pritchard.

"To your health, Marshal," Marleaux said, raising his glass.

"Call me Samuel," Pritchard said, raising his own.

Chapter Twenty-eight

"I've been pondering you," Marleaux said to Pritchard as they sipped whiskey.

"Somethin' about me you find vexin'?"

"Your reputation for spilling blood is most impressive," Marleaux said.

"Yours as well," Pritchard said. "You and your former commander, Captain Wirz, killed more Union soldiers at Andersonville through sickness and starvation than in just about every battle 'cept Chickamauga and Gettysburg."

"They called us monsters," Marleaux said. "I say we did our duty. All those thousands of prisoners we starved didn't return to the battlefield, did they? Some army commanders fought their battles with cannons. We fought ours with empty bellies. But the newly reformed Union didn't thank me or Captain Wirz for our victories. After the surrender, Grant hanged Wirz. I decided to avoid that fate and made a discrete exit."

"Can't fault a man for wantin' to keep his scalp."

"Some of the things credited to you, under the name Smokin' Joe Atherton, are the stuff of legend," Marleaux said. "Most of it is pretty hard to believe. I always assumed the tales were exaggerated in the telling, as such campfire stories tend to be. Frankly, until I met you, I didn't take stock in any of what was said about you. But two things have convinced me otherwise."

"What're they?"

"First of all, what Captain Mason and his troopers reported to me about your battle with the Crow. Captain Mason is a very practical man and not prone to exaggeration. Also, I know firsthand how formidable the Crow are in battle."

"I had help from Ned and Bonner. Those boys can shoot. And the second thing?"

"How you faced down McKinnon just now. He's one of the fastest gunmen I know, and I've a gang of more than two-dozen professional gunmen in my employ. I don't think I've ever seen any man move as fast as you did, and certainly not one as big as you."

"I had incentive," Pritchard said, tapping the scar on his forehead with his thumb. "I take it personal when folks point guns at me."

"I can see that," Marleaux said.

"He got lucky," McKinnon interjected hotly from across the room. "The big ox knew I wasn't really going to shoot him."

"If you weren't going to shoot him," Marleaux said, as if speaking to a recalcitrant child, "why did you point your pistol at him?"

218

"He . . . was unarmed," McKinnon stammered. "I couldn't just shoot him."

"I've seen you shoot plenty of unarmed men," Marleaux corrected him. "Women and children, too."

"Why, if Pritchard had been armed," McKinnon declared, "I would've—"

"You would've been shot dead," Marleaux cut him off. "Shut up, Daniel. We've heard enough of your mouth for one day. In fact, why don't you go and check on the guards at the corral and the mine? It would do you good to get some fresh air. It might even cool off your temper."

A red-faced McKinnon stood up, put on his hat, and stormed out under the eyes of all in the saloon.

Marleaux sighed. "Go with Daniel, Oleg, and keep an eye on him. You know how he gets when his blood is up. I don't want the crazy little Scotsman shooting any more of my workers than necessary. I'm already running low for this time of year."

The giant Russian wordlessly picked up his mallet and walked out.

"Sergeant Greenwald," Marleaux called out to a trooper at the bar. "Have you got a key to the leg irons?"

"I do."

"Turn Samuel loose, will you?"

"Are you sure you want to do that, Mr. Marleaux?"

"Are you afraid, Sergeant?" Pritchard asked. "I didn't forget you threatened to whip me like a rebel dog."

"I'm not afraid of him," Greenwald said unconvincingly. "But it doesn't do to have a prisoner walking about free."

Marleaux tilted his head. "What's he going to do, Sergeant? There's nowhere to run, and even the famous Smokin' Joe couldn't defeat all the guns which would turn against him were he to misbehave in Whiskey Falls." He turned to Pritchard. "Are you going to misbehave?"

"I'll behave," Pritchard said. "I have incentive."

"Remove the irons, Sergeant."

A moment later Pritchard was free.

"Come with me," Marleaux said, standing and collecting the whiskey bottle. "And bring the glasses."

Pritchard did as he was told, and followed Marleaux across the saloon to a private room in the back. Inside was a desk, several chairs, and an iron safe with the words Wells Fargo stamped on the door. After they entered Marleaux closed the door.

Both men sat, and Marleaux poured them each a fresh whiskey. Once both had taken a drink, he put his elbows on the desk and leaned forward.

"I have a predicament," Marleaux began, "and a proposition."

"You also have my attention," Pritchard said.

"Before I explain anything further," Marleaux said, "I'd like your opinion. You're a very young man, but I know you served the Confederacy, as I did, and traveled extensively as a Texas Ranger. You're much worldlier than your years. Tell me, what do you think of Whiskey Falls?"

"It's a very efficient operation, if'n you ask me. You run the place like a feudal empire. Whiskey Falls is situated perfectly to be both hidden and defended, yet is close enough to the Oregon Trail to allow you to plunder whatever you need in the way of material and manpower to keep it going. And your arrangement with the army, and theirs with the Crow, is pure genius. It keeps you protected in the heart of hostile Indian country. Finally, the escalatin' Indian troubles provide a convenient explanation to cover your doins' to the loved ones of those who've vanished."

"I'm flattered," Marleaux said. "Now tell me what's wrong with Whiskey Falls?"

"Whiskey Falls' days are numbered," Pritchard said flatly. "You may survive the winter, but not much longer. By spring, summer at the latest, you'll have to pack up and move out. That's if you can get out at all. The Sioux and Cheyenne are organizin' and buildin' their numbers for a fight with the government. By spring this territory will be crawling with more hostiles than the detachment at Fort Hall can handle. Which means the army will send more troops. A lot more. Whiskey Falls won't remain hidden for long."

"I'm impressed," Marleaux said. "You're right, of course." He leaned back in his chair. "Tell me why?"

"Thanks," Pritchard said. "Railroads are sproutin' new lines west every day. It's already faster, but soon it'll be cheaper to send folks and material by rail in days than it will be to haul 'em across the Oregon Trail in covered wagons in months. Your steady supply of slaves and pirated goods will dry up."

"What else?"

"Like I said, the Indian troubles are heatin' up. The army's pushin' the Sioux and Cheyenne hard, and they ain't gonna be pushed much longer. War is a-comin' between Reds and Whites. Fort Hall is only a small outpost. Soon there'll be many more troops, and much bigger forts, to protect the rail lines and you won't be able to stay hidden. Or maintain your 'arrangement' with the army."

"For a fellow who's only been in Whiskey Falls one day, you've given this a lot of thought."

"One of the reasons I'm still alive," Pritchard said, "is I've learned to scout out the terrain before me."

"Me, too," Marleaux said. "Is there any other reason why you believe Whiskey Falls is doomed?"

"The biggest one," Pritchard said.

"Which is?"

"The silver mine," Pritchard said. "It's played out."

"Outstanding," Marleaux said. "I knew when I first laid eyes on you, despite your physique and reputation, you were much more than a pair of fists and a fast gun. How'd you discover the mine is running dry?"

"I didn't," Pritchard said. "Ned Konig, the wagon master, did. He's done some prospectin'. Told me this mornin', while we were diggin', that there's no more silver comin' out of that hole."

"He's right," Marleaux said, draining his glass in one gulp. "What was thought to be a major strike which would bring up silver for years turned out to be nothing but a modest deposit. Barely two years later it's dried up."

"How many people in Whiskey Falls know?"

"More than I'd care to admit," Marleaux said. "Some of the miners, of course. I think Captain Mason suspects."

"If he finds out for sure?"

"If I'm lucky, he'll simply pack up, pull his troops and his Crow braves, and go back to Fort Hall. I have several hundred prisoners to watch over, and only about thirty men to do it. That's not enough to defend this town, not with high ground surrounding us on all sides. I certainly can't arm the prisoners. If Mason abandons us,

Whiskey Falls would be defenseless. It would be desperate enough without his troops, but without his Crow warriors to help keep out the Cheyenne and Sioux we'd be overrun in a matter of days."

"And if you ain't so lucky?"

"Captain Mason is fully aware that any resident of Whiskey Falls who returns to civilized society might potentially divulge what went on here. He knows his superior officers would look harshly upon his arrangement with me, and his complicity in what amounts to robbery, kidnapping, forced labor, and murder on an industrial scale. Rather than face a court martial and a firing squad, I fear the good captain might decide to turn his cavalry rifles and Crow tomahawks on the residents of Whiskey Falls, including me."

"Do you think Captain Mason would really massacre everyone," Pritchard said, "just to prevent someone here from spillin' the beans?"

"In his shoes," Marleaux said, "I would. He can't take the chance he'll be reported to the authorities. Mason's too smart to leave any survivors."

"Now I understand your predicament," Pritchard said.

"Make no mistake," Marleaux said, "it's your predicament, too. If you think Captain Mason would spare anyone in Whiskey Falls, slave or master, you're not as intelligent as I take you for."

"Perhaps," Pritchard said, "but my predicament doesn't feel quite the same as yours. You're sippin' whiskey in the sunshine, while I'm diggin' in the dark in a bled-out mine."

"Which brings us to my proposition," Marleaux said.

CHAPTER TWENTY-NINE

When Ned Konig and Laird Bonner exited the mine at dusk, at the conclusion of their twelve-hour shift, with forty-six other similarly-manacled, filthy, and exhausted prisoners, they were met with an unexpected sight. Standing before them was Samuel Pritchard. To their surprise, not only was Pritchard not wearing leg irons, he was wearing his guns.

Pritchard was bathed, shaved, clad in freshly-cleaned dungarees, a button-front shirt, shined boots, and his Stetson. Around his hips were slung his own revolvers, and both belts were fully re-stocked with cartridges to replace the ones he'd expended against the Crow. Over one shoulder was draped Ned's holstered .45 Colt Cavalry, and over the other was Bonner's pair of .44 Colt Open-Top revolvers.

"Good evening, boys," Pritchard said. "How was your day?"

"A mite less enjoyable than yours, I reckon," Ned said, staring at Pritchard as he handed his shovel to one of the prisoners entering the mine for the night shift.

"I'd have to agree with Ned," Bonner said, turning over his pickaxe.

Pritchard nodded to one of the guards, who bent down and unlocked the leg irons from Ned's and Bonner's ankles. Then he handed both men their gun belts.

"I don't get it," Ned said. "One minute we're galley slaves, and the next we're a-walkin' around free and armed?"

"Nothin' to get," Pritchard said cheerfully. "You're part of Henry Marleaux's gang now, just like me."

"Are you loco?" Ned exclaimed. "I wouldn't join up with that murderin' varmint—"

Pritchard cut him off. "Let's take a walk." He pulled Ned along by the arm, with Bonner following behind. He escorted the fuming wagon master away from the mine, toward the vast corral at the edge of town.

"Keep your lip latched," Pritchard said. "I'll explain when we're out of earshot."

"I don't need no explanation!" Ned protested. "I don't want nothin' to do with that prairie pirate!"

"Would you rather be back in irons in the mine?" Bonner said.

"Nope," Ned admitted, calming down. "I surely wouldn't."

The trio found a secluded area on one border of the corral where they could speak freely. The sound of their voices was muffled by the shuffling herd of livestock.

"Here's the lay of it," Pritchard began, as both men belted on their guns. "Marleaux approached me with a proposition this mornin'."

"What kind of proposition?" Bonner asked.

Pritchard briefly explained the contents of his conversation with Marleaux and what he'd learned about Whiskey Falls.

"So Marleaux's got hisself in a predicament," Ned said. "Both of his gravy trains, the mine and plunderin' wagon trains off the Oregon Trail, are played out? Can't say I'm heartbroke over his turn of bad luck."

"That's not the problem," Bonner said, grasping the situation instantly. "If Marleaux's luck runs out, so does ours."

"What are you talkin' about?" Ned said. Pritchard continued explaining, confirming Bonner's suspicions.

"Hell and tarnation," Ned said. "So what you're tellin' me, Samuel, is that either Captain Mason leaves Whiskey Falls defenseless, to be set upon by the Cheyenne and Sioux, or he sets his own troopers and redskins on us hisself? Is that what you're a-sayin'?"

"Them's the unvarnished facts," Pritchard said. "I ain't happy about throwin' in with Marleaux and his band of murderous coyotes any more than you are, Ned. But if we do, at least we have a fightin' chance of dealin' ourselves a way out of Whiskey Falls with our scalps attached. We hold no cards at all wearin' leg irons in the bottom of a hole."

"He's right," Bonner said. "Casting our lots with Marleaux, or at least pretending to, is our only chance."

"What's Marleaux got up his sleeve?" Ned asked.

"Tomorrow," Pritchard said, "is going to be Whiskey Falls' final auction. Marleaux plans to have every flesh-trader and stolen-goods merchant within fifty miles here for the festivities. He intends to sell off everything he can, and rake in as much money as possible, in one last haul. He'll add his takings to over one-hundred-thousand dollars in silver, plundered cash, and confiscated jewelry he's got tucked away in a stolen Wells Fargo safe inside his saloon, and flee forever."

"One-hundred-thousand dollars!" Ned whistled. "Are you joshin' me?"

"That's what he claims," Pritchard said.

"I wouldn't be surprised if that number was low," Bonner said. "Marleaux's been digging up silver, and robbing wagon trains, for over two years. Most people traveling the Oregon Trail by wagon sold everything they had back home to start their new lives out west."

"Where's Marleaux gonna go once he skedaddles from Whiskey Falls?" Ned said.

"He said he was going to California," Pritchard

said, "but he won't stop there. He didn't say it, but I'm certain he plans to head south into Mexico."

"How in tarnation is he gonna accomplish that?" Ned said. "You're tellin' me Marleaux's gonna sneak out of town unnoticed by Mason and his troops, and then get out of this valley past a couple of hundred Crow warriors a-campin' in the hills, all the while pullin' an iron safe in a freight wagon?"

"The wagon and a teams are no problem," Bonner said. "Whiskey Falls has an armada of stolen wagons and plenty of rustled horseflesh to pull them."

"Marleaux's already got a couple of sturdy wagons selected and loaded," Pritchard confirmed. "They're stocked with food, water, guns, ammunition, and other necessary travel provisions."

"He's got his escape all figured, don't he?" Ned said.

"That's not all he's got," Pritchard said. "I've been inside Marleaux's warehouse. He gave me a tour today. You won't believe what's stashed in there. Booty from a hundred waylaid wagon trains. Stores of grain, tools, furniture, not to mention dozens of barrels of whiskey, and an arsenal of guns and ammunition, including dynamite. Where do you think I got your guns from?"

Pritchard dug into his pockets. "That reminds me," he said, "I almost forgot what else I brung you." He handed Ned his tobacco pouch and Bonner a handful of his thin, black, cheroots. Bonner nodded his thanks, but didn't light a smoke. He didn't want to alert anyone to their whereabouts. Ned, however, greedily stuffed a wad of tobacco into his mouth.

"I still don't see how Marleaux's going to pull off a getaway?" Bonner said. "There'll be dozens of outsiders in Whiskey Falls for the big auction, not to mention all the soldiers and Crow braves. He can't possibly sneak himself, and a few wagons, out of this valley unnoticed."

"Marleaux believes he can," Pritchard said. "I'll wager he's right, too. Remember the barrels of whiskey I just mentioned?"

"I do," Ned said. "What of 'em?"

"One of the items Marleaux obtained from the countless waylaid wagon trains Captain Mason procured for him was several cases of laudanum."

"Laudanum?" Ned said. "What's that for?"

"He's going to spike the whiskey, isn't he?" Bonner said.

"You guessed it," Pritchard said. "Evidently on auction day whiskey flows like water. This auction day it'll be tainted. The soldiers and Crow will partake, as usual. But his own boys, which means us, will be drinkin' un-spiked liquor. It don't take much laudanum to put a man down. Mixed with whiskey, a little of that stuff will knock out a good-sized draft horse for a full day."

"Isn't he afraid," Ned asked, "of what the soldiers and Indians, not to mention his cheated auction buyers, will do to him when they eventually wake up, wise up, and come a-ridin' after him?"

"Marleaux told me he plans to be well away from Whiskey Falls by the time anyone wakes up."

"I don't believe him," Ned said. "Ain't no way that scoundrel is a-gonna leave a few hundred soldiers, Indians, prisoners, and jilted suckers alive to track him down. Especially after they wake up with headaches the next mornin' and find him and all their money gone. Henry Marleaux's too fox-clever, and too buzzard-mean, to let that happen. He's got somethin' nasty up his sleeve."

"I agree with Ned," Bonner said. "After what he's done in Whiskey Falls, Marleaux won't let anyone who can identify him stay above ground. You forget, Samuel, he was the second-in-command at Andersonville. He knows how to kill folks wholesale. No matter what he's told you, he's going to make certain no one follows him."

"I ain't arguin' with either of you," Pritchard said.

"So you're sayin'," Ned said, "that you believe Marleaux intends to—"

"Massacre everybody in Whiskey Falls?" Pritchard finished Ned's sentence for him. "I surely do. Once everybody is knocked out, I suspect he and his boys, which means us, are gonna shoot everybody dead like fish in a barrel. That's along with anybody else, such as the women and children, who won't lap up his hop-tainted booze. Then he'll toss all the carcasses in that old mine shaft to join the other poor souls him and Captain Mason have murdered over the last couple of years and ride out, pretty as you please."

"That would certainly be in keeping with Red Henry Marleaux's past behavior," Bonner concurred.

"Ain't he worried about gettin' jumped by the Sioux or Cheyenne," Ned said, "once out of this valley? And what about winter comin' on? It ain't too early for snow. Those ain't exactly small worries."

"It's only a hundred miles south to Promontory Summit," Pritchard said, "and the Union Pacific railroad depot there. He and his wagons shouldn't have any trouble makin' it before the snow sets in. In Promontory, he'll board the train to California. From there, Marleaux will go—"

"South to Mexico," Bonner finished. "Where U.S. law can't touch him."

"That's my guess," Pritchard agreed. "By the time the army figures out what happened to Captain Mason and his troopers from Fort Hall—"

"If they figure it out," Bonner interjected.

"Marleaux, his money, and what's left of his gang will be safe below the border."

"You still ain't explained how Marleaux's gonna get through a-hundred miles of Indian country on the way south to Promontory," Ned said. "The Sioux and Cheyenne might have a little somethin' to say about his travel plans."

"That's where we come in," said Bonner. "Right?"

"Right," Pritchard said. "Marleaux only came up with his grand escape plan after we arrived in Whiskey Falls. Captain Mason told him all about how the three of us, alone, wiped out more'n a-hundred Crow warriors in only a couple of hours. He figures with us three, his thirty men, and a wagon load of guns and ammunition, he stands a fair chance of gettin' to Promontory safely through Indian country with all his money, and his long red hair, intact."

"That's why he allowed you to set us free, isn't it?" Bonner asked. "You had to swear our loyalty to Marleaux."

"That's correct," Pritchard admitted. "I took the liberty of signin' you boys on with Henry Marleaux and Company."

"Henry Marleaux is the crookedest sidewinder I ever knew," Ned said, spitting tobacco juice, "and I've known a few in my day. What he's got in store for Whiskey Falls is the lowest, dirtiest, most underhanded scheme I ever heard of. A bullet's too good for that ginger-haired rat."

"Whoever called Henry Marleaux a monster," Bonner said, "was right on the money. If he hasn't earned every penny of the bounty on his head by now, he will after tomorrow."

"I have to be honest, fellers," Ned said, his jaw tightening, "I don't reckon I can partake of Marleaux's unholy plan. I've got no problem with puttin' down that thievin', murderin', army captain, nor his cowardly troopers and hired Crow scalphunters, especially after what they done to us. But I don't condone the murder of innocent men, women, and children, even if it is to save my own scalp. Nor am I gonna just ride off and leave captive prisoners to be butchered at the hands of Red Henry's men. I just plumb ain't a-gonna do it. You might as well put me back in irons, Samuel, and take me back to the mine."

"I'm in agreeance with Ned," Bonner said. "I'm a professional bounty-hunter. I've killed for money, true enough. But no matter what you two, or anyone else, think of me, I've never harmed hide-nor-hair of a woman, child, nor any other innocent person. Every man I ever put down, in war or for bounty, was armed and facing me. I'll not put a black mark on my soul by killing innocents now."

"What do you two lunkheads take me for?" Pritchard asked indignantly. "I don't abide the killing of innocent folks neither, nor would I tolerate such scurvy conduct from either of you. Did you boys actually believe I was gonna skungle off and leave the second-in-command at Andersonville free rein to massacre again without settlin' his hash? Frankly fellers, after all we've been through, I'd have thought you'd know me better by now."

"Sorry, Samuel," Ned said. "I should of knowed you wouldn't."

"I knew you wouldn't ride out and leave the prisoners to die," Bonner said. "You've been a lawman too long. It isn't in your nature."

"Forget it."

"Then what're we gonna do?" Ned asked. "You said we're part of Marleaux's gang now, ain't we? He's done set us free, and given us back our guns. Won't he be expectin' us to partake in his murderous deviltry?"

"We'll be partakin' in some deviltry, all right." Pritchard smiled. "It just won't be the deviltry Henry Marleaux is expectin'."

CHAPTER THIRTY

Pritchard left Ned and Bonner to get cleaned up, fed, and with a set of specific instructions. He told them they had a very important task to prepare for.

Pritchard informed them that tomorrow, which was Marleaux's big auction day, they were going to sneak into the storehouse. In addition to retrieving their gear, he tasked Bonner and Ned with a few other duties while inside. Afterward, they were to make their way to the horse corral where he'd meet up with them.

When asked by an indignant Ned how they were supposed to creep into a building whose front and back doors were guarded by armed men, steal their saddles and gear, load them up with food and provisions, do what else was required, and then get back out unnoticed, all Pritchard said was, "I'm gonna make sure everybody's attention is focused elsewhere."

Pritchard then walked alone to the large mess tent. It was dinnertime, and dozens of captive women toiled in two separate chow lines to feed the residents of Whiskey Falls. The prisoners were fed in one line from a large cauldron filled with beef-laced porridge, drank water from a bucket, and ate while seated on the ground outside the tent, all-the-while under armed guard.

Marleaux's men and Captain Mason's troopers were served steak and beer from a confiscated keg, and dined on tables set up inside. The Crow, nowhere in sight, chose not to eat in town with the White-Faces. Instead, they were allotted several head of beef each day, and elected to butcher their meat in the hills surrounding Whiskey Falls. Their cooking fires, visible at night and twinkling in the growing darkness on all sides of the valley, served as a warning to the Cheyenne and Sioux.

Pritchard quickly located Jolie and Rebecca. Rebecca was in the line serving prisoners, and Jolie was serving the soldiers and Marleaux's gang in the other. Both looked haggard and exhausted, and like all the women prisoners, tried to ignore the harassment of the men they served.

Most of the soldiers and gunmen leered at the women, some even making lewd comments and gestures. Pritchard walked boldly up, cut in line, took Jolie by the arm, and escorted her away from her duties. She was so surprised she didn't speak or resist.

Pritchard took her over to Rebecca's serving line, where he did the same with her. With a woman's arm in each of his large hands, he began to lead them away from the mess tent.

"Whoa there," Sergeant Greenwald said, standing up. "Where do you think you're takin' those two ladies?"

"None of your business," Pritchard replied.

"What if I make it my business?"

Pritchard released the women and turned to face the sergeant. Both of his hands were loosely at his sides. His thumbs brushed ever-so-lightly against the leather of his hand-tooled holsters.

"Be my guest," Pritchard said. "Anytime you feel ready to dig your pistol outta that widowmaker, start a-diggin'."

Sergeant Greenwald's Remington revolver was indeed buttoned-up in a standard-issue, cross-draw, full-flap-holster, commonly referred to as the widowmaker. Its nickname was earned for the inordinate length of time it took to draw the gun. The military scabbard was designed for protecting a pistol from the elements, with rapid accessibility a secondary consideration.

"You might want to tell that trooper sitting to your left," Pritchard said evenly, still staring directly at Greenwald, "if his fingers move any closer to his pistol under the table he'll get shot, too. After you get it, of course."

"Leave Mister Pritchard be," McKinnon spoke up in his Scottish accent from a nearby table. "Didn't you know, Sergeant? He's one of us, now."

"That's Marleaux's doing," Sergeant Greenwald spat, "not Captain Mason's. And certainly not mine."

"Then maybe you, and Captain Mason, and

your bloodthirsty mob of red savages should have dispensed with the marshal while you had the chance out on the Oregon Trail?"

"Go to hell, McKinnon," Greenwald said. McKinnon only laughed.

"I've got things to do," Pritchard said. "Make your play, Sergeant, or sit down, shut up, and mind your own business."

Sergeant Greenwald was in a quandary. He knew there was no chance of beating Pritchard to the draw with his army-issued flap holster. Yet most of his troopers were watching, as well as all the women serving food in the massive tent. Backing down was unthinkable.

In fact, the tent had grown almost totally silent. A moment before, the noisy clatter of several hundred people serving and eating dinner filled the tent. Now, virtually everyone had stopped what they were doing and were silently observing the drama unfolding before them.

"If you kill me," Greenwald said, "my men will cut you down seconds later."

"Sure they will," Pritchard conceded. "Everybody's gotta die sometime. But you won't be around to see it, will you? And I guarantee I'll take a few of your soldiers with me. I'll get a half-dozen, maybe more. Whyen't you ask your troopers which of 'em wants to join you in hell, Sergeant?"

A long minute transpired. The only sound was

the crackling of the fires and the boiling of the cauldron.

"There'll be another time," Greenwald finally said. He sat down and tried to look nonchalant. His reddened face indicated otherwise.

"Another time," Pritchard scoffed. "Hell, Sergeant, you've got almost a hundred troopers behind you. How many more will you need to back your play the next time? Two hundred? Three?"

Greenwald didn't answer, choosing instead to stare at his plate. Pritchard again took Jolie's and Rebecca's arms and began to escort them away from the mess tent. McKinnon left his table and caught up with them. Pritchard spun to face him.

"Easy there," McKinnon said. "I'm not issuing a challenge. I merely wanted to say, 'good evening' to the younger of the ladies."

"You stay away from my daughter!" Jolie snarled. She turned to Pritchard. "He's a vile pig. He's been saying the foulest things to Rebecca ever since we got here."

"I was planning on doing some of those things, too," he said to Jolie with a grin. "I can only assume that Marshal Pritchard is now going to be doing them in my stead?"

Pritchard's left fist snaked out a blisteringly fast hook, which struck the little Scotsman on the right side of his jaw. He spun one-hundred-and-eighty degrees, fell onto his face, and was unconscious before he hit the ground.

"Samuel! Look out!"

Rebecca's shouted warning came just in time. Oleg, the giant Russian, had come up behind Pritchard. His mallet descended from over his head.

Pritchard ducked, pivoted, and yanked his guns out as the huge hammer swooshed harmlessly past, close enough to knock off his Stetson. Had the mallet struck him, Pritchard's skull would have been instantly crushed. Oleg raised his mallet for another swing, as Pritchard cocked the hammers of both Colts and faced him.

A pistol shot rang out. Oleg halted his blow in mid-swing.

"Please don't kill him," Marleaux said, shaking his head. "I've grown somewhat fond of Oleg."

Pritchard turned around once again to find Marleaux with several of his men pointing their rifles at him. Marleaux holstered his smoking revolver and held up his hand. Oleg reluctantly lowered his mallet.

"You promised me you wouldn't misbehave," Marleaux said, wagging a finger at Pritchard. "Yet once again, you've decorated Daniel's face. I thought my instructions were clear."

"They were," Pritchard said, carefully lowering the hammers on his guns and holstering them. "You told me I could pick my own people. I'm doin' just that."

"You said Konig and Bonner," Marleaux

countered. "You didn't say anything about absconding with these two women."

"You didn't exactly say I couldn't," Pritchard argued. "I've just come back from freein' Ned and Bonner, like I told you I would, and now I'm recquisitionin' these two gals."

"Do you need both of them?" Marleaux said.

"I'm a large man," Pritchard said with a shrug and a grin. "I have large appetites."

"It seems like you're taking liberties with my good graces," Marleaux said. "I'd planned on putting both of these women to work in my comfort house tonight. I've already had two-dozen of my men, and most of the soldiers, offering me top dollar for a single poke. After Captain Mason and I broke them in, of course. And then I was going to auction them off tomorrow. I've got a feeling I'd get a pretty penny for each."

"You've got plenty of other women in your comfort house," Pritchard said. "You can spare these two."

"I'd like to let you have them," Marleaux admitted, "but I'm a businessman, and you don't have anything to trade for them."

"What do you want?" Pritchard asked.

"Not fair," Oleg interrupted, in his thick Russian accent. "Pritchard struck Daniel. Daniel fall down. Daniel is friend. I want to bash Pritchard."

"Calm down, Oleg," Marleaux said. "At the moment, I'm busy discussing business with Mister Pritchard. I realize you're fond of Daniel, but I'm also fairly sure Daniel himself had something to do with his current predicament." He nodded to his men, and a pair of them picked up the unconscious Scotsman. The remainder kept their rifles pointed at Pritchard.

"I declare," Marleaux said, shaking his head and taking the unconscious McKinnon's chin in his hand. "First you gave him a fat lip, and now you've blackened his eye. I fear Daniel will not be very pleased with you when he awakens."

"I'll try to get over it," Pritchard said. "Perhaps if'n he don't want to get slapped about he should mind his tongue or learn to duck?"

Marleaux signaled for the troopers to carry McKinnon off.

"Not fair!" Oleg repeated angrily. "Not calm down!" His nostrils flared, and his eyes blazed.

"Oleg's not very happy with me," Pritchard said.

"When Oleg gets this way," Marleaux said, "it's best to steer clear of him. He has a terrible temper. Sometimes it takes days for him to settle his blood. And he typically doesn't calm down until he's spilled someone else's."

"Speaking of Oleg," Pritchard said to Marleaux, "I do have something to trade for the gals. May I have a word in private? What I have to offer in exchange for these two women is best heard by you alone."

Marleaux motioned for his men to lower their rifles, and he and Pritchard moved apart from the others.

"I think I might have a way to satisfy Oleg's blood lust," Pritchard said in a hushed tone, "and serve your purpose at the same time."

"Go on," Marleaux said. "I'm listening."

"Seems to me," Samuel said, "you could do with a distraction while folks are consumin' your spiked whiskey?"

"They'll be food and liquor aplenty tomorrow," Marleaux countered. "Shouldn't that be enough incentive to drink?"

"What if the soldiers and Crow don't all drink at the same pace?" Pritchard asked.

"What do you mean?"

"The last thing you want," Pritchard went on, "is for some of the soldiers or Indians to succumb too quickly before others have partaken. Should that happen, their friends might get wise to the notion the booze is spiked. You could have a full-blown mutiny on your hands."

"I hadn't considered that possibility," Marleaux said, rubbing his beard. "But you're right. There's a risk some of Mason's men might figure out the whiskey is spiked before all fall to its effects. The troopers outnumber my men three-to-one, and that's not counting the Crow braves. What do you propose?"

"Let me fight Oleg."

"Are you mad?"

"Think about it?" Pritchard said. "Me and Oleg, goin' at each other bare-knuckle, on the auction stage in the square. That'll put everyone in town in one place with their eyeballs glued to one thing, instead of scattered all over Whiskey Falls sippin' in small groups in corners and alleyways, and succumbin' to the laudanum at different times."

"I like it," Marleaux said.

"All you have to do," Pritchard continued, "is advertise the bout, which ain't gonna be hard to do after word gets around that Oleg just tried to pound my head flat, and make sure to have your barrels of spiked whiskey strategically placed all around the square surroundin' the stage. The crowd's excitement, and their thirst, will do the rest."

Marleaux's eyebrows lifted. "Very clever," he said. "A gladiatorial bout, between two Herculean Titans. It's the perfect way to get everybody dosed with my tainted liquor at the same time. But aren't you concerned about Oleg injuring, or even killing, you? You may not know it, but in addition to his immense size, he's a professional brawler. I found him in New Orleans, working for a gambler, battling all challengers on the wharf.

He made his employer a fortune until I killed him and acquired the big Russian. You should know that Oleg has maimed or killed dozens of men in such matches, both in, and out, of the ring."

"Of course I'm concerned about Oleg doin' me harm," Pritchard said. "I'd be a fool not to be worried. But I'm sweet on these two gals, and a lot more concerned about you and me gettin' out of Whiskey Falls alive."

Marleaux turned back to Oleg, a smile erupting from beneath his beard. "Do you still want to bash Pritchard?"

"Oleg kill him," Oleg clarified. He glared down at Pritchard, which was something few men could do.

"Very well, my giant friend," Marleaux said, slapping Oleg on the shoulder. "Tomorrow, you and Pritchard shall fight on the stage for everyone in Whiskey Falls to see. What do you think of that?"

"Oleg happy," the Russian said, grinning hatefully at Pritchard.

"Do we have a deal?" Pritchard asked.

"The women are yours," Marleaux said. "Enjoy them tonight, for tomorrow Oleg will likely slay you."

CHAPTER THIRTY-ONE

"Are you plumb loco?" Ned asked. "You're tellin' us you actually volunteered to fight that gargantuan Russian bear?"

"It ain't 'cause I want to, Ned," Pritchard said sheepishly. "It's 'cause I have to. We need ourselves a diversion."

"He's right, Ned," Bonner said. "It's the perfect diversion. With everybody in Whiskey Falls in the town square watching the big gladiator fight, and gulping down Red Henry Marleaux's spiked liquor, it should be no trouble at all for us to sneak into that storehouse."

"You're forgettin' one thing," Ned said.

"What's that?" Bonner asked.

"Samuel gettin' his arms and legs tore off."

Pritchard, Bonner, and Ned had re-assembled in a private tent they had been allotted by Marleaux. Jolie and Rebecca were in the tent directly adjacent, where Pritchard could keep an eye on them. More important, he could keep the soldiers and Marleaux's men away.

"Don't worry about me," Pritchard said. "Just make sure you get into Marleaux's storehouse, get what we need, and stand ready. I've got a feelin' that tomorrow, one way or the other, there's gonna be hell to pay all around."

"I'm not arguin' with you there," Ned said, ejecting a glob of tobacco juice.

"In the meantime," Pritchard said, "I've got an appointment to keep."

"Your appointment wouldn't be with that yellow-haired gal who happens to be in the tent next door, would it?" Ned asked, grinning under his drooping mustache.

"Don't you nevermind who my appointment's with." Pritchard grinned back. "You lecherous old coot. But if you must know, I thought I'd take an evening stroll with Jolie. She wants to go down to the falls to take a bath, and I don't want her walkin' around unescorted in Whiskey Falls. What about you two? How do you fellers plan to spend your last night in Whiskey Falls?"

"Now that I'm free," Ned said, putting his thumbs under his suspenders, "I think I'll take a stroll over to Red Henry's saloon and get myself a drink before he pollutes the whiskey tomorrow. Care to join me, Laird?"

"No thanks," Bonner replied, lighting one of his cheroots. "I think I'll stay around and keep an eye on Rebecca. Quite a few of Mason's troopers and Marleaux's men are drunk and tomcatting around town. I think it best I stick close to her, at least until Samuel and his 'appointment' return from their evening stroll."

• • •

Pritchard walked Jolie across Whiskey Falls under a cloudless sky and in front of the envious and hateful eyes of Captain Mason's inebriated cavalry troopers and Henry Marleaux's hired gunmen. Most were lounging in front of the saloon, but a number of them wandered throughout the town carrying bottles.

Jolie clung nervously to Pritchard's left arm, leaving his right hand free to draw. She couldn't know it, but it didn't matter which of Pritchard's arms she held. He was equally skilled with either hand when it came to gun-handling.

They walked through the streets past the buildings, storehouse, mess hall, shacks, tents, huts, corral, and finally the mine. A pair of armed guards at the entrance stared at the pair as they walked past. Beyond the mine was the waterfall, cascading down from the cliffs above and emptying into a wide stream.

"Are you sure Rebecca will be all right if we leave her?" Jolie said.

"Don't worry," Pritchard said. "Bonner won't let any harm come to your daughter."

"How do you know?"

"He gave his word," Pritchard said.

"And you believe him?"

"I do. He's the kind of man who lives by a code."

"What kind of code?"

"A violent one," Pritchard said. "Most folks, especially those like Deacon Wilson, wouldn't understand. They'd consider Bonner's code uncivilized."

"And you don't?"

"Naw," Pritchard said. "I live by a fairly rough code myself."

"You two seem to have a lot in common. Is that why you've become friends?"

"We have a few common traits," Pritchard admitted. "We both served in the war, though on different sides. We both live by the gun; me for the law, and him for money. We may have fought alongside one-another against the Crow to save our scalps, and since comin' to Whiskey Falls have a mutual interest in workin' together, but I wouldn't exactly call us friends."

"Then what makes you so sure Rebecca is safe with him?"

"Because she'll be safer than without him," Pritchard said.

"Maybe we'd better go back," Jolie said. The concern was evident in her voice and on her face.

"Rebecca will be fine," Pritchard said.

"If you say so, Samuel."

"I say so."

"I don't know what Rebecca and I would have done," Jolie said, "if you hadn't rescued us today. We were both destined for Marleaux's cathouse tonight. One of the young women working there even warned me, at breakfast this morning, of the fate which awaited us."

"Who was she?" Pritchard asked.

"She said her name was Molly Fennerman," Jolie said. "She couldn't have been much older than Rebecca."

"Molly Fennerman?" Pritchard said, stopping in his tracks.

"Do you know her?"

"I do," Pritchard said. "She left Atherton, Missouri, a year ago last summer with her entire family. They were headin' west on the Oregon Trail to California. My sister Idelle taught her, and her brother and sister, in school. What did Molly say?"

"She said her wagon train was attacked by the Crow and taken by Captain Mason and his cavalry troopers, just like ours. She foretold of what was to become of Rebecca and I, here in Whiskey Falls."

"What else did she tell you?"

"She said Marleaux put Rebecca and I serving food in the mess tent our first day on purpose so all of his men, and Captain Mason's soldiers, could look us over. Once all the menfolk got a gander at us, and their appetites were whetted, Marleaux would have us taken to his bawdy house tonight and put us on our backs making him money. That's what happened to her."

"Did she say what befell her family?" Pritchard asked.

"She did," Jolie said solemnly. "She told me her father and both grandpas died laboring in the silver mine last winter. Her brother was shot dead trying to escape. Marleaux sold her ma, both of her grandmas, and her cousins at auction to a band of Comancheros this past spring. She doesn't know where they are now or even if they're still alive."

"What about her younger sister?" Pritchard said. "Maggie was her name, I believe."

A tear slowly ran down Jolie's cheek, glistening in the moonlight. "She said her little sister killed herself. Maggie cut her wrists with a piece of broken glass not long after being put to work in the saloon's whorehouse. She was only fifteen years old."

Pritchard put his arms around Jolie as she began to cry. He felt her body tremble, slowly at first, until she was practically shaking in his embrace.

"All day long," she wept into his chest, "as we served food to those pigs, my only thoughts were for Rebecca. Thinking about what Molly told me. The idea of my daughter being forced to submit to those grunting murderers, in Marleaux's house of filth, nearly drove me mad." She shuddered. "I tried to find a knife in the kitchen, but the guards don't allow any cutlery within reach of any of the women."

"What were you going to do with a knife had

you got your hands on one?" Pritchard said. He already suspected the answer.

"The same thing I was going to do with that pistol you gave me when the Crow overran our wagon train," she said. She looked up at Pritchard through tear-streaked eyes. "I wasn't going to let my baby girl die of disease and despair while slaking the desires of Henry Marleaux's and Captain Mason's murderous dogs. I'd have done her in, and then myself."

Pritchard held Jolie tighter and pressed her head against his chest. "We ain't a-gonna let that happen," he said.

Jolie looked up at Pritchard and wiped her eyes. "You are without a doubt the strongest, bravest, and toughest man I've ever known," she said, "and I bless you for saying that. But there's nothing you can do, Samuel. There's too many of them."

"Don't count me out yet," Pritchard said. "A helluva lot of fellers who did just that are below ground, and here I am walkin' the streets of Whiskey Falls with you."

"I trust you," Jolie said, "even though it seems you've somehow gotten yourself into Marleaux's good graces. Rebecca and I certainly benefited from your newfound relationship. I suspect you have a plan of some kind brewing, but be careful. You can't trust a man like him."

"I wrangled me, Bonner, and Ned into

254

Marleaux's confidence," Pritchard admitted. "I had no choice, if I want to find us a way out of Whiskey Falls."

"I won't ask how you did it," she said, "but you must know it's to no avail. Marleaux and Mason will eventually kill you, and Ned and Bonner, too. Marleaux needs you now, but when he doesn't, he'll end you just like all the other poor, captive souls he's brought in chains to this valley. This place is no different than Andersonville. Henry Marleaux's a madman and views people as nothing more than livestock to be worked, traded, or butchered. Nobody he brings to Whiskey Falls leaves alive."

"You mentioned how strong, brave, and tough I am." Pritchard grinned, attempting to change the subject and lighten Jolie's mood. "But you forgot to mention good lookin'." She released a weary smile.

"You're a hard man," Jolie went on, "especially for one so young. But even you aren't hard enough to survive Whiskey Falls. I fear nobody is. This is an evil place, Samuel. The devil thrives here, and his name is Henry Marleaux. He swallows up entire wagon trains and whole families, and those he doesn't kill he makes slaves and whores of. I don't mean to doubt you, but the simple truth is there's no salvation from Whiskey Falls. I'm going to die here. I can feel it."

"I'll hear no more of that talk," Pritchard said, releasing her from his embrace, taking her hand, and leading her toward the falls. "Whiskey Falls is a foul place. There ain't no disputin' that. And Henry Marleaux is as foul a bottom-feeder as ever walked the earth on two legs. But no matter how foul they are, Whiskey Falls is only a town, and Marleaux only a man. Both can be burned down. I know, because I've done it before."

"I pray you're right," Jolie said.

" 'Course I'm right," Pritchard soothed. "And as far as what you're a-feelin', it ain't the reaper's breath. It's only fatigue, and fear, and worry that's worn you down. Once we get you a bath, a solid meal, and a little sleep, you'll feel right as rain."

"I was thinking about something else I could use," she said, extending on her tiptoes to kiss him.

They walked through a narrow strip of woods, past a grove of trees, and down a short grade to the waterline. The falls loomed above them. They were fifty yards beyond the corral and mine and more than twice that distance away from Whiskey Falls, which put them beyond the eyes and ears of others.

"It's getting colder and colder each night," Jolie said, pointing to her breath. It was visible as vapor when she spoke. "And there's frost on the ground in the morning."

"September's nearly gone," Pritchard said. "I've heard it ain't uncommon to get snow in the Idaho Territory in October."

"I can't wait to wash the stink of that filthy kitchen off," Jolie said, as she slipped out of her shoes and dress, leaving her in only her petticoat. Pritchard unbuckled his guns, picked up Jolie, and waded into the stream. She gasped as the frigid water overtook them.

Still carrying her, Pritchard walked across the stream, which was chest-deep, and through the cascading water. Jolie giggled and cried out as they breached the waterfall and were drenched in the torrent.

On the other side of the falls, behind the crashing downpour, was a rock wall. At the base of the wall was a small opening, perhaps the size of a dinner plate. It was largely obscured by brush, and only visible in flashes reflecting from the whitewater created where the falls met the creek. Pritchard spotted the hole, realizing instantly it might be the lair of a mountain cat. He also realized, with some dismay, that his guns were lying at the water's edge, with their clothes, on the other side of the waterfall.

He released Jolie, swam over to the wall, and cautiously examined the opening. Once he neared it, he let out a sigh of relief. The hole in the rock, while large enough for a mountain cat, tapered sharply after a few feet into a fist-sized tunnel stretching deep into the ground. While the tunnel might accommodate a raccoon, fox, or groundhog, it was far too small for a mountain lion.

As he peered into the hole, a familiar scent reached his nose. Pritchard recognized the distinct smell of the burning, animal-fat, candles used in abundance in the silver mine. Clearly the hole led down into one of the mine's many tributaries.

A relieved Pritchard swam back to Jolie, who had emerged from underwater. Her hair swept back as she surfaced. She blinked water from her eyes, smiled at him, and glided into his arms. Their mouths met.

"Promise me," she said, speaking into his ear due to the waterfall's steady rumble, "no matter what happens to me, you'll protect Rebecca? Keep her safe? Get her far away from Whiskey Falls?"

"All I can do is try," Pritchard said.

"And if you can't get her out of this God-forsaken valley," Jolie continued, "show her the mercy her own mother would have shown her. End her life, and send her to heaven unspoiled. Do not let that monster, Henry Marleaux, despoil her, and trade her body, her life, and her soul, for his profit. Promise?"

"I won't have to commit such an act," Pritchard said, "because you, and her, are gettin' out of—"

"But if I don't make it," Jolie cut him off. "Promise me, Samuel. You'll end her?"

Pritchard closed his eyes and slowly nodded. "On my oath," he said.

CHAPTER THIRTY-TWO

Pritchard awoke well after dawn to the sounds of commotion outside the tent. He left Jolie asleep beneath a blanket and donned his boots, trousers, shirt, and Stetson. Belting on his guns, he stepped out into the brisk Idaho morning.

Laird Bonner was already standing outside his own tent and nodded a greeting to Pritchard. Bonner was fully dressed, including his pistols, and smoking a cheroot as he observed the bustle of activity under way in Whiskey Falls.

The main street was filled with people, and more were descending the steep valley trail every minute. Pritchard and Bonner watched as the day's shift of prisoners was herded to the mine past several hundred Crow Indians, almost one-hundred of Captain Mason's cavalry troopers, and dozens of outsiders Pritchard hadn't seen before.

The newcomers, undoubtedly the buyers who'd traveled to Whiskey Falls to partake in the auction, were all male, and to Pritchard's lawman's eye a most unsavory lot. He identified what looked like a collection of gunmen, pimps, cattle and livestock rustlers, Comancheros, slavers, and others untroubled by the constraints of law or humanity. As Henry Marleaux had explained to him, all had come to purchase stolen goods or captive flesh.

The food tent was in full operation, with a long line awaiting breakfast. The soldiers, Crow, and prisoners ate free, but the guests had to pay two-bits each. An armed guard with a bucket collected coins at the top of the line. In the street nearby, several head of cattle were being slaughtered by a group of male prisoners in preparation for the day's feast.

"Looks like Whiskey Falls is experiencin' a population explosion," Pritchard said, taking in the throngs of people milling about.

"It's become a regular boomtown," Bonner agreed.

"Where's Ned?" Pritchard asked.

"Haven't seen him yet today."

"Are you and Ned ready?"

"Can't speak for Ned," Bonner said, "since he hasn't surfaced yet. Don't worry, once you and that Russian Goliath start brawling, we'll get 'er done. Question is, are you ready for Oleg?"

"As ready as a feller can be to have his head stove in, I reckon," Pritchard said. "Meantime, it'd probably be best if the gals stayed outta sight. Some of these newcomers look less polite than you or me when it comes to how they treat womenfolk."

"I was thinking the same thing."

"Atherton! Smokin' Joe Atherton!" a man's harsh voice called out.

Pritchard and Bonner scanned the crowd and quickly located the voice's owner. Standing in the street, not ten feet away, was a squat man with shoulder-length hair, a chest-deep beard, wearing high boots and a fur hat. He looked to be in his forties, clearly hadn't bathed in a while, and wore a pair of Remington pistols at his hips. He also wore an expression of furious hatred on his grizzled face.

"Friend of yours?" Bonner asked, exhaling smoke.

"Never seen that feller before in my life," Pritchard said.

"He's evidently acquainted with you," Bonner said.

The man in the fur hat was accompanied by two other men, one on each side of him. The man on his left was lean, stoop-shouldered, and wore a faded Confederate kepi. A Leech & Rigdon black powder revolver was stuffed into his waistband. The man on his right, the tallest and heaviest of the three, was clad in a duster and wide-brimmed flop-hat and carrying a Henry rifle.

Keeping his eyes on the trio, Pritchard took two steps to his left. He wanted to get clear of both Bonner and the tents behind him, which contained Rebecca and Jolie Matheson.

"Do I know you, Mister?" Pritchard asked.

"Not directly," the man in the fur hat said, spitting tobacco juice. "But you sure as hell knew my brother."

"Ain't ringin' any bells," Pritchard said.

"You gunned him three years ago in Corpus Christi," the man said. "His name was Dell Chapman. I'm Max Chapman."

"I remember Dell," Pritchard said. "He and a couple of his friends raided a ranch on the Nueces River. Murdered the rancher, raped his wife, and beat the kids like rented mules before makin' off with the stock."

"So you say," Chapman said.

"So did a federal judge," Pritchard said. "Issued a warrant and ordered me to serve it."

"And how did you serve that warrant, Mister big-shot Texas Ranger?" Chapman said. "You shot down my little brother in cold blood, that's how."

"Kinda hard to call it 'cold blood' when a feller's shootin' at you," Pritchard said.

"That ain't how it happened," Chapman said. "You murdered him."

Jolie and Rebecca poked their heads out of the tent. "What's going on?" Jolie asked. Many of the men in the crowd ogled them hungrily.

Bonner stepped between the women and the crowd. "Get back inside," he ordered sternly, "lie flat on the ground, and stay there until I say otherwise." The women retreated into the tent.

"Hearin' you tell it," Pritchard said, turning his attention back to the man in the fur hat, "folks would be inclined to believe you were present when your brother expired. Which is a bit vexin', since I don't seem to remember you bein' there at all."

"I heard about what happened," Chapman said.

"If that's true," Pritchard said, "then you also heard how your gutless, yellow brother and his dry-gulchin' pals tried to bushwhack and backshoot me."

"You're a liar," Chapman said.

"Or maybe whoever told you the story is?" Pritchard said. "It sure wasn't your brother or his saddle-pals, 'cause I put all three of 'em under the snakes."

The pedestrians and onlookers parted and spread out, giving Pritchard and the three men facing him a wide berth.

"Now that you've introduced yourself," Pritchard said, "I'll bid you 'good-bye,' advise you to be on your way, and wish you a pleasant stay in Whiskey Falls. Can't say it was a pleasure makin' your acquaintance."

"You'll bid me no such thing," Chapman spat. "Our business ain't nearly concluded."

"I didn't know we had any," Pritchard said innocently.

"I'm a-gonna kill you," Chapman said. He put both hands on his holstered pistols. Behind him, his companion with the revolver snaked a hand toward his belt. The tall man with the Henry thumbed back the rifle's hammer and began to raise the barrel.

"Unlikely," Pritchard said, drawing.

Almost before anyone could detect the movement, Pritchard had his custom-barreled Colt .45s clear of their holsters and leveled. He fired his first two shots simultaneously, striking the two men on either side of Chapman in the face. The man in the kepi was struck just below his nose, and the man with the Henry rifle caught the .45 slug in his right cheek. Both dropped straight down, like marionettes with their strings cut, and were dead before they hit the ground. Chapman continued to draw as they toppled.

Pritchard's next two shots, discharged so close on the heels of the previous two as to be nearly indistinguishable, landed less than an inch apart from one another in the center of Chapman's chest. He dropped his guns, which had barely cleared their holsters, clutched his chest, buckled over at the waist, and went to his knees. From there he gazed up at Pritchard with a confused look, then fell forward onto his face. He twitched once and didn't move again.

Still keeping his guns leveled, Pritchard slowly scanned the crowd. No one else moved.

Henry Marleaux, flanked by Captain Mason, Daniel McKinnon, Oleg, and several of

Marleaux's hired gunmen, elbowed their way through the crowd. The entire right side of McKinnon's face was one continuous, black-and-blue bruise.

"What goes here?" Marleaux demanded. No one spoke.

"Sergeant Greenwald," Mason barked, recognizing his senior non-commissioned officer among the spectators. "Report!"

"Sir," Greenwald answered. "Those three," he pointed to the trio of fresh corpses, "just braced and pulled on Pritchard. It was a fair fight, Captain. Leastways as fair as three-against-one can be."

Marleaux appraised Pritchard, a wry grin appearing on his face. "Let that be a lesson to you all," he announced to the crowd. "Pulling on Mister Pritchard isn't a healthy practice."

"Apparently not," Sergeant Greenwald said, under his breath.

"Go on about your business, everyone," Marleaux continued. "The auction begins in less than an hour. Let's have no more gunplay, eh? This is a day for trading, not shooting at one-another."

Pritchard holstered his guns.

"And one more thing," Marleaux exclaimed, "for those of you just arriving. Tonight, once the auction's over, I have a special treat for your viewing entertainment. Mister Pritchard, who you've all just met, and my giant associate, Oleg, will be on the auction stage, in the town square, fighting a bare-knuckle duel. You don't want to miss it! Drinks will be on the house during the bout!"

A round of clapping and cheers broke out and faded. A moment later the crowd dissipated as if nothing had happened and witnessing three men shot dead in a matter of seconds was an everyday occurrence. Captain Mason motioned to his men, and they scooped up the bodies of Max Chapman and his two friends and carted them away.

"Helluva way to start the morning," Marleaux said to Pritchard.

"Had no choice," Pritchard said. "They—"

"I heard," Marleaux cut him off. "They pulled on you. Do me a favor, will you, Samuel? Don't shoot any more of my customers until after the auction? It's difficult to get money out of dead men."

"Not so much," Pritchard contradicted him. "Now, instead of goin' to the trouble of fleecin' Chapman and his boys durin' your auction, you can just empty their pockets while they feed the crows."

"Convenient." Marleaux laughed. "Perhaps I'll have you shoot everyone today?"

"Whatever you say," Pritchard said.

Marleaux laughed at his inside joke, signaled to his men, and started back to his saloon.

McKinnon and Oleg glared at Pritchard as they departed.

Once they were gone, Pritchard began to reload his left-hand revolver. Bonner finished his smoke and stamped it out under a bootheel.

"I caught a glimpse of your marksmanship abilities, with both rifle and pistol, during our fight against the Crow," Bonner said. "But this morning was the first time I had an opportunity to witness, firsthand, what I've heard said about your pistoleering from the draw."

"Meet your approval, did I?" Pritchard asked, without looking up from re-charging his guns.

"Some of the stories of your exploits were impossible to believe," Bonner said. "I'm definitely a believer now."

"If you want to collect that twenty-thousand-dollar bounty on my head," Pritchard said, re-holstering his now-reloaded right-hand pistol and looking up, "you're gonna have to earn it."

"Of that," Bonner said, "I'm certain."

CHAPTER THIRTY-THREE

It was a busy day in Whiskey Falls.

Marleaux began the auction after breakfast. Black-eyed Daniel McKinnon acted as his auctioneer, standing behind a podium on the stage with a gavel in his small fist. The stage itself was surrounded by most of Marleaux's men and the majority of Captain Mason's troopers. Oleg collected the money from the winning purchasers, a task overseen by Marleaux himself to ensure the counting was tabulated correctly.

A throng of over one-hundred excited buyers were massed around the stage, waving money in their fists and competing with one-another for the prizes on display. A swarm of Crow braves swarmed behind them, eagerly watching the transactions and awaiting the next, and most interesting phase, of the auction.

Throughout the day, Marleaux steadily sold all the livestock, excluding the horses to pull his pair of wagons, and the mounts belonging to his men, including Pritchard's, Bonner's, and Ned's horses. He also sold the remaining wagons, carts, and buckboards, and all the furniture, clothing, and personal possessions confiscated from the hapless travelers Captain Mason and his detachment of Crow braves waylaid on the Oregon Trail since the last auction, over a month ago.

The male prisoners who'd been working in the mine all night hadn't been allowed to sleep. Instead, the hollow-eyed and exhausted captives were pressed into service marking the livestock for buyers, bringing individual items to be auctioned from the storehouse to the stage, and loading up the various items for the buyers once they'd been purchased.

By noon, nothing remained in the storehouse but Marleaux's carefully-loaded wagons, the barrels of whiskey, crates containing guns, cases of ammunition, and boxes of dynamite.

Shortly after the midday meal, the real auction began. All the women in Whiskey Falls were lined up, under guard, and led to the stage. There were elderly women who'd been relegated to cooking and cleaning duties since their capture, and young children, too small to be assigned duties but old enough to be commodities. But the most valuable merchandise were the women between teen and middle-age.

Most of the females in this category had already been put to work in Marleaux's comfort house, some for many months. All were attired in garments carefully selected from the store of stolen clothing and wore freshly-applied make-up. The increased interest by the potential bidders, as indicated by the anticipation on their faces, was impossible to ignore.

The male prisoners who'd been relieved from the mine that morning, and who'd been laboring in the auction all day, were once more lined up and marched back to the mine under double-guard. Many of the women about to be put up for auction were sisters, daughters, wives, and mothers, and Marleaux wanted no desperate acts of chivalry to interrupt his money-making operation. Many of the women, looking out into the crowd of hard-faced, leering men waiting to buy them, began to weep.

Pritchard, Bonner, and Ned observed the morning's proceedings from a distance, choosing to stick near the tent Jolie and Rebecca Matheson occupied. Pritchard and Bonner had obtained food for them that morning at the breakfast line and insisted the women remain out-of-view. Jolie and Rebecca didn't argue.

Ned had showed up around mid-morning after the auction was well under way. He had his trademark wad of tobacco in his jaw, but added bloodshot eyes to his craggy features.

"Enjoy your sleep?" Pritchard asked him.

"What I remember of it," he said. "My last recollection was the bottom of a bottle. What'd I miss?"

"Nothing but Henry Marleaux selling everything in Whiskey Falls that ain't nailed down," Pritchard said.

The three men watched as the night-shift prisoners were marched to the mine and forced to join their brethren working the day-shift inside. They noted the number of guards outside the mine's entrance had been tripled. With the guards was one of Marleaux's men, smoking a pipe and carrying a satchel over his shoulder.

"What's that all about?" Bonner asked, pointing to the mine.

"When I was walkin' over here," Ned said, "I heard one of the guards a-tellin' the prisoners they was bein' kept in the mine until after the auction. He said, as soon as the women had been sold, they'd let the prisoners out."

Bonner looked at Pritchard and Ned. "Do you believe that?" he asked.

"I'm only reportin' what I heard," Ned shrugged.

Once the women's auction began, pandemonium erupted. Men argued, shoved, and fought as they tried to outbid each other for the individual women displayed on the stage. More than once, a pair of Mason's cavalry troopers had to push into the crowd with their rifles to break up a fight.

Once a transaction was completed, the woman being auctioned was escorted back to Marleaux's saloon and comfort house where she would remain under guard. The purchaser was not allowed to take his merchandise at the time of purchase. Instead, the woman was marked with a number, and the buyer given a similarly-numbered poker chip as a receipt. The new owner would have his property turned over to him on the way out of town, and not before. This was to prevent the inevitable violence that would have ensued had the women been allowed to accompany their new owners out-and-about among so many other men in Whiskey Falls.

Some of the prices the women commanded were quite high, while others brought in less than a single head of cattle auctioned off earlier that morning. Marleaux enraged many of the Crow by refusing to accept pelts or scalps as currency. It was cash money only with no IOU's accepted. By evening, just as the sides of beef that had been roasting all day were being sliced up and served, the last of over one-hundred and fifty women and girls were sold.

"That concludes the auction, gentlemen," Marleaux declared. "I thank you for your business, and invite you to partake of my beef and whiskey, courtesy of Henry Marleaux and the town of Whiskey Falls!"

Marleaux gave a signal to McKinnon, who in turn signaled groups of Marleaux's men. Kerosene torches were lit and placed around the stage. Next, a dozen whiskey barrels were rolled out from the storehouse and set up, along with boxes containing cups, mugs, and glassware of every type. A pair of Marleaux's men stood vigil at each barrel.

"Is time?" Oleg anxiously asked Marleaux.

"It's time," Marleaux nodded. "Samuel?" he called out.

Pritchard, Bonner, and Ned approached. "How'd you make out?" Pritchard asked.

"By my count," Marleaux said, beaming, "over thirty-thousand dollars. Our most lucrative auction yet. Too bad it had to be the last. Are you ready to meet Oleg on the field of honor?"

"I reckon it can't be avoided," Pritchard said. He handed Bonner his hat, neckerchief, shirt, gun belts, and revolvers.

"Come along then," Marleaux said, laughing and slapping Pritchard on the back. "Those who are about to die, salute you."

Oleg was already on the stage when Pritchard and Marleaux ascended the steps. He also had his shirt off, and his massive, hair-covered chest, equally-hairy arms and back, and shaved head lent him the appearance of a giant, albino gorilla.

Pritchard, at six-foot-six inches tall and almost two-hundred and thirty pounds, was no small man. But compared to Oleg, he seemed almost a dwarf.

The murmuring crowd closed in on the stage, as Marleaux raised both hands for silence and attention. All the men in Whiskey Falls—the auction guests, Marleaux's gunmen, Captain

Mason's troopers, and the Crow warriors, with the exception of the prisoners in the mine—were in the town square. To a man, their focus was riveted on Red Henry Marleaux and the pair of gladiators about to engage in combat before them.

"Gentlemen," Marleaux began, in his booming voice, "I offer, for your entertainment, a clash of Titans. On my left, standing almost seven feet tall, and weighing nearly four-hundred pounds, hailing from New Orleans by way of Russia, is a champion who has beaten many a man to death with his bare hands. I give you, Oleg the Man-Crusher!"

The crowd cheered, clapped, and shouted their approval.

"On my right," Marleaux continued, "at six-and-a-half feet tall, and weighing over one-hundred-and-fifty pounds less than his opponent, is a warrior of no less repute. A hero of the Confederacy, former Texas Ranger, Missouri lawman, and famous mankiller, formerly known to many as Smokin' Joe Atherton. I give you, Samuel Pritchard!"

This time, the crowd booed, hooted, and cursed, and nobody clapped. Pritchard wasn't sure if he was disliked personally, or if the crowd simply didn't like lawmen of any stripe. In either case, he recognized what everyone else in Whiskey Falls already knew—there was a clear favorite, and he wasn't it.

"This is a fight until one man yields," Marleaux explained, "either by surrender, injury, or death. Would anyone care to place a bet as to which of these worthy combatants is victorious?"

"Ten dollars on Oleg!" someone from the crowd shouted.

"Twenty on the Russian!" another shouted.

"I'll take some of that action!" others chimed in.

"Captain Mason will take your bets," Marleaux said, gesturing to where the cavalry captain stood with several of his troopers. His bugler kept a notebook, and recorded the wagers while another trooper took in the money. A line soon formed.

"When all the bets are placed," Marleaux said, "the match will commence."

Pritchard and Oleg stood awaiting the signal to begin fighting in opposite corners of the stage. Ned stood at Pritchard's corner, and McKinnon at Oleg's.

"Any words of advice for me?" Pritchard asked Ned.

"Nope," Ned said, spitting a glob of tobacco. "You're about to get killed, Samuel, or maimed to where you wish you were. Ain't much more there is to say about it."

"That's plumb encouragin'," Pritchard said. He lowered his voice to a whisper. "Don't forget to slip away durin' the fight, meet up with Bonner, and get into that storehouse."

"I didn't forget," Ned said.

Mason signaled to Marleaux that all bets had been placed. Marleaux drew one of his revolvers, cocked the hammer back, and held it aloft.

"Are you ready?" Marleaux asked each of the combatants.

"I reckon so," Pritchard answered.

"Oleg kill," Oleg said.

"At the sound of this pistol shot," Marleaux said, "not only will the bout begin, but the kegs will be tapped and the whiskey served. Help yourselves, gentlemen, and enjoy the fight."

Marleaux pulled the trigger.

CHAPTER THIRTY-FOUR

Oleg came straight at Pritchard, throwing a looping roundhouse that arrived faster than expected for someone so large. Pritchard ducked under it, but made an immediate mental note not to underestimate his opponent's speed on the basis of his size. He had too much experience in the ring for such an assumption.

Due to his own size, which came early to him, Pritchard had entered the Jackson County Fair's bare-knuckle wrestling contest every summer since the age of thirteen. He'd never lost a match. His father was a peaceful, religious, man who eschewed firearms, but was nonetheless a highly-skilled boxer and wrestler. He began imparting these skills to his only son as soon as he could stand.

In addition to training his son in wrestling and boxing, Thomas Pritchard owned a lucrative lumber business where Samuel was employed since he was able to walk. Carrying buckets of nails and sawdust as a toddler, hauling lumber as a boy, and felling trees as a youth, had packed layers of hard muscle on Pritchard's outsized frame. By age seventeen, he was widely known as one of the largest, strongest, and most-feared fist-fighters along the Missouri River.

That was over ten years ago. Before his father was murdered by Union raiders disguised as rebel outlaws, their sawmill was "commandeered," his mother and sister were taken, and the Pritchard family home was burned to the ground.

What followed was a blood-soaked year fighting as a Confederate guerilla and nearly a decade as a Texas Ranger, both under the name Joe Atherton. During that time he'd ended countless men by rifle, pistol, knife, and his bare hands. But tonight, in Whiskey Falls, deep in the Idaho Territory, Samuel Pritchard fought in an arena before spectators for the first time since an innocent seventeen-year-old, back in the summer of 1863.

Oleg lunged. After Pritchard ducked again, he sidestepped and landed an overhand left hook that took Oleg in the right temple. It was an awkward punch, but one of Pritchard's most effective, and the first time he could remember using it on someone taller than himself. The blow seemingly had no effect, other than making his hand feel like he'd just punched a barn door.

Pritchard had fought many men who outweighed him, but few who had longer reach. The length of Oleg's reach was deceptive; his thick arms gave the impression they were short, but at nearly seven-feet-tall, he had half-a-foot more arm-distance than Pritchard.

Pritchard feinted left, darted right, and stepped

inside. He threw a three-punch combination to Oleg's gut. It was like punching one of Marleaux's kegs of laudanum-tainted whiskey, and again, seemingly had no effect on the wild-eyed Russian.

Oleg responded to Pritchard's attack by throwing another roundhouse. Backing away, Pritchard thought he'd slipped the punch, but was forced to bunch his shoulder to ward it off when he realized the Russian moved too fast as he retreated. Oleg's massive fist glanced off his shoulder, sending a wave of pain coursing the entire length of his arm, and grazed the edge of his right cheek.

An explosion of fireworks flashed momentarily before Pritchard's eyes, and he staggered backward. It took three long steps before he regained his balance and cleared his head. The crowd roared its approval.

Outside the stage, Pritchard saw Marleaux's men feverishly laboring to serve cups of whiskey to the eagerly waiting crowd. Each of the kegs was being mobbed by swarms of spectators, with the cavalry troopers and Crow braves among the first in line.

"Oleg crush you," the Russian declared, grinning. "Oleg squeeze guts out through mouth."

"That's the spirit," McKinnon shouted from his corner. "Smash him like a bug!" Another loud cheer erupted from the crowd.

Pritchard ignored the mob cheering for his defeat, shook his head, and risked a look to his corner. Ned was gone.

Now all Pritchard had to do was prolong the fight for as long as he could, to give Ned and Bonner the time they needed to enter Marleaux's storehouse and retrieve their saddles and gear. Unfortunately, as was evident to everyone in the crowd, Oleg had a different agenda.

Oleg wanted to kill Pritchard and do it in a way that maximized the lawman's pain and suffering.

Once more, Oleg charged.

As soon as the fight began, Bonner gave one of his Open Top Colt .44s to Jolie, along with a reminder to stay hidden inside the tent. He ignored her and Rebecca's inquiry as to where he was going and went back outside, ostensibly to have a smoke.

After reassuring himself that everyone in Whiskey Falls was in the town square, guzzling free whiskey and observing the fight on the stage, Bonner extinguished his smoke and made his way toward the storehouse. Ned was nowhere in sight, and he assumed he would meet up with the salty wagon master somewhere near their mutual destination.

It had by then become full dark, the sun having already dipped well below the valley walls. Bonner wove his way silently past buildings, through mazes of tents, and avoided the main street until he reached the storehouse. He was working his way around to the rear of the large building when Ned materialized from the darkness. He was carrying a whiskey bottle.

" 'Bout time," Ned whispered. "I was startin' to think you weren't a-comin'."

"I'm here now," Bonner whispered back. "How's it look?"

"Two guards at the big barn doors, up front," Ned reported, "but only one in back. All of 'em have rifles."

"Then the back door it is."

Both men quietly circumnavigated the storehouse until they reached the back door. From the shadows, they observed a forlorn-looking guard. He stood alone, a lantern and cigarette his only company.

Bonner started to draw his knife, but Ned stayed his hand, shook his head, and held up the whiskey bottle. Bonner nodded.

"Evenin'," Ned said, stepping out into the light by himself. The guard, a stern-faced fellow in his early forties, wheeled to face him. He leveled his Winchester. "Who goes there?"

"Easy now," Ned said, keeping his voice low so not to alert the other two guards at the opposite side of the building. "I'm a friendly. Marleaux sent me down to see how you boys are a-doin."

"You can tell Red Henry we're just swell," the guard grumbled, lowering his rifle. "Ever-body else is in the town square a-sippin' whiskey and watchin' the big fight, and it's just my luck to draw guard duty all the way out here."

"That's why I brung you this," Ned said. "To ease your sufferin'."

"Henry don't like us to drink on duty," the guard protested.

"He said it's okay, just this once," Ned said. "Seein' how it's our last night here, and he done sold off everything in the storehouse anyways." He extended the bottle. "Go on ahead. It's getting' a mite cold out, and a nip or two ain't a-gonna hurt you none."

"Henry didn't sell everything," the guard said, accepting the bottle. He leaned his rifle against the storehouse door and uncorked it. "He's still got two big freight wagons in there, loaded up with guns, whiskey, and whatnot. You think he'd have us a-guardin' an empty barn?"

As soon as the guard put the bottle to his lips, and tilted his head up to drink, Ned drew his revolver and clubbed him over the head. He caught the whiskey bottle as it dropped from the guard's hands. When he stumbled to his knees, Ned clubbed him once more with his Colt. The guard went down on his face and didn't stir. Ned waved Bonner over.

Taking a drink while Bonner relieved the unconscious guard of his pistol and rifle, Ned opened the storehouse door and they went inside. Bonner dragged the guard in after them and closed the door. Using the guard's lantern, he surveyed the interior of the vast storehouse. The guard had been right; the place was largely empty, but not entirely.

Against one wall were cases of goods Marleaux had elected not to sell. Among these items were ammunition, dynamite, laudanum, and even the crate of Bibles confiscated from the Indiana Quakers.

There were two sturdy Conestoga freight wagons in the middle of the storehouse, each heavily laden. Both were stocked with canned goods, grain, barrels of water, whiskey, crates of ammunition, and boxes of rifles.

Against the opposite wall were several dozen saddles, all lined up and awaiting Marleaux's men.

All Marleaux had to do tomorrow morning, after the slaughter tonight, was hitch up teams of horses to his pair of wagons, mount up his men, and ride out for the Utah Territory.

"C'mon," Bonner said, quickly locating his and Pritchard's saddles. "Let's get these outfitted."

Bonner and Ned got to work. They busied themselves filling canteens and stuffing food and ammunition into five sets of saddlebags on five separate saddles. They loaded his and Pritchard's saddles, one for Ned, and two more for Jolie and Rebecca.

Pritchard and Bonner's rifles were still in their

scabbards. Ned helped himself to a couple of bottles of whiskey, while Bonner pilfered several bundles of dynamite and a bottle of laudanum.

Bonner hefted both his and Pritchard's saddles over his shoulders. "Grab a couple of saddles," he instructed Ned. "We'll stash them in the woods by the corral and come back for the other."

Ned followed Bonner out of the storehouse, and the two men scurried along in the darkness under the weight of their heavily loaded saddles. When they reached the woodline near the falls, almost one-hundred yards away from the storehouse, Bonner was slightly out-of-breath, but Ned was panting heavily. Bonner concealed the saddles in heavy brush and covered them with fallen branches and leaves.

"I'll go back for the last saddle," Bonner offered. Ned was bent at the waist and looked as if he was going to vomit.

"I'll . . . let . . . ya," Ned panted.

"You get on back to Pritchard's corner," Bonner suggested, "before you're missed. I'll catch up with you two later."

Ned nodded, too winded to speak, and stumbled off toward Whiskey Falls.

Bonner made his way back to the rear door of the storehouse. He drew his gun, in case the guard had awakened, but found him snoring inside on the floor in the same position as when they'd left.

Bonner started to pick up the fifth saddle, but then stopped, distracted by a glance at the wagons. His curiosity got the better of him. He put down the saddle and clambered aboard the nearest one.

Holding the lantern with one hand, Bonner lifted the tarpaulin. While examining the boxes of rifles, crates of food and ammunition, and other traveling sundries, he noticed a strongbox under the wagon's seat.

He pulled it out and opened it, which wasn't difficult. The hasp had been pried off, and he could only assume the box was damaged when it had been forced open by Mason's or Marleaux's men after being taken from a wagon train.

Bonner found the strongbox stuffed with paper cash. The money wasn't new bills in neat bundles, but worn, well-handled, currency undoubtedly swiped from the dozens of wagon trains pirated by Captain Mason and Red Henry Marleaux over the past two years. By his quick estimation, there must have been tens of thousands of dollars inside.

Bonner climbed aboard the second wagon and found a similarly damaged strongbox under the seat there, as well. Upon lifting its lid, he discovered that it, too, was loaded with thousands of confiscated dollars.

Henry Marleaux was cleverer than Bonner had given him credit for. While he had no doubt that the Wells Fargo safe in Marleaux's saloon was probably stuffed with money, including by now most of his profits from today's lucrative auction, Bonner realized he was hedging his bets. He didn't want all his eggs in one basket, so to speak, in the event he encountered some unforeseen misfortune during his journey to Promontory. By splitting his money between the safe, and two strongboxes in two separate wagons, Marleaux tripled his chances of getting at least some of his ill-gotten fortune safely out of Whiskey Falls.

Bonner suddenly had an idea. He leapt from the wagon and retrieved a pair of empty saddlebags and a coiled lariat he'd previously spotted among the pile of saddle tack staged against the wall.

Bonner knew he'd have to work fast. But if he hurried, and Pritchard was as tough as he looked, he might just have enough time.

CHAPTER THIRTY-FIVE

Pritchard evaded another looping punch and threw two of his own. His first struck Oleg in the kidney as he darted behind the huge Russian, and the second was a right-hook that landed squarely on his granite jaw. The only effect of either punch, much to Pritchard's chagrin, was that the look of fury on Oleg's face became more prominent.

The fight had been going on in this manner for over ten minutes. Oleg would charge, and Pritchard would evade the onslaught like a matador evades a charging bull. As he weaved and dodged after each attack, Pritchard would invariably land at least one punch, if not several, on the giant Russian's massive head, neck, or torso. Yet none of these successfully landed blows seemed to be wearing the Russian down. A frustrated Pritchard felt as if he was punching an oak.

Pritchard himself was no lightweight puncher. As an eighteen-year-old prisoner-of-war, he once killed an abusive guard with a single blow to the head. The incident was witnessed by his friend Ditch Clemson, who then saved his life when another guard attempted to backshoot him. As a result, both youths found themselves as the guests-of-honor at a firing squad. Had an enemy attack not befallen the encampment just before the order to fire was given, neither would have survived the day.

All around the makeshift ring, soldiers, Crow braves, and the guests who had come to Whiskey Falls for the auction guzzled free whiskey and shouted with enthusiasm.

Henry Marleaux, along with a contingent of rifle-armed men who were not serving whiskey, stood back from the stage and took it all in. Captain Mason was nowhere in sight.

Oleg suddenly spun around in a circle, swinging both arms, and caught Pritchard with a backfist. Pritchard absorbed the blow, which felt like he'd been hit with an axe handle. If he hadn't raised his forearms to block the wildly swung strike, his head would have absorbed it, and the fight would have ended then and there.

Even blocked, the Russian's blow sent Pritchard stumbling backward again. This time, he wasn't able to maintain his balance. He crashed to the stage and landed on his back.

As the crowd shrieked in drunken glee, Oleg pounced. Before a dazed Pritchard could roll to his feet, Oleg dove across the stage. He was barely able to cover his throat with one hand, and his groin with the other, before Oleg fell upon him.

Even with a split-second to gather air and tense

his body in preparation for the impact, Pritchard was nearly rendered unconscious when Oleg landed. The breath was driven from his lungs, and his body reeled from the driving weight of nearly four-hundred pounds of infuriated Russian brawler.

Oleg straddled him and clamped both hands around his neck, just as Pritchard lowered his chin. The vice-like grip immediately began to tighten. Pritchard got both of his hands over Oleg's, trying desperately to loosen their grasp. The Russian was incredibly strong, and it took every bit of the formidable strength in his own shoulders, arms, and hands to keep his adversary's fingers from working their way under his chin to his throat.

"I rip head off," Oleg growled in his broken English.

Pritchard vaguely noticed the crowd moving in closer, pressing against and surrounding the stage. The men were in a frenzy as they sensed the bout's imminent conclusion, after over ten minutes of what they considered little more than ballroom dancing as Pritchard ducked, dodged, and evaded his oversized opponent.

From the corner of his bulging eyes Pritchard saw dozens of soldiers, Crow warriors, and auction buyers, delirious with bloodlust, holding aloft their cups and cackling in delight as Oleg closed in for the kill.

Yet despite Pritchard's dire predicament, he

also noticed something else on the faces of the rowdy spectators closing in and rooting for his defeat. They all appeared extremely drunk. More than drunk, actually, for how little time they'd been drinking. Many looked as if they'd been boozing all night, and they leaned on one another as they noisily cheered for Oleg to end him.

Henry Marleaux's concoction of whiskey and laudanum was clearly taking effect. Pritchard had no idea how much of the opium-based potion he'd poured into each keg, but by the rapidity with which the hundreds of onlookers were descending into blind intoxication, he presumed it was plenty. Some of the observers in the front of the crowd slumped forward over the stage. Others began to sink to a sitting position. Still others were beginning to fall.

Pritchard caught a glimpse of Henry Marleaux, flanked by his men, wearing a look of smug satisfaction on his face. He wasn't able to enjoy the image long, as Oleg's enormous fingers were snaking ever closer to getting under his chin and around his throat.

"Howdy, Samuel," Ned's voice suddenly said from the corner behind him. Pritchard couldn't even turn his head to acknowledge him.

"If'n I were you," Ned said, "I'd get myself out from under that there big Russian feller. He's likely to tear your noggin' off."

"Thanks . . . for . . . the . . . advice," Pritchard

was able to squeeze out, as he pitted all of his strength against the Russian's.

"Quite a party," Ned remarked, looking around. Spectators were dropping over right and left. The laudanum-laced whiskey was taking its toll. A Crow brave bumped into Ned as he crumpled to the ground, and he had to step back to avoid a pair of soldiers as they dropped. "I declare," he went on, as men toppled all around him, "none of these fellers seem able to hold their liquor."

A gunshot rang out, and then another. A pair of soldiers who had elected not to partake had come to the realization the liquor their fellow soldiers were consuming was spiked. One trooper drew his revolver, and was instantly shot down by one of Marleaux's men. The other, who wasn't wearing a pistol, tried to run and was shot in the back by another of Marleaux's gang.

One of the Crow warriors let out a war cry, which was followed by several more, and the sound of men shouting. Henry Marleaux's booming voice was then heard barking orders, and a dozen or more shots erupted from various points in the town square.

At the sound of the shots, Oleg, who was still straddling Pritchard's chest, flinched. He momentarily paused to look up from where he'd been busily attempting to throttle his prey, and unconsciously relaxed his grip. It was the opening Pritchard needed.

He took his hands from Oleg's, reached down, and grabbed the colossal Russian's crotch. He squeezed with every ounce of strength he could muster. This act had the desired effect.

Oleg let out a resounding howl and instinctively grabbed for the offending hands, which meant releasing Pritchard's throat. It also meant shifting his weight, which left him off-balance. Sensing the shift in the Russian's balance, Pritchard bucked his hips and threw him off.

Pritchard then sprang to his feet. His speed was fueled by fear, adrenaline, and the realization that if he didn't beat Oleg to a standing position, he might again find his gigantic quarry's hands around his neck.

The Russian was slower to get up. Though not as strong as Oleg, Pritchard was himself extremely strong. When he squashed his opponent's genitals, he nearly paralyzed him, if only for a moment.

Oleg looked up at Pritchard from where he crouched, preparing to piston his legs and spring once more upon the smaller man. If his face wore fury before, it was now wearing a mask of uncontrollable, homicidal, rage.

Pritchard reacted by kicking Oleg squarely in the face. The Russian's bear-like head snapped back, and before it rolled forward Pritchard kicked him in the face again.

Though Oleg was likely unconscious, by the

way his eyes rolled back and his arms dropped, Pritchard wasn't in the mood to take chances. As Oleg fell, Pritchard gave him a third kick, again, squarely in the face. The giant flopped backward with his nose and mouth covered in blood. When he hit the floor, the entire stage shook.

Daniel McKinnon rushed onto the stage to Oleg's side. "What have you done?" he demanded of Pritchard, cradling his friend's head.

"Nothin' Oleg wasn't a-tryin' to do to me," Pritchard said, rubbing his neck.

"You might have killed him."

"Don't worry none," Pritchard said. "He ain't hurt bad. He'll come around soon enough."

"Not before I end you," McKinnon snarled, standing up. He drew one of his revolvers and cocked the hammer back.

"That's quite enough, Daniel," Marleaux said, taking the stage. Several of his carbine-wielding men were beside him. "Put your gun away, please."

"But you saw what he just did to Oleg?"

"It was a fair fight," Marleaux said. "Besides"—a grin broke out under his red beard—"Pritchard's one of us now."

"I don't believe it," McKinnon argued. "I never did."

"Actually," Marleaux said, his grin becoming a smile, "I don't, either." He snapped his fingers and pointed at Pritchard. A half-dozen rifles were suddenly aimed at him.

CHAPTER THIRTY-SIX

"You didn't really think I'd fall for your claims of loyalty to me, did you?" Marleaux asked Pritchard.

"I had hopes." Pritchard shrugged.

"You forget your reputation precedes you."

The town square was littered with hundreds of unconscious men. Cavalry troopers, Crow Indians, and the criminals who'd come to Whiskey Falls to trade in goods and slaves all lay motionless where they'd fallen. So potent was the drugged whiskey, and so laden with laudanum, that many would never wake up.

A couple of dozen men, those who hadn't consumed any of Marleaux's potion, had been shot dead. But the rest of Whiskey Fall's menfolk, excluding Marleaux's gang and those still in the mine, were strewn about like leaves fallen from an autumn tree.

While two men covered Pritchard with their rifles, a third bound his hands behind his back.

"Whether Smokin' Joe Atherton, or Marshal Samuel Pritchard," Marleaux went on, "one thing about you is clear; you're an honest, law-abiding, man. As far as I've heard tell, you've never killed anyone except in military combat or a fair fight, even when your own life was at stake. Yet I'm supposed to believe that you're suddenly willing to join my gang and help me finish off several hundred men lying defenseless on the ground? I think not, Samuel."

"It was worth a try," Pritchard said.

"Search all the bodies," Marleaux commanded his men. "Recover any firearms, valuables, and ammunition."

While some of his gang began searching the downed men, several others began distributing military rifles, with bayonets attached, which had once belonged to Captain Mason's cavalry troopers.

"You're gonna stick 'em?" Pritchard said, motioning to the bayonets with his chin. "You're not even gonna show 'em the mercy of a bullet?"

"Bullets are precious," Marleaux explained. "I believe you ran out of ammunition when Captain Mason's Crow detachment attacked your wagon train, did you not?"

"We did," Pritchard confirmed.

"I don't plan to suffer the same fate on the way to the Utah Territory. We'll save every bullet we can for use on those who can fight."

"That's right economical of you," Pritchard said. "Not to mention, cowardly."

A group of men came walking down Whiskey Fall's main road. At the head of the assembly was Laird Bonner, Captain Mason, and Sergeant

Greenwald. All three had been disarmed, and their hands were bound behind their backs. Behind them were several of Marleaux's men holding guns on them.

"What's the meaning of this?" Captain Mason demanded, when they'd reached the town square and were led over to Marleaux. He stared in anger at his troopers, lying inert among the braves and auction buyers before him.

"Why have you done this to me?" a furious Mason said to Marleaux. "And what have you done to my men?"

"The 'why' should be obvious, Captain," Marleaux said. "And what I've done to your men will be done to you, soon enough."

"We had a deal," Mason argued.

"I made myself a new one," Marleaux answered. "One that doesn't involve sharing my money with you."

"Without me and my men," Mason insisted, "including my Crow braves, you'll never get out of this valley alive. Do you have any idea how many Cheyenne and Sioux roam this territory?"

"I have over thirty men," Marleaux said, "a lot of guns, including your men's, and plenty of ammunition. What I don't have, is a desire to have your troopers and braves butcher me."

"I would do no such thing," Mason declared.

"You're a Yankee liar," Marleaux said. "You'd slaughter me and my men, all right, without a second thought. If not for the money, you'd wipe us out to keep anyone from disclosing our arrangement, and your association with Whiskey Falls."

"I wouldn't," Mason insisted, the first signs of panic creeping into his voice. "I swear. I'd stay silent."

"I know you'll stay silent," Marleaux said. "Because I'm personally going to see to your silence."

"All the bodies have been searched," McKinnon said, extending a burlap bag of money for Marleaux's inspection. The bag contained cash, coins, and what items of jewelry the troopers, braves, and buyers had on them. Their guns and ammunition had been collected in a crate.

"You know what to do," Marleaux told him. "Get on with it."

McKinnon whistled, and those of Marleaux's men not guarding Pritchard, Bonner, Mason, and Greenwald at gunpoint began walking among the unconscious men and bayonetting them. They moved systematically, stabbing each comatose body through the chest. Some of the men twitched, others cried out once, but most didn't move at all when the bayonets entered their body, mercifully anesthetized by the laudanum-infected whiskey.

Sergeant Greenwald sank to his knees. "Oh, dear God," he began to sob.

"You cryin' for your men or yourself?" Pritchard asked him. He got no answer.

"Just like Andersonville," Bonner said, as they watched the massacre. "Defenseless men being murdered by the bushel at Red Henry Marleaux's hand."

"Once you kill enough men," Marleaux said, "a few hundred more, here or there, doesn't bother you at all. I'm surprised you, of all people, Mister Bonner, don't know that."

"All my killing has been done one-on-one," Bonner said, "eyeball-to-eyeball. I've never killed a defenseless man."

"Perhaps that's why you're going to die today," Marleaux said, "and I'm going to ride out of Whiskey Falls in a wagonload full of money?"

He turned away and walked over to the stage to count the money in the bag. Oleg sat sulking nearby. The big Russian held a blood-soaked towel to his face and glared through swollen eyes at Pritchard.

"I'm sorry I let you down," Bonner whispered to Pritchard. "I got jumped coming out of the storehouse. Marleaux's men were there waiting for me."

"I know," Pritchard said quietly. "Ain't your fault. You didn't stand a chance."

"How did they know I was there?"

"Why don't you ask Ned?" Pritchard said, gesturing with his shoulder.

The wagon master stood by himself, at the edge of the stage, chewing tobacco and watching in silence as several hundred helpless men were impaled on the ground before him.

"I might just do that," Bonner said, "seeing as how Ned hasn't been tied up yet, and is still wearing his gun."

CHAPTER THIRTY-SEVEN

"I'm disappointed in you, Ned," Pritchard said. "I thought you were a better man."

"I'm disappointed in you, too," Ned said, spitting a glob of tobacco. "I put down a twenty-dollar bet on Oleg to whomp you. Looks like both of us lost out."

"What made you sell me out?" Pritchard asked.

"Us out," Bonner added.

"It'd be smarter to ask why I didn't throw in with Marleaux sooner?" Ned said. "In truth, Samuel, you never stood a chance. After we survived that attack by the Crow, and got brung here to Whiskey Falls in chains, I figured we was gonners. When you got yourself into Red Henry's graces, and got us outta the mine, I was right grateful to you."

"You're welcome," Pritchard said.

"But then you figured on double-crossin' him," Ned continued, "and I knew I couldn't play along. I realize you're a federal marshal and all, and tryin' to do the right thing, but what you were askin' of me was suicide. You wanted me and Laird to help you go up against Red Henry, all his men, plus Captain Mason's troops, and a couple of hundred Crow braves who already tried once to separate us from our hair out on the Oregon Trail? You was fixin' to get us all killed, Samuel, plain-and-simple. You was just too self-righteous, stubborn, and lunk-headed to know it."

"I ain't never been accused of an abundance of brains," Pritchard admitted.

"Look around you," Ned said. "You see all them dead fellers, lyin' about, getting' stuck? That wasn't gonna be me."

"Dyin' ain't the worst that can befall a feller," Pritchard said. "To my mind, sellin' out your friends, and your soul, to a sidewinder like Henry Marleaux is a helluva lot worse. Isn't that what you called him? The 'crookedest sidewinder' you ever knew?"

"I said a lot of things," Ned said. "Mostly whatever I had to."

"I must say," Bonner said, "you had me convinced with your speech about how you couldn't partake in Marleaux's 'unholy' plan. You remember the one? When you told me and Pritchard you couldn't condone the murder of innocent men, women, and children?"

"I still don't condone it," Ned said, moving his tobacco from one side of his cheek to the other. "But if'n it's a choice between them or me, I'll stay above ground every time."

"I pity you," Pritchard said. "Judas hanged himself, remember?"

"His conscience bothered him," Ned said. "Mine don't."

"Ned's not going to get a chance to hang himself," Bonner said. "Because I'm going to kill him."

"I couldn't care less for your moral reproaches, Samuel," Ned said, "nor for your threats, Laird. Marleaux offered me more money than I ever seen in my life, and I took it. I'm sorry things went south for you two, but you each made your choice, just like me. My choice is gonna let me ride out of Whiskey Falls alive and rich. Your choice is gonna end you both today. Now if'n you boys'll excuse me, I've got work to do."

Ned led a group of Marleaux's rifle-armed men off to the mine. Marleaux came back over to where Pritchard, Bonner, and Captain Mason stood and Sergeant Greenwald knelt. Greenwald was quietly crying.

"What's going to happen to us?" Captain Mason asked. "Are you going to bayonet us, too?"

"Out of respect for our previous business relationship," Marleaux said, "I thought I'd give you the option of choosing the manner in which you meet your end. I can offer you the bayonet, Captain, if you wish to go out the way your men did? Or perhaps you'd prefer a bullet? How about the rope? As you can see, my gallows is still standing and operates perfectly."

"You son-of-a-bitch," Mason hissed.

"Or maybe you'd like to end your days with a sip of my whiskey?" Marleaux asked. "A glass of my laudanum-spiked rye, and you'd simply fall asleep? You wouldn't feel the blade or bullet or rope at all."

"Please," Greenwald sobbed, "I don't want to die."

"Do you have any idea," Marleaux said, rolling his eyes, "how many times I heard exactly that pathetic plea at Andersonville? Thousands of times, that's how many. What a dreary phrase. Please, Sergeant, out of respect to your uniform, don't beg? It's unbecoming of a soldier, and gives me a headache."

Suddenly a shot rang out, and then two more, followed by men shouting and a woman's scream. The sounds came from the line of tents where Jolie and Rebecca Matheson were hiding.

Marleaux signaled to his men, and several of them ran to the tents. A moment later they emerged. Two of his gunmen came out carrying a third man, and two more were dragging Jolie Matheson's lifeless body. Another was tugging Rebecca Matheson by the hair. They shoved the weeping Rebecca to the ground at Marleaux's feet, and dumped Jolie's body beside her. Rebecca fell across her mother in grief.

"What the hell happened?" Marleaux asked.

"We was searchin' the tents," one of Marleaux's

men began, "like you told us, when we found these two gals a-hidin'. Big Don grabbed the young one, I presume to have hisself a bit of fun. The older one pulled out this pistol," he held out Bonner's Open Top .44, "and shot Don right through his pumpkin. Then me and Bob shot her."

Marleaux took the revolver from his man and examined it. "I believe this is yours?" he said to Bonner.

"I must have misplaced it," Bonner said.

"I also believe," Marleaux said to Pritchard, "these are the two females you convinced me to leave in your care?"

Pritchard said nothing to Marleaux. Instead, he walked over to where Rebecca lay sobbing over her mother's body and knelt beside her. Unable to put his arms around her to comfort her since they were bound behind his back, all he could do was say, "I'm sorry, Rebecca."

"Put her," Marleaux pointed to Rebecca, "in the saloon with the others." One of his men grabbed her by the arm and tugged her away.

Pritchard stood up. "Damn you to hell, Henry Marleaux," he said.

"The name's Red Henry," Marleaux said. "And speaking of hell, you've just given me an idea on how to end you."

Ned came back with Marleaux's men and a line of fifty leg-manacled, prisoners from the mine.

They were leading a half-dozen large freight wagons, each being pulled by a team of horses. The prisoners began loading bodies into the wagon, to be taken back to the mine and dumped in the old shaft. One of the first bodies placed in the wagon was Jolie's.

"I've changed my mind," Marleaux said, addressing Pritchard, Bonner, Mason, and Greenwald. "I've got good news and bad news. The good news is, you lads no longer have to be burdened by deciding how you're going to die. Thanks to Samuel cursing me to hell, I've decided your fates for you."

"What are you going to do to us?" Greenwald said, fear and dread lighting his tear-streaked face.

"The bad news," Marleaux chuckled, "is I'm going to send you all straight to hell. Or at least as close to hell as I can get from Whiskey Falls."

CHAPTER THIRTY-EIGHT

The remainder of the evening was spent loading several hundred bodies onto wagons and hauling them to the mine, where they were unceremoniously tossed down into a deep, played-out, vein. The manacled prisoners, under the watchful eyes and ever-ready guns of Marleaux's men, labored under the grim task of picking up the dead soldiers, Crow warriors, and auction buyers strewn around the stage and carting them away.

Pritchard, Bonner, Captain Mason, and Sergeant Greenwald sat on the stage, bound and guarded by McKinnon and Oleg, and observed the macabre proceedings. Henry Marleaux oversaw the mass burial with a glass of whiskey in his hand.

Greenwald finally stopped crying and stared glumly off into the distance with a blank expression on his face.

Eventually, the last of the bodies was shipped off. Marleaux's men returned without the wagons.

"It's finished," one of Marleaux's men reported. "The carcasses have all been dumped, and the prisoners returned to the mine. There're men guarding the entrance, a-waitin' your instructions."

"Very good," Marleaux said. "You boys get on down to the saloon. The women folk are all there. Have the women I didn't elect to keep sent over here. There're boys waiting for the word to bring them. Then get yourselves something to eat and have a bit of whiskey, but don't partake too heavily. Remember, we ride out at dawn."

"We didn't forget," the man said. "Let's go, boys." He led the other men off.

"Speakin' of the women," Pritchard said, "what's to befall them?"

"I may as well tell you," Marleaux said, "since there's nothing you can do about it. Most of the women, the old, withered-up ones, and the children, are going to end up with the men in that mine."

"And the in-between ones?" Bonner asked, thinking of Rebecca.

"I'll bring them along on my trip to the Utah Territory," Marleaux explained. "I have plenty of wagons at my disposal because the men who bought them, paying me good money by the way, seem to have abruptly left this earthly plane." He chuckled to himself at his own joke. "The women can entertain my men on the journey, and if we encounter any hostile Indians, they might prove valuable in trade."

"You realize," Captain Mason said, "that by

now the Sioux and Cheyenne will have taken notice of the lack of Crow cooking fires in the hills surrounding this valley? It won't be long before the scouts report back to their lodges. You'll soon be up to your neck in war parties after your scalp. You're going to need every man, and every gun, you've got."

"Nice try," Marleaux said. "I've plenty of guns and more than enough men."

"Not men like me," Mason argued. "I'm a professional Indian fighter. You need me, Henry, if you plan on getting through a-hundred miles of Indian-infested territory to Promontory."

"I'm not a fool, Captain," Marleaux said. "Do you really think I'd give you a gun after wiping out all of your men?"

Mason didn't answer, merely hanging his head in defeat.

"I had intended to allow Marshal Pritchard and Mister Bonner to accompany me," Marleaux said, "since they'd already demonstrated their extreme proficiency in combat against the redskins. But they foolishly chose to double-cross me, instead."

"We're not fools," Pritchard said. "Yours was a devil's bargain."

"Even if we had gone along with you," Bonner said, "we know you'd never let us reach Promontory alive. You'd have used us to get you there, then found a way to finish us off."

Marleaux sipped his whiskey. "Unfortunately

309

for you, you're both right." He chuckled. "But if you'd stuck to your bargain with me, at least you'd have survived this day."

A procession of females approached from the saloon, escorted under guard by Marleaux's men. There were over one hundred of them. Most were over forty years of age or younger than ten.

"This is all the ones you marked," one of the guards reported to Marleaux.

"Come along." Marleaux gestured to Pritchard, Bonner, Mason, and Greenwald. "Let's join these ladies on their stroll to the mine."

The terrified women and girls held hands, and each other, as they were prodded along by the rifles of Marleaux's men. Pritchard, Bonner, Mason, and Greenwald fell in behind the procession, with several more of Marleaux's gunmen, along with McKinnon and Oleg, at their backs. Ned and Marleaux brought up the rear. Oleg pushed a wheelbarrow containing a keg of whiskey.

They walked the short distance to the mine, and when they arrived were greeted by a half-dozen more of Marleaux's men bearing rifles. They began hustling the womenfolk, sobbing and pleading, into the mine.

"Maybe they're not going to kill us?" Greenwald blurted in desperation. His eyes were wild, and he appeared on the verge of full-blown panic. "Maybe Marleaux's just going to keep us locked up in the mine until they leave in the morning?"

"Wishful thinking," said Bonner. "I saw Marleaux's men stashing something at the mine's entrance earlier this evening."

"Dynamite?" Pritchard said.

"That would be my guess," Bonner nodded.

Soon all the women were inside the mine, and the only prisoners remaining outside were Pritchard, Bonner, Captain Mason, and Sergeant Greenwald. McKinnon motioned for them to enter.

"NO!" Greenwald shouted. "Marleaux isn't going to seal me in a rathole to die!" He started to run, but was easily grabbed and restrained by two of Marleaux's men. He thrashed and struggled, howling in terror, frantically trying to keep from being herded into the mine's opening.

"The sergeant evidently doesn't want to go into the mine," Marleaux said.

"I don't want to die!" Greenwald screamed hysterically.

"And I don't want to listen to your pathetic whining anymore," Marleaux said. "It makes my ears hurt. Oleg?"

Oleg nodded, set down the wheelbarrow, stepped forward, and punched Greenwald in the gut. The cavalry sergeant grunted, sunk to his knees, and slumped forward because his hands were bound behind his back. The huge Russian lifted his heavy mallet overhead and brought it crashing down on Greenwald's skull, pulverizing it in one, mighty blow.

Captain Mason averted his eyes in horror and disgust. Even some of Marleaux's men turned away from the pulped remains of what was only a moment before Sergeant Greenwald. McKinnon chuckled, and Marleaux smiled.

"Is there anyone else who doesn't want to go into the silver mine?" Marleaux asked.

Neither Pritchard, Bonner, nor Mason answered.

"Very well," Marleaux said triumphantly. "In you go."

Pritchard, Bonner, and Mason slowly entered.

"One moment," Marleaux said. He again nodded to Oleg, who tipped the wheelbarrow, rolled the whiskey barrel to the entrance, and kicked it inside. Marleaux tossed a tin cup on the ground alongside the keg.

"I wouldn't want you gentlemen to meet your ends thinking Red Henry Marleaux is completely without humanity," Marleaux said. "That whiskey barrel's full of my special laudanum recipe," he continued. "There's more than enough for everyone inside the mine, even the children and the Quaker teetotalers."

"I'll not drink your hemlock," Mason spat.

"I'll wager you do," Marleaux said, "once the air runs out, and your lungs begin to burn, and the wails and cries of the women and children in there with you in the dark become aggravating enough."

"You'll burn in hell for this," Mason said.

"Says the man who spent two years murdering pilgrims and collecting slaves on the Oregon Trail for me." Marleaux laughed. McKinnon laughed along with him.

"So long, Ned," Pritchard said. "Be seein' you."

"I reckon not," Ned said, spitting tobacco juice. "But I do thank you, Samuel, for savin' me from them highwaymen, and the Crow, when we was out on the trail. I reckon you're haulin' some regret for that, right about now, ain't ya?"

"Never was one for regrets," Pritchard said.

"You do realize," Bonner said to Ned, "that Marleaux isn't going to let you reach Promontory alive? He'll use you to get him there then double-cross and murder you, just like he's doing to Captain Mason and did to his troops."

"If Oleg and McKinnon ain't worried," Ned said, "neither am I."

"Good-bye," Marleaux said, signaling to McKinnon. The diminutive Scotsman lit a match.

"If I were you lads," McKinnon said gleefully, "I'd get myself a bit farther into the mine. In a moment, it's going to get very loud, and very messy, here at the entrance."

He lit the long fuses of two bundles of dynamite

that were deposited on opposite sides of the mine's opening.

"Let's go," Pritchard said to Bonner. He turned and headed deeper into the mine. Captain Mason scrambled after them.

CHAPTER THIRTY-NINE

Pritchard, Bonner, and Captain Mason found over one-hundred-and-fifty miners, along with more than one hundred older women and small children, huddled in the space between intersecting tunnels approximately seventy-five feet into the mine. In the dull glow of kerosene lanterns and candles surrounding them, the fear was visible on their soot-covered faces.

"Everyone get down," Pritchard ordered. "Marleaux's going to blow the entrance."

"Blow the mine?" someone exclaimed. "He can't! We'll be trapped!"

"That's the idea," Pritchard said. "Do as I say."

Samuel and Bonner ducked against the wall. Mason followed suit. Many of the others began wailing and crying but huddled down together against the walls, as well.

A thundering boom erupted. The sound was ear-splitting, and the vibration could be felt through the walls and floor of the mine. People cried out in terror as a tidal wave of billowing smoke, flying dirt, and cascading debris poured through the exit tunnel toward them.

Darkness ensued, as all the lanterns and candles

went out. The air was suddenly thick with dust, and it took several long minutes to settle.

"Get the candles and lanterns lit again," Pritchard ordered, standing up. The sounds of people gasping, coughing, and retching emanated around him. A moment later, a candle flickered on and then another.

"Is everyone okay?" Bonner asked. "Anybody hurt?"

"Just a little dusty," a voice called out. "I think everyone's all right." More candles were lit and finally lanterns.

"Someone take a lantern back toward the entrance and check it out," Pritchard said. "And untie our hands."

"Hold on a minute," a familiar voice said. A filthy Deacon Wilson emerged from the crowd. "You aren't giving any orders here, Marshal Pritchard. And you're certainly not getting untied."

"I haven't time for your foolishness, Deacon," he said. "If we want to get out of here alive, we need to work together. Untie me."

"I will not," Wilson said.

"Okay," Pritchard said, as he headbutted the deacon. The diminutive Wilson fell to the ground, stunned. He turned to face the others. "Untie me," he said, "or I'll start kickin' teeth out."

"I'll be helping him," Bonner said.

Several men untied Pritchard and Bonner.

Captain Mason turned around, waiting to be untied, but no one moved.

"What about me?" Mason said.

"You and your men attacked our wagon train," a tall man holding a pickaxe said. "We were just peaceful Iowa farmers. You killed my brother."

"You brung us here as slaves to work in Red Henry Marleaux's mine," said another man, carrying a shovel.

"Your men raped me and my daughter," a woman said.

"Your Crow Indians murdered half my family," said another. "Scalped 'em, too, after they done it."

"We may die in this mine," said a woman, "but before we do, we'll see you die first."

"Get him," the first man who spoke said.

"NO!" Captain Mason screamed, as the mob descended.

Pritchard and Bonner could do nothing but step aside as Captain Mason, formerly of the U.S. Cavalry assigned to Fort Hall, was beaten and hacked to death by a pack of enraged miners with shovels and picks. He shrieked and howled as he was dismembered, until what was left of him lay rendered and silent.

The man who'd taken a lantern to scout the entrance returned. "The entire entrance is caved in," he announced. "Must be under fifty feet of solid rock. Even if we could dig through, it'd take weeks. We'll never get back out that way."

Gasps and moans resonated throughout the crowd. Several women began to cry.

"We're gonna suffocate down here," a man's voice declared. "With the opening blocked, and this many of us, there can't be more'n one or two days' worth of air in here. We're done for."

"There's a barrel of whiskey got rolled in," someone pointed to the keg. "At least we won't die thirsty."

"It's tainted with laudanum," Bonner said. "That's Red Henry Marleaux's idea of mercy. Don't drink it unless you want to die."

"That filthy monster," a man cursed. A chorus of others joined in.

"Everybody calm down," Pritchard said. "We ain't licked yet."

"You can't shoot your way out of this one, Marshal," a miner said. "We're gone goslin'. That's a plain fact. Hell, we're even buried."

"Maybe not," Pritchard said. "Who here knows this mine?"

A short, thin man stepped forward. "My name's Sven Jorgensen," he said. "Been diggin' here over a year," he said. "I guess I do, as well as anyone."

"This main tunnel runs crossways to the creek, don't it?" Pritchard asked.

"It does," Jorgensen confirmed. "The slew is just outside the mine."

"Do you have any shafts that steer toward the direction of the falls?"

"We have a couple of branches that go thataways," the miner said. "But they didn't play out, so they don't go in too deep."

"Bring a candle and show me," Pritchard said.

"What do you have in mind?" Bonner whispered, after pulling Pritchard aside.

"It's just a hunch," Pritchard said, keeping his voice low, "but I may know a way out. Stay here and keep everybody calm. I'll be back as quick as I can."

Pritchard followed Jorgensen, who led him down the main shaft approximately fifty yards. Then they turned right, and began heading into a tributary shaft. They walked for another fifty yards, by his estimation, before the tunnel began to narrow.

The channel got progressively smaller as they advanced. Jorgensen had to stoop at the waist, and Pritchard duck-walk, as they scooted through. They stopped when they reached a point where they'd have to crawl on their bellies to proceed any farther.

"This was one of the mine's earliest offshoots," Jorgensen said. "It must've been dug by the original claimholders before Marleaux and his boys jumped 'em and stole it. As you can see, they abandoned it because this burrow wasn't bringin' up any silver."

"Keep goin'," Pritchard said.

"Are you loco?" Jorgensen said. "The shaft's so small now, you'd practically have to slither like a snake to go on. Besides, it don't go anywhere. It just ends."

"Crawl in as far as you can," Pritchard told him, "and hold up that candle."

"What for?"

"Just do it," Pritchard said. "I'd go myself, but I'm too damn big."

Jorgensen shrugged and began to crawl in. He got another twenty feet and stopped.

"That's as far in as I can go," he called back.

"Hold out that candle," Pritchard said, "and hold your breath."

"What?"

"Do as I say," he ordered.

A long minute of silence ensued.

"Jumpin' Jehosaphat!" Jorgensen excitedly shouted. "There's air a-movin' in here!" He scooted himself back out of the tunnel and grabbed Pritchard's shoulder.

"How did you know?"

"I had occasion to explore the pool behind the falls," Pritchard explained. "Found what I thought was a bobcat hole, but turned out to go deeper in. By my reckonin', the end of this here shaft is only ten or so feet, at the most, from that openin' behind the waterfall."

"We've got the tools," Jorgensen said, "fellers

320

who're even smaller than me, and we sure as hell know how to dig. If your reckonin' is correct, Marshal, we could be dug out of here in a few hours."

"Then let's get 'er done," Pritchard said.

CHAPTER FORTY

"You can't just leave us down here!" Deacon Wilson exclaimed.

"I can," Pritchard said, "and I will."

It was long past midnight when the first miner broke through to the surface behind the waterfall. Fifteen minutes later the exit was bored out big enough for Samuel to fit through.

The miners worked feverishly all night, digging, scraping, and hauling dirt from the tunnel. Those too big to get into the chamber and dig hauled out the dirt in a daisy-chain of buckets. If there was one thing their tenure as slaves in Henry Marleaux's mine had taught them, it was how to dig and haul dirt.

Once they got into a rhythm, it went much faster than Pritchard and Bonner anticipated. When the lead miner finally broke through, he turned to his fellow miners and let out an exultant yell. "Yee-haw! We're free!"

Samuel scrambled into the shaft after him, grabbed the giddy fellow by his ankles, and dragged him roughly out.

"What's the big idea?" the indignant miner asked.

"I'd ask you the same question." Pritchard

said. "Are you tryin' to alert the guards outside?"

"Uh . . . I guess I forgot."

"Forget again, and I'll silence you permanent. Those men out there already tried to kill us once. I ain't givin' 'em a second chance."

"Sorry, Marshal."

Pritchard presumed the noise of the falls would quell any sound before it reached the nearest building, which was the storehouse, but didn't want to take any chances. He also presumed the guard Bonner and Ned had overpowered earlier would have been discovered. He suspected a new one would have been posted in his place, though with all the residents of Whiskey Falls besides Marleaux's men either dead, buried in the mine, or prisoners in his comfort house, the need to guard the storehouse might be moot.

Bonner reminded him, however, that Marleaux was too suspicious and greedy to leave his storehouse full of booty unguarded, particularly with the Sioux and Cheyenne potentially in the vicinity lurking about.

All those in the mine assembled at the intersection of the main tunnel and exit shaft, anxiously awaiting their turn to get out.

"Nobody's goin' anywhere," Pritchard said. "At least not yet."

"What're you talkin' about?" Deacon Wilson asked. "We dug this opening, and we're getting out of this mine."

"And go where?" Pritchard asked.

"Right back into the waiting guns of Marleaux's men," Bonner said, "that's where."

"And this time," Pritchard said, "he wouldn't put you all back in the mine. He'd have you shot on sight."

"The marshal's right," Jorgensen said. "If we all go out now, we'll just get rounded up again."

"What are we going to do?" a woman asked.

"Stay here a bit longer," Pritchard said. "Give me and Bonner a chance to sneak outside and get our hands on some guns. Then we'll have a fightin' chance against Marleaux and his men."

"Do you need some help, Marshal?" a man asked.

"You got us this far," another said. "Tell us what to do, and we're with you."

"I could surely use a hand," Pritchard said. "But any man who comes along with me has to follow my orders without backtalk, and can't be squeamish about killin'. Anybody here fit the bill?"

A dozen men stepped up. Pritchard and Bonner smiled. "All right, boys," Pritchard said. "Let's go."

"Wait a minute." Deacon Wilson pushed through the crowd. The bump on his forehead was visible, even in the dim light. "How do we know you'll come back for us?"

"I reckon you'll just have to trust me."

"I certainly will not," Wilson said. "As you have proven countless times, you're nothing but a violent heathen."

"Maybe so," a woman said, "but I reckon the marshal knows how to deal with men like Red Henry a sight better than you, Deacon. What we must do calls for bullets, not Bibles."

"Violence is never the answer," Deacon said smarmily.

"Perhaps it ain't the ideal answer," Pritchard said, "but it beats feedin' the crows at the hands of another."

"Why don't you tell us your plan, Deacon?" Bonner said.

"I say we all get out of this infernal mine, right now, and then we can decide a course of action once we're above ground."

"There ain't room for everybody to hide behind the falls," Pritchard said. "You think Marleaux's men ain't gonna notice a couple a hundred people millin' about in the dark? There're guards on the herd, at the storehouse, and I'm bettin' walkin' the streets right now, due to all the Crow Indians in the hills bein' gone and the Sioux and Cheyenne about. Not to mention, we're only an hour or so from sun-up. Anything we do has to be done now; not after a town hall meetin'."

The people in the mine murmured their assent.

"I disagree," Wilson said. "And I'm not staying underground one more second than I have to."

"I'll tell you what," Pritchard said, loud enough for everyone to hear, "why don't you let the folks decide? Leave now, under Deacon Wilson's leadership, or hunker down in here a bit longer and give me and the boys a chance to make a play?"

"I'm for the marshal's idea," somebody said.

"Me, too," a woman said. "Especially since we now have a way out."

"Shut up, Deacon," another said.

"It's settled then," Pritchard said. "We're burnin' dark." He turned to Jorgensen. "Guard the hole, keep everybody quiet, and make sure nobody gets out; at least for now."

"I will," he agreed. "For how long?"

"Give us an hour," Pritchard said. "If we ain't back for you all by then, I reckon you'll have to assume you're on your own and make a play for yourselves."

Jorgensen nodded. "Good luck, Marshal."

Pritchard squirmed through the opening and found himself in the space behind the waterfall. The last time he'd been there he was in Jolie Matheson's arms. Now she was dead.

Bonner emerged behind Pritchard, and a dozen miners followed behind him. The air was cold, and Pritchard estimated the sun would be rising soon.

"The storehouse is full of guns and ammunition," Bonner said. "We just have to get to it."

"Sure wish we had a gun or two now," Pritchard remarked, "in case we're spotted crossin' open ground."

"We do," Bonner said. "Follow me."

Bonner led Pritchard and the men silently through the falls. The water was frigid, but refreshed them, and washed away the dirt of the mine. When they came out on the other side, they remained in the creek with only their heads above water and waded to the opposite bank.

"While you were dancing with Oleg," Bonner explained quietly, "Ned and I stashed our saddles under some brush over yonder. Our rifles, too. Come on."

Bonner led the way, crawling on his belly, with Pritchard right behind him. The men remained behind. A few yards from the falls, they found the five saddles Bonner had secreted. One of them was supposed to be for Jolie.

"Something else I should show you," Bonner said to Pritchard, "while we're alone."

He searched through the brush until he found a concealed rope. One end was tied to a tree, and the other disappeared into the creek. Bonner pulled on the rope, and a bulging set of saddlebags came out of the water. He opened them, revealing the money he'd taken from Marleaux's wagons.

"There's over one-hundred-thousand dollars in here," Bonner said. "It was stashed in boxes concealed under the seats of his wagons. I switched the cash out for Bibles. If I was a betting man, I'd wager there's nothing inside Marleaux's safe."

"Right clever," Pritchard said, "and just like Red Henry to cheat his boys out of their share of the loot. They think his money's in the safe, which means they'll be guardin' it with their lives on the way to the Utah Territory. But before they reach Promontory, he'll have a way to end them, like he did Captain Mason, his soldiers, and the Crow, to keep all the cash for himself."

"That's how I figured it," Bonner said, returning the bags to the water.

Pritchard and Bonner wasted no time retrieving their rifles, still in their scabbards. They loaded the weapons, and stuffed their pockets with cartridges from their saddlebags. Bonner also withdrew a Bowie knife and revealed the dynamite he'd pilfered from Marleaux's storehouse. He stuffed the bundle in his shirt, along with a box of matches.

"Figured it might come in handy," Bonner whispered.

"I reckon you figured right," Pritchard said. He produced a bottle of whiskey from his bags, took a slug, and handed it to Bonner. "Just a nip," he said, "to take off the chill."

The bounty hunter helped himself to a quick gulp, and handed the bottle back to the men behind him. Each man took a successive drink.

"Okay boys," Pritchard whispered. "Me and Bonner are gonna make our way to the back door of that storehouse. Wait for our signal to start makin' your way in."

The men nodded, and Pritchard and Bonner departed. They continued to crawl on their stomachs until they reached the edge of the corral, thirty yards away. It was slow going, but neither man wanted to stand until they had the livestock herd to cover them.

Bonner pointed to one of Marleaux's men, smoking a cigarette and standing watch. He was leaning against a fencepost, and had a Henry rifle cradled in one arm. Pritchard nodded, borrowed Bonner's knife, and crept around the circumference of the corral fence until he came up behind him.

The sentry never knew what killed him. One of Pritchard's massive, powerful, hands clamped over his mouth, and the other used the Bowie to cut his throat. Pritchard held him in place until he stopped moving, then gently lowered him to the ground to avoid creating any sound. He wiped the blade on the man's shirt, took his pistol belt and rifle, and signaled for Bonner to join him.

"I don't see another livestock guard," Bonner said.

"Don't need more'n one," Pritchard said, "with all the stock in a corral."

The guard at the rear door of the storehouse

was even easier to deal with. Evidently believing there was little threat since Captain Mason's troops and the Crow had been wiped out, and all the male prisoners were supposedly sealed in the mine, he was snoozing away in a chair propped against the storehouse's back door. His rifle was across his lap, and Pritchard and Bonner simply walked up to him.

"Almost hate to take the fool so easy," Pritchard whispered.

"I've got no reservations," Bonner whispered back. "Didn't bother his slumber any, burying women and children in a mine to die."

Pritchard relieved Bonner of his Sharps rifle and handed him back his Bowie knife. The bounty hunter stepped in, swung the knife like he was throwing a roundhouse punch, and buried the blade hilt-deep in the sleeping sentry's temple. He took hold of the body as it slumped from the chair, again to avoid any sound, while Pritchard caught his rifle.

Bonner quietly opened the storehouse's back door and dragged the body inside. Pritchard waved to the miners to start coming in. Then Bonner motioned for Pritchard to follow him, and both men skirted around the large building until they came around to the front.

This guard was awake, and pacing back-and-forth in the cold air to ward off the chill. As soon as he turned his back, Pritchard stepped around the corner and was on him in two steps. One punch from his rock-hard fist and the guard collapsed, instantly unconscious. Pritchard ducked under him, threw him over his shoulder, and carried him back around the corner of the building. By the time they got to the back door again, all the miners were inside. Bonner pointed them to the weapons and ammunition stashed in the two wagons.

"The other guard is in front of the comfort house," Bonner said, peering out the cracked barn doors. "I can just see him from here. I'm guessing he's the only one left in town who's awake."

"How do you want to take him?"

Bonner reached down and took off the coat, gun belt, and hat from the guard Pritchard had just clobbered and donned them. "Give me a minute," he said.

Pritchard handed him the sentry's rifle and Bonner slipped out. He watched the bounty hunter walk nonchalantly down the main road, waving casually as he approached the final guard posted in front of the saloon.

When he got within arm's reach, Pritchard saw a brief flash as Bonner's Bowie came out. An instant later, the guard was over Bonner's shoulder and he was scurrying back to the storehouse.

"Right nice work," Pritchard said, as Bonner

re-entered the storehouse. "I didn't hear a thing." Bonner dumped the body on the floor and shrugged out of the blood-soaked coat.

"A couple of you fellers get on back to the mine," Pritchard said, "and lead the rest of the folks here to the storehouse. Hurry 'em along, and keep 'em quiet. We don't know when the guard is supposed to change, and more of Marleaux's men might come to relieve these guards."

Two men jogged off.

"What about the rest of us?" the other miners said.

"Get yourself a gun," Pritchard said, "stock up on cartridges, and be ready to use it."

CHAPTER FORTY-ONE

Thirty minutes later, all those who'd been in the mine had been shepherded into the barn-like storehouse. Marleaux's food stores were opened, and the wet, starving people ate hungrily.

It was crowded, and dark, but Pritchard forbade light and insisted on total silence. Bonner kept watch at the front doors, where he could observe the saloon.

Pritchard and Bonner distributed weapons to all the men, and now had well over one-hundred, armed, former prisoners at their disposal. They'd also located their own gun belts in the stacks of confiscated firearms. Pritchard checked his revolvers, gratified to be wearing his custom-barreled Colts again. Only one of Bonner's 1872 Open Top revolvers was in his holsters, the other having been taken by Henry Marleaux's men from Jolie Matheson.

The guard Samuel knocked unconscious slowly came around, as the men readied their weapons and ate. He'd been gagged, bound hand and foot, and was seated against one wall next to the bodies of the herd guard, rear guard, and street patrol.

Pritchard knelt next to him with his Bowie in his hand.

"Take a gander," he said to the wide-eyed guard as he stared at the bodies of his fellow guards. "I'm a-gonna ask questions, and you're a-gonna answer 'em. If'n you don't, or I don't like your answers, you'll be joinin' your friends in hell. Comprende?"

The guard nodded enthusiastically.

"Where's Marleaux sleep?"

"Upstairs at the comfort house, above the saloon," the guard said, after Pritchard lowered his gag. "Room at the end of the hall. It's the only one with a window."

"What about his men?"

"A couple of 'em are in the comfort house, like McKinnon and Oleg, to watch over the women, but the rest of Henry's boys sleep in the bunkhouse next door. It's the big building with the stovepipe chimney stickin' up through the canvas roof."

"Any of his men posted anywheres else?"

"Nope," the guard said. "Just the stock guard, the two guards at the storehouse, like I was, and the sentry in front of the saloon."

"When does the shift change?"

"We'd normally get relieved at dawn," the guard said, "but since we're pullin' out today at sun-up, I reckon everybody'll be up and packin' and there won't be need for guards no more."

"How soon till dawn?" Pritchard asked Bonner, who was looking out through the main doors.

"Less than half-an hour," he said.

"Are you gonna kill me?" the guard asked.

"Like you and your friends tried to do to me," Pritchard answered, "and all these innocent folks?"

The guard hung his head. Pritchard put the gag back in place.

"All right, fellers," Pritchard said, getting everyone's attention. "I need a couple of dozen of you men to stay here, ford up, and protect the women and children. If'n the rest of you fellers are of a mind, you can come on down to the comfort house with me and Mister Bonner to greet Red Henry and his boys."

Grins broke out on a hundred dirty faces, as men checked and readied their guns. "We're right behind you, Marshal Pritchard."

Bonner nodded, handed Pritchard his Winchester, and pushed open the big barn doors. The faintest glow of sunrise was beginning to show over the eastern crest of the valley.

Pritchard and Bonner led a procession of a hundred armed men down the main street. When they reached the comfort house, the group split into separate parties. Bonner took half the men, and placed them strategically around the bunkhouse. The rest encircled the saloon.

"Gimme a chance to go inside and visit with Red Henry," Pritchard said. "Mayhaps we can avoid further bloodshed."

"Some of these miners have been digging like slaves for over a year," Bonner said. "All of them have lost loved ones. I don't think many are of a mind to avoid bloodshed."

"Don't forget," Pritchard said, "there are forty or fifty women held captive in the rooms upstairs in that big saloon. Rebecca is one of 'em. We start a shootin' war with them gals inside, plenty of 'em ain't comin' out alive."

"Good point," Bonner said, removing the bundle of dynamite from inside his tunic and lighting himself a cheroot. Several other miners produced similar bundles they'd obtained at Bonner's direction. "We'll hold for your signal, or as long as we can. But at the first sign of Marleaux's boys rousing out of that bunkhouse, I'm giving my boys the order to cut loose."

"Fair enough," Pritchard said. He handed Bonner his Winchester.

"You don't want your rifle?"

"I'm better with my wheel guns indoors."

"I'll not dispute that," Bonner said.

Pritchard hauled his huge frame silently up the steps and into the comfort house. The saloon downstairs was vacant. He ascended the stairs, a revolver in each hand.

On the second floor, just like the guard had said, were a series of rooms. Pritchard passed them all, tiptoeing as softly as he could, until he reached the door at the end of the hall.

None of the doors had locks. Pritchard holstered his left-hand gun and slowly turned the latch, pushing the door open with his shoulder.

Henry Marleaux was asleep in his long-handles, his immense belly rising with each snoring breath. His guns, and an empty whiskey bottle, lay on a table nearby, along with Bonner's other Open Top Colt. On the floor, next to his boots, was a bulging leather satchel.

Rebecca Matheson lay fully clothed next to him, both hands manacled to the bedpost. She had a black eye, and looked up at Pritchard as he entered.

He put a finger to his lips, holstered his other gun, and drew his knife. In one swift movement Pritchard pounced on Marleaux, clamped his left hand in an iron grip around the sleeping man's throat, and brought the tip of his Bowie to rest against his bulging left eye.

"If you make a sound," Pritchard said, "I'll gut you like a Mississippi catfish."

Marleaux nodded. Pritchard stood up, hauled him to his feet by his long red hair, and moved the blade to his throat.

"Where're the keys to her chains?" he asked. Marleaux pointed to a ring on the table.

"Unlock her," he ordered, releasing Marleaux.

Marleaux retrieved the keys and unlocked Rebecca. The instant she was free she began punching and slapping Marleaux's face in a furious rage.

"Settle down," Pritchard said, restraining her.

"You don't know what he tried to do to me," she sobbed.

"I can guess," he said. "Calm down, or you'll wake up the house."

Marleaux seized upon the distraction caused by Rebecca's outburst to lunge for the Open Top Colt on the table. His fingers had barely touched the revolver's butt when Pritchard's Bowie knife pinned his right hand to the tabletop. He opened his mouth to scream, but the sound never came out. A hammer-like fist slammed into his solar-plexus, knocking the wind out of him and silencing him instantly. Marleaux sunk to his knees, his hand still pegged to the table top.

Footsteps echoed down the hallway. "You okay in there, Boss?"

Pritchard drew one revolver, cocked it, and stuck the barrel behind Marleaux's ear. The other he aimed at the door.

"I'm . . . all . . . right," Marleaux sputtered. "This . . . gal's . . . spirited . . . that's all."

"Whatever you say, Boss," the voice outside the door said. "I'm goin' back to bed."

An instant later the door flew open. One of Marleaux's men, barefoot and wearing only trousers and suspenders, dashed in. A Colt Navy, modified to fire metallic cartridges, was in his right hand with the hammer back.

Pritchard shot him in the face as he brought his gun up.

"Let's get out of here," he told Rebecca, as he removed the spent casing and reloaded his Colt. He pulled out his Bowie from both the table and Marleaux's hand, and wiped the blade on the bed. Marleaux fell to the floor, clutching his profusely bleeding hand.

"Can you hear me, Bonner?" Pritchard yelled out the window.

"I can," came the reply. "Sounds as if folks are waking up in there."

"They are," Pritchard said. "You and the boys feel free to start the fireworks."

CHAPTER FORTY-TWO

Bonner lit the short fuse of the dynamite bundle with his cheroot and hurled it through a bunkhouse window. The other former prisoners with dynamite bundles did the same. Men could be heard cursing inside, and a few seconds later the windows, doors, and canvas roof blew out in a tremendous series of explosions.

The walls teetered, and the entire structure caught fire. Charred and stunned men staggered out, stumbling and bleeding, and were shot down by guns belonging to the miners surrounding the bunkhouse.

A minute later, the flaming walls of the bunkhouse collapsed. More than twenty-five of Henry Marleaux's gang perished in the blast and subsequent fire, or were gunned down by Bonner's riflemen as they attempted to flee.

Bonner rallied the jubilant miners, and sent them to join their comrades with Pritchard at the saloon.

While Rebecca manacled Marleaux's hands behind his back with the same chains he'd used to tether her to the bed, Pritchard examined the contents of the satchel. He found it packed with money. A quick perusal put the total, by his estimate, to be at least fifty-thousand dollars.

"I wonder why Henry didn't tuck all this auction money away in his safe, downstairs?" he asked.

"Who knows why this filthy animal does what he does?" she said.

Pritchard tucked Bonner's gun in his belt, snatched the keys from the bed stand, and yanked the owner of Whiskey Falls to his feet by his red hair. He handed Rebecca the satchel.

"We're leavin'," Pritchard said to Marleaux, "but you're goin' first. You're gonna tell your boys to throw down their guns and go outside with their hands up."

"My men won't do it," Marleaux snarled. "They'll kill you first."

"Didn't you hear them explosions?" Pritchard said. "That was your bunkhouse, and everybody in it, goin' to hell in flames. Which means you don't have more'n a handful of men left."

"Perhaps" Marleaux said, "but they're men willing to die for me, like McKinnon and Oleg."

"We'll see about that," Pritchard said. "Once your boys get a gander at their dead brothers outside, and the hundred-or-more angry men with rifles surrounding this saloon, I reckon that loyalty might falter. Especially after they learn you planned to cheat them out of their share of the booty you've collected these past two years."

"What are you talking about?"

"I happen to know that safe of yours downstairs is empty. That's why you kept your takins' from yesterday's auction with you in that satchel-bag, and didn't put it into the safe."

"That's ridiculous."

"I think not," Pritchard said. "You were gonna lug that big iron safe out of Whiskey Falls, in a freight wagon, to fool all your boys into thinkin' that's where the fortune was. But we both know it's really stashed in strongboxes under the seats of your wagons. Or at least it was. Those boxes are full of Bibles, now."

Marleaux's face reddened in anger. "That money is mine!" he said.

"Like hell," Pritchard said. "Every penny of that money was stolen from others, the same way you stole that silver mine. And every penny is goin' back to them it belongs to."

"You have no right to take it!"

"Let's go," Pritchard said, ignoring Marleaux's hypocrisy and prodding him toward the door with his guns. Rebecca fell in behind them.

When they got to the top of the stairs, they found McKinnon, Oleg, Ned, and six other men holding guns on all the women in the saloon. They'd herded them downstairs from their rooms, and had them huddled together against the bar.

"Good mornin', Marshal Pritchard," McKinnon said jauntily in his Scottish accent. "Didn't expect to see you again. I must say, your reputation for being a hard man to kill is certainly well-deserved."

"Nice to see you again, fellers," Pritchard answered the greeting. "Especially you, Ned. Told you we'd meet again."

Ned's face was drained of color.

"By the way boys," Pritchard went on, "you've got me above you, a hundred guns outside a-waitin' for you, and if you couldn't tell by the fireworks, the rest of your gang has been bedded down. I recommend throwin' down your guns and givin' yourselves up."

"You forget, Marshal," McKinnon said, "we have these women."

"Keep 'em," Pritchard said, causing Rebecca to gasp. "Shoot 'em all, if'n you want. Don't mean a whit to me. But it won't save any of you, if'n you do."

"You're bluffing, Marshal," McKinnon said. "Your famed code of honor won't allow you to stand idly by while innocent women are gunned down."

"Call my bluff, Scotsman," Pritchard said. "Shoot one of 'em, and see what it gets you."

"Samuel," Rebecca said behind him, "you can't mean—?"

"Be silent," Pritchard whispered over his shoulder to her. "Trust me."

"Seems like we're at a standoff," McKinnon said.

"Not hardly," Pritchard said. "Them boys

outside the saloon with rifles ain't a-gonna shoot me. They're surely primed to shoot you, though. Even if you plug all the womenfolk and kill me, you'll still die."

"He's got you over a barrel, Daniel," Marleaux said.

"I propose a bargain," McKinnon said. "We all want to live, do we not? In exchange for the lives of these women, and your own, you allow Marleaux, me, Oleg, and what's left of my boys to take the safe, pack a wagon, and ride away?"

"Fair enough," Pritchard said. "But before you go, you might want to take a look inside that safe." He threw the ring of keys taken from Marleaux's bedside table over the railing.

McKinnon caught the keys, and looked quizzically up at Marleaux. "What's the marshal talking about, Henry?"

"I don't know what the fool is talking about," Marleaux said nervously. "Don't listen to him, Daniel. It's a trick."

"Go on," Pritchard chided McKinnon. "Take a gander into the safe. What're you afraid of? What doesn't Red Henry want you to see?"

"Shut up!" Marleaux snapped at Pritchard.

"Keep the women covered," McKinnon said to his men and started for Marleaux's office.

"Don't listen to him," Marleaux repeated. "Pritchard is only trying to rattle you. He wants to sow distrust between us."

"Somebody sounds worried," Pritchard said. "Must be somethin' in that safe Ole' Henry doesn't want you to find?"

"Makes a man wonder," McKinnon said, "doesn't it?" He unlocked Marleaux's office door and disappeared inside.

Bonner and several miners with rifles materialized in the saloon doorway. "Having a saloon social, are we?" he asked, taking in the scene before him.

"Just a little friendly conversation," Pritchard said, "with guns. Come on in, and join the party."

He holstered one of his guns, and tossed Bonner's second Colt down to him. The bounty hunter deftly caught it, checked the load, and inserted it back into his vacant cross-draw holster.

"Good morning, Ned," Bonner said.

Ned looked nervously from Pritchard, on the stairs above him, to Bonner, at the door. His face grew paler.

"Look fellers," he said, working his chaw, "it wasn't nuthin' personal. I just figured I had a better chance at survivin' if I throwed in with Marleaux, that's all. It was you two, up against an army of them. Nobody in their right mind would've reckoned you'd have come out on top against Marleaux's gang and Captain Mason's troops and Indians. I only done what anyone would've, in my boots. I never meant to cause you fellers no intentional grief."

"Of course not," Bonner said. "Blasting us inside a silver mine to suffocate and die was just your way of being neighborly, I suppose?"

"Speaking of Mason," Marleaux said, "where is the captain? Last I saw of him, he was in your company, Marshal?"

"After you buried us in your mine," Pritchard said, "the good citizens of Whiskey Falls decided to express their feelins' about gettin' kidnapped off'n the Oregon Trail, seein' their loved ones raped, murdered, and scalped, and bein' forced to dig in your mine or whore in your saloon. As you can imagine, those feelins' weren't especially cordial."

"What did they do to him?" Marleaux asked, his face slackening.

"All I can tell you," Pritchard said, "was that he didn't die pretty, and he didn't die quick."

"Nor quietly," Bonner added.

McKinnon emerged from Marleaux's office wearing a bemused look. He'd holstered his gun, and was spinning the key ring on his trigger finger.

"Guess what?" he asked Marleaux. "There wasn't anything but empty space in that safe." He faced Pritchard. "How'd you know, Marshal?"

"Doesn't matter," Pritchard said. "Important thing is, you didn't."

"Where's the money?" McKinnon demanded. "By my estimate, it's well over one-hundred-thousand dollars."

"Where you'll never find it," Pritchard said. He neglected to mention the satchel Rebecca was carrying behind him.

McKinnon turned to Marleaux. "You were going to double-cross me, weren't you, Henry? Oleg, too, and the rest of your boys? Do us all in on the trail to Utah? You planned to keep every penny of that money for yourself, didn't you?"

"Nonsense," Marleaux said unconvincingly. "Don't listen to Marshal Pritchard, Daniel, he's lying. Sure, I stashed the money, but only for safekeeping. I wanted to keep it hidden for us; for you, me, and the boys. I was afraid Captain Mason and his men might plunder the safe and make off with our money."

"Of course, you were," McKinnon muttered, shaking his head.

"I'm done talkin'," Pritchard said, holstering his guns and descending the stairs. He pushed Marleaux ahead of him. "I ain't makin' any deal with you, McKinnon. Lay down your arms and live. Keep 'em and die. Ain't no other choice before you."

"There is other choice," Oleg suddenly declared, stepping forward with his mallet. "You and I fight again, Marshal Pritchard. This time, I smash you."

"Oh, shut up," Pritchard said. "I've grown right tired of your bullyin'."

Oleg howled, raised his mallet, and charged.

Pritchard drew and fired in less than the blink of an eye, shooting the giant Russian between the eyes. His gargantuan body fell to the ground with a resounding thud. His large mallet thudded next to him.

McKinnon gasped and went to his knees alongside his giant dead friend. His head slumped, as he patted Oleg's lifeless back.

"He was a gentle soul, at heart," McKinnon said softly.

"Sergeant Greenwald would disagree," Bonner said, "if he could."

McKinnon's head snapped up. He glared hotly at Bonner but said nothing.

"I'm tired, hungry, and plumb angry," Pritchard said, facing McKinnon, Ned, and the half-dozen surviving members of Marleaux's gang. Bonner moved to stand next to him.

Two men, a lawman and a bounty hunter, stood shoulder-to-shoulder. Each were wearing a pair of Colts at their hips and resolute expressions on their faces.

"Drop them guns," Pritchard said, "or make your play. But do it quick, or I'm gonna start shootin'."

"You might as well keep your gun, Ned," Bonner said. "I'm going to kill you no matter what you do, just like I told you I would."

Ned dropped his revolver and raised his hands. "If'n you're a-gonna shoot me, Laird, know you're killin' an unarmed man. You told me once you never killed nobody that wasn't in battle durin' the war, or facin' you and armed. I reckon' you won't make me your first."

All six of Marleaux's remaining men made a different choice and went for their guns. One started to bring his already-drawn pistol to bear on Pritchard but never finished the act. A .45 slug fired from Samuel's right-hand pistol struck him through the breastbone, and a second from his left gun pierced the top of his head as he fell forward.

The second of Marleaux's men aimed at Bonner, but took three, fan-fired, .44s from the bounty hunter's crossdraw belt gun for his effort. He twitched as each bullet found their mark, the final one entering his chin. He was dead before he hit the barroom floor.

The third of Marleaux's men to refuse to surrender almost got off a shot. He'd just thumbed the hammer of his revolver back when he succumbed, like his two companions, to the lightning-fast, and deadly accurate, fire from Pritchard's Colts. A pair of simultaneously-fired bullets tore into his chest. He dropped his gun, sunk to the ground, and began his death rattle.

The final trio of Marleaux's men were cut down in a hail of gunfire from the rifles belonging to the former prisoners who'd entered the saloon with Bonner. Their riddled bodies flopped to the floor.

"How about you, McKinnon?" Pritchard said, through the haze of gunsmoke, which now filled the room. "Care to try your hand?"

"Perhaps with Laird," McKinnon said. He grinned, stood up, and unbuckled his guns. "But not with you, Marshal Pritchard. You've got the hands of the devil."

Bonner motioned to the miners, who already had chains ready. McKinnon and Ned were manacled and their guns collected.

Rebecca ran to the formerly captive comfort house women, and they all swarmed around her. Many began crying.

"Is it true?" a pretty young woman asked Pritchard. "Are we finally free?"

"It's true, all right," he said. "You're free." The crying then became general among the women, their tears mixing relief with joy.

"Marshal Pritchard!" a breathless miner suddenly burst in through the saloon doors. "Best come outside, quick!"

"What's the trouble?" he asked. He and Bonner were busy reloading their guns.

"Up on the hill," the miner said. They followed him from the saloon.

The miner pointed with his rifle to the crest of the valley, where the sun was just beginning to rise. "Indians! A helluva lot of 'em!"

CHAPTER FORTY-THREE

"They're Sioux," Pritchard said, shielding his eyes from the rising sun. He scanned the ridge above on all sides of the valley. "And there's plenty of 'em."

"What're we gonna do?" the miner asked.

"Get everybody down to the storehouse," Pritchard ordered, "pronto. Fortify the doors, distribute ammo, take up positions all around the building, and be ready. It won't be very long before they're on us."

"Wouldn't it be better to ford up here at the saloon?" Bonner asked.

"I don't reckon so," Pritchard answered. "There's only one passable trail into this valley, and it comes out in the middle of town. That's where this saloon is, and in here we're surrounded by other buildings which'd give the Sioux cover as they approached. They'd be able to attack from all sides without us seein' 'em until they were on us. The storehouse is on the opposite end of Whiskey Falls, farthest from the trail, sittin' all by itself. We'll be able to see 'em and shoot at 'em from farther out."

The miner scurried off to carry out Pritchard's orders.

"You're right," Bonner agreed. "The storehouse is also plenty big enough to hold everybody, backed up against the valley wall on one side, the creek on the other side, and the corral on still another. To get to us, they'll have to either cross the creek, navigate a herd of cows, or come straight at us over open ground. Each of those routes will make them splendid targets. Besides that, we've got plenty of food, water, and ammunition stashed in there, not to mention dynamite. If we're going to hold off an army of Sioux warriors, that's the place to do it."

"That's how I figured it," Pritchard said.

Bonner elbowed Pritchard, and pointed to the scaffold in the town square. While they were surveying the hills and debating where to make their stand, they hadn't noticed a large group of miners herding a reluctant Marleaux, McKinnon, and Ned roughly out of the saloon at gunpoint.

"What're you fellers a-doin'?" Pritchard called out.

"We're fixin' to hang Red Henry and these two of his boys," one of them shouted back.

"We haven't time for such frivolity," Pritchard retorted. "You see them Sioux braves a-comin' down the trail?"

"It won't take us but a few minutes to string 'em, Marshal."

"We ain't got a few minutes," Pritchard said. "Get 'em down to the storehouse with the others.

We can string 'em later, if we're still above ground ourselves." The miners grumbled but complied.

"Thank you," McKinnon said with an insincere smile, "for saving my life."

"Wasn't me who saved your hide this mornin'," Pritchard said. "Thank the Sioux. They'll be here soon enough."

"Might I make a suggestion, Marshal?" Marleaux said, as he was being shoved past Pritchard.

"I'm listenin'."

"The whiskey barrels," Marleaux said. "As you may remember, they're heavily-laced with laudanum. Leave them out in the middle of the main street. Who knows? Maybe the redskins will partake, and save you some bullets?"

"That's not a bad idea," Bonner said.

Pritchard gave the order, and a group of miners scurried off to set out the kegs.

"Why are you suddenly bein' so helpful?" Pritchard asked.

"I have no more desire to be scalped than you do, Marshal."

"In your case," Pritchard said, "it'll likely only be a reprieve. Even if we do fend off the Sioux, I doubt you'll fend off all the folks in Whiskey Falls you've abused. If they do to you what I watched them do to Captain Mason, you've got a right messy end comin'."

"Isn't it your duty," Marleaux said with a smug grin, "as a lawman, to see me delivered safely back to the proper authorities for trial?"

"Whyn't you ask Oleg?" Pritchard said. Marleaux's grin vanished.

While everyone hastened to the storehouse, Pritchard and Bonner returned to the creek and retrieved their saddles, taking Marleaux's satchel with them. Then they went into the corral and fetched their horses. Rusty was as happy to see Pritchard as he was to be reunited with the big Morgan. They walked their animals into the vast lot where the stolen wagons were stored and tied them to a freight cart deep within a row of dozens of others.

"That's the best we can do for 'em," Pritchard said. "If the Sioux get into the corral, steal the horses, and stampede the herd, hopefully they'll miss these two hidden out among the wagons." He hid the satchel underneath his saddle, retrieved his spyglass from his saddlebags, and they returned to the storehouse.

The storehouse was bustling with activity. Sacks of grain, bales of hay, and every type of crated goods imaginable were being piled up along the interior to create bulwarks. While men busily hacked and cut firing ports through the walls, others scrambled to barricade the big barn doors and rear door, and stack food, guns, ammunition, water barrels, and medical supplies in the center, where the women and children were assembled.

Marleaux, McKinnon, and Ned, along with the last remaining member of Marleaux's gang, the storehouse guard Pritchard had earlier taken prisoner, were seated against one wall. They were all still chained, and being watched by several armed women supervised by Rebecca Matheson. Marleaux's punctured hand had been bound, and he smiled lecherously up at Rebecca as she stood over him.

Pritchard and Bonner located their rifles, hats, and the cartridges to stoke their weapons from the abundant supply Marleaux had accrued. Pritchard stocked up on .45 for his Colts and .44-40 for his Winchester. Bonner found .44 Henry cartridges for his Open Tops, and .50-90s for his Shiloh Sharps. Some of the other men wielded .44 Henrys, Winchesters, and various rifles confiscated from wagon trains waylaid on the Oregon Trail, but most of the miners were armed with U.S. Army–issued Trapdoor Springfield carbines once belonging to Captain Mason's cavalry troopers, for which a large supply of ammunition was obviously available.

"Keep a knife handy to pry out your cartridge cases," Bonner advised those using the Springfield. He knew, as a former army officer, that the copper cases of the standard, .45-70 caliber army ammunition would expand when the Trapdoors heated up, which often occurred during rapid firing, and become stuck in the chamber. He suspected there would be much rapid firing today.

Pritchard peeked out through the slats of the main doors with his telescope. He recognized the Sioux's fringed buckskin tunics and leggings, the unique feathered headgear they wore as a symbol of honor and accomplishment, and saw they were painted up for war. He also noted only braves in the column, no women or children, and that no more than approximately half of the riders appeared to be in possession of firearms.

Pritchard collapsed his scope and examined the nearly three-hundred anxious faces looking back expectantly at him.

"Are we gonna die today?" a woman asked bluntly. He could read the same unspoken question on the faces of many others around her.

"Damned ironic, ain't it?" a man said. "We gain our freedom and lose our lives on the same day."

"We ain't lost our lives yet," Pritchard corrected. "Quiet that defeated talk. If you keep your heads about you, and your hands steady, we'll make it."

"I appreciate your confidence, Marshal," the first woman said, "but have you looked outside?"

"I have."

"There's close to a thousand of those Indians out there," she said. "We don't stand a prayer."

"What's the point?" someone else asked. "We all know how this is gonna end."

A murmur of agreement rumbled through the crowd.

Pritchard held up his hand for silence. "I know you've all had a rough time of it," he began. "Attacked and snatched off the Oregon Trail by soldiers sworn to protect you. Forced to watch as your loved ones were murdered and scalped. Dragged to this hellhole, Whiskey Falls, to serve as slaves to a madman who learned how to ply his wicked trade in the sufferin' and misery at Andersonville."

Everyone glared at Marleaux, who merely stared back in defiance.

Pritchard removed his hat. The bullet scar on his forehead, over his right eye, was once more visible to all.

"I also know you're hungry, tired, and beat down, and the last thing you figured on this mornin', after just achievin' your freedom, was bein' beset upon by a horde of warring Sioux. Some of you, perhaps those of a religious nature, are probably wonderin' why God has abandoned you? Why he chose you folks, out of all his children, to endure such torment?"

Pritchard recognized Deacon Wilson's bruised face, across the storehouse, staring at him intently.

"Truth is," Pritchard continued, "I don't know.

Nor do I care. Ain't my place to know God's business. I reckon my place, same as yours, is to play the cards he's dealt the best I can. Whether I end up busted or flush, nobody can say."

He wiped his brow and returned his hat to his head. "There's a couple hundred of us in here, and what look to be a thousand Sioux warriors out there. But we've made it this far, haven't we? We've got plenty of food, water, and cartridges, and this building is solid. I can't speak for anybody else, but I'm still game, and I'm a-gonna fight. Whether I see tomorrow's sunrise, or get finished today, I ain't a-quittin'. If this be my last day, I'll spend it on my feet, a-fightin' to the end, and won't hear another word from anybody about the fight bein' over before the first arrow's flown."

Deacon Wilson stepped forward. "The marshal's right," he said. "It's taken me a while to realize it, but God does indeed help those who help themselves. Is not our plight exactly the same as the Israelites fleeing Egypt from the persecution of the Pharaohs?"

Wilson looked up at Pritchard. "And did not God send Moses, to deliver the Israelites?"

The deacon walked over to the stack of weapons, picked up a Trapdoor carbine, pulled back the hammer, opened the gate, and inserted a cartridge.

"Been a Quaker, and a conscientious objector,

my entire life," he said. "Always thought it was wrong to kill. Henry Marleaux and Marshal Pritchard taught me different. Sometimes, to protect the innocent and to fight evil, killing is necessary. Righteous, even."

"Amen," Pritchard said.

"I was wrong about you, Marshal," Deacon Wilson said. "I'm powerful sorry for that. I hope you can forgive me."

Samuel nodded to Deacon Wilson, who returned his nod, and silently began stuffing his pockets with .45-70 cartridges from an open case.

"Hold your fire until you're sure of your targets," Bonner said, as the men began to take up their firing positions along the fortified walls. "If you need ammunition, call out, and a runner will deliver it. We're well-protected from spear and arrow in here, so aim first for those braves bearing firearms or fire. Squeeze those triggers, don't jerk 'em, and good luck."

"The Sioux just broke the trail," a lookout announced. "They're only a half mile from the edge of town."

"Welcome to Whiskey Falls," Pritchard said, topping off his Winchester.

CHAPTER FORTY-FOUR

"What's on your mind," Bonner asked Pritchard.

The big lawman stood with his hat tipped back, one hand on his hip, and the other rubbing his jaw. He was taking stock of the supplies stacked in the center of the storehouse's vast room. He paid particular attention to the cases of ammunition and dynamite.

"Just had me an idea," Pritchard answered.

"I'm listening," Bonner said.

"The way I figure," he began, "the Sioux know everyone's forded up at this end of town in the storehouse."

"Undoubtedly," Bonner said. "Their scouts must have seen the Crow abandon their positions in the hills yesterday morning, when they all came into town for the auction. I presume they've been observing Whiskey Falls continually since then."

"Which means," Pritchard went on, "they'll likely ignore the town, and start the fracas with an all-out attack on the storehouse."

"Just like the Crow did against our wagon train on the Oregon Trail," Bonner said.

"Exactly," Pritchard said. "But I'm bettin' that after we repel their first assault, the Sioux will back off, just like the Crow did. They'll retreat, probably to the town square, re-group, and come at us again."

"And again," Bonner agreed, "and again. What's your point?"

"With the food, water, and cartridges we have stockpiled, we can hold out for a few days," he said, "perhaps a week, but not indefinitely. We've got a few hundred folks to feed. I'm confident we can stave off their initial attack. But eventually, if the Sioux are determined enough, we'll either run out of ammunition, get overrun, or starve."

"Agreed," Bonner said. "What's your idea?"

"What if a few of our boys, armed with dynamite, were a-lyin' in wait back at the town square? We wouldn't hit 'em during their first assault; we'd wait until they pulled back to regroup. By then they'd be shot all to hell, bunched up together, and ripe for a proper dynamitin'."

"Where would these men hide out?" Bonner asked. "It's certain the Sioux will search the town on the way in."

"Under the stage," Pritchard said.

"Not bad," Bonner said. "Kind of like the Trojan Horse in reverse. Instead of a small band of Greeks sneaking into Troy hidden inside a wooden horse, we'd be already hiding under a wooden stage in the town square, waiting to ambush the invaders after they entered."

"I reckon," Pritchard said, "we could thin their numbers considerably."

"What about the men conducting the attack?" Bonner asked. "After they strike, they would be exposed, outside the storehouse, and have to fight their way back through what's left of the Sioux war party."

"I thought of that," Pritchard said. "It'd be no picnic, that's for sure."

"It's a worthy plan," Bonner said. "But if we're going to implement it, we'd better do it quick. The Sioux are almost here. I'll gather some volunteers, get the dynamite, and get started."

"Not a chance," Pritchard said. "You're a-stayin' here. You were a regular army officer. You know how to lead men in battle, conduct proper firing sequences, and repel a siege on a fortified position. You'll be needed to command inside this storehouse, if this ragtag band of prisoners is to successfully stave off repeated Indian attacks. I'm better off leadin' the dynamite crew. I was a horseback guerilla and Texas Ranger, remember? Gunnin' and runnin' is my specialty."

Pritchard's logic was unassailable. "All right," Bonner said. "Being that I've still got a game leg from that Crow arrow, and can't run very fast anyway, I'll stay and hold the fort. I'll allow you to go out, blast the Sioux, and get yourself killed."

"Figured you'd see it my way," Pritchard grinned. "Of course, if the Sioux end me, you won't get to collect on Cottonmouth Quincy's bounty."

"It's a wash," Bonner grinned back. "If we don't fight off the Sioux, I won't even get to collect a tomorrow."

Pritchard whistled, to get the attention of the people in the storehouse. "I'm goin' out with a case of dynamite," he announced, "to bushwhack them Sioux braves. I could use a couple of volunteers to lend a hand."

"You're going out into Whiskey Falls," Rebecca asked, "with only a few men, against all those Indians?"

"Has to be done," Pritchard said.

"I'm with you," Jorgensen said without hesitation. He stepped forward. "If it wasn't for you, Marshal, I'd be suffocatin' in that silver mine. I can shoot, and I know how to set a short fuse."

"Grab that roll of fuse then, and a case of dynamite. Who else is with me?"

No one else answered. The silence was both awkward and deafening.

"I'll go along with you, Marshal," McKinnon finally said.

"Count me in," Ned said. "If'n I'm a-gonna die, I might as well go out game."

"What about you, Henry?" Pritchard asked.

"I believe I'll stay right here," Marleaux said,

with a foul smile, "and keep Miss Matheson company, like I did last night. I'm sure she'd miss me if I left."

Rebecca kicked the seated, manacled, Marleaux squarely in the mouth. His head snapped back, then rolled forward. Blood, along with all four of his upper and lower front teeth, dribbled down his chin.

"Sorry to leave you short-handed," she said to Pritchard.

"No apology necessary," he said. "We'll manage without Henry."

"You're really going to trust McKinnon and Ned with guns?" Bonner asked. "Those boys want to end you. Hell, they both already tried."

"You wanted to end me," Pritchard said, "and I gave your gun back, didn't I?"

"True enough," Bonner admitted. "That still doesn't mean you should let Ned Konig or Daniel McKinnon get their hands on a gun."

"Got no choice," Pritchard replied. "They're some of the best shots we've got. Besides, what're they gonna do? I already told 'em if they try to come back to the storehouse without me, you'll shoot 'em on sight."

"You can bet I will," Bonner said.

Ned and McKinnon had been released from their manacles, were given back their guns, and were busy loading up with cartridges. Jorgensen and a group of a dozen miners were cutting fuse into inch-long lengths and inserting them into dynamite sticks, which they tied together in bundles of three and returned to the cases. Bonner, meanwhile, had found a ladder and posted two dozen of what he hoped were his best marksmen on the storehouse's roof, along with a case of rifle ammunition which had been hauled up by a rope.

"You boys ready?" Pritchard asked Jorgensen, Ned, and McKinnon.

"Right behind you, Marshal," Jorgensen said.

"Ready as I'll get," Ned said, "I reckon."

"I was born ready," McKinnon said.

Bonner opened the barn doors and four men scurried out. They jogged across town not on Whiskey Falls' main street, but behind the rows of buildings and tents. Pritchard carried a case of dynamite over each muscular shoulder, and Ned and McKinnon each brought Henry rifles, along with shoulder bags filled with .44 rimfire cartridges. The quartet scrambled one-hundred yards to the town square and clambered under the stage.

It was less cramped than Pritchard thought, as the four men lay on their bellies and waited for the ponies of almost one-thousand Sioux warriors to ride past. They didn't have to wait long.

"Here they come," Bonner announced. "Hold your fire until I give the order."

Just before they reached the town limits, a

bonneted chief raised his spear and released a blood-curdling howl. An instant later an army of mounted Sioux warriors coaxed their horses to a gallop and charged into Whiskey Falls.

They met no resistance when they poured into town. As they flooded in, braves on both sides of the street leaped off their horses and ran into tents and buildings. They emerged moments later, and signaled to their chief that no White-Faces had been found inside.

The whiskey kegs were located immediately, sitting out in the open around the town square with stacks of mugs. Braves whooped and howled in glee. They swarmed the barrels, smashed open their tops with their rifle butts, and eagerly drank. Those who didn't grab a mug scooped handfuls of whiskey and slurped.

Within minutes, the streets were filled with Sioux. Eventually the main body reached the storehouse, eyeing the herd of cattle and horses corralled behind it. They bunched up in a massive crowd before the storehouse, whooping and hollering. They knew the White-Faces were hiding inside, and anxiously awaited the order from their chief to attack.

"Fire!" Bonner commanded. One-hundred-and-fifty guns opened up, and over one-hundred braves, and dozens of horses, went crashing to the ground.

The Sioux's war cries intensified as their chief

gave his own order. By then, countless more braves were shot from their horses under the withering, point-blank, fusillade from inside and above the storehouse.

Bonner started, and kept up, a brutally efficient firing regimen. He posted women behind the riflemen inside the storehouse to hand them ammunition, which drastically sped up their reloading and diminished the time between shots. Consequently, their gunfire was steady, rapid, accurate, and devastating. The unspoken goal was not merely to ward off the Indian attack, but to put down as many of their attackers as possible before they retreated to the town square to re-group.

The Sioux began firing back sporadically, but the haze of dust and gunsmoke, along with the general melee of having dozens of horses and men continually falling dead all around them, prevented accurate or sustained return fire. And the large size of the Sioux war party, densely packed into such a small area, made it difficult for the shooters in the storehouse to miss.

The riflemen on the roof were especially effective. Bonner had selected them from miners who'd served in the military, were veterans of the war on either side, or claimed to be proficient hunters. With a bird's-eye view from above the battle, and unimpeded by the dust and smoke at ground level, they unleashed a blistering volley of accurate fire down upon the attacking Sioux.

One of the first to fall at the hands of the rooftop sharpshooters was the chief. Again, with their crow's-nest perspective, they could easily identify the Sioux leaders and chieftains by their elaborate bonnets, similar in purpose to the uniform insignia worn by American and European military officers to distinguish their rank.

But where the rooftop marksmen were most effective, was in countering attempts by the Sioux to burn the storehouse. Every time a group of braves attempted to light a fire, to provide flame to those warriors with resin-soaked arrows, they were instantly cut down. At the first sign of flame, a rifleman would take aim and extinguish that flame by extinguishing the man attempting to wield it.

So effective were the rooftop riflemen, that Bonner diverted another twenty armed men from the two sides of the storehouse under the least onslaught and sent them up the ladder. He also sent up another case of .45-70 ammunition.

Within fifteen minutes of the start of the attack, no more mounted Sioux could even get near the storehouse. There were simply too many dead horses and corpses piled up on the perimeter around the building. The horsemen trying to navigate their mounts through the carnage made ridiculously easy targets, and were cut down like ripened wheat under a farmer's scythe.

Warriors on foot then attacked en masse, but were slowed as they advanced for the same reason. They stumbled over the carcasses of warrior and horse alike and were easily repelled. Hundreds of them joined their fellow braves in death.

They were also slowed considerably by Marleaux's tainted whiskey. It became obvious, early on in the battle, that many of the braves were becoming lethargic. They were stumbling, and in some cases, collapsing, even before struck by bullets.

The now-reinforced rooftop sharpshooters continued to be incredibly successful in their efforts to decimate the ranks of the Sioux war party. By the time a surviving chieftain signaled for the warriors to retreat, less than an hour after the first bullet was fired, over four-hundred Sioux braves, and over two-hundred horses, lay dead or dying on the ground before the storehouse. Four of those braves were killed at the hands of Deacon Wilson.

The rooftop shooters continued to pick off Sioux as they retreated down the main street, back toward the town square. The firing gradually stopped, but only because there were no more targets left in-range to shoot. The silence, after almost a constant hour of gunfire, was stark.

A rousing chorus of cheers broke out among the men and women in the storehouse.

"Anybody hit?" Bonner called out. No one answered. Another round of cheers ensued.

"We sure as hell showed 'em!" a man hollered.

"We must've killed half of 'em!" another man shouted.

"Bring 'em on!" still another bellowed.

"We can do this all day," a voice triumphantly yelled, "and twice on Sunday!"

"Keep your heads about you," Bonner ordered. "Reload, and stand ready for another attack." He walked along the firing line, patting men on the shoulder and reassuring them. "We'll likely be hearing some blasting soon," he said, "from the vicinity of the town square, so don't be alarmed. Keep a sharp eye out for the marshal when he returns. You boys at the gate be prepared to let him in."

Bonner walked over to Rebecca and gave her a reassuring smile.

"Does Samuel have a prayer of getting back here alive?" she asked.

"We'll know soon enough," he said.

CHAPTER FORTY-FIVE

The remaining Sioux warriors, almost five-hundred of them, thundered back into the town square from the rout at the storehouse. They created a massive dust cloud as they rode in and dismounted. Pritchard, Ned, Jorgensen, and McKinnon were hiding under the big wooden stage in the middle of the square, and welcomed the additional concealment.

They'd listened to the battle at the other end of Whiskey Falls from under the stage for nearly an hour. When they heard the firing die down, they knew the Sioux were in retreat. Sure enough, no sooner had the gunfire ceased than the thunder of approaching hooves took its place. Within minutes, the town square was again filled with angry Sioux. This time, however, there were far fewer of them.

The braves were yelling and chattering at one another in their native Lakota tongue as they thirstily mobbed the whiskey kegs again. Throngs of Sioux warriors shoved and pushed one-another as they competed for access to the liquor barrels.

"I reckon they're about as bunched up as they're gonna get," Pritchard whispered. "You fellers ready?" In response he got three grim nods, and Jorgensen lit a cigar.

"All right, boys," he said. "You each know what to do. Let's give 'em hell!"

Pritchard, Ned, Jorgensen, and McKinnon slithered out from under the stage. No one noticed the four white men hunkered down behind it, the billowing dust cloud concealing them. The braves were occupied by arguing over the whiskey, taking out their frustration on one another at having their attack on the storehouse so effectively thwarted.

More than a few warriors who'd consumed the laudanum-tainted whiskey before the battle had already succumbed, and lay inert on the ground. Others, who'd only recently imbibed, were beginning to stagger about drunkenly in the town square.

Using his cigar, Jorgensen began lighting the bundles of dynamite that had been prepared back at the storehouse and tossing them to Pritchard. Their fuse lengths were carefully cut to allow for only a few seconds' burn. Ned and McKinnon shouldered their rifles and awaited the first detonation.

Pritchard caught each lit bundle as it was tossed to him by Jorgensen and immediately lobbed it into the pack of Sioux. The first dynamite bundle had no sooner landed when it exploded with an ear-splitting boom. Braves, horses, and dismembered parts of both flew through the air in a mushroom cloud of dirt, blood, bone, and debris. A few seconds after the first explosion the second one came, and then the third, and so on.

When the first blast ripped through the square, Ned and McKinnon began firing. They fired their repeating rifles rapidly and accurately, and with every shot a brave fell. Every few shots they stoked the loading gates of their rifles with more cartridges from the bags at their sides. This kept their weapons constantly charged, and thus continually in action.

Pritchard spread out his throws, flinging the bundles of explosive expertly into each part of the square where the Sioux were clumped the thickest. He carefully gauged the direction in which the braves fled from each blast. Consequently, after each explosion, the surviving and terrified Sioux warriors typically fled one blast by running directly into another.

There were twenty bundles of dynamite in each case. Forty times, in the span of less than ten minutes, Pritchard chucked a dynamite package into the Sioux war party. Several of the whiskey kegs also exploded in flames, dousing those braves unfortunate enough to be near them in burning liquid.

The cacophonous reports of the repeated blasts, mixed with the screams of the burning, wounded, and dying braves, baying horses, and steady gunfire from Ned's and McKinnon's rifles, belied the brutally systematic nature of their work. Like the fight at the storehouse that preceded it, the dynamite attack on the re-grouping Sioux war party was less of a battle and more of a massacre. Only a few braves were able to return fire. Those not killed outright were stunned and unaware, due to the tainted whiskey and incessant explosions, where the death raining down upon them was emanating from.

Pritchard hurled his last bundle of dynamite and drew his revolvers. When the final explosion's echo faded, there was so much dirt, dust, smoke, and debris in the now immense cloud over the town square that visibility was only a few feet in any direction. His ears were ringing, and he couldn't even see Jorgensen, only a few feet behind him, or Ned and McKinnon on either side.

Pritchard couldn't know it, but well over three-hundred Sioux braves lay dead or dying in Whiskey Falls' town square. While the majority obviously perished as a result of the explosives, more than fifty of the dead had been killed by the withering fire from McKinnon's and Ned's Henry rifles, and more than a few from Marleaux's potion.

"Jorgensen?" Pritchard called out through the haze. "Ned? McKinnon? We'd best be gettin' back to the storehouse while we've still got this blanket of dust over us. Where are you?"

"I'm right behind you, Marshal," McKinnon's Scottish-accented voice came out of the smoke.

Pritchard instantly dropped to the ground, a split-second before the sound of a pair of shots rang out. He heard Jorgensen cry out in pain.

He rolled, came up in a crouch, and fired both of his guns in the vicinity the gunfire came from. He had no way to know if he'd hit anything. All Pritchard could see, in every direction, was dust and smoke.

"Sorry, Marshal," Ned's faceless voice came out of the vapor. "We ain't goin' back to the storehouse with you. Me and Daniel will be a-leavin' Whiskey Falls directly. Don't you bother comin' after us, you hear?"

"Like Bonner told you once before," Pritchard answered, "we'll meet again."

"I hope so," McKinnon's voice replied. By the sound of it, he was already moving farther away. "You and I have a bit of a score to settle. Not to mention, there's that tempting bounty on your head."

"Whyn't you show yourself and try to take my head now?"

"Not quite yet, Marshal Pritchard. I've seen you and your guns in action. I'll bide my time, and wait for a more opportune moment."

"You mean when you can backshoot me?"

"Perhaps."

"Until our trails cross," Pritchard said.

"Over here, Marshal," Jorgensen said. Pritchard followed the sound until he found the diminutive miner lying on the ground near the stage. He'd taken a bullet to his lower leg.

"Ned shot me," Jorgensen said, tying his handkerchief around the wound to staunch the flow of blood. "That dirty, bushwhackin', skunk."

"Curse him later," Pritchard said, as he scooped him up. "We'd best get a-movin' before this smoke clears." He threw Jorgensen over his shoulder and headed back to the storehouse at a run.

CHAPTER FORTY-SIX

"Here comes the marshal!" a lookout on the roof called down.

"Open the doors," Bonner commanded, "and stand ready to fire on pursuers."

Several men moved the items barricading the big barn doors and opened them, while many others covered with their rifles. Pritchard carried Jorgensen inside the storehouse. No Sioux followed. Once inside, Pritchard set down the wounded miner, whose injury was immediately attended to by several of the women. The doors were closed the instant they entered.

"Thank you, Marshal," Jorgensen said solemnly to Pritchard. "That's twice in one day you saved my life."

"It'll cost you a beer," Pritchard smiled, as he caught his breath.

"Watched the whole shooting-match from the roof," Bonner said. He handed Pritchard his telescope. "Your plan worked magnificently. You four men, alone, decimated several-hundred Sioux warriors."

"That dynamite surely came in handy," Pritchard agreed. "From what I saw on the way in, it looks like you got your share of scalps at

377

this end, too. I had to run over a field of carcasses to get back in here. Ain't seen this many dead in one place since the war."

"It was a turkey shoot," Bonner admitted. "They came in all together, as we expected, and bunched up right in front of the storehouse. Practically begged to get shot. Reminded me of Fredericksburg."

"Between the two of us," Pritchard said, "you here in the storehouse, and me in the square, I reckon we damn-near wiped most of them Sioux out."

"That was quite a dust cloud you put up," Bonner said, "but from what I could tell through your spyglass there couldn't be more than a hundred braves left. Many of those appear to be wounded or under the influence of Marleaux's poisoned liquor. They turned tail, headed back up the trail, and departed Whiskey Falls in a hurry."

"You're welcome," Marleaux said to them.

"What have we to thank you for?" Pritchard said.

"My dynamite, gunthz, and cartridgeth, of courth," the lisping Marleaux said through his missing teeth. "Without what wath in thith store-houth, you'd all be dead."

"You'll get no gratitude from me," Pritchard said, "nor anyone else. You'd be dead, too, if'n it wasn't for us."

"Where's Konig and McKinnon?" Bonner asked.

"After we blasted the Sioux to perdition," Pritchard said, "but before the dust settled, they turned on us. McKinnon tried to gun me, and Ned shot Jorgensen. Those two snakes then slunk away in the smoke. I'm guessin' they've rounded up a couple of mounts by now, and are makin' tracks out of Whiskey Falls to Promontory."

"Why not head to Fort Hall?" Bonner said. "It's only forty miles northwest from here. If they rode hard enough, they could be there in a day or two. Promontory's almost a-hundred miles south."

"Because Ned's smart," Pritchard answered. "He knows the Cheyenne are gettin' ready to mount a campaign against the army and are likely circlin' Fort Hall, a-waitin' to strike. He also knows something the soldiers at Fort Hall don't. Half of the troops who were stationed there—"

"Captain Mason's men and his Crow contingent," Bonner cut in, "are a-rottin' away at the bottom of a mine. They ain't gonna be any help stavin' off Indian attacks. Ned and McKinnon don't want to get caught in Fort Hall and face another one. Also, the rail line's in Promontory. They can head south and make for California."

"So what's our next move?" Jorgensen said.

"Our next move, Pritchard said, looking at the anxious faces of the men, women, and children in the storehouse staring at him expectantly, "is to move out."

"Now?" a woman asked.

379

"But we're safe in here," another woman offered, "and we've plenty of food. Why would we leave now?"

"Shouldn't we at least rest a while?" a man asked. "We just dug our way out of a mine, fought off an army of Sioux, and most of us ain't slept in a couple of days."

"We ain't got a couple of days," Pritchard said, "and we ain't gonna be safe in here for long. Those Sioux we just fought off ain't gonna take a clobberin' sittin' down. Not to mention, they've seen the livestock herd here in Whiskey Falls. They sure as hell ain't gonna run off and abandon it, and all the grain and plunder in this storehouse, with winter a-comin' on. They'll round up another batch of warriors, maybe even join up with the Cheyenne, and be back in Whiskey Falls in a day or two. If'n we want to keep our scalps, we'd best move now and rest later."

"Marshal Pritchard's right," Bonner added. "They've retreated for the time being, but the Sioux aren't licked. They'll be back, and soon."

"Now's the time to make our departure," Pritchard said, "while the Sioux are on their heels. If we push hard, and leave the herd behind, we can be in Promontory in four or five days."

"What if we encounter more Sioux or Cheyenne on the trail?" a man asked.

"Chances are," Pritchard explained, "if we do encounter a war party on the trail, it'd likely be a small one; no more than a hundred braves, at most. That's if'n we leave now, and get out of this valley before they can muster in force. We've a couple of hundred rifles ourselves, and we'd be able to repel such an attack. But if we wait here and give the Sioux time to join up with other war parties, they could easily have a couple of thousand warriors mustered."

"And the next war party surely won't fall for the same tricks," Bonner said. "They won't bunch up and attack this storehouse all at once, like before, nor let themselves be dynamited. They'll slink in, in small groups, and hit us continually, all day and all night. They'd eventually wear us down and burn us out. That's a fact."

"You heard the marshal," Deacon Wilson called out to everyone. "If you all want to keep your hair, we'd best get to work. It isn't yet noon; there's plenty of daylight left." Pritchard gave the deacon a nod of approval.

And work they did. Carrying their guns, work crews left the storehouse. Teams of men were tasked with moving the hundreds of bodies to clear the road, filling barrels of water from the creek, collecting wagons from the vast lot of stolen carts, rounding up horses and oxen to pull them, and hitching the animals up. A pair of lookouts were posted on the storehouse roof, given Pritchard's telescope, and orders to alert everyone at the first sign of the Sioux's return.

Once a wagon was hitched and ready, it was steered past the creek to collect water, then driven to the storehouse where it was loaded with food, ammunition, and other critical supplies from Marleaux's stash of stolen goods.

Pritchard and Bonner left unobserved, retrieved their saddles and horses, the bag of cash from Marleaux's auction, and the two sets of saddlebags stuffed with money from the creek. At Pritchard's insistence they loaded the three bags of money, unnoticed due to the bustle of activity, into the back of the wagon Rebecca and Jorgensen were to ride in.

Pritchard pulled Jorgensen and Rebecca discretely aside. "Once we're on the road, I want you two to count it," he told them, as they stared wide-eyed at the money. "We'd best know how much there is before we turn it over to the government."

By evening, the exhausted people of Whiskey Falls had loaded up and were ready to depart. Fifty wagons were lined up on the road. All the men, women, and children had boarded and were awaiting the signal to go.

"Are you sure getting started before dark is a good idea?" Bonner asked Pritchard. "Perhaps we should wait until morning?"

"I don't like travelin' by prairie schooner at night any more'n you do," Pritchard said, "especially up and over that narrow pass out of the valley. But there's a solid moon, no clouds, and now that we've loaded up all our supplies into the wagons, we have to go. If we were attacked now, we couldn't get much more than ourselves back into the storehouse before bein' set upon."

"You're right," Bonner conceded. "Now that we're packed, we need to get out of this valley and onto flat ground if we're going to defend ourselves."

"Then let's quit jawin' and get movin'," Pritchard said. He mounted Rusty, signaled to the lead wagon carrying Rebecca and Jorgensen, and waved his hat to the lookouts still on the storehouse roof to come down.

Pritchard was about to give the command to move out when one of the lookouts began excitedly shouting.

"Injuns!" he yelled, his eyes glued to Pritchard's spyglass. "On the ridge over the valley! Thousands of 'em!

CHAPTER FORTY-SEVEN

"They're Cheyenne," Bonner announced, as he squinted through the compact telescope, "with what look to be some Lakota Sioux. And the lookout was right; there're thousands of them."

Bonner and Pritchard had gone up to the roof after ordering the people to dismount the wagons, unload the supplies as quickly as they could, return to the storehouse, and prepare for another attack.

"Why do you suppose," Bonner asked, already knowing the answer, "there's suddenly such a large pack of Cheyenne in the vicinity?"

"I reckon it has something to do with the Cheyenne bein' on the warpath," Pritchard said, "and musterin' for an attack on Fort Hall."

"There're too many of them," Bonner continued, handing the scope to Pritchard. "That's a plain fact. We can hold them off for a while, but not forever. A couple of days, at best. They're going to defeat us this time, and they know it."

Pritchard scanned the ridge and found nothing to contradict Bonner's declaration.

"You thinkin' about makin' a run for it?" Pritchard asked. "A solo horseman just might sneak his way out of Whiskey Falls unnoticed once the fight commences."

"And leave Rebecca and the rest of these folks to die?" Bonner retorted. "What kind of a man do you take me for?"

"One who was going to kill me for money."

"Haven't done it yet, have I?"

"That's only because so many others have been tryin' to do it for you," Pritchard said, collapsing the spyglass.

"So what's our plan this time?" Bonner asked, changing the subject. "You can bet those Cheyenne are going to learn from what the Sioux told them about this morning's battle. They won't bunch up and make polite targets for our bullets or dynamite."

"I don't know what 'our' plan is," Pritchard said, "but 'my' plan, is to go out, meet their chief, and try to parlay for our scalps."

"Are you insane? After what we did to their fellow warriors earlier today you'll be scalped on the spot. Besides, you don't have anything to trade with."

"Maybe not," Pritchard said, "but if'n I don't at least try, I'm gonna end up done in and minus my hair anyways, ain't I? And as far as trade goods you've played poker, haven't you?"

"I have."

"Then you know it ain't the cards you're holdin' that count," Pritchard said, "it's the cards your opponent thinks you're a-holdin'."

"I can't argue that," Bonner conceded.

Pritchard and Bonner descended the ladder.

"Stay here and prepare to fight," Pritchard announced to the expectant people in the storehouse. "I'm goin' out to meet with them Indians." He plucked a white cloth from a stack of bandages cut up from sheets before the first battle and tied it to the muzzle of his Winchester. Then he made sure the weapon was fully-loaded, checked his revolvers, and started for the door.

"You aren't really going out to negotiate with those savages, are you?" Deacon Wilson asked.

"You and Reverend Farley tried to talk me into doin' it once before," Pritchard said. "Figured I'd take your advice this time."

"I don't think that's a good idea," Wilson said.

"I don't either," Rebecca said.

"Hell," Pritchard said, lowering his voice to ensure others didn't hear, "neither do I. But if there's a chance it might work, I've gotta try. Truth is, we ain't got a prayer against that many braves."

"I once compared you to Moses," Wilson said, "when we were trapped in the mine, and you delivered us. You delivered us this morning, too. But honestly, Marshal, I think Moses had a better chance at parting the Red Sea than you'll have at reaching an accord with those savages."

"They might not be as savage as you think," Pritchard said. "Either way, I reckon I'm about to find out."

Pritchard nodded for the men at the door to open it. He walked out to Rusty and mounted up. To his surprise, Bonner followed him and mounted his horse as well.

"Where're you goin'?" Pritchard asked him.

"With you," he answered, drawing his Shiloh-Sharps rifle and laying it across his pommel. "There's a bounty on your head, remember? I've got to protect my investment."

"Suit yourself," Pritchard said.

The duo rode through the abandoned town of Whiskey Falls, passing scores of stacked bodies on a dirt road stained brown with blood. Pritchard held his rifle up with one arm, resting the stock on his thigh, as they slowly left the town and began to ascend the grade up the valley wall. The sun was just beginning to touch the crest of the ridge.

Up ahead, they watched as a group of fifteen riders began descending the trail to meet them. Twenty minutes later they were face-to-face with thirteen mounted Cheyenne warriors and a pair of Sioux braves.

Pritchard and Bonner halted their horses and allowed their counterparts to ride up to them. All but one of the Indians were painted for war and carried rifles, not spears or bow, which they directed at the pair. The one without a weapon was very old, and sat on a painted horse in the rear of the pack, where he couldn't be easily seen.

The leader was obvious by his long, feathered, bonnet. "I am Iron Sky, of the Dog Men," he said, in passable English. "You ride under a white flag."

"I am Samuel," Pritchard said. "I ask you to hear my words, Iron Sky."

"You have no words I wish to hear," Iron Sky said. "I have come to kill you, and your soldiers, and the Crow who slay my people."

"They are not my soldiers," Pritchard said. "I, and the people down in the village of Whiskey Falls with me, were set upon by those same soldiers, and their Crow allies, as your people have been. We were made slaves and forced to work in the mine."

"Where are the soldiers?"

"We defeated them, and the Crow who rode with them. We won our freedom. Their bodies lie deep in the mine."

Iron Sky looked to one of the Sioux. He nodded in affirmation.

"What is it you want, Samuel?"

"I want my life, and the lives of those with me. We are not soldiers, and have only killed to protect our scalps. We are slaves, women, and children."

"You are no slave, Big One," Iron Sky said. "You, and the one who rides with you, are warriors."

"We've been such in the past," Pritchard admitted.

"You killed many Sioux today," Iron Sky said.

"The Sioux attacked us," Pritchard said. "They gave us no chance to speak, as you and I are speakin' now."

"If I give you your lives," Iron Sky said, "what do I get in return?"

"We'll give you the entire herd; over a thousand head of cattle. We will also give you all the grain and food in the storehouse. Your people will not starve this winter."

"These things you offer," Iron Sky said, "I can take without giving your lives."

"True enough," Pritchard said. "But if we are to die, we will fight. Look below, at the countless dead Sioux in the valley before you. To defeat us, you will lose a great many of your Dog Men. These are warriors you will need to fight the White-Face army."

"My warriors are not afraid to die."

"Didn't say they were," Pritchard said, "but I reckon if they don't have to, they don't want to. If you attack us, Iron Sky, you will win. We know this. So we will have no need for the food in our possession. I will have my people burn the storehouse, and all the grain and food within it, before you defeat us. I will also have them shoot all the cattle, which means you will have meat, but not nearly as much, since you will have to carry it with you as you travel instead of drivin' it. Your people's bellies will be empty this winter. Do you want your people to go hungry?"

"My people have known great hunger," Iron Sky said.

"They have," the old Indian in the rear of the group suddenly spoke up. He rode forward. "As you well know, Samuel of the White-Faces."

It was Avanaco, the elder Cheyenne he'd met on the Oregon Trail. Pritchard smiled and waved.

"Haaahe, Avanaco," Pritchard said. It was suddenly clear to him that the ancient Cheyenne was the true chief, and not the bonneted Iron Sky. Bonner looked quizzically at Pritchard.

"I told you your gift would not be forgotten," Avanaco said, smiling back.

"You also warned me to 'beware the falling whiskey,' " Pritchard said. "I didn't know what you meant, Great Chief, until I was captured and brought here to Whiskey Falls."

"This is a place of evil," Avanaco said. "The spirits here scream in the night."

"No longer," Pritchard said. "We have silenced them."

Avanaco spoke in Algonquian to Iron Sky, who nodded in deference.

"Take your people," Iron Sky said to Pritchard and Bonner, "and go. Leave at dawn, and do not return. Do not take the herd, and take only the food you will need for your journey. Do not go to the place called Fort Hall. If you do, you will perish."

"I thank you, Iron Sky," Pritchard said, "for

your kindness and mercy. We will leave much that your people can use, and will do as you say; we will not go to the fort. We will go south, and return to your lands no more." Iron Sky merely nodded again.

"And one more thing," Pritchard said. "Do not let your people drink the whiskey in town. It has been tainted."

"So we have learned," Avanaco said. "Good-bye, Samuel of the White-Faces."

Pritchard said, "Good luck."

Pritchard and Bonner were met by Deacon Wilson and Rebecca at the storehouse door when they returned.

"What happened?" Wilson asked.

"Remember that ancient Cheyenne brave we found a-starvin' on the Oregon Trail," Pritchard asked, "along with them squaws and kids?"

"I remember," Wilson said. "You gave them two of our stock."

"He's the Cheyenne Chief. Let that sink in, Deacon."

"Thanks to Marshal Pritchard," Bonner announced to everyone, "it looks like we'll get to keep our scalps." A chorus of cheers broke out.

"Not a bad bargain," Pritchard said to the deacon, "for the price of a couple of cows."

CHAPTER FORTY-EIGHT

It took five days for Pritchard, Bonner, and the other refugees from Whiskey Falls to reach Promontory. Pritchard pushed the wagon train hard. Without a herd of cattle to slow them, the travelers easily made twenty miles a day.

When one of the men, a cattleman before being kidnapped and imprisoned at Whiskey Falls, complained about allowing the Cheyenne to keep all the livestock, Pritchard merely asked him, "Which would you rather keep? Them cows or your scalp?"

The wagon train was fortunate in only encountering one squall on their third day south. Heavy rains were feared as much as snow, as a sodden trail would bog down the wagons and slow their progress.

But the rain passed in an hour, and the wagons steadily moved forward. Pritchard and Bonner took turns scouting ahead, armed men kept a watchful eye, and the train slogged south. The pilgrims ate sparsely from the stores of canned goods and other sundries they'd packed, and weren't bothered by the need to cook beef each night, since they had no stock to slaughter.

Few complained. All had been subsisting on

meals of beef-laced gruel, even the women and children, for the duration of their stay in Whiskey Falls. Jerky, canned vegetables, and jarred preserves were a welcome addition to their diet.

Rebecca Matheson and Jorgensen surreptitiously counted the money inside the covered wagon, then packed it all inside a box filled with linen. They discretely reported to Pritchard and Bonner the amount; over one-hundred-and-seventy-eight-thousand dollars. A tremendous fortune, collected in blood, suffering, misery, and death by Henry Marleaux during his reign in Whiskey Falls.

Marleaux himself remained shackled, riding alone in the back of a wagon filled with sacks of feed grain for the horses.

Pritchard also asked Jorgensen and Rebecca to compile a list of names of everyone in the company, and the names of those, to the best of the survivor's remembrance, who had died at the hands of Captain Mason on the trail or under Marleaux's cruelty at Whiskey Falls.

Just before noon, on the fifth day after they departed Whiskey Falls, Pritchard halted the wagon train. They'd reached Promontory Summit and beheld the town below. The tracks of the Transcontinental Railroad and the Central Pacific Railroad Station beckoned to them.

A chorus of cheers broke out among the travelers. Some laughed and danced, others cried and held each other. Henry Marleaux looked glum. Deacon Wilson approached Pritchard, who had dismounted Rusty to stretch his legs.

"You delivered us," the deacon said. "Just like Moses. Our prayers were answered." A crowd of grateful people swarmed around Pritchard.

"I believe it was guts and bullets," Pritchard said to them, "and not prayers, that brought us deliverance. But I reckon the prayers were helpsome, too."

"Thank you, Samuel," the deacon said. They shook hands.

"Gather around, everybody," Pritchard ordered. He nodded to Jorgenson, who brought out the cash box. He opened it to reveal the contents for all to see.

"There's almost one-hundred-and-eighty-thousand dollars in this box," he announced to the assembled pilgrims. "It's the blood money Red Henry Marleaux collected in Whiskey Falls."

The crowd collectively gasped and whistled. It was more money than any of them had ever seen in one place.

"I figure this money can go one of two ways," Pritchard went on. "I can take it all down into Promontory, turn it over to the marshal, and let the territorial courts decide who's to get what. It could take months to settle claims. I reckon most of you folks don't fancy lingerin' in the Utah Territory all winter."

The crowd murmured and nodded in agreement.

Everyone wanted to either get back home to where they'd come from, or go on to where they were headed, before being waylaid on the Oregon Trail and diverted to Whiskey Falls.

"The other way this could go," Pritchard continued, "is I could divvy up this money among you now? There's two-hundred-and-sixty-two folks here. That reckons out to about seven-hundred dollars per person. Some of you might have had more than that when you started out on the Oregon Trail, but I reckon most of you had less, otherwise you'd have been takin' the train west instead of goin' by wagon. This cash might get you where you're a-goin', and perhaps give you a stake when you get there. You can buy a train ticket down there in Promontory, be on your way, and put the memory of Whiskey Falls behind you. I'll leave it up to you."

"We'll take the money now, Marshal," a man said.

"Hell, yeah!" another said. Everyone else enthusiastically agreed.

"Start divvyin' it up," Pritchard told Rebecca. People lined up, and she and Jorgensen began counting out and distributing the money. "Don't hold out any for me," he said. "Put my share into the pot and dole it out."

"Right generous of you," Bonner said to Pritchard. "Distribute my share, as well," he told Rebecca. She smiled at him.

"Too generouth, if you athk me," Marleaux lisped through his missing teeth. He jumped up from where he sat fuming in anger as Rebecca and Jorgensen handed out the cash.

"Thath my money," he snarled, spraying slobber. "You have no authority to give it away to theeth peathants, you filthy bathtards!"

"Shut your yam-hole, Henry," Pritchard said, "or you'll surrender more teeth."

"Speaking of Red Henry," Bonner said. "Do you remember us discussing the ten-thousand-dollar bounty on his head?"

"I recall the conversation," Pritchard said. "I also recall a conversation about a twenty-thousand-dollar bounty Cottonmouth Quincy put up on my scalp. Which if I ain't mistaken, was what brung you out on the Oregon Trail, posin' as a U.S. Marshal, to begin with."

"I was thinking," Bonner said, ignoring Pritchard's jab, "if I collected the ten-thousand-dollar bounty on Marleaux, I might be persuaded to return the ten-thousand-dollar down-payment Cottonmouth Quincy gave me as an advance on the twenty-thousand to put you down?"

"Why not just kill me," Pritchard said, "and take Red Henry in? You could walk away thirty-thousand-dollars richer?"

"I've considered that," Bonner said.

Pritchard turned slightly to face Bonner. His giant frame appeared relaxed, his expression was neutral, and both of his hands hung loosely at his sides. His thumbs lightly brushed the case-hardened steel of his holstered Colt revolvers. But to Bonner's trained eye, the big marshal looked anything but tranquil.

Bonner laughed. "I could put you down, all right," he said. "But I've grown to like you, Samuel Pritchard. I believe I'll allow you to live."

"Right generous of you," Pritchard said evenly.

"You've done something I thought impossible," Bonner continued. "You've restored a bit of my lost faith in humanity. That was no small feat. Not to mention, I'm indebted to you. I didn't forget about you saving my life. Besides, the way I figure, my life's worth more to me than twenty-thousand, anyway. Also, Rebecca might get mad at me if I ended you."

"She just might, at that," Pritchard agreed.

Bonner stuck out his hand. Pritchard nodded once and shook it.

"You figure there's a federal marshal down in Promontory to turn Henry over to?" Jorgensen asked.

"Don't need a federal marshal in Promontory," Bonner said, drawing one of his Open Top Colts. "You're a federal marshal, aren't you, Samuel?"

"I am," Pritchard confirmed.

"All I need to do is turn in Red Henry Marleaux's head," Bonner said. "To hell with

397

the rest of him. Samuel and I can swear out statements it's his noggin, and then we're ten-thousand-dollars richer."

"Luggin' in Henry Marleaux's brain-bucket is certainly preferable to luggin' him in alive," Pritchard said. "It would spare folks the grief and expense of a trial."

"That's a fact," Bonner said, as he thumbed the hammer back.

"Thtop!" Marleaux pleaded. He held up his manacled palms. "You can't juth thoot me in cold blood! You're a lawman, Marthal Pritthard! You have to take me in to the authoriteeth!"

All of the two-hundred-and-sixty-two former prisoners of Whiskey Falls stopped what they were doing to behold the spectacle.

"Don't shoot him," a woman said to Bonner.

"She's right," a man said. "You can't just plug him."

"It wouldn't be right," another said.

"Thee what I mean?" Marleaux exclaimed triumphantly. "These folkth are Christianth. They won't allow you to exthecute me. They underthtand the conthept of merthy."

"Mercy, hell," Rebecca spoke up. "Shooting Red Henry is too quick an end. He deserves to suffer for what he's done."

"Hell, yes!" a man shouted.

"String him," another man yelled, "like he strung my brother!"

"Let him dangle!" a women hollered. Everyone else joined in, shouting their concurrence.

"So much for Christian mercy," Pritchard said to Marleaux. "Somebody fetch a rope."

Bonner shrugged, lowered his revolver's hammer, and holstered it. "Fine by me," he said, "as long as you folks don't damage his head."

CHAPTER FORTY-NINE

Lieutenant Red Henry Marleaux, former executive officer at Andersonville, and former mayor of Whiskey Falls, was hanged from the bough of a cottonwood tree overlooking Promontory. He howled, shrieked, sputtered, and spat as he was put upon a horse and a noose was looped around his neck.

"I curth you all to hell!" he raged, as those he'd once enslaved and abused stood witness to his impending hanging.

"I condemn you, Henry Marleaux," Pritchard said, "to the flames of hell for what you've done to the poor souls who perished in Whiskey Falls, and for the crimes against those you couldn't murder who stand before you today. I ain't a-gonna ask God to have mercy on your soul. 'Tween you and me, I hope the Devil's stokin' his fires with fresh-dug coal."

"Roast in hell, Red Henry," Bonner added, "for those at Andersonville."

Pritchard slapped the horse's flank. All watched in rapt silence as the horse trotted out from under a wide-eyed Marleaux.

Since he wasn't dropped from a gallows, and his neck instantly broken, he struggled mightily.

He flailed and kicked, dancing at the end of the rope, as his face discolored and his tortured gasps transformed into a death rattle. It took over a minute of agony for Red Henry Marleaux to finally depart the earthly plane.

Pritchard ordered the others away while he and Bonner cut down Marleaux's corpse. Bonner beheaded it with an axe, drained the grisly trophy, and stuffed it into a burlap bag which he lashed to his saddle. A crew of men hastily buried what was left, and the wagon train continued on into Promontory.

Townsfolk came out to stare as fifty wagons, bearing over two-hundred-and-fifty gaunt, exhausted, and jubilant travelers, rolled into town. Pritchard and Bonner made straight for the marshal's office. Bonner carried his burlap bag over his shoulder.

Both men swore out statements to the marshal that the head in the burlap bag belonged to Former Confederate Army Lieutenant Red Henry Marleaux, wanted by the U.S. Government for war crimes committed during his time as the executive officer of the Andersonville prison camp. The marshal, a salty old lawman named Corbett, took their statements, but told Bonner and Pritchard that while he didn't doubt their word, he had a better way to verify their claim.

Marshal Corbett explained that the town's blacksmith had been imprisoned in Andersonville during the war. He sent a local boy to the forge to fetch him.

While they waited, Pritchard got directions to the telegraph office. A few minutes later, a burly fellow about Bonner's age entered the marshal's office. His face and hands were covered in sweat and soot.

"What's goin' on, Marshal?" the blacksmith asked.

"Sorry to trouble you, Mike," Corbett said, motioning for Pritchard and Bonner to be silent. "If'n you don't mind, would you take a look inside that there burlap bag on my desk? It's only fair to warn you, there's a man's head in there."

"A man's head?" the blacksmith asked incredulously.

"Yup," the marshal drawled, as if disembodied heads in burlap bags on his desk were a daily occurrence.

"What for?"

"I'd surely like to know if you recollect the name of the feller who was once attached to that head."

"Why ask me?"

"Indulge me, will you Mike?"

"Whatever you say, Marshal," the blacksmith said. He approached the desk, peeled back the burlap, and his eyebrows lifted. He looked over at Pritchard and Bonner.

"You know him?" Corbett asked.

"This here's Lieutenant Henry Marleaux," the blacksmith said without batting an eye. "Or what's left of him. Red Henry, we used to call him at Andersonville. He was in charge under Captain Wirz. He enjoyed our sufferin'."

"You sure about that?" Corbett asked.

"I'd know that face till the day I die," the blacksmith said.

"That'll be all," Marshal Corbett said. "Thanks for stoppin' by, Mike."

"Did you kill him?" the blacksmith asked Pritchard and Bonner. Pritchard nodded.

"How'd he die?"

"Exactly the way a polecat like him should've," Pritchard said. "Danglin' from a tree and dancin' like a piñata dodgin' a stick."

"Wish I could've been there to see it," the blacksmith said, and walked out.

"I'll wire the federal government," Corbett said, wrapping the burlap bag back up. "You boys should have your money within a couple of days."

"Give it all to him," Pritchard said, pointing at Bonner with a thumb. "I've got a wire of my own to send out."

"Suit yourselves," Corbett said.

"Tell me, Marshal," Pritchard asked, "you haven't had a couple of strangers ride into town the last couple of days, have you?"

"Promontory is a railroad town, Marshal

Pritchard," Corbett said. "We get strangers passin' through all the time. What do these two fellers look like?"

"One of 'em's a little Scotsman, wears a bowler hat and a pair of revolvers slung low. The other is a scruffy-lookin' feller about fifty, with a beard. They would've come in by horseback together, not more'n two days ago."

"Seems like I've seen a couple of fellers like that, but in truth, I can't be sure. Lotta folks come and go around here. You might try askin' down at the hotel and saloon."

"It's only fair to warn you," Pritchard said, "that these two fellers are associates of Marleaux's, and wanted for attempted murder. If'n I locate 'em, there's likely to be gunplay."

"Who'd they try to murder?" Corbett asked.

"Me, and Bonner here, and everybody else who came in on that wagon train."

"You two look like you can handle yourselves," Corbett said. "Try not to shoot any bystanders, and have at 'em. Jail's here, and the undertaker's office is down the street, by the livery."

"I like the way you conduct business, Marshal Corbett," Pritchard said. He and Bonner thanked the lawman and left his office.

"You don't really think Ned and McKinnon are still here in Promontory, do you?" Bonner asked, once they got outside.

"Where're they gonna go?" Pritchard answered.

"They left Whiskey Falls with only a half-day's start on us. Even figurin' that a pair of horsemen can ride faster than a wagon train, they couldn't have arrived more'n a day or two ahead of us. Neither of 'em had any money that I know of, so I doubt they could afford a train ticket. I reckon it's more'n likely they're still here in Promontory, tryin' to scrape up enough for a stake to get out."

"If they're in Promontory," Bonner said, "you can bet they know we are, too. Everybody in town watched our wagon train pull in."

"I reckon you're right," Pritchard said, scanning the street.

Both men checked their revolvers, and each added a sixth cartridge to the cylinders of their guns.

"McKinnon's an arrogant blowhard," Bonner said, "but that doesn't mean he isn't fast out of the holster. I've seen him shoot."

"Ned ain't fast," Pritchard said, "but he's a backshooter. Ask Jorgensen."

"I guess that means we should stick together for a bit," Bonner said. "If you don't mind, of course."

"I'll tolerate your company," Pritchard said.

CHAPTER FIFTY

Pritchard and Bonner didn't have to wait long to encounter Ned Konig and Daniel McKinnon.

The lawman and bounty hunter were coming out of the telegraph office, an hour after leaving the marshal's office, when they found McKinnon standing across the street. He was leaning against the post of a saloon called the Double Deuce with a half-empty bottle of whiskey in his hand, a cigarette dangling from the corner of his mouth, and his bowler tipped to the back of his head.

Pritchard and Bonner had gone to the telegraph office to wire Governor Woodson. Pritchard tersely related what had transpired in the course of his investigation over the past few weeks, both on the Oregon Trail and in Whiskey Falls. He further advised the governor to contact the army and warn them of the impending attack on Fort Hall. He finished his wire by advising he would be returning to Missouri forthwith, on the next train east from Promontory, and would make a full report in person in Jefferson City.

Pritchard and Bonner decided to get a bath and a shave, and were heading to the Hotel Promontory to do just that, when they were confronted by McKinnon.

"Good afternoon, Marshal Pritchard," McKinnon said. "And to you, as well, Mister Bonner." His words were slightly slurred, and when he pushed himself off the post he was leaning against he swayed slightly before regaining his balance. "Fancy meeting you here."

"You know what he's doin'," Pritchard whispered to Bonner, "don't you?"

"Of course," Bonner whispered back. "Distracting us. Mind McKinnon. I've got your bobtail."

"Didn't expect to find you in Promontory," Pritchard said to McKinnon. "Thought by now you'd have skedaddled."

"I'd surely like to be gone," McKinnon admitted, "but find myself a bit short of funds to purchase a railroad ticket. Which reminds me, I heard a rumor that you gave away all of Henry Marleaux's money? You shouldn't have done that. Some of that money was mine."

"That's not a rumor," Pritchard said. "It's a fact. And it weren't your money any more than it was Marleaux's."

"I also heard you hanged Ole' Red Henry and unburdened him of his head?"

"That's also a fact. By the way, where's Ned? Last I saw, you and him were a-ridin' out of Whiskey Falls together."

"Ned's around here somewhere," McKinnon said. "I want my share, Marshal. I earned it."

"Looks like you're plum out of luck, Daniel," Pritchard said. He slowly walked toward McKinnon from across the street. Pedestrians and bystanders recognized the imminent confrontation and scattered in all directions. "Your luck ran out when you tried to shoot me in the back and missed."

"Isn't backshootin' a lawman against the law?" McKinnon said with a grin.

"It is."

"Are you going to arrest me, Marshal Pritchard?" McKinnon said.

"Nope," Pritchard said. "Gonna gun you."

"Is that legal?"

"If it ain't," Pritchard said, "it's sure enough proper."

"Good-bye, Marshal," McKinnon suddenly said. His mirth instantly disappeared, his features hardened, and his eyes looked up.

Above them, leaning out of the hotel's second floor window above the saloon, was Ned Konig. He was aiming a Henry rifle down at Pritchard.

A shot rang out, and then another. Neither came from Ned's gun.

Two rimfire .44s, fired from Laird Bonner's Open Top Colts, struck Ned Konig twice in the head—once in the mouth, and once in the forehead. He dropped his rifle and tumbled from the window, landing with a thud at McKinnon's feet.

"Thank you," Pritchard said to Bonner, over his shoulder.

"Don't mention it," Bonner said, holstering one gun and casually reloading the other.

"Looks like it's just you and me now," Pritchard said, as he took several steps closer to the Scotsman. He stopped ten paces from the diminutive gunman.

McKinnon's face turned ashen. He stared numbly down at Ned's corpse.

"You look a bit peaked," Pritchard said. "Somethin' botherin' you?"

"I should have killed you in Whiskey Falls," he mumbled, "when I had the chance."

"Too bad for you," Pritchard said, "this ain't Whiskey Falls. I ain't no unarmed Quaker."

McKinnon dropped the whiskey bottle, which shattered at his feet. "I'm not afraid of you," he said. His voice said differently.

"You're wearin' a brace of pistols," Pritchard said. "If'n you ain't afraid, use 'em."

"If I go for my guns, you'll kill me. We both know it."

"I'm a-gonna kill you anyways," Pritchard said. "Like you said, you 'earned it.' You might as well go out game, facin' me, instead of tryin' to backshoot me from behind."

McKinnon's face twisted into a snarl and he did exactly as Pritchard suggested. He reached for his guns, but didn't even clear the holsters. Two .45

slugs, fired simultaneously from Pritchard's Colts, cut the Scottish gunman down. His mouth opened but no sound came out. He slowly fell to his knees, and then onto his face. He twitched once, and moved no more.

"I must say," Bonner remarked, holstering his second reloaded revolver, "for a youngster, you're a pretty fair hand with those pistols."

"Been told that before," Pritchard said, as he reloaded.

CHAPTER FIFTY-ONE

Pritchard stepped off the train and stretched, grateful to be on solid ground again. Bonner disembarked behind him and lit a cheroot. It was a cool evening in St. Louis, and the October trees were resplendent in their autumn bloom of red, orange, yellow, and brown.

Pritchard and Bonner had been traveling for the past nine days. After squaring things with Marshal Corbett and the local magistrate in Promontory in the wake of Ned Konig's and Daniel McKinnon's deaths, they boarded an eastbound train. Five days later they got off in Omaha, unpacked their horses, and booked passage for themselves and their horses again on a riverboat heading south on the Missouri to Kansas City.

Two days later, they boarded another train in Kansas City and arrived in Jefferson City the following afternoon. There they met with Governor Silas Woodson, his Attorney General, Henry Ewing, several high-ranking army officers, and members of the governor's staff.

Over an excellent steak dinner at the governor's mansion, Pritchard reported in detail what had transpired since being dispatched by Woodson two months previously to investigate the disappearances of so many wagon trains on the Oregon Trail. Bonner, who was known to the army officers present, fully corroborated Pritchard's account.

Governor Woodson was delighted that the elusive Henry Marleaux had finally been located and brought to justice after so long as a fugitive, though deeply dismayed at the loss of life and property suffered by so many at his hands. He ordered his staff to contact the individuals on the list of the names of Whiskey Falls survivors provided by Pritchard, and obtain their statements and tabulate additional victims for the purposes of notifying next-of-kin. He had already reached out to the governors of several neighboring states by telegraph to notify them of the status of Pritchard's investigation, and offered assurances that further information on their jurisdiction's missing pilgrims would soon be forthcoming.

The army officers, one of whom was a general officer, advised the governor that robust military expeditions were already en route to reinforce Fort Hall, as well as the uncharted location Pritchard and Bonner identified as the valley containing what was once the town of Whiskey Falls.

Attorney General Ewing wasn't particularly pleased that Pritchard had distributed nearly two-hundred-thousand dollars of illicit money to the Whiskey Falls survivors, preferring to have had the cash turned over to government coffers in Missouri for what he called, "proper distribution of the funds under the auspices of the courts and the authority of the law."

Pritchard respectfully told the attorney general that at the time he doled out the money to two-hundred-and-sixty destitute refugees, all of whom had lost loved ones and had barely escaped with their lives, he himself was the only "authority of the law," and that he couldn't give a whit about the "auspices of the courts." He politely reminded Ewing there were no judges or courts on the Oregon Trail, or in Whiskey Falls, when Captain Mason and Red Henry Marleaux were kidnapping, enslaving, and murdering innocent travelers.

After dinner they retreated to the governor's study and were treated to brandy and cigars. Pritchard deferred on the cigar, as he didn't smoke, and requested whiskey instead of brandy. There the conversation turned to another matter.

Bonner explained to those in attendance the unique circumstances by which he'd come into Marshal Pritchard's acquaintance. He then turned over the ten-thousand dollars paid to him by Dominic Quincy, formerly the owner of the Quincy Detective Agency, as down-payment on a verbal contract to hunt down and murder Deputy U.S. Marshal Samuel Pritchard.

Bonner wasn't heartbroken at the loss. He'd

collected $10,000 on the bounty for Henry Marleaux.

Governor Woodson was furious that Cottonmouth Quincy, while out on bail and awaiting trial for previously paying bounty-killers to murder Marshal Pritchard, had blatantly tried to do so once again. He remembered bristling at the time that Quincy was granted bail after his arrest, undoubtedly a result of his money and influence with a particularly corrupt St. Louis magistrate.

The governor immediately demanded Ewing revoke Quincy's bail. He also ordered the properties Quincy put down as collateral for his bail, including his imposing riverside offices and opulent Westmoreland Place mansion, impounded, along with any funds still at his disposal. Attorney General Ewing was only too happy to do so.

Woodson further ordered Ewing to issue a warrant for Quincy's arrest on the new charges of attempted murder of a law enforcement official and commanded Pritchard to execute it.

"It'd be my pleasure," Pritchard told the governor. "How hard can it be to find a one-armed Irishman?"

"Don't underestimate him," Woodson cautioned. "Cottonmouth may not be so easy to track down, even for a lawman as formidable as you."

Governor Woodson reminded Pritchard that

Dominic Cottonmouth Quincy was an extremely dangerous and resourceful adversary. He pointed out that Quincy's reputation for ruthlessness was earned as a Union spy and riverboat captain during the war, and in the decade since he built a detective agency only second in prominence to Pinkerton. This helped him cultivate a national network of spies and loyalists whose supporters included everyone from wealthy and powerful railroad, steel, and newspaper magnates, to some of the most dangerous criminals in America.

"Though we will confiscate all of his property and funds that we know of, and make him a wanted criminal," the governor said, "I have no doubt that Quincy still has at his disposal significant resources."

"He spent ten years collecting dirt on the rich and powerful," Pritchard agreed. "He'll be collectin' on those markers."

"You can be certain," Attorney General Ewing added, "that once Quincy discovers his plot to kill you has failed, and that not only are you alive, but he is officially listed as a fugitive, he will go to ground. He will not only disappear, Marshal Pritchard, but redouble his already-Herculean efforts to see you dead. You as well, Mister Bonner, for he will view your turning him in to the authorities as a betrayal."

"Quincy told me as much," Bonner said, "when he hired me."

"Which means," Governor Woodson said, "despite the fact that you've just returned from a grueling mission which nearly cost you your life, and I'm sure you would welcome a long rest back home in Atherton, you might want to begin your pursuit of Cottonmouth Quincy immediately."

"I reckon so," Pritchard said. He turned to Bonner. "Wanna come along?"

"I've got nothing else on my calendar," Bonner said, blowing a smoke ring. "Old Cottonmouth is going to be just as angry at me for double-crossing him as he is mad at you for taking his right arm. In the interests of my health, I'd best see him put behind bars or below ground."

So after a particularly restful night as guests of the governor at his mansion, and an even better breakfast, Deputy U.S. Marshal Samuel Pritchard and Bounty Hunter Laird Bonner boarded a train for St. Louis. By evening, they'd arrived.

The lawman and the bounty hunter rode side-by-side through the bustling streets of St. Louis. Their destination was the offices of the Quincy Detective Agency, an imposing brick building with a view overlooking the Mississippi waterfront.

Both men checked their revolvers before entering. The last time Pritchard was in Quincy's office, he was forced to shoot the enraged Irishman, costing him an arm. And the last time Bonner visited with Quincy in that same office, he was commissioned to hunt down and kill Samuel Pritchard, and threatened with death if he failed.

Pritchard and Bonner asked the stunning young receptionist to see Quincy. The receptionist, who remembered both of them, had been Quincy's mistress before he abandoned her in romantic pursuit of the vengeful Evelyn Stiles, who at the time went under the alias Eudora Chilton. She icily announced that Dominic Quincy had left St. Louis, and his whereabouts were currently unknown.

"You figure he got word we were a-comin' for him?" Pritchard asked Bonner.

"Of course, he knew you were coming," the receptionist cut in before Bonner could answer. "Dominic has eyes and ears everywhere. He knows you're still above ground, Marshal Pritchard, and he knows Mister Bonner took his money and double-crossed him. He also knows all about your meeting with the governor, and that you'd both be coming for him."

"Cottonmouth's well-informed," Bonner said. "He must have a spy or two on Governor Woodson's staff."

"I reckon so," Pritchard said. "Probably got 'em everywhere."

"He'll hound you both," she laughed. "You two fools think you're the ones hunting Quincy, but now he's hunting you. You'd best start making your funeral arrangements, because you'll be departing this earth soon."

417

"Maybe so," Pritchard said, tossing a copy of the governor's writ on the receptionist's desk, "but meantime you're out of a job. This building, and everything in it, is hereby confiscated by the State of Missouri. Quincy's house is impounded, too. I reckon you'll have to return to the dance hall he found you in."

Her eyes widened, then narrowed in anger. She stood and gathered her reticule and hat. "Do you think that'll stop him?" she asked as she donned her coat. "Taking all his possessions?"

"I doubt it," Bonner admitted. "I'm sure he's got money stashed. At least the other ten-thousand he was going to pay me. Old Cottonmouth is too cagey not to have an escape plan. But now he's going to have to operate underground. It'll make things more difficult for him."

"You'll never find him," she said smugly. "He'll find you, first. Dominic Quincy is the greatest detective in America."

"Allan Pinkerton might disagree with you," Bonner said.

"Go to hell," the receptionist said, as she stormed out. Both men tipped their hats, nonetheless.

"Charmin' young gal, ain't she?" Pritchard said sarcastically.

"She's loyal," Bonner said, "I'll give her that. She's also right about Cottonmouth Quincy not going to be easy to find."

"How hard can it be?" Pritchard asked. "How many murderous, one-armed, bent-nosed, Irishmen you expect to be walkin' around Missouri?"

"Quincy may be a madman," Bonner said, "but he didn't build a nationwide intelligence network and detective agency by being a fool. If he doesn't want to be found, he won't be found. Frankly, I'm not even sure where to start looking." He paused to light a cheroot. "Where would you go, if you were Dominic Quincy?"

"If I was Dominic Quincy," Pritchard said, "I'd still be sore at me. I'd be wantin' revenge."

"Something his secretary said has me riled," Bonner said. "She said, 'You two fools think you're the ones hunting Quincy, but now he's hunting you.'"

"I recall her sayin' that," Pritchard said.

"If Quincy got word from one of his spies that we were back in Missouri yesterday," Bonner said, "he'd have plenty of time to catch a train west. He could—"

"Already be in Atherton," Pritchard finished Bonner's sentence. "In my home town. Do you think he knows I have a pregnant sister livin' there?"

"Quincy's a detective," Bonner answered. "What do you think?"

"We'd best get a-movin'," Pritchard said, tightening his jaw.

CHAPTER FIFTY-TWO

Dominic Quincy stepped up into the buggy and accepted the whip from Buck Gibson, the young liveryman on duty at the stables. He was sixteen years old, and the nephew of the stable's owner.

"You sure you can handle this rig okay," Buck asked, "bein' how's you have only one arm and all? You've rented a right spirited horse."

Quincy arrived in Atherton on the 4:40 from Jefferson City. He was directed to the local stables by the conductor and went there directly. He wore an expensive bowler, equally expensive suit and shoes, and carried a suitcase in his only hand. At the livery he commissioned a horse and buggy, specifying a strong, fast, animal.

"I'll have no trouble with the buggy, young man," Quincy answered with a smile. "But I thank you kindly for your concern."

"Did you lose your arm in the war?" Buck couldn't help but ask.

"Something like that," Quincy said.

He tipped the youth a dollar. As the wide-eyed attendant gleefully pocketed the unexpected windfall, Quincy asked, "You wouldn't happen to know where Mrs. Idelle Clemson's residence is, would you?"

"Why do you wanna know?"

"My name's Hendershot," Quincy said. "I'm a real-estate attorney from Jefferson City. Mrs. Clemson sent for me, and is expecting my arrival today. I have business matters of some importance to conduct with her."

Idelle Clemson, formerly Idelle Pritchard, was the ex-mayor of Atherton, Marshal Samuel Pritchard's younger sister, and current Mayor Ditch Clemson's wife. She was also seven months pregnant with her first child. If a boy, she and Ditch pledged to name him Samuel.

"Everybody knows where Idelle lives," Buck said, seemingly placated. "She used to be the mayor, before she got hitched. The Clemson place is actually on what used to be called the Old Pritchard place. She lives there with her husband, Ditch. He's Atherton's mayor now. He's out of town, though."

"I believe I'll go on out to see Mrs. Clemson directly," Quincy said. "Where did you say her place was?"

"The property's just north of town on the main road. It's a big brick mansion. You can't miss it. Now if'n you'll excuse me, I've gotta go ring the church bell. It's part of my duties, sometimes, to ring the bell."

Quincy tipped his hat, cracked the whip, and pointed his rented buggy north.

421

• • •

"May I help you?" Idelle asked.

It was suppertime, and Idelle responded from the kitchen to answer a knock at the front door. She wore a flour-covered apron over her distended belly, and wiped her hands on a towel. She found a distinguished-looking, one-armed, man of about fifty years of age, wearing fancy city clothes, standing on her porch. He held a handkerchief in his only hand, and used it to wipe his runny nose.

"Am I in the presence of Mrs. Idelle Clemson?" Quincy asked in his Irish accent. He politely removed his hat.

"You are," Idelle said. "And who might you be?"

"My name's Hendershot," Quincy said. "I'm acquainted with your brother, Samuel. Is your husband at home, by chance?"

"He is not," Idelle said. "He and Deputy Strobl rode to Missouri City yesterday morning in pursuit of two men who tried to rob the payroll over at the sawmill."

"It is truly tragic," Quincy said, shaking his head, "what a lawless land this has become."

"You're Irish, aren't you?" Idelle asked.

"You've a fine ear," Quincy said. "I am indeed."

"What can I do for you, Mister Hendershot?"

"The question," Quincy said, returning his

422

hat to his head, pocketing his handkerchief, and drawing a Colt Baby Dragoon from his vest, "is not what you can do for me, Mrs. Clemson? The question is, 'What can I do to you?' "

"I don't understand?" Idelle said, a confused look alighting her face. She slowly stepped back into the house.

"There's not much to understand, my dear," Quincy said. "Your brother took from me. Now I'm going to take from him." He cocked the Colt's hammer back, but held the gun down at his side as he followed her into the house. The engraved pistol was a gift from a grateful client.

"What did Samuel take from you?" Idelle asked, still backing up.

"Only the woman I loved, my right arm, my detective agency, my home, my fortune, and soon my freedom. Because of your brother, I've lost everything."

"Killing me isn't going to bring those things back," Idelle said.

"I know," Quincy said. "But with your death, and the death of your unborn child, Samuel Pritchard will know something of my pain. That's enough for me." He raised the revolver and aimed it at Idelle.

"Good-bye, Mrs. Clemson," Quincy said. "Know I'll be sending your brother to hell on your heels."

The gunshot that followed wasn't the sharp

crack of a .31 caliber, black-powder, ball fired from a Baby Dragoon, but instead the ear-splitting roar of two 00 buckshot rounds fired from a 12-gauge, double-barreled coach gun.

Dominic Cottonmouth Quincy's chest exploded. He flew backward through the open front door, tumbled down the porch steps, and landed on the front lawn. His sightless eyes stared unblinkingly up into the evening sky.

Deputy Tater Jessup stood in the kitchen doorway, his shotgun smoking in his beefy hands. He had blueberry pie stains around his mouth, on his fingers, on the napkin tucked into his collar, and on his overalls.

Idelle took in, and let out, a deep sigh of relief. She turned to Tater, trembling, and nodded her thanks. He set down the weapon and scurried to her side, taking her arm and escorting her back into the kitchen to sit down.

"You and the baby all right?" Tater asked, his face framed with worry. He poured her a glass of water from a pitcher on the table.

"We're both fine," Idelle said, rubbing her tummy and giving the portly deputy's arm a squeeze. "Thanks to you and the warning bells from the church in town. What about you, Tater? Are you okay?"

"Gunfire ain't exactly good for my digestion," Tater said, "but I reckon I'm all right. Why wouldn't I be?"

"You just had to kill a man," she said. "That can be a mite upsetting."

"Weren't nothin' upsettin' about riddin' the world of a varmint like Cottonmouth Quincy," Tater scoffed. "I've shot hydrophobic skunks what gave me more regret. Far as I'm concerned, gettin' shot's too good an end for the likes of a feller who'd point a pistol at a pregnant woman. Hell, I might just reload my two-eyed blunderbuss, go outside, and shoot what's left of him again on general principle."

"I'm sure grateful you were here, Tater," Idelle said. "Samuel will be mighty grateful, too."

"Tweren't nothin'," Tater said sheepishly. "When Samuel—I mean Marshal Pritchard—sent that telegram last night tellin' us to look out for Cottonmouth, and askin' me to watch over you, I wasn't never gonna leave your side, and that's a fact. Of course"—he grinned, showing blue teeth—"the fact that you've been bakin' pies today don't hurt none, neither."

"Samuel's telegram said he'll be back tonight," Idelle said. "Hopefully Ditch and Florian will return, too. Then things'll be right in Atherton again."

"I reckon so," Tater agreed. "Meantime, do you mind if I have another slice of your blueberry pie?"

"Help yourself," Idelle said, shaking her head in disbelief.

CHAPTER FIFTY-THREE

By the time Pritchard and Bonner got off the train in Atherton, Mayor Ditch Clemson and Deputy Florian Strobl had already returned. They were waiting to greet the duo at the station, accompanied by Idelle and Tater.

Ditch and Strobl had ridden into town, with a pair of manacled prisoners, not long after the lethal confrontation at the Clemson home. Seth Tilley and his son Simon, Atherton's only undertakers, drove their wagon out and picked up Dominic Quincy's body. It lay in Tilley's shop, awaiting instructions from Marshal Pritchard.

"Welcome home, Marshal," Tater greeted his boss, who was busy receiving a fierce hug from his sister. "Nice to see you again, Marshal Johnson," he said to Bonner.

"About my name, Deputy Jessup," Bonner said. "I have some explaining to do."

"Let's do it over a drink," Pritchard suggested. "It's been a long, hard few weeks. I don't know about you fellers, but I'm powerful thirsty."

"Don't have to ask me twice," Ditch said, as he ushered everyone toward the Sidewinder Saloon.

As the group walked from the train station to the saloon, they passed the undertaker's office.

Simon Tilley, nearly as tall as Pritchard and skeletally thin, emerged to hail the marshal.

"Marshal Pritchard," he said. "What do you want me to do about this one-armed feller I got in my shop? I don't even know his name?"

"His name was Cottonmouth Quincy," Pritchard answered. "Put that on his stone. And make sure he's planted in Sin Hill and not the Churchyard."

"Whatever you say, Marshal," Tilley said.

"I can't wait to hear all about your adventures," Idelle said to her brother. "Where, exactly, have you been all these past weeks?"

Pritchard's eyes met Bonner's, and the two men shared a moment of silent understanding.

"Whiskey Falls, little sister," Pritchard said. "I've just come from Whiskey Falls."

ACKNOWLEDGMENTS

I wish to express my heartfelt gratitude to the following individuals for their support in the writing of this novel:

Gary Goldstein. My friend, editor at Kensington Publishing, and the fellow who first prodded me into writing westerns. I only wish I could write a character as wise, salty, and true as him.

Scott Miller. My friend, my literary agent at Trident Media Group, and a man of honor who always keeps the faith.

The fine folks at the Western Writers of America, who welcomed me so generously.

The Calaveras Crew: Chris the Stallion, also known as Vergon, Emperor of the Dragons (18th Level Ninja of Tongular Flippage), Lothar the Merciless, Russ the Gunfighting Urologist, Canadian Todd, Barry the Duke, Savage Ed, Rodeo Eric, Rick Boat, and the inimitable Frank Brownell. Sidehackers all, and men to ride the river with.

The Usual Suspects, whose support is deeply appreciated. If it takes a village, ours is the Village of the Damned.

Lastly, and most importantly, my wife Denise,

daughter Brynne, and son Owen. They are the greatest blessings ever bestowed on a fellow. I am humbled every day. Today, tomorrow, and forever; you know the rest.

SEAN LYNCH grew up in Iowa, served in the army as an enlisted infantryman, and spent almost three decades as a municipal police officer in the San Francisco Bay Area. During his law enforcement career, he's been a motorcycle officer, firearms instructor, S.W.A.T. team member, sex crimes investigator, and homicide detective. Learn more about Sean at seanlynchbooks.com.

Books are produced in the United States using U.S.-based materials

Books are printed using a revolutionary new process called THINKtech™ that lowers energy usage by 70% and increases overall quality

Books are durable and flexible because of Smyth-sewing

Paper is sourced using environmentally responsible foresting methods and the paper is acid-free

Center Point Large Print
600 Brooks Road / PO Box 1
Thorndike, ME 04986-0001 USA

(207) 568-3717

US & Canada:
1 800 929-9108
www.centerpointlargeprint.com